TEXT BY MONIQUE PETERSON

DESIGN BY JONATHAN GLICK

Disney

The Little Big Book of

Family Classics

welcome
BOOKS

NEW YORK • SAN FRANCISCO

NOTE: All the activities and recipes within this book are to be conducted and made with appropriate adult supervision. Care must be taken by parents and guardians to select activities that are appropriate for the age of the children. The writer and the publisher shall have neither liability nor responsibility to any person or entity with respect to any mishaps or damage caused, or alleged to be caused, directly or indirectly by the information contained in this book.

Published in 2004 by Welcome Books®
An imprint of Welcome Enterprises, Inc.
6 West 18th Street
New York, NY 10011
(212) 989-3200; Fax (212) 989-3205
www.welcomebooks.com

Publisher: Lena Tabori
Editor: Alice Wong
Designer: Jonathan Glick
Text by Monique Peterson
Project Assistant: Deidra Garcia
Art Assistant: Amanda Hirschfeld
Line Illustrations on pages 23, 51, 79, 92-93, 107, 121, 135, 148, 162, 177, 233, 247, and 261 by Kathryn Shaw
Recipe testing by Millie Walraven and Hazel Peterson

Distributed to the trade in the U.S. and Canada by
Andrews McMeel Distribution Services
U.S. Order Department and Customer Service
Toll-free: (800) 943-9839
U.S. Orders-only Fax: (800) 943-9831
PUBNET S&S San Number: 200-2442
Canada Orders Toll-free: (800) 268-3216
Canada Order-only Fax: (888) 849-8151

© Disney Enterprises, Inc.
A Bug's Life; Finding Nemo; Monsters, Inc. © Disney Enterprises, Inc./Pixar Animation Studios

The Little Big Book Series © Welcome Enterprises, Inc.
Design © Welcome Enterprises, Inc.

101 Dalmatians: Based on the book *The Hundred and One Dalmatians* by Dodie Smith, published by The Viking Press.

The Jungle Book: Based on the Mowgli stories in *The Jungle Book* and *The Second Jungle Book* by Rudyard Kipling.

Winnie the Pooh: Based on the "Winnie the Pooh" works, by A. A. Milne and E. H. Shepard.

All rights reserved. No parts of this book may be reproduced or utilized in any form or by any means, electronic or mechanical, including photocopying, recording, or by any information storage or retrieval system, without permission in writing from the publisher.

Library of Congress Cataloging-in-Publication Data on file.

ISBN 1-932183-16-7

Printed in Singapore

First Edition

10 9 8 7 6 5 4 3 2 1

CONTENTS

Foreword 10

101 Dalmatians
Story 14
Q & As 20
Activity: Dalmatian Plantation Puppies
.... 22
Lines from the Film 24
Recipe: Puppy Paw Print Cookies 26

Aladdin
Story 28
Q & As 34
Activity: Aladdin's Magic Carpet 37
Lines from the Film 38
Recipe: Abu's Finger Food 41

Alice in Wonderland
Story 42
Q & As 48
Activity: Mad Tea Party Toppers 50
Lines from the Film 52
Recipe: Alice's Unbirthday
Tea Party 54

Bambi
Story 56
Q & As 62
Activity: Bambi & Thumper on Ice ... 64
Lines from the Film 66
Recipe: Thumper's Salad 68

Beauty and the Beast
Story 70
Q & As 76
Activity: The Beast's Enchanted Rose
.... 78
Lines from the Film 80
Recipe: Be Our Guest Appetizers 82

A Bug's Life
Story 84
Q & As 90
Activity:
Egg Carton Insects 92
Lines from the Film 94
Recipe: Ant Trail Mix 97

Cinderella

Story	98
Q & As	104
Activity: Cinderella's Castle	107
Lines from the Film	108
Recipe: Pumpkin Coach Cupcakes	110

Dumbo

Story	112
Q & As	118
Activity: Casey Jr.'s Circus Train	120
Lines from the Film	122
Recipe: Dumbo's Circus Popcorn	125

Finding Nemo

Story	126
Q & As	132
Activity: Nemo's School of Fish	135
Lines from the Film	136
Recipe: Nemo's Fish Puzzle Sammies	138

Hercules

Story	140
Q & As	146
Activity: Dress of the Gods	148
Lines from the Film	150
Recipe: Hercules' Strengthening Sports Drink	152

The Jungle Book

Story	154
Q & As	160
Activity: Slithering Kaa	163
Lines from the Film	164
Recipe: Bare Necessities Banana Bread	167

Lady and the Tramp
Story 168
Q & As 174
Activity: Clothespin Doggy 176
Lines from the Film 178
Recipe: Tony's
Spaghetti Especialle 180

Lilo & Stitch
Story 182
Q & As 188
Activity:
Lilo's Hawaiian Hula Skirt 190
Lines from the Film 192
Recipe: Stitch's Hawaiian
Fruit Smoothies 194

The Lion King
Story 196
Q & As 202
Activity: Savanna-orama 204
Lines from the Film 206
Recipe: Timon & Pumbaa's
Hot & Gooey Grub Logs 208

The Little Mermaid
Story 210
Q & As 216

Activity: Ariel's Wishing Stars 218
Lines from the Film 220
Recipe: Ariel's
Bottom-of-the-Sea Soup 223

Monsters, Inc.
Story 224
Q & As 230
Activity: Boo's Closet Door 233
Lines from the Film 234
Recipe: Abominable Snowman's
Lemon Snowcones 237

Mulan
Story 238
Q & As 244
Activity:
The Indestructible Mushu 246
Lines from the Film 248
Recipe: Mushu's
Happy-to-See-You Porridge 250

Peter Pan
Story	252
Q & As	258
Activity: Tick-Tock Croc	260
Lines from the Film	262
Recipe: Watermelon Pirate Ship	264

Pinocchio
Story	266
Q & As	272
Activity: Marionette & Puppet Theater	275
Lines from the Film	276
Recipe: Pleasure Island Root Beer Floats	279

Pocahontas
Story	280
Q & As	286
Activity: "Colors of the Wind" Leaf Rubbings	288
Lines from the Film	290
Recipe: Meeko's Cornmeal Crackers	292

Sleeping Beauty
Story	294
Q & As	300
Activity: Prince Phillip's Shield of Virtue and Sword of Truth	303
Lines from the Film	304
Recipe: Aurora's Sweet Sixteen Birthday Cake	306

Snow White and the Seven Dwarfs
Story	308
Q & As	314
Activity: Stick Dwarfs	317
Lines from the Film	318
Recipe: Snow White's Gooseberry Pie	321

Toy Story
Story	322
Q & As	328
Activity: Alien Squishies	330
Lines from the Film	332
Recipe: Pizza Planet Mini Pizzas	335

Winnie the Pooh
Story	336
Q & As	342
Activity: Pooh's Honeypots	345
Lines from the Film	346
Recipe: Sticky Pooh Bear Buns	348

FOREWORD

This is the twentieth Little Big Book and the tenth that I've worked on. Welcome has produced two Disney titles (*The Little Big Book of Disney* and *The Little Big Book of Pooh*), but this is the series' first Disney title exclusively for children. Disney and children is a classic and unbeatable combination. Even as a child of immigrant parents who did not speak English, Disney was big in our household in Chinatown, New York. The only videotapes my parents ever bought for my brothers and me were Disney's animated movies. They trusted Disney even though they didn't understand the language. My parents worked long hours with little vacation time, but whenever relatives from overseas came to visit, they would throw everyone in the car (or two) and drive down to Walt Disney World in Orlando, Florida. Of all the things in America our relatives could see, every one of them chose Walt Disney World. My brothers and I never complained!

I am the mother of three little ones now, ages 2, 6, and 8. It is with much nostalgia I enjoy old favorites again and I look forward to every new, soon-to-be classic that comes out. We've gone through many obsessive stages: when the theme song from *Winnie the Pooh* was the only song played in the car; when *Toy Story* was the only video request for what seemed like a year; when my eldest insisted she was a Dalmatian and wanted to be fed dog food. I still laugh at the time, a few years ago, when the favorite playground game of my two older children was acting out the scene from *The Lion King* when Mufasa hangs on to the side of the cliff. "Help me, brother," Chi Chi would gasp to Sylvia while hanging on to the top of slide. Sylvia would then clamp down on Chi Chi's hands: "Long live the King!" and give a shove. Then comes the very dramatic and long "Arghhhhhhhh..." as Chi Chi slides slowly down the slide on her belly. A more beautiful memory to balance this is the two of them on summer vacation on a secluded rocky island off Lake Huron. The vision I treasure is the two of them jumping and climbing on boulders by the vast water and against a dazzling blue sky, flinging out their arms and singing out to nature the few lines they knew from *Aladdin*'s "A Whole New World."

I love Disney's animated films. This project was conceived because of it. As a parent, I appreciate all the learning that can come out of something children really enjoy. If your children are watching a favorite movie over and over, engage them in a conversation afterwards. The questions and answers in this book are a fun way to start. Let your children act out the favorite scenes or memorize the favorite lines also found in this book. Have fun with the activities and recipes. The littlest ones will enjoy making Dalmatian puppies, Nemo's pet-rock fish, and playing with alien squishies. Older children will like the challenge of making the Beast's enchanted rose, and may have so much fun making Dumbo's circus train or Cinderella's castle, you may find them creating a huge complex from cardboard all afternoon. Tempt your children with Hercules' strengthening drink in the morning or a rabbit-shaped salad made with Thumper's favorite munchables for lunch. Maybe your children will even try spinach "seaweed" for the first time in Ariel's bottom-of-the-sea soup. May this book fill you and your children's days with much fun, laughter, and tasty treats.

—Alice Wong, Editor

ONCE UPON A TIME, two Dalmatian dogs named Pongo and Perdita lived in London with their pet humans Anita and Roger Radcliffe. Their family was a very happy one, for Perdita had just given birth to a litter of fifteen puppies.

101 Dalmatians

One afternoon, Anita's rich and glamorous old school chum Cruella De Vil paid a visit. She barged into the house without even saying hello. "Where are they?" she demanded, blowing cigarette smoke in Anita's face.

"Who?" asked Anita.

"The puppies!" snapped Cruella. "I'll take them all. Just name your price." Cruella was used to getting whatever she wanted—and she wanted fur coats. She was dead set on owning a white one with black spots.

"We're not selling them," Roger said firmly. Cruella stormed out of the house in a furious rage. "You'll be sorry, you fools!"

One evening, Roger and Anita took their usual stroll in the park with Pongo and Perdita. While they were away, Cruella's henchmen, Horace and Jasper Badun, broke into the house and stole the puppies.

The next morning, newspaper headlines screamed DOGNAPPING!

"Scotland Yard is no help," said Roger angrily.

Pongo knew it would be up to the dogs to find their puppies. "We must use the Twilight Bark," he told Perdita.

That night, Pongo barked out an All Dog Alert. The message traveled from one dog to another, across all of London and far into the countryside.

By dawn the barks had made their way to a farm in Suffolk. "News from London!" alerted Sergeant Tibs the barnyard cat. Colonel the English sheepdog lifted his ear. "Fifteen spotted puppies dognapped from London!"

Tibs remembered hearing barking a few nights ago at Hell Hall, the old abandoned De Vil place. He and Colonel investigated and overheard Cruella talking to Horace and Jasper. "We can't wait—the police are everywhere. I don't care how you kill the little beasts, but do it now!"

Colonel reported their findings to London immediately. Meanwhile, Tibs broke in and found the fifteen stolen puppies...plus eighty-four more! He helped the puppies escape through a hole in the wall.

Before long, Horace and Jasper caught the puppies trying to sneak away. Soon they had the pups cornered with

crowbars. Just then Pongo and Perdita broke through a window and attacked Cruella's thugs, scaring them away.

What a happy reunion Pongo and Perdita had with their puppies. But there were so many others! "They were going to make dog-skin coats out of us," one pup said.

Pongo and Perdita couldn't believe their ears. "We'll take them home with us," Pongo said. "All of them."

So, Pongo, Perdita, and the ninety-nine puppies trudged through the cold winter snow. They made it as far as Dinsford, where a black Labrador found a ride for them back to London in a moving van.

Meanwhile, Cruella was hot on their trail. "They've got to be near here somewhere," she told Horace and Jasper. "Find them!"

The dogs were hiding in a blacksmith's shop when Cruella drove by. "Pongo," cried Perdita. "What shall we do?" They would never be able to get the puppies into the moving van without being noticed.

Then Pongo got an idea when he saw two puppies rolling around in the blacksmith's ashes. "Look," he said. "We'll all be Labradors!" So all the puppies got good and dirty until none of them had spots.

It worked, and soon Perdita and Pongo had loaded all the puppies into the moving van, right under Cruella's nose. But when some snow dripped on one of the pups and washed the soot away, Cruella spotted her Dalmatians!

"My coats!" Cruella screamed as the van drove off. "After the little mongrels!" she shouted. Cruella drove like a maniac to catch them, but in the midst of the high-speed chase, Horace and Jasper accidentally sideswiped her with their car and forced her into a ditch.

In London, Roger and Anita couldn't understand why Pongo and Perdita had run away.

Suddenly, Nanny heard a ruckus outside. She opened the door, and in stampeded scores of blackened puppies. "One hundred and one!" Roger counted.

"We'll have to get a big place in the country," said Anita.

"A plantation," said Roger. "A Dalmatian plantation!" Then one hundred and one Dalmatians joined Roger and Anita around the piano as they sang and played happily throughout the night.

101 DALMATIANS

1. What is the name of Cruella De Vil's abandoned property in the country?
2. How many puppies do Pongo and Perdita originally have?
3. What do Pongo and Perdita use to send their message about the stolen puppies?
4. How do Jasper and Horace disguise themselves to steal the Dalmatian puppies?
5. How do Pongo, Perdita, and all the puppies disguise themselves to trick Horace and Jasper?
6. How do Pongo, Perdita, and the puppies get back to London after they escape Hell Hall?
7. Who finally hears the Twilight Bark message that can help Pongo and Perdita find their missing puppies?
8. How does Cruella know where the puppies have gone after they escape Hell Hall?
9. What do Roger and Anita decide to do after they adopt eighty-four more Dalmatian puppies?
10. Why does Cruella want Roger and Anita's puppies?

Q & As

1. Hell Hall
2. Fifteen
3. The Twilight Bark
4. As men from the electric company
5. They roll in soot to look like black Labradors.
6. They get a ride in the back of a moving truck.
7. Sergeant Tibs, the cat; the Colonel, the English sheepdog; and Captain, the horse
8. She follows their footprints in the snow.
9. Have a Dalmatian plantation in the country
10. To make a black-and-white spotted fur coat for herself

Dalmatian Plantation Puppies

Pongo and Perdita can't find their puppies. With a little paper and glue, you can make a whole litter of pups. See how many you can spot and rescue from the clutches of Cruella De Vil.

black and white construction paper, scissors, glue, googly eyes, markers

To make the puppy's head, cut out a square piece of white construction paper and fold diagonally in half to create a triangle. Along the fold of the triangle, fold down both corners to make flaps. These flaps are the puppy's ears. To make the body, cut out a rectangular piece of white construction paper and glue one end to the back of the head. Cut out white triangles to glue on for legs and a tail. To add spots, cut different sized black circles and glue them onto the face, ears, and body of your puppy. Glue on googly eyes. Use markers to add a nose and mouth. How many spots does it take to make 99 Dalmatian puppies?

"I live for furs. I worship furs. After all, is there a woman in all this wretched world who doesn't?" –Cruella De Vil

"Fifteen Dalmatian puppies stolen!" –Twilight Bark

"Fifteen spotted puddles stolen. Oh, balderdash." –Colonel

"We'll have a plantation.

Puppy Paw Print Cookies

MAKE PUPPY TRACKS just like your favorite Dalmatian puppies with these paw print cookies. Then, one by one, you can help the puppies escape Cruella De Vil by making those tracks disappear!

½ cup butter, softened

1 cup sugar

1 egg

½ teaspoon almond extract

1 ½ cups flour, sifted

¼ teaspoon soda

¼ teaspoon cream of tartar

about 2 dozen chocolate kisses with the tips broken off

about 72 chocolate chips

1. Preheat oven to 375° F.
2. In a large bowl, mix butter and sugar until fluffy.
3. Beat in egg and almond extract.
4. Stir in flour, soda, and cream of tartar until mixture forms into dough.
5. Shape teaspoonfuls of dough into balls, and place on ungreased cookie sheet. Flatten dough gently with the bottom of a glass so that the cookies are about ¼ inch thick.
6. For each cookie, invert one chocolate kiss and press into the cookie, just below the center. Then, invert three chocolate chips above the kiss to form a paw print shape.
7. Bake for ten minutes, or until edges are golden brown.
8. Cool on wire rack. Then watch how quickly the paw prints disappear!

Makes about 2 dozen.

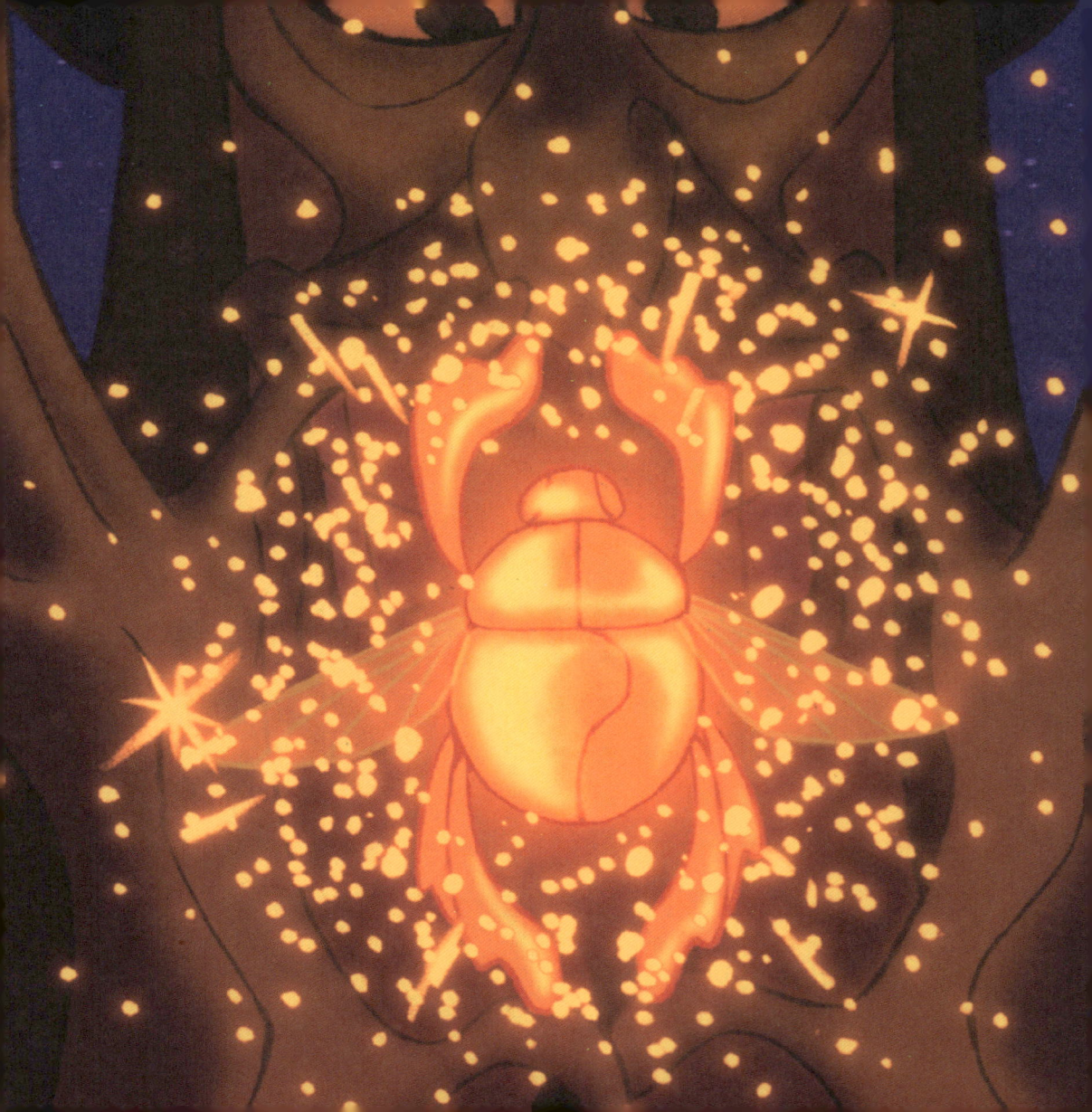

Aladdin

IN A FARAWAY LAND, under the moonlit Arabian night, Jafar, the Sultan's evil advisor, clutched a stolen scarab in his palm. After all these years of searching, he finally held the key to the Cave of Wonders!

"Who disturbs my slumber?" asked the Cave. "Only one whose worth lies far within may enter here: a Diamond in the Rough."

"I must find this Diamond in the Rough," said Jafar.

In the marketplace, Aladdin stole a loaf of bread. Every day he had to eat, so every day, he had to steal. But when Aladdin and his monkey friend Abu saw two hungry children, they gave them their bread. "Someday, Abu, things will change."

Inside the palace wall, Princess Jasmine shooed suitors away. According to law, she had to wed by her next birthday—only three days away.

The desperate Sultan asked his trusted advisor for help. "Of course I can find a suitor for the princess," Jafar assured him, "with the help of the Mystic Blue Diamond on your finger." The Sultan looked into Jafar's snake staff and gave up his ring.

"I will only marry for love," Jasmine declared. So, unknown to the others, she slipped outside the palace and went to

29

the marketplace for the first time. There, she took an apple without knowing to pay for it. Aladdin and Abu tried to help, but guards, under orders from Jafar, came and locked them up.

In the dungeon, Aladdin and Abu met an old prisoner who spoke of a Cave of Wonders. Aladdin didn't know it was the evil Jafar in disguise. The old man led Aladdin out of the dungeon and into the cave. "Touch nothing but the lamp and then you shall have your reward," he promised.

In the cave, Aladdin and Abu made friends with a Magic Carpet who flew them past piles of royal treasures. When Aladdin spotted the lamp, Abu spotted a glittering ruby red gem and grabbed it. Suddenly, a great rumbling shook the cave. Aladdin grabbed the lamp and the Carpet flew them back to the cave's edge.

The old man grabbed the lamp from Aladdin's hand. "At last!," he shouted and pushed Aladdin and Abu into the cave a moment before the cave sank into the ground.

They were trapped! But Abu chittered happily. He pulled the lamp he had stolen back from the old man out of his shirtsleeve. "You hairy little thief!" said Aladdin. "This looks like a worthless piece of junk." He took the lamp and rubbed its side. In a swirl of blue smoke, a genie appeared. "Right here for your wish fulfillment," he said. "Three wishes to be exact, and ix-nay on wishing for more wishes."

"What would *you* wish for?" Aladdin asked.

"Freedom," Genie admitted. But that would only be possible if his master wished it.

"I'll set you free," said Aladdin.

"Here's hoping," said Genie. "Now, what is it you want most?"

"Well, there's this girl," said Aladdin. "But she is the princess. I need to be a prince to have a chance to marry her."

"Hang onto your turban," Genie told Aladdin. "We're gonna make you a star!"

Soon, Aladdin was Prince Ali Ababwa, riding an elephant with an entourage and musical parade all the way to the Sultan's palace. "I have journeyed from afar to seek your daughter's hand," Aladdin told the Sultan.

Prince Ali impressed Jasmine with a magic carpet ride.

"You remind me of someone I met in the marketplace," Jasmine told Prince Ali.

"You couldn't have met me," Aladdin lied.

Meanwhile, Jafar had his own ideas for the prince. Guards took Aladdin and tossed him deep into the sea. Genie saved Aladdin from drowning, at the cost of another wish.

Aladdin returned to the palace to tell Jasmine the truth. While Aladdin searched for the princess, Jafar's parrot Iago stole Aladdin's lamp. Now Jafar was the Genie's master.

The palace rumbled as Genie granted Jafar his first wish: to rule as Sultan. "Bow to me!" Jafar commanded Jasmine and the Sultan.

They refused.

"Then you will cower before a sorcerer!" said Jafar. "Genie, my second wish!" The sorcerer Jafar sent Aladdin to the ends of the earth and kept Jasmine as his royal slave.

But the Magic Carpet rescued Aladdin and Abu, making Jafar's wrath greater than before. Jafar rose into a great serpent poised to strike Aladdin. Aladdin used his wits to outsmart Jafar. "The Genie has more power than you!" Aladdin shouted. "You're second best."

"Not for long!" said Jafar. "I wish to be an all-powerful genie!"

Genie granted Jafar his wish and Aladdin showed the new genie his new home—an itty bitty living space in the oil lamp. "Ten thousand years in the Cave of Wonders ought to chill him out," whispered Genie.

"I still have a wish," Aladdin reminded Genie. "I wish for your freedom." Genie couldn't believe his ears. He was finally free. So was Jasmine— to marry whom she pleased. She chose Aladdin.

And under the moonlit Arabian night, Jasmine and Aladdin soared into a whole new world.

1. Where does Aladdin find the Genie?
2. What kind of pet does Princess Jasmine have?
3. What are the three wishes the Genie cannot grant?
4. What object does Abu befriend in the Cave of Wonders?
5. What is the wish the Genie would have if he could make a wish?
6. What are Aladdin's three wishes?
7. What are Jafar's three wishes?
8. What kind of hat does the Genie wear after Aladdin sets him free?

ALADDIN

9. Why is the Sultan eager to find a husband for Jasmine?
10. How does Jafar make the Sultan do what he wants?

Q & As

1. In the Cave of Wonders
2. A Bengal tiger named Rajah
3. He can't kill anybody, he can't make anybody fall in love with anybody else, and he can't bring people back from the dead.
4. A magic flying carpet
5. To be free
6. To become a prince, to save his life from drowning, and to set the Genie free
7. To become a sultan, to become the most powerful sorcerer, and to become an all-powerful genie
8. A "Goofy" hat
9. Because, according to the law, she must be married by her next birthday
10. By hypnotizing him with his magical staff

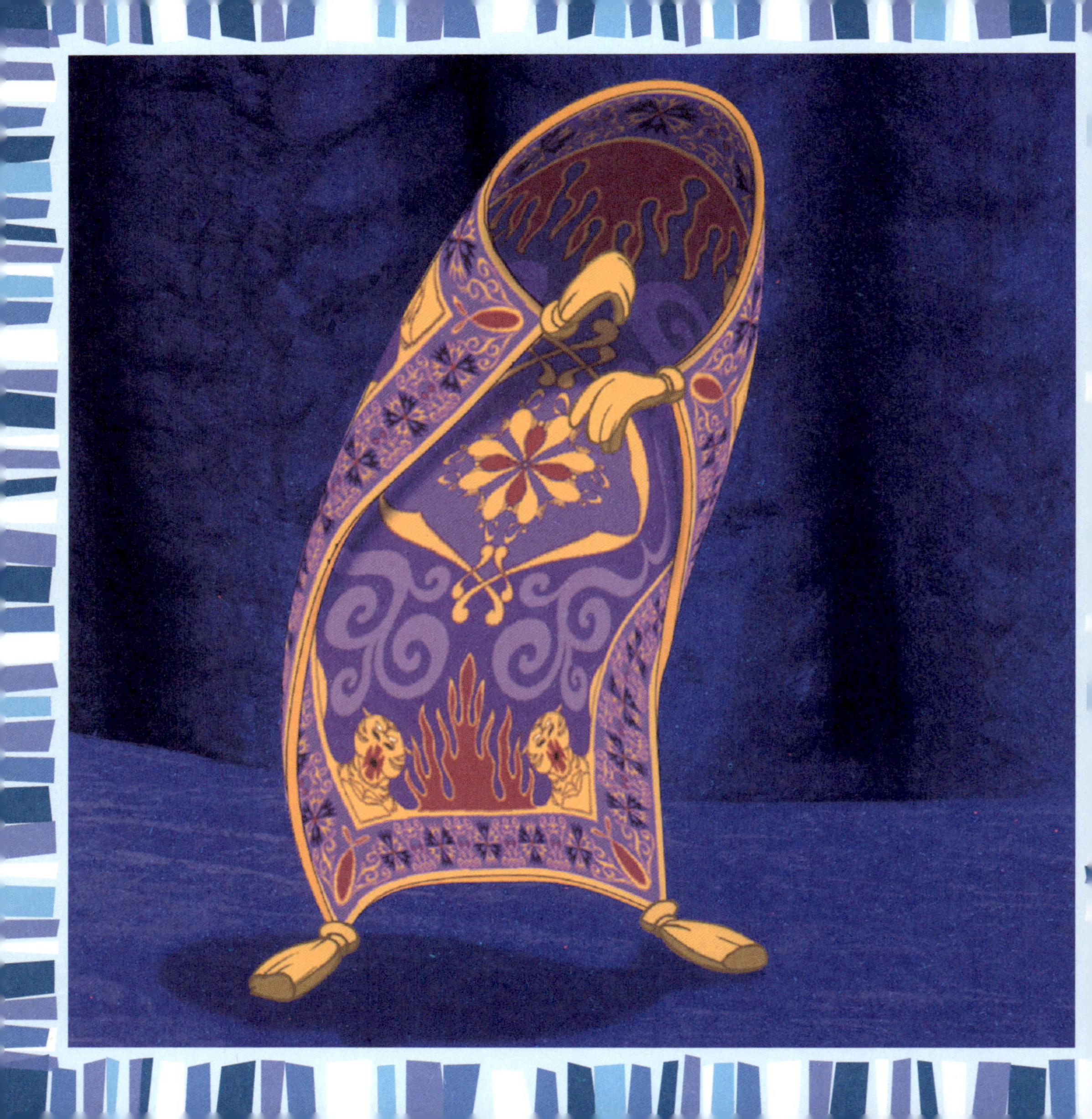

Aladdin's Magic Carpet

The Magic Carpet will fly you to dazzling places all over the world. Where do you want to go? Just hop on and enjoy the ride!

brown wrapping paper, scissors, pencil, ruler, newspaper, poster paints, paintbrush, yellow yarn. Optional: glue, gold glitter, 8½ x 11 copy paper, crayons

Cut a rectangular piece of brown wrapping paper about 3 x 5 feet or 5 x 8 feet. Mark a 5-inch border around edge with pencil and ruler. Draw flowers, swirls, and other decorative shapes on the paper. Place paper carpet on top of newspaper on the floor. Paint carpet with purples, reds, yellows, or whatever colors you wish. Let dry. For a bit of "magic" add a thin layer of glue and gold glitter on the edge of the carpet. Let dry. Make yarn tassels and glue to each corner. Take off your shoes, hop on, and decide where you are flying to.

For younger children, try the above on a smaller scale with 8½ x 11 copy paper and crayons. Do not add the tassels. Hold the finished carpet horizontally in the air and let go. Watch the Magic Carpet drift to the ground.

JASMINE: Do I know you?

ALADDIN: <As Prince Ali> Uh, no. No.

JASMINE: You remind me of someone I met in the marketplace.

ALADDIN: The marketplace? I have servants who go to the market for me. I even have servants who go to the market for my servants. You couldn't have met me.

JASMINE: I guess not.

GENIE: <As a bee, to Aladdin> Enough about you. Talk about her. She's smart, fun. The hair, the eyes, anything!

ALADDIN: Princess, you're very…

GENIE: <As a bee, to Aladdin> Wonderful, magnificent, punctual.

ALADDIN: Punctual!

GENIE: Sorry.

ALADDIN: Beautiful.

GENIE: Nice recovery.

JASMINE: I'm rich, too, you know. The daughter of a sultan.

ALADDIN: I know.

JASMINE: A fine prize for any prince to marry.

ALADDIN: Right. A prince like me.

GENIE: Warning!

JASMINE: Right, a prince like you… and every other stuffed shirt swaggering peacock I've met.

GENIE: Mayday! Mayday!

JASMINE: Just go jump off a balcony!

GENIE: Stop her! Want me to sting her?

ALADDIN: Buzz off.

GENIE: Okay, fine. But remember, be-e-e-e yourself.

ALADDIN: Yeah, right.

JASMINE: What?

ALADDIN: You're right. You aren't just some prize to be won. You should be free to make your own choice. I'll go now.

LINES FROM THE FILM

<Aladdin steps off the balcony and onto the Magic Carpet.>

ALADDIN: What?

JASMINE: How are you doing that?

ALADDIN: It's a Magic Carpet.

JASMINE: It's lovely.

ALADDIN: Want to go for a ride? We could leave the palace. See the world.

JASMINE: Is it safe?

ALADDIN: Sure. Do you trust me?

JASMINE: What?

ALADDIN: Do you trust me?

JASMINE: Yes.

<She gets on the carpet and they fly around the world.>

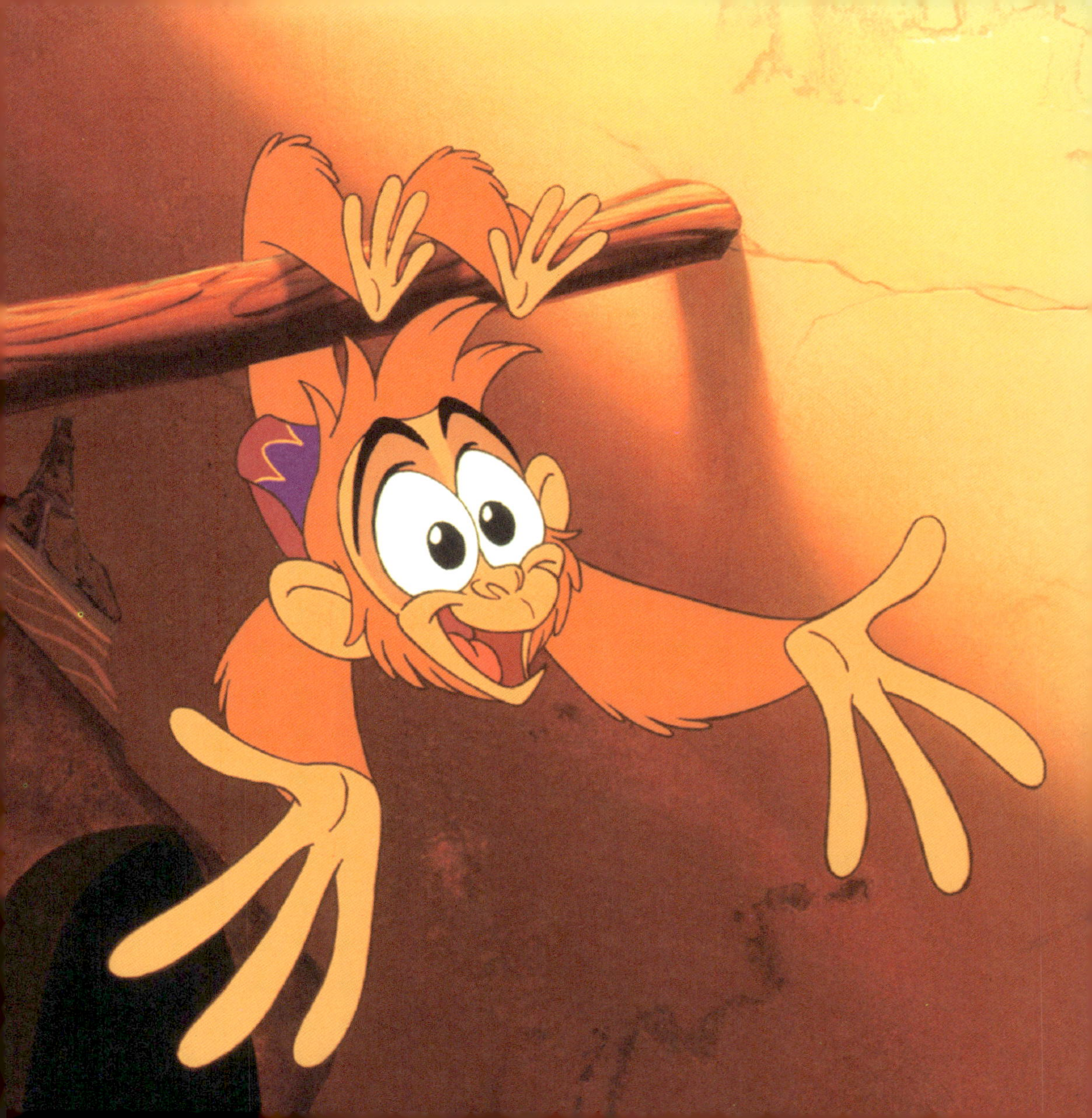

Abu's Finger Food

THE OPEN MARKET is full of good finger foods, especially when Abu has his hand in things. Try your hand with these tasty pickings and savory dip that's a snap to make.

HUMMUS:
1 cup garbanzo beans
2 to 3 tablespoons lemon juice
1 clove garlic, crushed
1 teaspoon cumin
salt to taste
water

FINGER FOODS:
1 cucumber, peeled and sliced
2 large carrots, cut into sticks
8 radishes
2 stalks celery, cut into sticks
1 zucchini, sliced
16 plum tomatoes
16 olives
4 pieces pita bread, cut into triangular wedges

1. Put all the hummus ingredients in a blender. Add enough water to make the hummus dip a thick and moist consistency. Blend until creamy.

2. Serve hummus in a dip bowl on a large serving platter. Arrange finger foods on the platter around the bowl.

3. Serve immediately and eat with fingers.

Makes 8 servings.

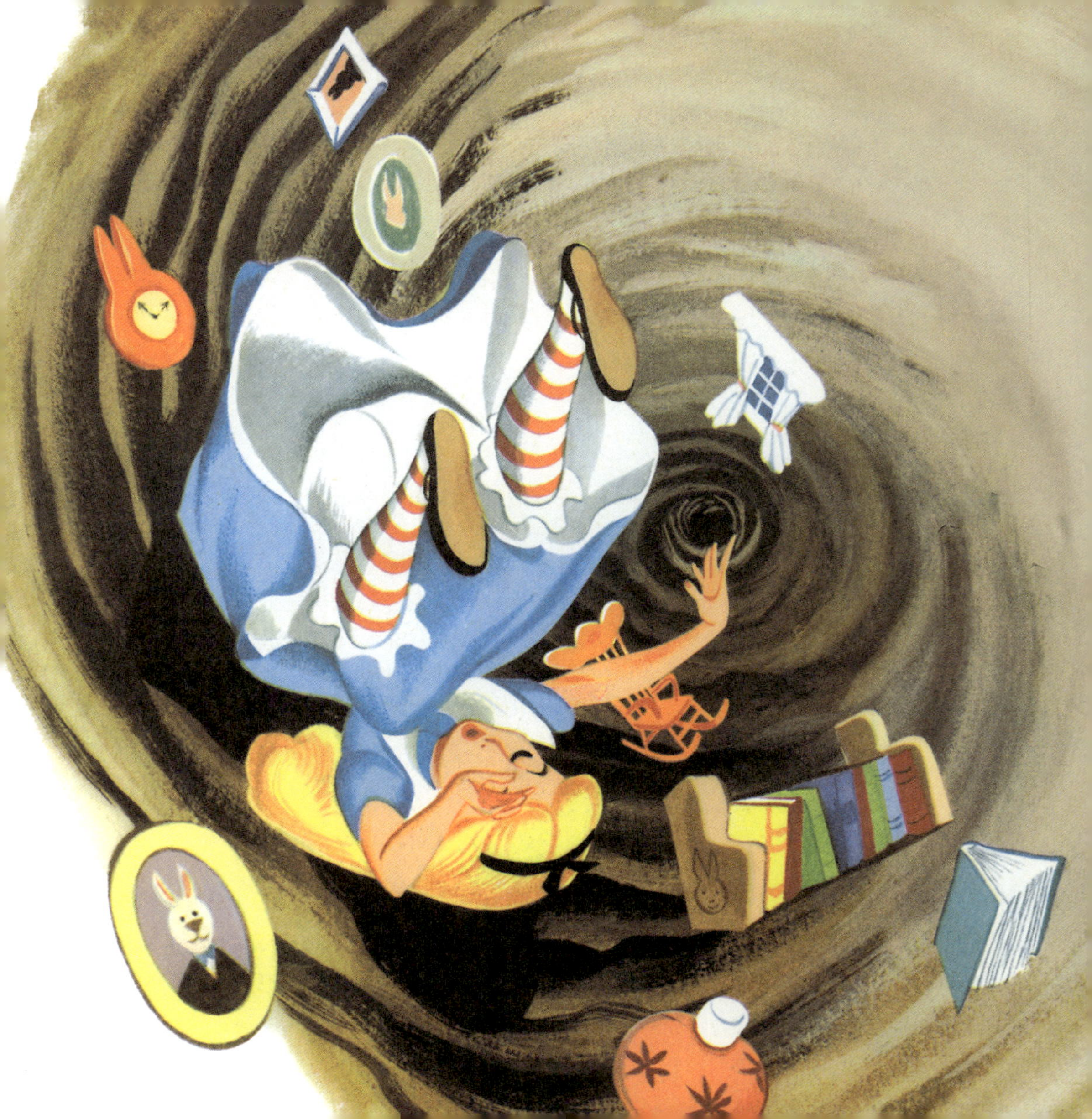

Alice in Wonderland

ONE SPRING DAY, young Alice lounged on a tree branch near the riverbank with her cat Dinah while her sister read her lessons. Alice wasn't listening. She was too busy daydreaming.

A White Rabbit wearing a waistcoat scurried by. "I'm late for a very important date!" he cried. Alice jumped out of the tree and followed the peculiar creature down a dark rabbit hole.

"Perhaps he's going to a party," thought Alice.

"I shall think nothing more of falling down stairs!" Alice said as she floated down a very long hole. At the bottom, the White Rabbit disappeared behind a very small door.

"Look on the table," the Doorknob told Alice. She found a bottle that read Drink Me. With one sip she shrunk down to ten inches. Now she was too small to reach the door key on the table!

"Try one of those," said the Doorknob, pointing to a box of cookies that read Eat Me.

With one bite, Alice shot up nine feet. She burst into tears and soon, she filled the room with a sea of monster-sized teardrops.

The "Drink Me" bottle floated by. Alice took a sip and shrank small enough to swim through the keyhole.

Alice washed ashore and met the oddest twins, Tweedledum and Tweedledee, who demanded Alice pay attention to their silly songs and nonsense poems.

Alice saw the White Rabbit as they recited "Father William," and snuck away to follow him.

Soon Alice came upon the White Rabbit's house. "Marianne!" he shouted to her. "I need my gloves!" Alice looked for them and found another box of "Eat Me" cookies. She ate one and suddenly her arms and legs burst out of the house.

"Let's smoke the monster out!" shouted the White Rabbit's friends. But before they could light a match to her toes, Alice ate a carrot out of the backyard and shrank down small enough to escape.

She chased the White Rabbit into a lush garden and quickly lost her way amidst bread-and-butterflies and talking flowers. There, she followed a trail of smoke to a caterpillar lounging atop a mushroom. "Exack-ticaly what is your problem?" he asked.

"Three inches is such an awful height to be," Alice explained.

"Three inches is exack-ticaly my height!" said the caterpillar as he rose to his full tallness and transformed into a butterfly.

As he flew away, he said: "One side of the mushroom will make you grow taller ... the other side smaller."

Alice broke off two pieces and saved them.

Looking about the woods, she spotted a toothy grin floating above a tree branch. Then a pair of eyes...then pink and purple stripes. "Why, you're a cat!" said Alice.

"Cheshire Cat," corrected the puss. "If I were looking for the White Rabbit," he mused as he faded away, "I would ask the Mad Hatter. Or the March Hare."

Alice found the Mad Hatter and the March Hare having an Unbirthday party. "Clean up! Move Down!" they shouted every time they offered Alice tea.

Alice never got her tea. She stormed off, quite ready to go home.

The more Alice tried to go back the way she came, the more lost she became. Quite unexpectedly, the Cheshire Cat appeared again.

"I can't find my way," Alice said.

"All ways are the Queen's ways," explained Cheshire. "You must meet her!" The curious cat opened a passageway to the Queen of Hearts' royal garden. "She'll be mad about you!"

The White Rabbit announced the arrival of the Queen of Hearts. "Do you play croquet?" the Queen asked Alice. "Let the game begin!"

Alice swung her flamingo mallet, trying to hit a hedgehog ball through the playing-card wickets. Suddenly, the Cheshire Cat tripped the Queen.

"Someone's head is going to roll for this!" shouted the Queen. She pointed to Alice. "Off with her head!"

The King insisted that Alice have a trial. "Sentence first, verdict afterward. Off with her head!" shouted the raging Queen. A mad chase ensued. Alice ran through all of Wonderland back to the Doorknob to escape. When she looked through the keyhole, she saw herself, fast asleep.

"Wake up!" said Alice's sister. "It's time for tea." With a gentle stretch, Alice found herself back on the riverbank with her sweet cat Dinah, very happy to be back home.

1. What happens when Alice eats a cookie from the box marked "Eat Me"?
2. What peculiar figures recite poetry and want to play hide-and-seek with Alice?
3. What does Alice look for in the White Rabbit's house?
4. What do the talking flowers think Alice is?

ALICE IN WONDERLAND

5. How tall is the caterpillar that Alice meets in the woods?
6. What kind of party are the Mad Hatter and March Hare having?
7. What are the playing cards doing in the Queen of Hearts' garden?
8. What do Alice and the Queen of Hearts use to play croquet?
9. Who does Alice follow into Wonderland?
10. What does the Queen of Hearts say if someone makes her lose her temper?

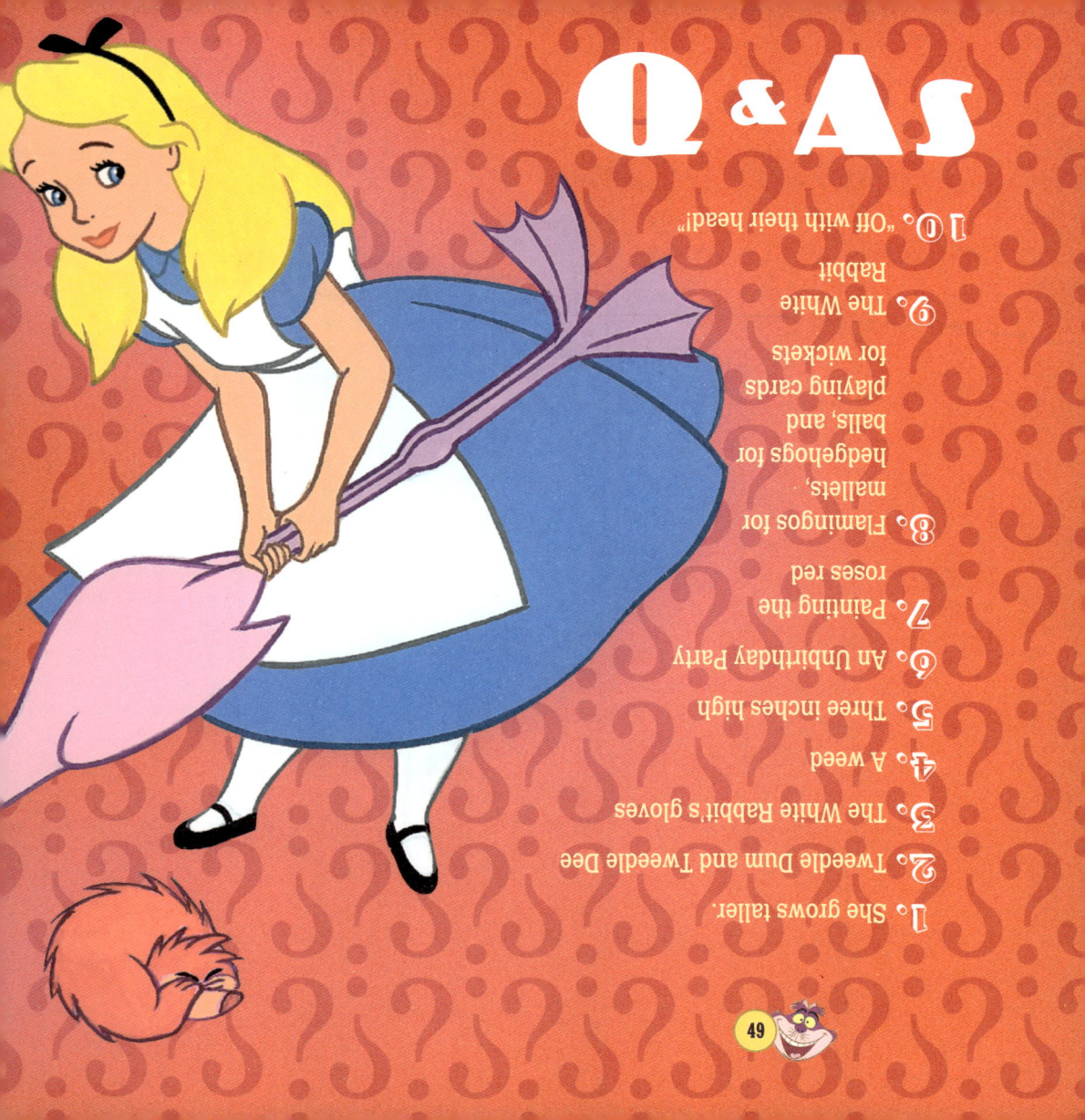

Q & As

1. She grows taller.
2. Tweedle Dum and Tweedle Dee
3. The White Rabbit's gloves
4. A weed
5. Three inches high
6. An Unbirthday Party
7. Painting the roses red
8. Flamingos for mallets, hedgehogs for balls, and playing cards for wickets
9. The White Rabbit
10. "Off with their head!"

Mad Tea Party Toppers

The next time you're invited to a mad tea party, put on some March Hare ears or a Mad Hatter hat. Then pour some tea, and don't forget to wish everyone a very merry unbirthday!

posterboard paper, scissors, construction paper, glue, tape, markers

MARCH HARE EARS

Cut a strip of posterboard about 4 inches wide and long enough to wrap around a child's head. Cut two rabbit ear shapes out of construction paper, about 8 inches long. To make the inner ears, cut out two smaller rabbit ear shapes and glue them in the center of the bigger rabbit ears. Tape the ears to the inside of the headband. To wear, wrap the headband around the head and tape the ends together.

MAD HATTER HAT

Cut a rectangle of construction paper about 7 inches wide and long enough to wrap around a child's head. Tape the ends together to make a tube. To make the top, trace one end of the tube on construction paper. Draw four rectangular tabs around the edges of the circle and cut the tabs and circle out (see illustration on left). Fold the flaps down and tape inside the top of the tube. To make the brim, trace another circle on construction paper, then draw another circle around it about three inches larger in diameter. Cut out along the larger circle. Within the smaller circle, draw four bisecting lines through the circle to make eight triangles (see illustration on right). These will be flaps. Cut on the lines, but do not cut on the outline of the smaller circle. Tape the triangular flaps to the inside of the bottom of the hat to attach the brim. Cut a 2-inch-wide band out of construction paper to wrap around the hat above the brim. Add a card that says "$10/6$" to tuck into the band.

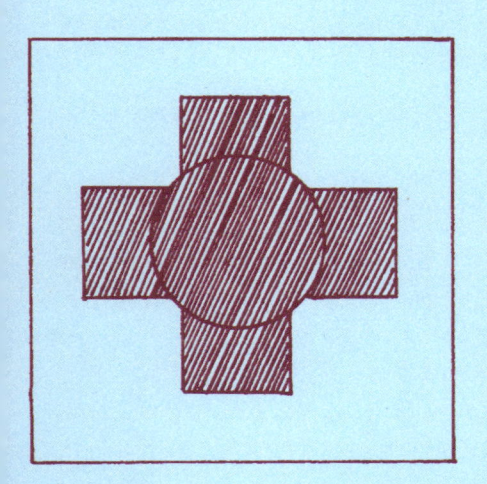

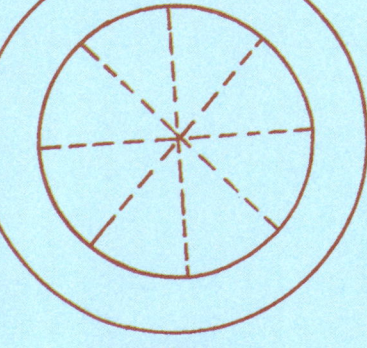

LINES FROM THE FILM

"Curiouser and curiouser…" —Alice

"Most everyone's mad here. You may have noticed that I'm not all there myself." —Cheshire cat

"After this, I shall think nothing

"Move down. Move down. Clean cup, clean cup. Move down!" —March Hare

"Don't let's be silly!" —Mad Hatter

"You're much too big. Simply impassible." —Doorknob

"of falling down stairs." —Alice

Alice's Unbirthday Tea Party

WITH 364 UNBIRTHDAYS to celebrate, almost every day out of the year can be just right for an Unbirthday Tea Party. Serve up the perfect pot of tea with shortbread teacakes, and have a mad time!

Tea:
2 teaspoons loose-leaf black tea or 2 tea bags
4 to 6 ounces warm milk
honey

For tea:

1. Have an adult bring a fresh pot of cold filtered or spring water to a boil. Remove from heat when water is just boiling.

2. Pour some water into teapot and let sit for a minute to warm the pot. Remove water.

3. Place tea leaves or bags in teapot. Pour 10 to 12 ounces water into teapot.

4. Allow to steep for 3 minutes.

5. Pour tea into teacups, filling the cups halfway. If brewing loose tea, be sure to pour tea through a strainer.

6. Add warm milk and honey. Sip slowly and enjoy.

Makes 2 servings.

For shortbread:

1. Preheat oven to 325° F.
2. Mix ingredients together until dough is thoroughly blended.
3. Pat into a 9 x 11" baking pan. Score the surface with a knife so that it can be easily cut into 24 pieces. Poke with a fork to add decorative marks.
4. Bake for about 30 minutes or until golden brown. Serve warm.

Makes 12 servings.

Shortbread:

1 ½ *cups all-purpose flour*
1 *cup butter, room temperature*
½ *cup powdered sugar*
½ *teaspoon almond extract*

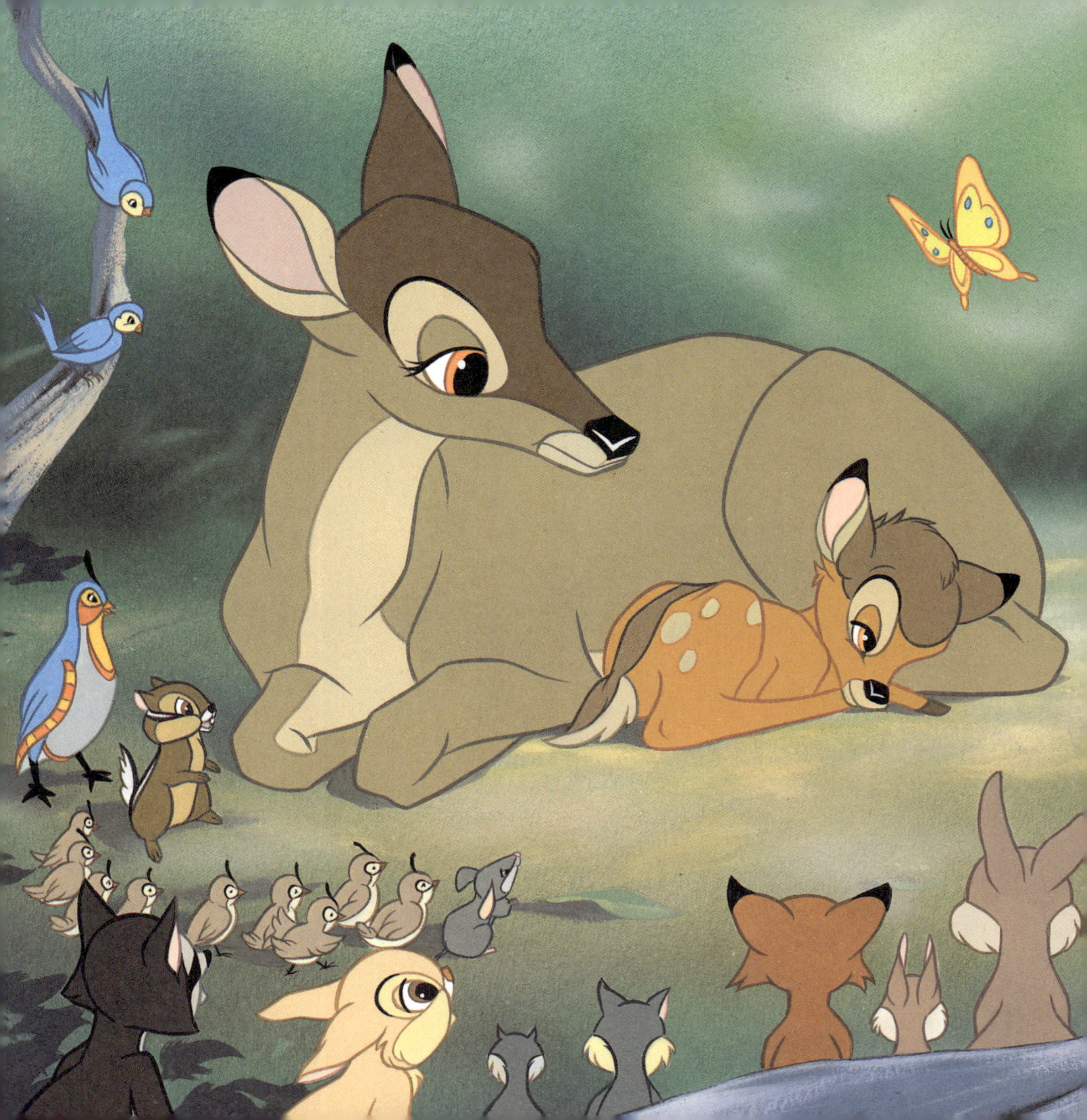

Bambi

ONE BRIGHT SPRING MORNING, Thumper the rabbit woke to the sound of birds singing a special song. "The new prince is born!" said Thumper. "Let's go see him!"

Squirrels, chipmunks, rabbits, and birds all gathered around the thicket. There, nestled by his mother's side, was a newborn fawn, sleeping. "This is quite an occasion," said Friend Owl. "It's not every day that a prince is born."

"Hello little prince!" said all the animals when the fawn awoke.

"Whatcha gonna call him?" Thumper asked the mother deer.

"Bambi," she said.

Soon Bambi was frolicking through the woods, making new friends. He met Mother Opossum, who liked to hang upside down with her little babies. Then Mr. Mole popped his head out of the ground to say hello. Even Mrs. Quail and her chicks stopped to say good morning.

Bambi had the most fun with Thumper and a shy skunk named Flower. They played together in the woods all day.

One day after a spring rain shower, Bambi's mother said he was old enough to go to the meadow. There, Bambi saw birds flying low over the tall grasses and ducklings swimming across the creek. A hopping frog led Bambi to a pond, where he met a playful fawn named Faline.

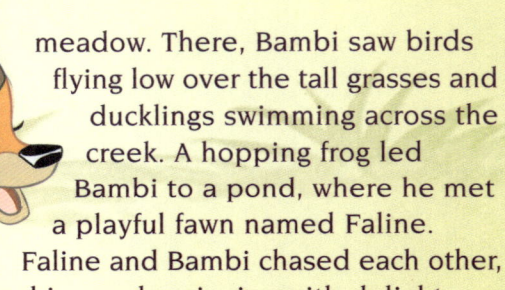

Faline and Bambi chased each other, laughing and springing with delight. Soon the meadow was filled with leaping young stags. Bambi watched the older deer and tried running and jumping the way they did.

Summer and fall ended, and winter's snow soon blanketed the forest. At the lake, Bambi found Thumper gliding across the ice. "The water's stiff," Thumper explained. He thumped the frozen lake with his foot to show Bambi. Before long, Thumper and Bambi were skating across the ice and playing in the snowbanks.

But winter was not all fun and games. As the cold days and nights continued, food became scarce. Bambi and his mother had to eat bark off the trees to survive. One day, after it seemed like there was nothing left to eat, Bambi discovered new shoots of spring grass.

As they hungrily ate, Bambi's mother sensed danger. "Quick, to the thicket!" she warned. They ran through the falling snow and heard the sound of gunshots.

"We made it, Mother!" Bambi said when he returned home. But his mother wasn't there.

Bambi searched through the storm and found his father, the Great Prince. "Your mother can't be with you anymore," the stag explained. "You must be brave and learn to walk alone."

By springtime, Bambi had sprouted antlers. Lovebirds filled the treetops with their wooing songs, as it was the time of year when forest animals fall in love. "They're twitterpated," Friend Owl explained. "It can happen to anybody."

It happened to Flower first. A giggling girl skunk peeked at him through the flowers. She kissed him, and then they were twitterpated! Then it happened to Thumper. A sweet girl bunny fluttered her eyelashes. She kissed him, and soon he was twitterpated, too!

Bambi didn't think it could happen to him. Then he saw Faline. With one kiss, Bambi was twitterpated, too. They frolicked together as if they were dancing on clouds.

But Bambi was not the only buck who liked Faline. A rival named Ronno challenged Bambi to a fight. They charged and locked antlers over and over in a fierce struggle. Finally, Bambi won. From that day on, he and Faline were always together.

One day, a fire broke out in the woods. The flames leaped to the trees and spread quickly throughout the forest. "Man is here again," the Great Prince told Bambi. "To the stream!" They ran to safety with all the creatures in the forest. Bambi met Faline waiting for him on the island in the lake. Together they watched the destruction man had brought to the forest.

Soon another spring arrived, with fresh flowers and new growth in the woods. "Wake up, Friend Owl!" said Thumper. "It's happened!" So Friend Owl, Thumper and his baby bunnies, and Flower and his baby skunks went with all the woodland animals to the thicket. There, nestled in the very same spot Bambi had been born, Faline rested with her new twin fawns.

High on the hilltop, Bambi and the Great Prince watched with pride. "My time is done," the Great Prince told Bambi. "It is now your time to be the Great Prince of the forest." And so Bambi stood alone and proud, watching over the thicket, his heart filled with love.

1. How did Thumper get his name?
2. Why does Thumper tell all the forest animals to gather at the thicket?
3. What is Bambi's first word?
4. Who does Bambi discover in a bed of flowers?
5. Which place does Bambi's mother say is dangerous?

BAMBI

6. Who is the bravest and wisest deer in the forest?
7. What happens to Bambi's mother?
8. What does Thumper teach Bambi to do in the winter when the water gets stiff?
9. What does Owl say happens to Bambi, Thumper, and Flower in the springtime?
10. Who does Bambi rescue Faline from in the forest?

Q & As

1. By the way he thumps his foot loudly on the ground
2. To welcome the new prince of the forest, Bambi
3. Bird
4. Flower, the skunk
5. The meadow, where there are no trees or bushes to hide behind
6. Bambi's father, the Great Prince
7. She gets shot by a hunter.
8. How to ice-skate
9. They get twitterpated.
10. Ronno

Bambi & Thumper On Ice

Can Thumper and Bambi skate gracefully on the ice? Or will they slide into a snowbank? Twirl the magnetic figures on a foil lake and see for yourself.

tracing paper, crayons, paper cement, white posterboard, scissors, 2 small metal paper clips, tape, 2 small round magnets, shoebox lid, aluminum foil, cotton balls, glue, bar magnet

Trace Bambi and Thumper onto tracing paper and color. Apply a small amount of paper cement to the back of the tracing paper and paste onto poster board. Have a grown-up help you cut out the figures. (Cut to the curved outline under Bambi's legs; do not cut out the area between his legs.) Bend one end of each paper clip so it forms a 90 degree angle. Tape one end of each paper clip to the base of each figure. Tape the other end of the paper clip to the top of a small round magnet. To make the ice-covered pond, cover the top of a shoebox with foil for ice and glue cotton balls around the edges for snow. Place Bambi and Thumper on the "ice" and move a bar magnet underneath the shoebox lid to make them slip and skate on the lake. Watch out for the snowdrifts!

LINES FROM THE FILM

BAMBI: Thumper!

FLOWER: Hi, fellows!

BAMBI: Flower!

FLOWER: Yeah!

<They notice birds twittering above.>

FLOWER: Well, what's the matter with them?

THUMPER: Why are they acting that way?

OWL: Why, don't you know? They're twitterpated!

BAMBI, THUMPER, FLOWER: Twitterpated!

OWL: Yes! Nearly everybody gets twitterpated in the springtime! For example, you're walking along minding your own business, you're looking neither to the left nor the right, then all of a sudden, you run right smack into a pretty face! Woo woo! You begin to get weak in the knees, your head's in a whirl, and then you feel light as a feather. And before you know it, you're walking on air! And then, you know what? You're

BAMBI: Hello, Friend Owl, don't you remember me?

OWL: Why, it's—it's the young prince, Bambi! My, my, how you've changed! Turn around there. Let me look at you. I see you've traded in your spots for a pair of antlers. You know, just the other day I was talking to myself about you and we were wondering what had become of you.

THUMPER: Hello, Bambi! Remember me?

knocked for a loop. You completely lose your head.

THUMPER: Gosh. That's awful!

FLOWER: Gee whiz!

BAMBI: Terrible!

OWL: It can happen to anybody. So you'd better be careful!

Thumper's Salad

THIS SALAD, made from some of Thumper's favorite munchables, is as much fun to look at as it is to eat. With a little imagination, it may even hop right off the plate and into your mouth!

2 pieces curly leaf lettuce
1 ripe pear, cored and peeled
2 dried cranberries
4 raisins
4 almond halves
2 scoops cottage cheese

1. Arrange lettuce leaves on two plates.

2. Place pear halves, cut side down, on top of each lettuce leaf.

3. Make small slits near the small end of each pear for eyes, ears, and nose. Then add a cranberry for the nose, raisins for eyes, and almond slices for ears.

4. Place a scoop of cottage cheese at the other end to make a tail.

Makes 2 servings.

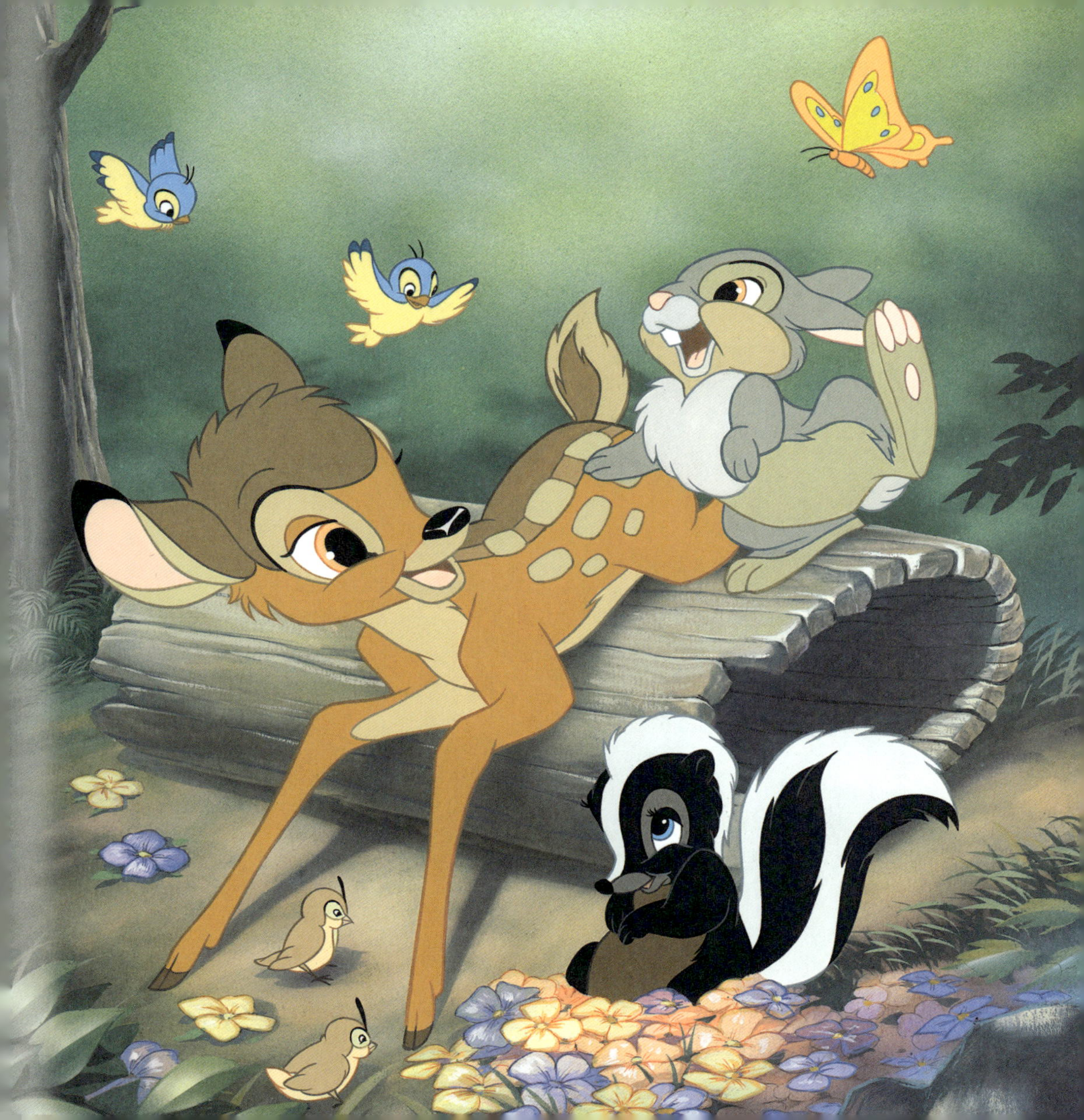

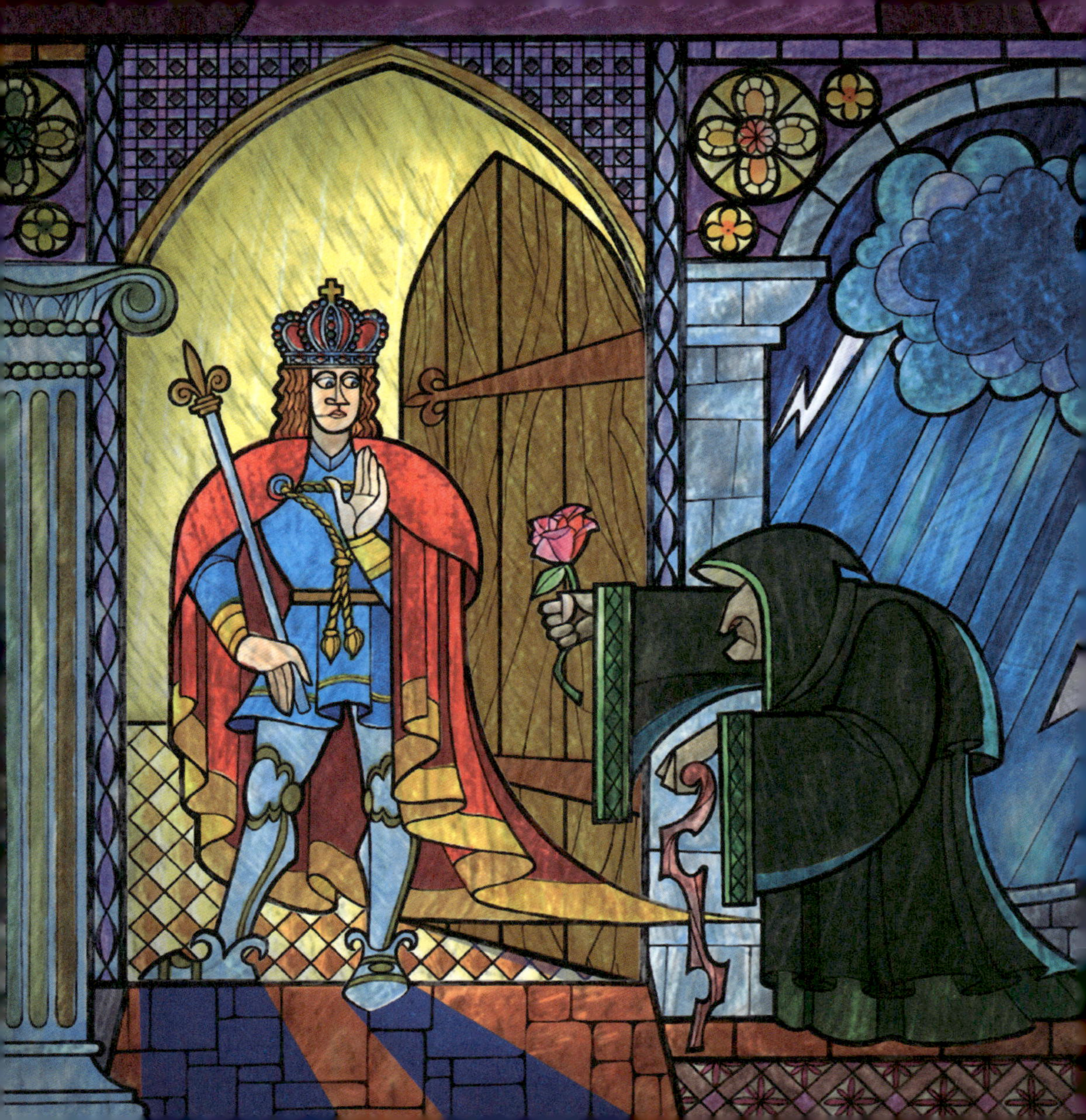

ONCE UPON A TIME, there lived a spoiled young prince who was so selfish and unkind that an enchantress turned the prince into a horrible Beast and placed a powerful spell over the entire castle.

She gave the Beast an enchanted rose that would bloom until his twenty-first year. During that time, if he could learn to love and be loved in return, the spell

Beauty & THE Beast

would be broken. If not, the prince would remain a Beast always.

Nearby, in a little village, lived the beautiful young Belle. The hunter Gaston wanted Belle for his wife, but she could never marry such a vain and arrogant man. She would rather read and dream about life outside her town.

One evening, Belle's father, Maurice, and his horse, Phillipe, got lost in the woods on the way to a fair. They stumbled upon a fierce pack of wolves that chased them all the way to a strange castle.

Maurice ran inside for help, but froze in horror when he saw the Beast. "Are you staring at me?" roared the Beast. He dragged Maurice to a dark tower in the castle and threw him into a dungeon.

"Where's Papa?" Belle cried when his horse came home alone. "Take me to him at once!" Together, she and the horse raced to the gates of the Beast's castle. Inside, Belle met the Beast. Frightened but brave, she begged for her father's life. "Take me instead," she offered.

"But you must promise to stay here forever," growled the Beast.

"You have my word," said Belle. Then, Maurice was freed. But instead of a dungeon, the Beast showed Belle to her own room.

The Beast's enchanted objects welcomed Belle with joy. They knew that if Belle could love the Beast, they would be set free. Cogsworth the clock and Lumiere the candlestick gave her a tour. Mrs. Potts the teapot poured her tea. All the pots and pans served a grand dinner just for her.

Time passed, and the Beast became kind to Belle. He showed her the best room in the castle: a huge library. "I've never seen so many books!" Belle said with delight.

"They're all yours," he told her.

Belle started to see a sweetness in the Beast that hadn't been there before. They read together, danced together, and shared meals together.

The day came when the last few petals remained on the enchanted rose. Time would soon run out to break the spell. That evening the Beast planned a romantic dinner with Belle. "Are you happy?" he asked.

"Yes," she said. "But I miss my father."

The Beast held up a magic mirror so that Belle could see her father. When she saw that he looked ill, she cried, "I must go to him!"

The Beast looked at his enchanted rose. He had lost his hope to break the spell. "I will set you free," the Beast told Belle. He gave her the mirror. "Look back and remember me," he said.

"I will never forget you," smiled Belle as she rushed off to be with her father.

The enchanted objects were shocked at the news. "How could you let her go?" asked Cogsworth.

"Because...I love her," said the Beast. And he roared in pain.

Meanwhile, when Maurice told the townsfolk about the Beast, they called him crazy. But when Belle returned, she held up her magic mirror and showed everyone that he was real.

"Let's kill the Beast!" shouted Gaston.

"He's not dangerous!" Belle pleaded. But Gaston didn't listen. He locked her inside the cottage and led an angry mob to the castle, but Belle eventually escaped.

Gaston found the Beast gazing sadly out the window. He drew his arrow and shot. The Beast fell to the terrace below and slumped over, with no desire to fight.

"No!" shouted Belle. The sound of her arrival lifted the Beast from despair. He grabbed Gaston. "Leave!" he ordered. Then he turned to Belle. "You came back." He smiled.

Gaston, jealous of Belle's affection for the Beast, stabbed him in the back. The Beast flailed in pain, causing Gaston to lose his grip and tumble off the edge to his death. The Beast fell at Belle's feet, gravely wounded. "Don't leave me," she wept. "I love you."

Suddenly, a swirling light transformed the Beast into a human once again. Belle looked into the eyes of a prince. "It's me," he said, and she knew it was true. The prince held her in his arms and they kissed. The servants, free from the spell, danced and cheered, for everyone knew the Prince and Belle would live happily ever after.

1. Why do the townsfolk think Belle is strange?
2. What does Belle's father invent to bring to the fair?
3. Why is the Beast a beast and his castle enchanted?
4. How long does the Beast tell Belle she must stay in the castle?
5. Where is the one part of the castle that the Beast forbids Belle to go?
6. How many eggs does Gaston eat a day?
7. How long will the Beast's enchanted rose continue to bloom?
8. What happens to Belle when she tries to run away from the castle?
9. What is Belle's favorite room in the Beast's castle?
10. What does Gaston do to try and get Belle to marry him?

BEAUTY AND

Q & As

1. Because she likes to read
2. An automated wood chopper and piler
3. Because an enchantress put a spell on him for having no love in his heart.
4. Forever
5. The West Wing
6. Five dozen
7. Until his twenty-first year
8. She's surrounded by wolves and the Beast saves her life.
9. The library
10. He plans to throw her father into an asylum.

THE BEAST

The Beast's Enchanted Rose

Will the Beast find true love before the last rose petal falls? Now you can make your own enchanted rose that will never wilt, and give Belle plenty of time to save her prince. Although this activity may be too challenging for very young children, it does produce beautiful flowers.

large paper clip, red and green masking tape, scissors

To create the stem, unfold the large paper clip into a long wire. Take a long strip of green tape and wrap it tightly around the wire to make the stem. To create a rose petal, cut a 2-inch-square strip of red tape. Fold over one corner so that the tip of the corner is in the center of the square, leaving stickiness along two sides. Fold an adjacent corner over in the same way, leaving stickiness along one remaining side. Hold the rose petal so that the triangular part is at the top. Wrap the petal around the tip of the stem, making sure not to wrap it too tightly. Repeat the steps to make additional petals, then wrap each new petal around the center petals until the rose has as many petals as you like. Finally, wrap one strip of green tape around the bottom of the rose to secure the stem in place. Let your enchanted rose bloom in a special place as Belle and the Beast's love for each other blooms.

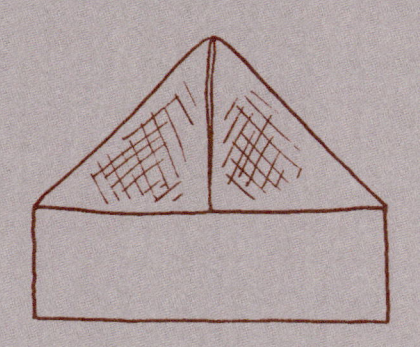

LINES FROM THE FILM

BEAST: I told you to come to dinner!

BELLE: I'm not hungry.

BEAST: You come out or I'll break down the door!

LUMIERE: Master, I could be wrong… but that may not be the best way to win her affections.

COGSWORTH: Please. Attempt to be a gentleman.

BEAST: <*to Cogsworth*> But she's being so difficult!

MRS. POTTS: Gently. Gently.

BEAST: <*to Belle*> Will you come down to dinner?

BELLE: No!

COGSWORTH: Suave, genteel.

BEAST: <to Belle> It would give me great pleasure... if you'd join me for dinner.

COGSWORTH: Say "please."

BEAST: Please.

BELLE: No, thank you.

BEAST: You can't stay in there forever!

BELLE: Yes, I can!

BEAST: <to Belle> Fine! Then go ahead and starve!

BEAST: <to group> If she doesn't eat with me, then she doesn't eat at all!

MRS. POTTS: Oh, dear. That didn't go very well at all.

Be Our Guest
Appetizers

LET LUMIERE be your host and arrange a tray with a colorful display that's good enough to eat. Everyone will feel welcome when these tasty tidbits dance off the plate and into their mouths.

1 dozen assorted table crackers
1 tablespoon cream cheese
6 cucumber slices
1 tablespoon mayonnaise
¼ teaspoon lemon juice
¼ teaspoon dill
3 grape tomatoes, quartered
3 very thin ham slices
3 slices pineapple
3 two-inch-long thin slices turkey breast
1 tablespoon cranberry sauce

1. Spread cream cheese on 3 crackers, layering with 2 slices of cucumber each.

2. Mix mayonnaise, lemon juice, and dill together and spread onto 3 crackers. Fan grape tomato slices on top.

3. Layer pineapple and ham on 3 more crackers.

4. Place turkey slices on the remaining crackers and top with cranberry sauce.

Makes 4 to 6 servings.

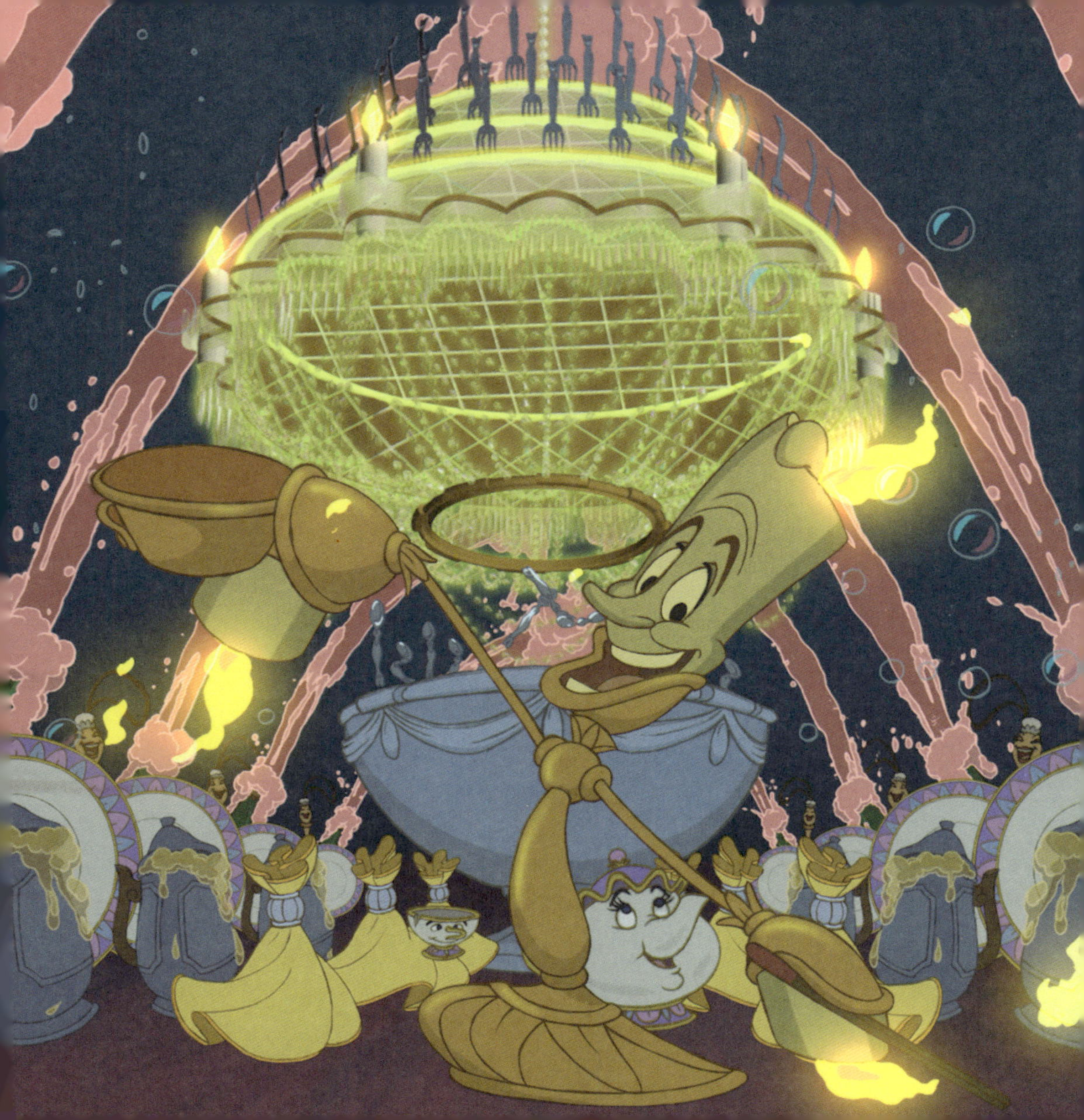

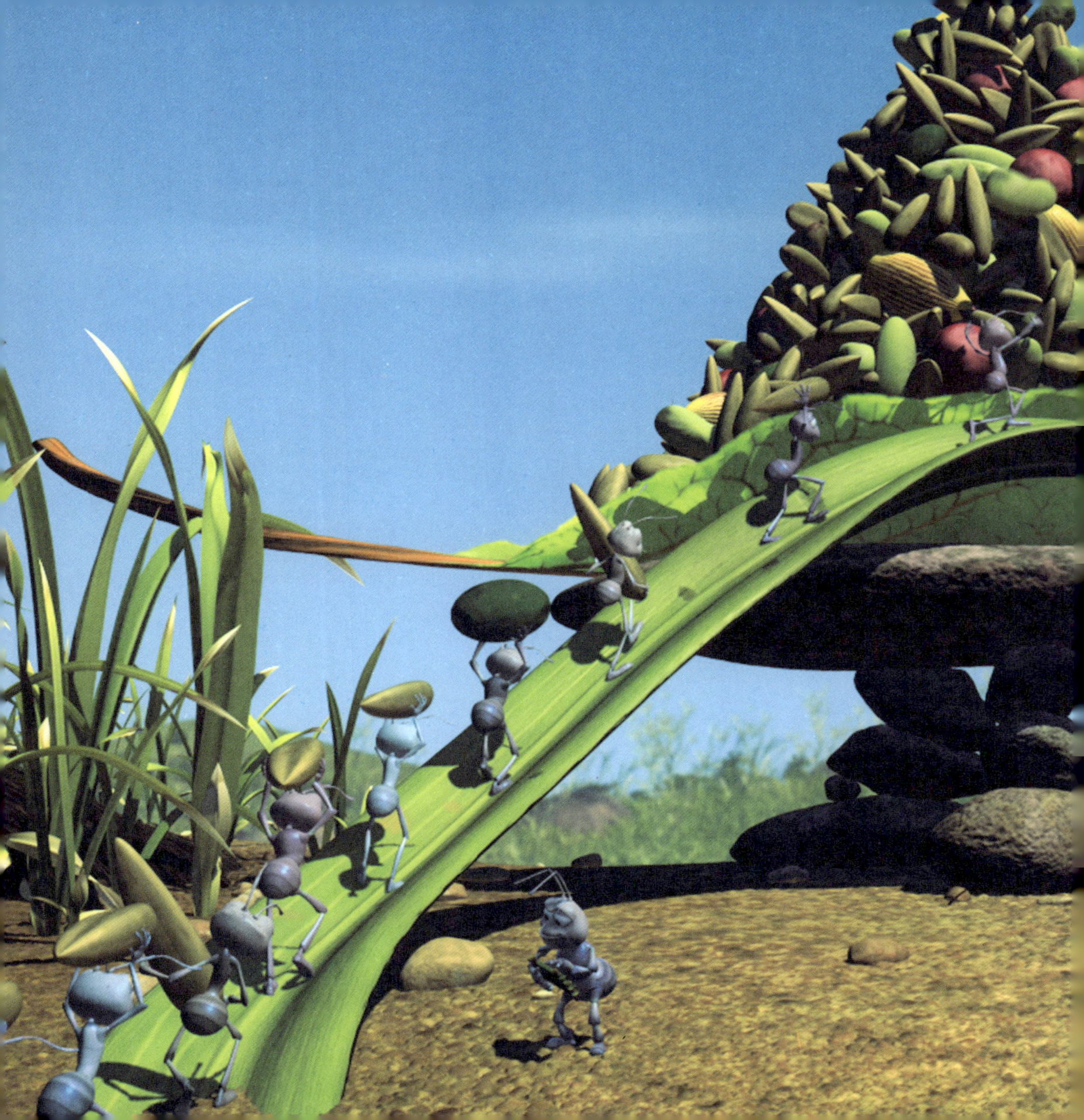

ONCE UPON A TIME, on a grass-covered island in the middle of a stream, a thriving colony of ants lived happily under a benevolent queen. Their only hardship was their annual offering of grain to the evil grasshopper Hopper and his clan.

A Bug's Life

One spring morning, as the ants were completing the offering, Flik showed off his new super-speedy, grain-gathering contraption. All the ants laughed at his silly invention—except Princess Atta and her little sister, Princess Dot.

Suddenly the sky was filled with the buzz of approaching grasshoppers, sending the ants running for the anthill. Flik unloaded his grains, but when he ran for the hill, his grain harvester slipped .... and CRASH! The annual offering tumbled into the river below!

Hopper and his gang stormed the anthill in a rage. "There's

still a few months before the rains come," he told the Queen. "If you don't keep your end of the bargain, someone might get hurt." The ants knew there wasn't enough time to gather grain for the grasshoppers and still have enough left over to survive the winter.

When the grasshoppers left, Flik volunteered to find bigger, meaner bugs to fight the grasshoppers. The colony cheered when he left, but Flik did not know it was because they were happy to be rid of him.

A few days later, to everyone's surprise, Flik returned with an army of warriors. The colony threw a celebration in their honor. But when the new bugs learned that they would be fighting grasshoppers, they told Flik they had to leave. "We're really part of a flea circus," they explained. "The whole warrior thing is an act."

But Flik had a plan. "Hoppers are afraid of birds—so we'll build one that we can operate from the inside. But I need your help," he told them. The circus crew agreed. They convinced the colony of the idea, and soon everyone stopped gathering food for the grasshoppers to build a bird instead.

As the summer months passed, the grasshoppers lazed about eating and drinking to their hearts' content in a cantina south of the border. With so much food at their disposal, some of the grasshoppers wondered why they should bother going back to Ant Island. "It's not about food, it's about keeping them in line," Hopper said. And he rallied the grasshoppers back to Ant Island.

Meanwhile, a stranger arrived on Ant Island with a big wagon. It was P. T. Flea, looking for his missing circus troupe. Suddenly, the entire colony saw that the warriors were really circus performers and that Flik was really a fraud. "Go!" said Queen to the circus performers. "And don't come back," Princess Atta told Flik.

Soon thereafter, Hopper's gang returned to Ant Island. When they didn't find their food, Hopper took the Queen hostage. "Get every scrap of food on this island," he demanded. "Or I'll squish her."

As the ants scrambled for food, Dot flew to P. T. Flea's caravan and told Flik what Hopper had done.

Discouraged, Flik didn't think his plan could work. But the troupe cheered him up, and soon they were on their way back to Ant Island.

By the time P. T. Flea's circus returned, the grasshoppers had rounded up all the ants and stolen every last scrap of food. "We've been specially invited by Princess Atta to perform for you," P. T. Flea told Hopper. Flattered, the grasshoppers sat down to watch the show.

Meanwhile, Flik and a group of ants climbed into their hidden weapon. With one swoop of the mechanical bird, chaos ensued and the grasshoppers fled for safety. In the confusion, the bird collided with P. T. Flea's Flaming Death act and caught fire. When Hopper saw the bird was a fake, he attacked Flik and carried him off.

In a daring rescue attempt, Princess Atta freed Flik from Hopper's grasp in midair. They dropped into the grass and found themselves next to a real bird's nest. "I have an idea," Flik said, and they hid among the grass.

Hopper buzzed down and was ready to kill them, when he heard a bird chirp behind him. Thinking it was another trick, Hopper approached the bird.

But Hopper was mistaken—the bird plucked him off the ground and fed him to her hungry chicks!

As the end of summer approached, the sun smiled on Ant Island. In the field, ants harvested more grain than ever with the help of Flik's harvesting machines. With all well, the time had come for the circus troupe to set off for new adventures. As they waved good-bye, the ants saluted them with fireworks of grain in celebration of victories and happiness.

A BUG'S LIFE

1. What are the names and types of all ten circus bugs?
2. What does Flik invent to speed production for the ant colony?
3. What is Flik's plan to defeat Hopper?
4. What is P.T. Flea's most popular circus act?
5. What does Flik think the circus bugs are when he first meets them?
6. What is the name of Dot's club of young ants?
7. What eventually becomes of Hopper?
8. What do the circus bugs do to make the colony think they're warriors?
9. Where do the grasshoppers go in the spring while the ants are working?
10. What materials do the ants use to make their mechanical bird?

Q & A's

1. Rosie, the black widow; Dim, the rhino beetle; Heimlich, the caterpillar; Francis, the ladybug; Slim, the walking stick; Gypsy, the gypsy moth; Manny, the praying mantis; Tuck and Roll, the two pillbugs; P.T. Flea, the flea
2. A grain harvester
3. To build an artificial bird that they can operate from the inside and use to scare off the grasshoppers
4. Flaming Death
5. Warriors
6. The Blueberry Troop
7. He becomes lunch to a nest of baby birds.
8. They save Dot from being eaten by a bird.
9. They go to a cantina south of the border.
10. Twigs, branches, Rosie's silk, a snail shell, and leaves

Egg Carton Insects

Make more insects! Flik, Atta, Dot, and their friends from P. T. Flea's circus troop need all the help they can get to save Ant Island from Hopper's raiding gang of grasshoppers.

egg cartons, scissors, tempera paint, paintbrushes, pipe cleaners, googly eyes, markers

Ant: 3 cups, 2 antennae, 6 legs; blue paint
Caterpillar: 4 to 6 cups, 2 antennae; green paint
Ladybug: 1 cup, 2 antennae, 6 legs; red and black paints
Spider: 1 cup, 8 legs; black paint

To make egg carton insects, cut one to six cups from an egg carton. Decorate with tempera paint and let dry. To make legs, poke a hole in the side of each cup and insert pipe cleaners. To make antennae, poke two small holes in the top of the first cup and insert pipe cleaners. Glue on googly eyes and draw on a mouth. Will the insects save the colony, become warriors, or just join the circus?

LINES FROM THE FILM

"You always cast me as the broom, the pole, the stick, a splinter." —Slim

"I hate performing on an empty stomach." —Heimlich

"That's how my twelfth husband died. So now I'm a widow. I mean, I've always been a black widow— now I'm a black widow widow." —Rosie

"So being a ladybug automatically makes me a girl, is that it, flyboy?" —Francis

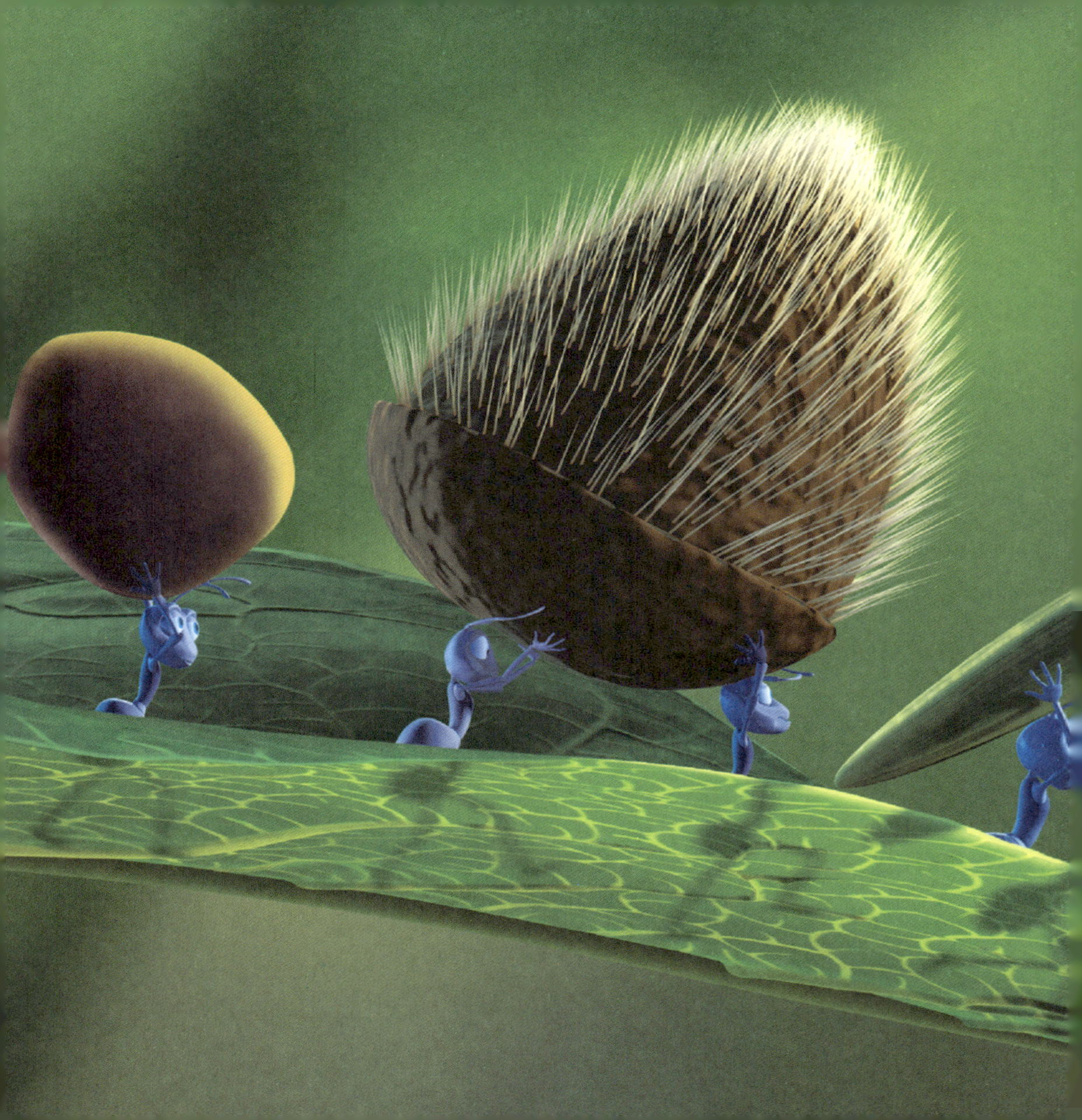

Ant Trail Mix

AS FLIK, Dot, and her Blueberry Troop of junior ants know, eating right is what it takes to make strong harvesters. This meal will last all winter long, and is a great source of energy to hike up any trail.

1 cup sunflower seeds
1 cup pecans or walnuts
1 cup hazelnuts
1 cup peanuts
1 cup yogurt-covered raisins
½ cup shredded coconut
1 cup dried cranberries
½ cup dried cherries
½ cup dried apricots
½ cup dried apples
½ cup banana chips

1. Mix all ingredients together in a large bowl.

2. Store in individual snack packs and seal in an airtight container.

3. Grab a snack pack when you're on the go and munch along the way.

4. Ant Trail Mix will last up to 4 months on the shelf.

Makes about 8 cups.

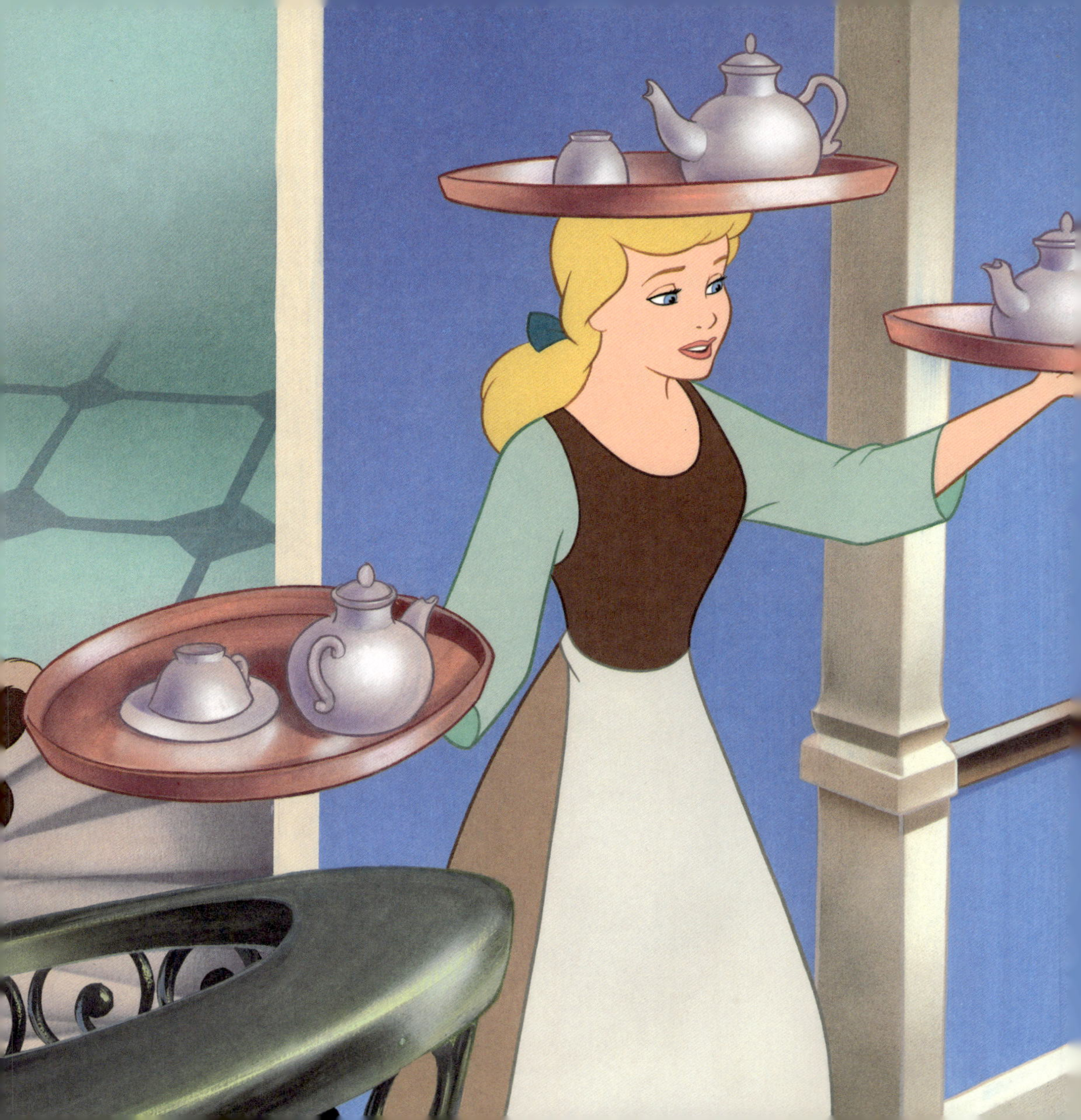

ONCE UPON A TIME, in a faraway kingdom, there lived a widowed gentleman and his daughter, Cinderella. He felt she needed a mother's care, so he married Lady Tremaine, who had two young daughters, Drizella and Anastasia. Unfortunately, Cinderella's father met an untimely death. Soon after, Cinderella's Stepmother showed her true, wicked, nature—as did her stepsisters.

Cinderella

One morning, like every other morning, Cinderella awoke to a day of chores and her stepsisters' annoying requests that she bring them tea. Cinderella didn't see that Lucifer the cat was tormenting her two mice friends, Jaq and Gus. When the stepsisters found the mice hiding under their teacups, their shrieks could be heard all the way to Lady Tremaine's room. "Apparently, you have time for vicious practical jokes," she scolded Cinderella. "For that, you shall clean the entire house, do all the mending and laundry—and see that Lucifer gets his bath."

Meanwhile, the King of their land was thinking about his future grandchildren. "It's high time my son settles down and gets married!" he said. "We need to arrange the right conditions for him—a ball to celebrate!" The Grand Duke saw to it that every maiden of marriageable age would be there.

That afternoon, Lady Tremaine received an invitation. "A ball tonight at the palace— eight o'clock!"

Drizella and Anastasia twittered with ungraceful glee.

"I'm an eligible maiden," said Cinderella. "That means I can go, too!"

The stepsisters grew fierce. "No, Mother! Don't let her come!"

But Lady Tremaine told Cinderella, "IF you get all your work done, and IF you can find something suitable to wear, then yes, you too may go."

Overjoyed, Cinderella ran to her room. She pulled out an old dress that her mother had worn. "With a little trim, I'm sure that I can make it work!" But the stepsisters kept her busy with their needless demands.

Cinderella dutifully returned to her chores, while the stepsisters grumbled about clothes. They tossed out an old sash and string of beads that they swore they'd never wear again. Eight o'clock came around too quickly, and Cinderella hadn't had one moment to work on her dress.

But when she arrived in her room, her animal friends surprised her! The mice and birds used the stepsisters' sash and beads to turn her mother's dress into the loveliest gown she had ever seen.

"Thank you so much!" Cinderella cried. The dress fit perfectly.

When the jealous stepsisters saw their old things on Cinderella's gown, they tore it to shreds. Drizella and Anastasia went to the ball with their mother, and poor Cinderella ran into the garden to cry.

At that moment, Cinderella's Fairy Godmother appeared out of a sparkly cloud. "Don't cry, dear," she said. With a few waves of her magic wand, the Fairy Godmother transformed a pumpkin into a coach, Cinderella's mice friends into horses, a horse into a coachman, and Bruno the dog into the footman. With a final touch of her wand, the Fairy Godmother turned Cinderella's torn rags into a dress fit for a princess, and added a pair of dainty glass slippers.

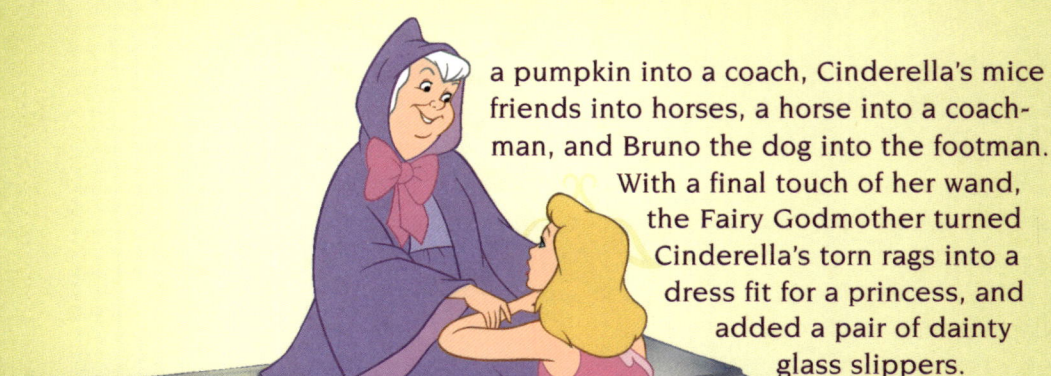

"Return not a minute past midnight, for the spell will be broken," she warned. "Hurry along!"

The moment the Prince laid eyes on Cinderella, it was as if no one else were at the ball. He danced with Cinderella all night long. The King was thrilled to see them falling in love. But when the clock began to strike midnight, Cinderella ran away. In her haste, she lost a glass slipper on the staircase. The Prince ordered his footmen to chase her, but at the stroke of twelve, the spell was broken and her coach turned back into a pumpkin. Cinderella and her animal friends just missed the royal horsemen as they rode by and trampled the pumpkin.

The next day, Cinderella hummed and danced happily about her chores unaware of her stepmother's watchful eye. When Lady Tremaine heard that the Grand Duke was searching for the one woman whose foot would fit the missing glass slipper, she locked Cinderella in her room. Luckily, Gus and Jaq stole the key and freed Cinderella in the nick of time. She ran downstairs to try on the slipper, but Lady Tremaine tripped the Footman and shattered the shoe into pieces. "But you see," cried Cinderella pulling something out of her pocket, "I have the other slipper!"

The King couldn't have been more pleased. Church bells rang across the kingdom as Cinderella and the Prince wed. The couple rode off in their wedding coach and lived happily ever after.

1. What does Anastasia discover under her teacup when Cinderella delivers her breakfast?

2. What do Anastasia and Drizella throw away that Gus and Jaq take for Cinderella's dress?

3. What talents do Anastasia and Drizella show off during their music lesson?

4. Under what conditions is Cinderella allowed to attend the ball?

5. What do Cinderella's mice and bird friends do to surprise her when she is forced to do chores all day?

CINDERELLA

6. What do Anastasia and Drizella do when they see their old sash and beads on Cinderella's dress?

7. What does Cinderella's Fairy Godmother use to make the coach that will take her to the royal ball?

8. What does the Prince do when he sees Cinderella at the ball?

9. Where does Cinderella lose her glass slipper?

10. What does Cinderella do when the Footman trips and breaks the glass slipper before she can try it on?

Q & As

1. Gus the mouse
2. A sash and a string of beads
3. Drizella sings and Anastasia plays the flute.
4. That she finishes all the chores and that she finds something suitable to wear
5. They alter her mother's old dress into a beautiful gown for her to wear to the ball.
6. They tear her dress to shreds.
7. A pumpkin for the coach, mice for horses, a horse for the coachman, and Bruno the dog for a footman
8. He dances with her for the rest of the night.
9. On the steps of the royal palace
10. She pulls the matching glass slipper out of her pocket, proving that she is the one the Prince wants to marry.

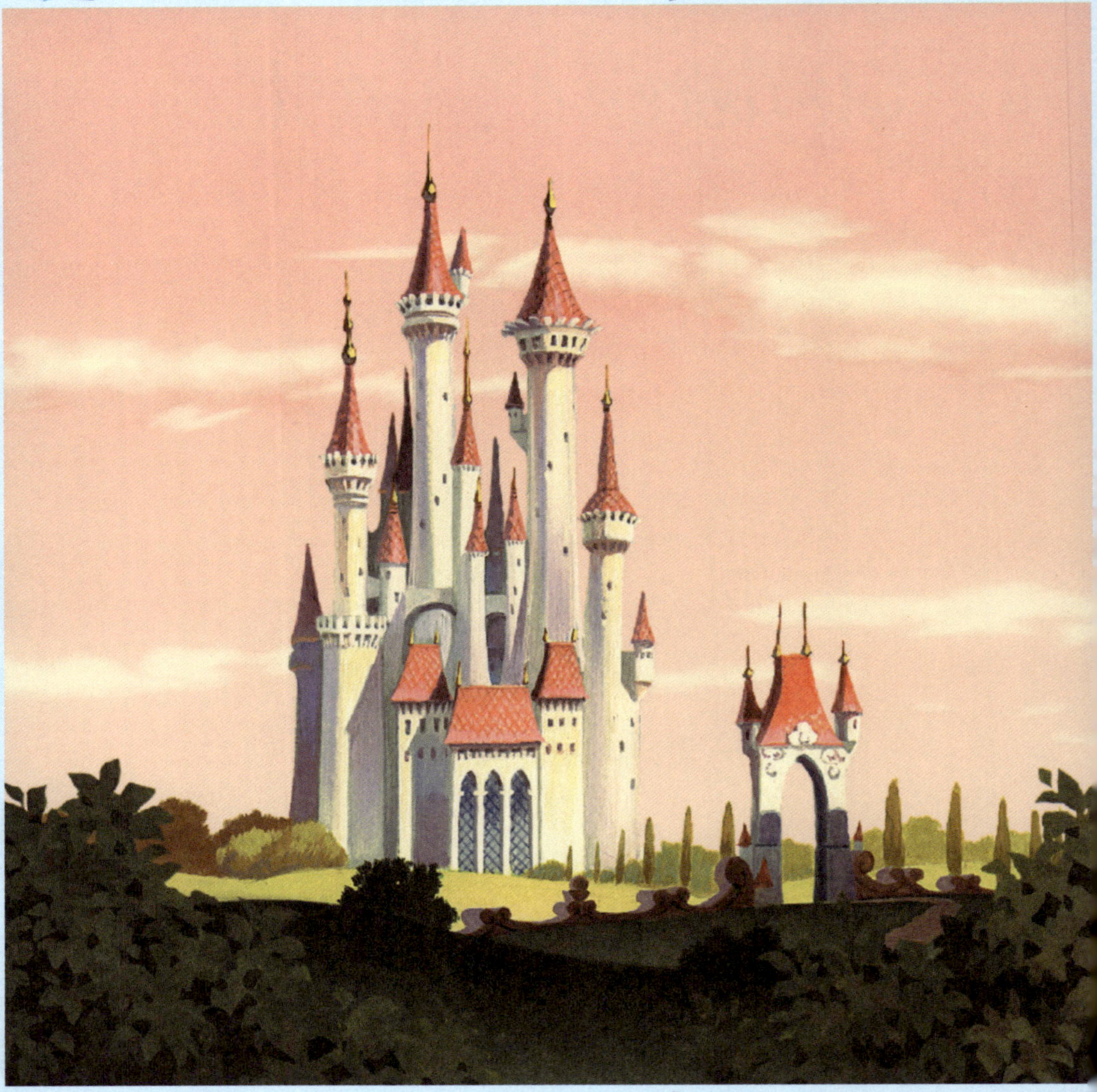

Cinderella's Castle

Thanks to the Fairy Godmother, Cinderella meets the prince of her dreams and lives happily ever after in a magnificent castle. With a little creative magic of your own and help from an adult, you can have a ball making a castle where dreams come true.

4 paper-towel tubes, scissors, square tissue box, poster paint, paintbrush, construction paper, glue, markers, plastic drinking straw

Trim the paper-towel tubes so that they are three inches taller than the tissue box. Cut 8 evenly spaced 1-inch-deep slits around the top of each tube. Fold every other tab down to create castle turrets. Paint the turrets and the tissue box and set aside to dry. Cut castle doors and windows out of construction paper. When the paint is dry, glue doors and windows onto the tissue box and turrets. Then glue the turrets to the four corners of the tissue box. To make a flag, cut out a construction-paper triangle and decorate it with a marker. For the flagpole, cut a slit in the top of the drinking straw and slide the flag in to the slit. Glue the straw onto the inside of one of the castle turrets. Your castle now awaits Cinderella and her prince!

"And don't forget the garden, then scrub the terrace, sweep the halls and the stairs, clean the chimneys, and of course, there's the mending and the sewing and the laundry." —Lady Tremaine

"We'll have to hurry because even miracles take a little time." —Fairy Godmother

"Did you ever see such a beautiful dress? And look... glass slippers! Why, it's like a dream. A wonderful dream come true!" —Cinderella

LINES FROM THE FILM

"But you see, I have the other slipper." —Cinderella

Pumpkin Coach Cupcakes

HAVE A BALL decorating these miniature versions of Cinderella's magical coach. The outside may be frosted to look like a ride for a princess, but one bite will tell you that this coach is really pumpkin.

CUPCAKES:
2 cups flour
2 teaspoons baking powder
1 teaspoon cinnamon
1/2 teaspoon ground ginger
1/2 teaspoon nutmeg
1/4 teaspoon salt
1/2 cup vegetable oil
1 1/4 cups sugar
2 eggs
1 teaspoon vanilla extract
1 cup mashed cooked or canned pumpkin

1. Preheat oven to 350°F.
2. In a large bowl, sift together all the dry ingredients except sugar.
3. In a separate bowl, stir oil and sugar together. Whisk in eggs and vanilla.
4. Pour wet ingredients over dry ingredients and mix. Stir in pumpkin until blended.
5. Spoon into a well-greased muffin pan.
6. Bake for 25 minutes or until tester comes out clean.

FROSTING:

1 8-ounce package cream cheese, room temperature

$\frac{1}{4}$ cup butter

1 pound confectioners' sugar, sifted

2 teaspoons vanilla extract

red and yellow food coloring

vanilla wafers

decorative cake toppings, such as cake sparkles, edible glitter, nonpareils

1. Beat together cream cheese, butter, sugar, and vanilla until smooth.

2. Wisk in about 4 drops of red food coloring and 12 drops of yellow to make the frosting orange.

3. Spread tops of cupcakes with frosting.

4. Add vanilla wafer wheels to sides of cupcakes, using frosting as paste.

5. Decorate with cake sparkles, edible glitter, nonpareils, or similar toppings.

Makes 12 cupcakes.

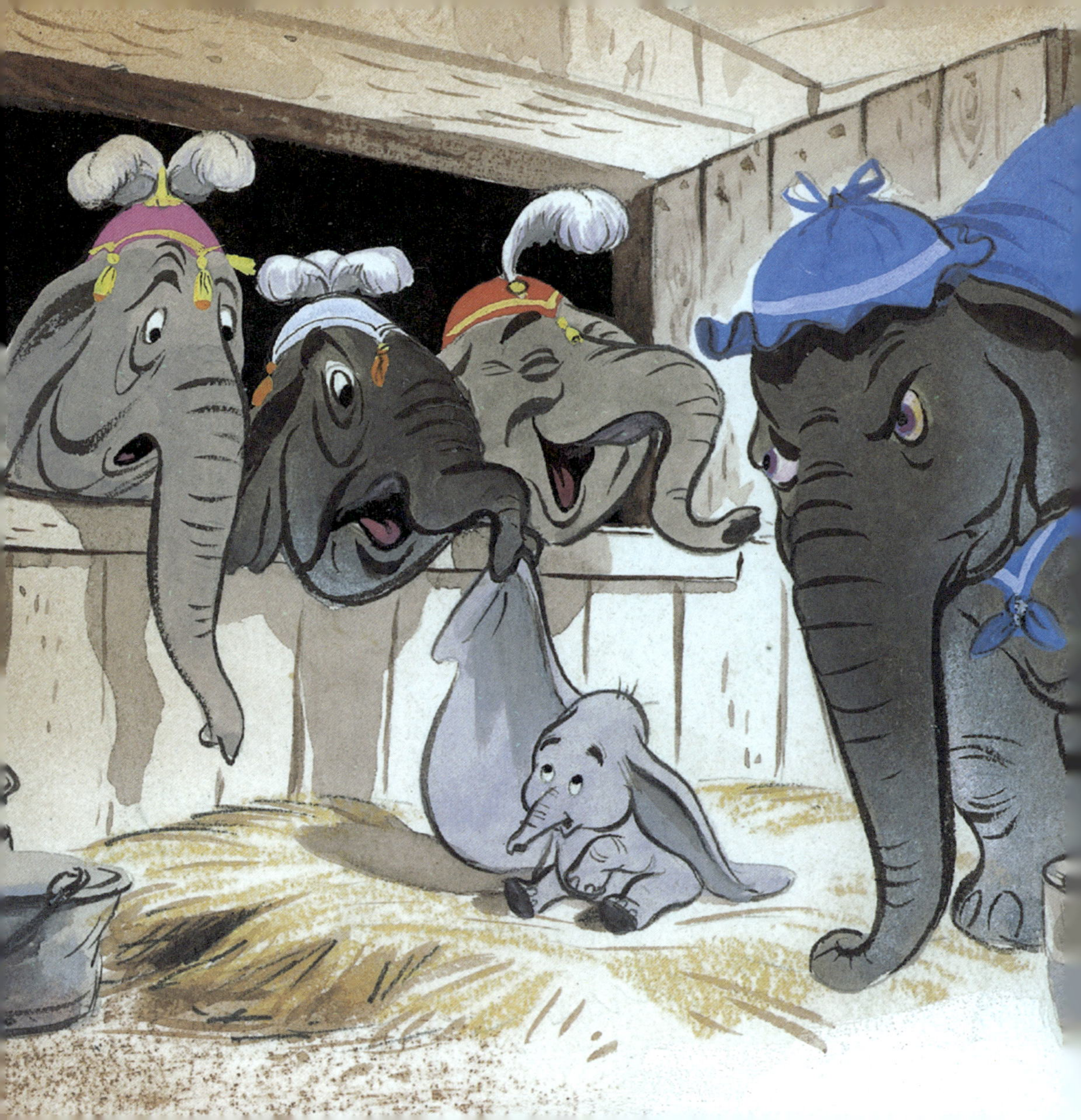

Dumbo

THE FIRST DAY OF SPRING was growing near, and all the circus animals knew it was time for special deliveries. The storks made their way through the last of the winter snow and sleet, bearing special bundles for all the expectant parents.

One by one, all the new circus babies got delivered: bear, kangaroo, tiger, hippo, giraffe. Mrs. Jumbo, the elephant, was expecting a delivery, too.

"All aboard!" shouted the ringmaster. Casey the train blew his whistle. Time to get rolling! As the train pulled out of the station, Mrs. Jumbo's stork flew aboard. The new mother unwrapped the bundle the stork brought her to see the sweetest blue-eyed baby looking up at her. "Happy Birthday, Jumbo Junior," sang the stork.

"He's adorable," said one elephant. "Better than I expected," said another. A third elephant tickled him with her trunk, and … ACHOO! Out popped the largest ears any elephant had ever seen. All the elephants roared with laughter. "He should be called Dumbo!"

But Mrs. Jumbo ignored them and lovingly cradled her new son.

When the train arrived at the first town, all the animals got out and helped pitch the big tent. In the morning, a big parade marched through town announcing the circus.

Inside the big tent, some boys began making fun of Dumbo. Mrs. Jumbo got angry and spanked one of the boys with her trunk. Suddenly, pandemonium broke out. When the ruckus ended, Mrs. Jumbo was locked away in a cramped cart, with a sign that read DANGER, MAD ELEPHANT.

"It's all the fault of that F–R–E–A–K," said one of the other elephants. "With ears only a mother could love!"

Timothy the mouse couldn't see what was wrong with Dumbo. He found the sad little elephant under a bale of hay. "Too bad you don't trust me, 'cause I thought we could get your mother out of the clink," said the mouse. Dumbo poked his head out of the hay. "All we have to do is make you a star."

That night, Timothy snuck into the ringmaster's tent and climbed onto his pillow. "I am the voice of your inspiration," he whispered into the ringmaster's ear. "The little elephant with the big ears will be the climax of your show. Dumbo..."

The next evening the ringmaster was pleased to announce a grand spectacle. "Seven magnificent pachyderms will now form a pyramid atop this ball."

But when the time came for Dumbo's grand finale, he tripped on his ears and sent elephants flying everywhere.

When the circus came to the next town, Dumbo was dressed as a clown and rescued from a burning building. That night the other clowns celebrated a show well done with many glasses of champagne.

Dumbo was not happy about being a clown. Timothy decided to cheer him up by taking him to visit his mother. Mrs. Jumbo could only reach her baby with her trunk through the bars of her cage, but she rocked little Dumbo gently and comforted him.

The next morning, a crow woke Timothy. He and Dumbo were sleeping in a tree! "How do you suppose we got up here?" Timothy wondered. "Maybe you flew up," laughed the crow.

"That's it, Dumbo!" Timothy shouted. "Your ears! You can fly!" So Dumbo and Timothy spent some time practicing flying with the crows. Just to be sure, one of the crows gave the little elephant a "magic" feather and told Dumbo the feather would allow him to fly. The feather wasn't really magic—the crow just wanted to help Dumbo.

That night, Dumbo clutched his feather for his big act and dove through the air. But the feather slipped from his grip and suddenly he and Timothy were falling fast. "The magic feather was just a gag!" shouted Timothy, clutching his hands together. "You can fly!"

Suddenly, over a group of astonished clowns, Dumbo flapped his ears and soared on his own through the big tent. With a big power dive he forced all the clowns to leap for safety into a big bucket of water. The crowd went wild!

The next day, Dumbo made headlines across the nation. His ears were insured for $1,000,000 and the circus was renamed "Dumbo's Flying Circus." But best of all, Dumbo got a personal streamlined railcar, with a special seat just for his mother, Mrs. Jumbo.

1. What does Mrs. Jumbo do when a boy makes fun of Dumbo?
2. What is the name of the circus train?
3. How many elephants is Dumbo supposed to balance on top of during the pachyderm pyramid act?
4. What happens to Dumbo after the circus tent collapses?
5. What do the crows give Dumbo to help him fly?
6. What stunt do the clowns make Dumbo do?

DUMBO

7. What is Dumbo's original name?
8. What happens to Dumbo's mother for protecting her son?
9. How much are Dumbo's ears insured for?
10. What is the new circus called once Dumbo becomes a star?

Q & As

1. She spanks the boy with her trunk.
2. Casey Jr.
3. Seven
4. The Ringmaster makes Dumbo a clown.
5. A magic feather
6. Jump from a burning building
7. Jumbo Junior
8. She is chained in a cage labeled "mad elephant."
9. One million dollars
10. Dumbo's Flying Circus

Casey Jr.'s Circus Train

Take a ride with Casey Jr. and Dumbo's Flying Circus. Make a car for each animal in the circus, then shout "All Aboard!" and chug along to the next town for a big-top circus thrill.

small pantry-item boxes (such as empty tea or cracker boxes), scissors, brown wrapping paper, tape, paintbrushes, finger paint, markers, glue, buttons, large paper clips

Collect small boxes as cars for bears, kangaroos, tigers, giraffes, lions, elephants, and other circus animals. Cut brown wrapping paper and use tape to wrap it around each box. With finger paints, make thumb and finger prints along the sides of the boxes to create various animal bodies. Then use a marker to draw animal eyes, ears, tails, and feet on the thumbprint bodies. Using paintbrushes, add bars to the circus cars and decorate the tops and ends of each car. Glue buttons on each car to make train wheels.

To connect the cars, straighten paper clips and bend each end to point down at a 90-degree angle. Poke holes in the ends of each car, then insert paper clip ends into the holes to link the cars together. Get ready to step right up and see the big-top show!

LINES FROM THE FILM

<Dumbo is on edge of cliff being pushed by crows>

CROWS: Let's go! Let's go! Heave ho, heave ho!

TIMOTHY: Let's go, Dumbo!

CROWS: Let's go!

<Timothy slides down Dumbo's trunk with magic feather clutched in it>

CROWS: Let's go, heave ho!

TIMOTHY: Come on, now. Up, down, up down, one, two, one, two, one, two—faster!

CROWS: Heave ho!

<Dumbo flaps his ears, waving a cloud of dust>

TIMOTHY: Faster! Get up to flying speed! Retract your landing gear. Raise your fuselage! Take off!

<A huge cloud of dust covers them as Dumbo continues flapping his ears>

TIMOTHY: Aw—it's no use, Dumbo! I guess it's just another one of their—

<Timothy jumps in the air and points>

TIMOTHY: Look!

<They see Dumbo's shadow on the ground below>

TIMOTHY: Hot diggity! You're flying! You're flying!

ONE CROW: Ha! Ha! Ha! Ha! Why, he flies just like a' eagle! Better than a' airplane!

SECOND CROW: Well, now I've seen everything!

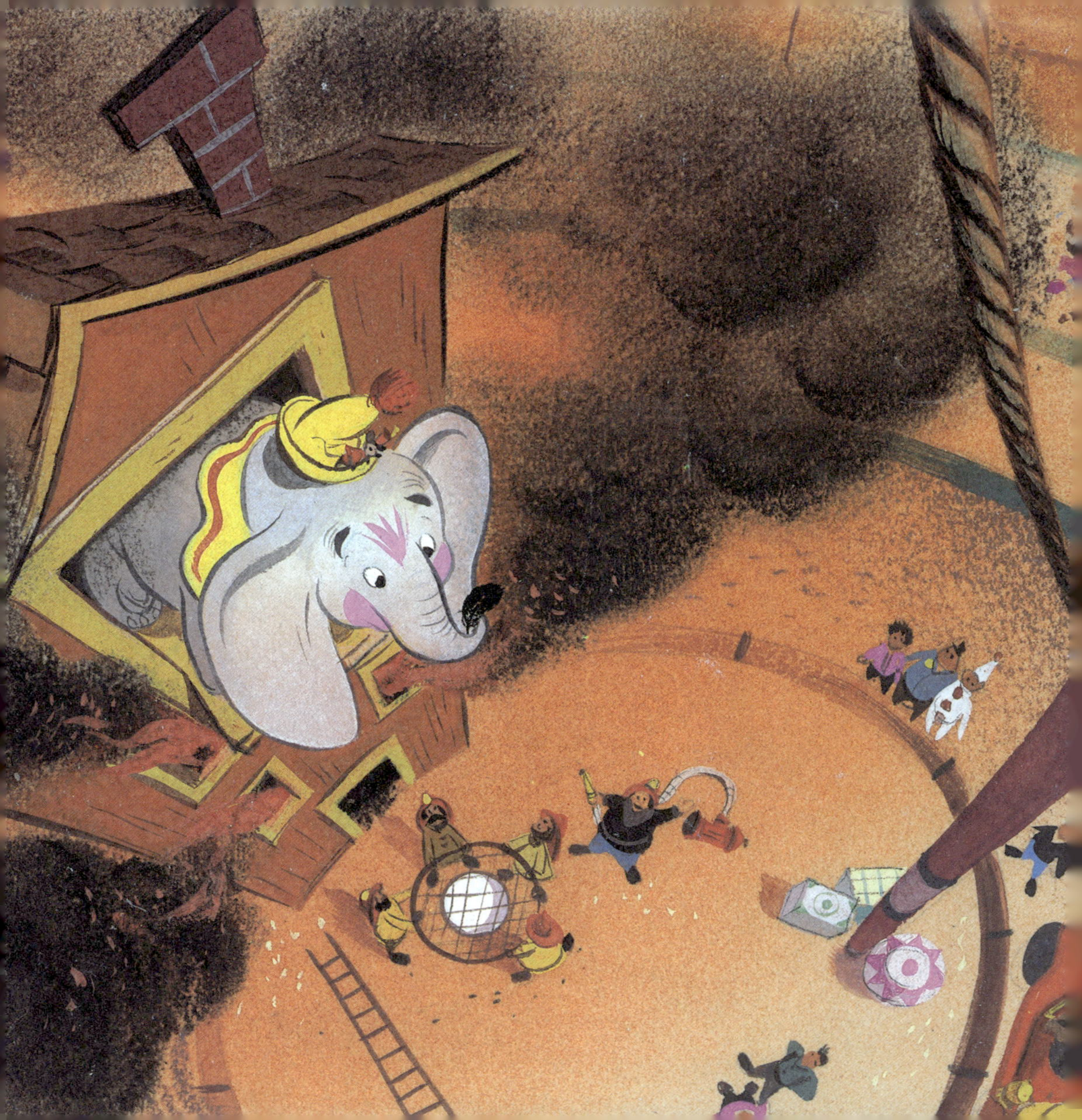

Dumbo's Circus Popcorn

WHEN IT'S TIME to see Dumbo the Flying Elephant under the circus big top, what better way to enjoy the show than with Dumbo's sticky popcorn? This snack will have you licking your fingers, so be sure to save a peanut for your favorite elephant before it all disappears.

8 jumbo-sized marshmallows
⅓ cup butter
⅓ cup brown sugar
½ cup popcorn, freshly popped
1 cup salted peanuts

1. Melt butter and brown sugar together in a microwave on high in 30-second increments until melted.

2. Add 4 marshmallows and microwave on high for 20 seconds. Add remaining marshmallows and microwave for another 20 seconds. Stir every 20 seconds until melted together.

3. Allow mixture to cool for about one minute.

4. In a large bowl, toss popcorn and peanuts.

5. Pour caramel mixture over the popcorn and mix well.

6. Serve immediately.

Makes 4 to 6 servings.

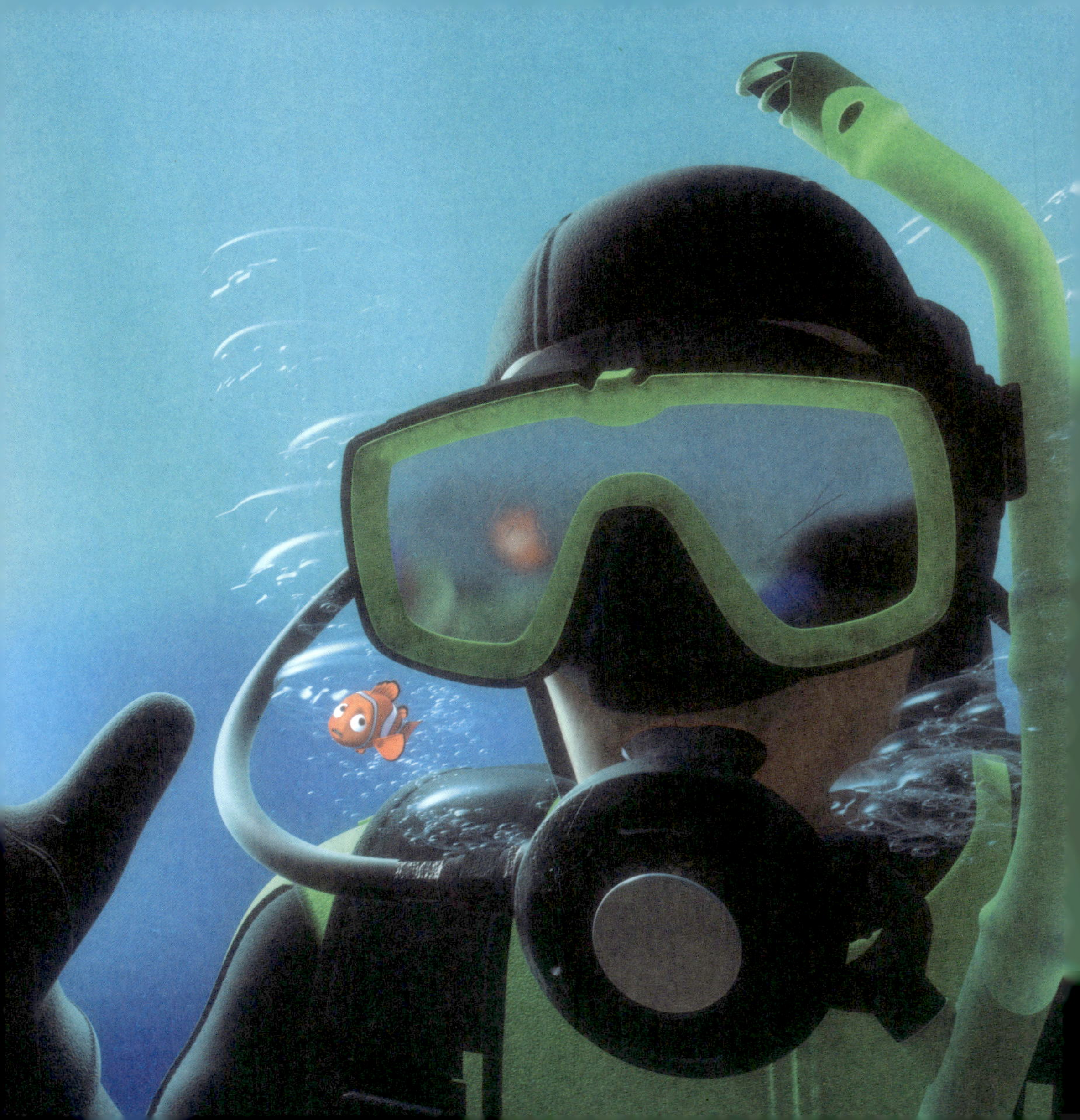

IN THE HEART OF AUSTRALIA'S Great Barrier Reef lived the clownfish Marlin and his son Nemo. Marlin had recently lost his wife and more than four hundred eggs in a ruthless barracuda attack. Ever since, he worried constantly about Nemo, and wouldn't let him do anything on his own.

One day, Marlin's greatest fears came true. Nemo swam out in the open waters and got captured by a diver. Marlin immediately forged out into the deep sea to find his son. A regal blue tang fish named Dory offered to help:

Finding Nemo

"The boat went that way!" But suddenly, Dory forgot what they were doing. "I suffer from short-term memory loss," she explained.

What Dory lacked in memory, she made up for in friendliness. Soon they were swimming to a "party" with Bruce the shark. On the way, Marlin spotted the mask of the diver who had kidnapped Nemo. It had writing on it.

During a narrow escape from a reformed fish-eating shark, an exploding minefield, an abyss, and a deadly anglerfish, Dory had remembered that she could read!

The mask read: P. Sherman, 42 Wallaby Way, Sydney.

Meanwhile, Nemo was making friends in the fish tank of P. Sherman, a dentist in Sydney. He learned that the dentist planned to give him to his fish-torturing niece. So, with the help of a scarred fish named Gill, Nemo planned an escape.

"We have to take the East Australian Current to get to Sydney," Dory told Marlin. A school of fish pointed the way.

Soon they came to a trench. "Look, something shiny!" Marlin pointed upward.

"Let's go!" shouted Dory. Before Marlin could stop her, they were playing tag in a forest of jellyfish above the trench in order to escape the stinging tentacles. They passed out.

Sometime later, Marlin awoke on the back of a sea turtle named Crush. "Dude, you really took on those jellies!" Crush said with awe. Marlin told Crush about his son Nemo. "We need to find the East Australian Current," he said.

"You're riding it," Crush told him.

News of Marlin's travels made their way to Nigel, a pelican who frequented the window of the dentist's office. And when Nigel squawked Marlin's brave story to the Tank Gang, Nemo couldn't believe his ears. These stories didn't sound like the overprotective father he knew.

Feeling a surge of pride, Nemo was more determined than ever to escape. He swam up the filter and jammed the gears just as Gill had instructed. Soon the tank would get dirty and the dentist would have to clean it. They simply had to wait to be bagged on the counter, ready to roll out the window to sea.

After Marlin and Dory left the sea turtles, they needed directions. Dory asked the next creature they saw, which happened to be a very large whale. "I speak Whale," Dory assured Marlin.

But the whale swallowed them. Dory spoke to the whale. "We should move to the back of the throat, or he wants a root beer float," she translated. The answer was clear when suddenly Marlin and Dory shot out of the whale's blowhole into Sydney Harbor.

The next morning, in the dentist's office, the tank was spotless. The dentist had installed an automated cleaner, wiping out any chances for escape. Then he bagged Nemo for his niece, who was reclining in the dental chair. Just then, Nigel flew to the window carrying Marlin and Dory in his beak. In a daring rescue, Nigel bombarded the dentist, and Nemo slipped away from the screaming niece down the spit basin into the open sea.

Nigel released Marlin and Dory back into the harbor, and soon Nemo found his father among a school of groupers. "Daddy!" Nemo cried.

"NEMO!!" shouted Marlin. They raced toward each other in a happy reunion, when suddenly a big net scooped up the groupers and captured Dory, too. Before Marlin could stop him, Nemo swam into the net and told the fish to swim down. "It's the only way we can save Dory," Nemo said. "I can do this." Marlin realized his son was right. "I know you can," he said proudly. And Nemo did.

Thereafter, Marlin and Nemo shared many happy times in their cozy anemone in the Reef. Nemo had a father he could be very proud of, and Marlin knew that he wouldn't have to worry about his son anymore.

And far away, on the other side of the East Australian Current, a group of individually bagged fish from P. Sherman's fish tank rolled out the window and across the street from P. Sherman's dentist office into the harbor below.

FINDING NEMO

1. How old is Crush, the sea turtle?
2. What kind of sea creature is Nemo's teacher?
3. Where does Nemo live?
4. What happens to Nemo when he swims past the "Drop-off"?
5. Which current does Marlin need to ride to find Nemo?
6. How do Marlin and Dory finally make it to the harbor in Sydney?
7. What talents does Dory have that help Marlin?
8. Where does Nemo get taken after his capture?
9. What nickname does Nemo earn after he swims through "the ring of fire"?
10. What is Gill's foolproof plan for Nemo new friends to escape the fish tank?

Q & As

1. 150 years old
2. A manta ray
3. In a sea anemone
4. He gets captured by a scuba diver.
5. The East Australian Current
6. They get blown out of the spout of a whale.
7. She can read, and she can speak whale.
8. To P. Sherman's fish tank in his dental office at 42 Wallaby Way, Sydney
9. Sharkbait
10. They jam the filter and get the tank filthy, so the dentist needs to clean it himself. Once the dentist puts the fish in separate plastic bags to clean the tank, they can roll down the counter, out the window, off the awning, into the bushes, across the street, and into the harbor!

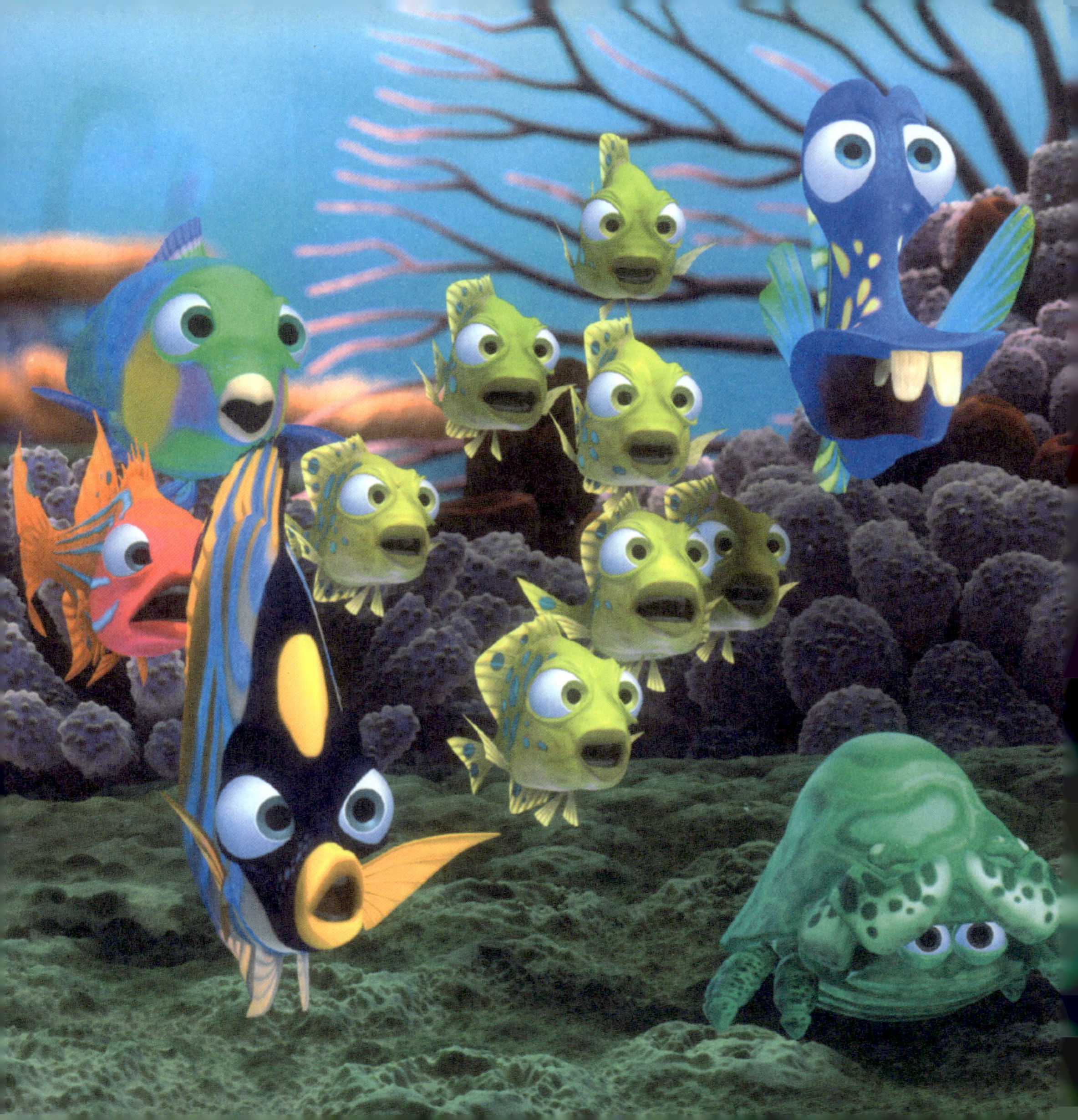

Nemo's School of Fish

Join Nemo and his fish friends as they swim away with Mr. Ray in science class. You can turn rocks with fun shapes into fish, crabs, octopi, or any other favorite sea creature.

various shaped rocks, tempera paint, paintbrushes, varnish, scissors, construction paper, glue, googly eyes. Optional: fan-shaped shells, pipe cleaners, yarn

Paint the rocks with a base color of tempera paint. Let the paint dry, then paint a second layer of stripes, polka dots, or other designs. When the layers are dry, coat the rocks with varnish. Once the varnish has dried, cut out construction paper fins and tails (or use fan-shaped shells) and glue them onto the rocks. Add googly eyes. You can also glue on tentacles and tails made out of pipe cleaners or yarn. Now you can make a splash with Mr. Ray's explorers!

CRUSH: Duuude! Duuuude. Focus Dude! Duuuude…

MARLIN: Oh-hhhh!

CRUSH: He lives! Hey dude!

MARLIN: What happened—?

CRUSH: Oh, saw the whole thing, dude. First you were like—whoa. And then we were all like—WHOA! And then you were like—whoooooa…

MARLIN: What are you talking about?

CRUSH: You, mini man. Takin' on the jellies. You got serious thrill issues, dude…awesome.

MARLIN: Oh, my stomach. Ohhhh…

CRUSH: Oh, man, no hurling on the shell, dude, O.K.? Just waxed it.

MARLIN: So Mr. Turtle—

CRUSH: Whoa. Dude. "Mr. Turtle" is my father. Name's Crush.

MARLIN: Crush? Really? O.K., Crush. Listen, I need to get to the East Australian Current. E. A. C.?

CRUSH: Dude…You're riding it, dude! Check it out. 'Kay, grab shell, dude.

MARLIN: Grab whaaAAAAA—?

CRUSH: Oh-ho! Righteous! Righteous! Yeah!

LINES FROM THE FILM

Nemo's Fish Puzzle Sammies

NEMO AND HIS SCHOOL OF FISH friends know that they need brain food to be at their best for Mr. Ray's science classes. Feed *and* work your brain with these tasty and fun sandwiches.

4 large hard-boiled eggs, cooled, shelled, and sliced

2 tablespoons mayonnaise

3 tablespoons plain nonfat yogurt

2 tablespoons pickle relish

dash salt

dash pepper

2 raisins

4 whole wheat or rye bread slices

1. Combine all ingredients except bread and raisins in a small bowl.

2. Spread egg salad on two slices of bread and top with two other slices. Press down gently.

3. Cut two oval shapes from the two sandwiches for the fish bodies. Cut two large triangular tails and four smaller triangles for two dorsal (top) and two pectoral (side) fins.

4. Serve oval sandwiches with the triangle pieces and raisins. Let children piece together their fish puzzle sandwiches and add raisins for eyes.

Makes 2 sandwiches.

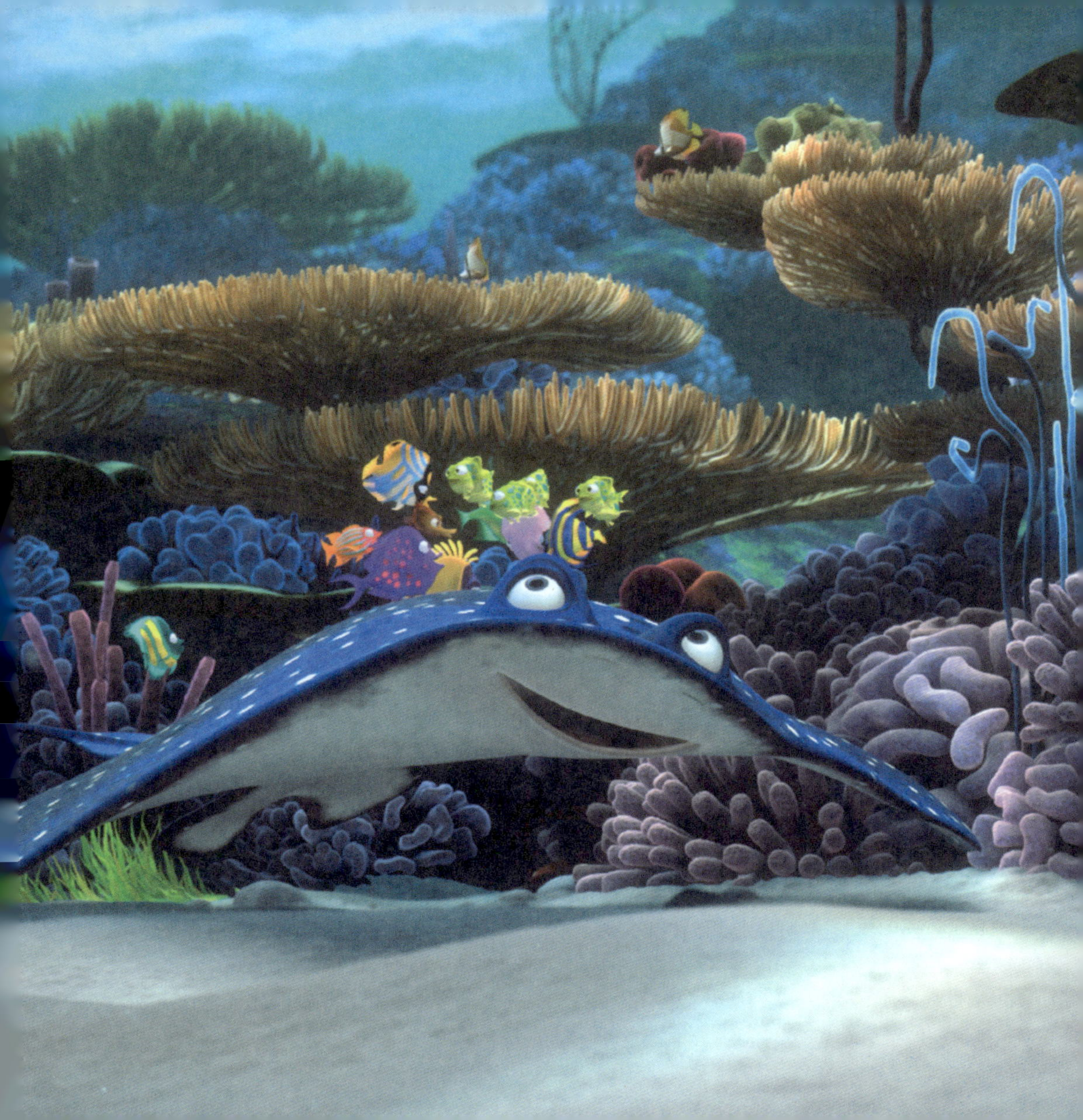

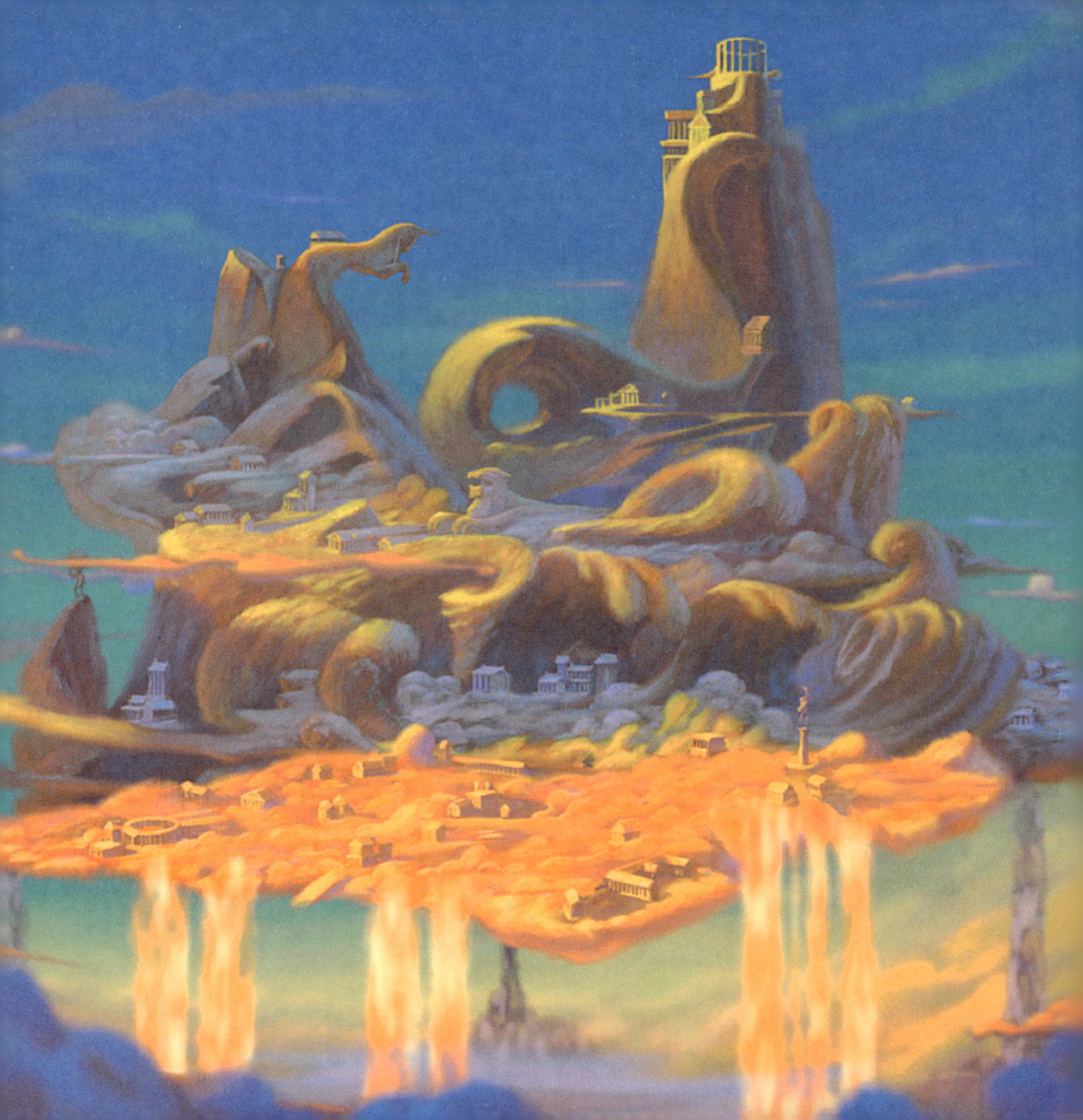

LONG AGO, Zeus tamed the world by defeating the mighty Titans and locking them up. Thereafter, Zeus ruled from Mount Olympus, where all the gods and goddesses lived. One day Zeus and his wife, Hera, celebrated the birth of their boy Hercules, who had special powers of strength.

Meanwhile, Hades, the god of the underworld, wanted to take over Mount Olympus. The Fates told him that in eighteen years the planets would align and that Hades could then unleash the Titans on Zeus. "One word of caution," the Fates warned. "If Hercules fights, you will fail."

Hercules

That night, Hades ordered his henchmen, Pain and Panic, to kidnap Hercules. They fed him a potion to make the baby god mortal. But before Hercules finished the bottle, a couple found the baby and raised him as their own.

Hercules grew into an unusually strong but awkward young man. He created catastrophe everywhere he went. "I'm a freak," he told his parents. "I feel like I don't belong here."

Finally, one day, his parents told Hercules how they found him. They showed him the gold medallion that he had worn as a baby. "It's a symbol of the gods," they said.

So Hercules went to the temple of Zeus and prayed. "My boy!" The statue of Zeus came to life and embraced his son. "The only way you can return to Mount Olympus is if you prove to be a true hero on Earth."

Hercules trained with Philoctetes the satyr to become the best hero ever. One day, Phil thought Hercules was ready to prove himself. "We're going to Thebes," he said.

On the way, Hercules rescued the beautiful and spunky Megara from a vicious centaur attack. Hercules had never seen such a beautiful woman. Meg had never seen such a wonderful boy. They fell in love.

But Hercules did not know that Meg worked for Hades. When Hades learned how strong Hercules was, he went up in flames. He used Meg to lure Hercules into fighting the many-headed Hydra. In a battle of true strength and courage, Hercules fought the monster and won.

Thebes had a hero! Suddenly Hercules saw his name all over the city. He shared the news with Zeus. "Being famous is not the same thing as being a hero," Zeus said. "You must look into your heart."

Now Hades wanted to destroy Hercules more than ever. He sent Meg to find his greatest weakness. "Hercules doesn't have any weaknesses," said Meg. But Hades saw that Hercules had fallen in love. "I think he does," Hades sneered.

Hades tied Meg up and threatened to harm her unless Hercules gave up his powers for twenty-four hours. "Meg's a fraud," warned Phil. "She doesn't love you!" But Hercules had already agreed to Hades' bargain. His strength was gone.

At that moment, all the planets fell into alignment and Hades set the Titans free. Leaving behind a wake of pure destruction, the Titans captured all the gods on Mount Olympus. Zeus's throne could finally belong to Hades!

Meanwhile, Hades sent the Cyclops after Hercules. The one-eyed monster destroyed all of Thebes. Without his strength, Hercules could not stop the Cyclops.

Then Phil told Hercules to tie the feet of the Cyclops together to make him fall. It worked! But the

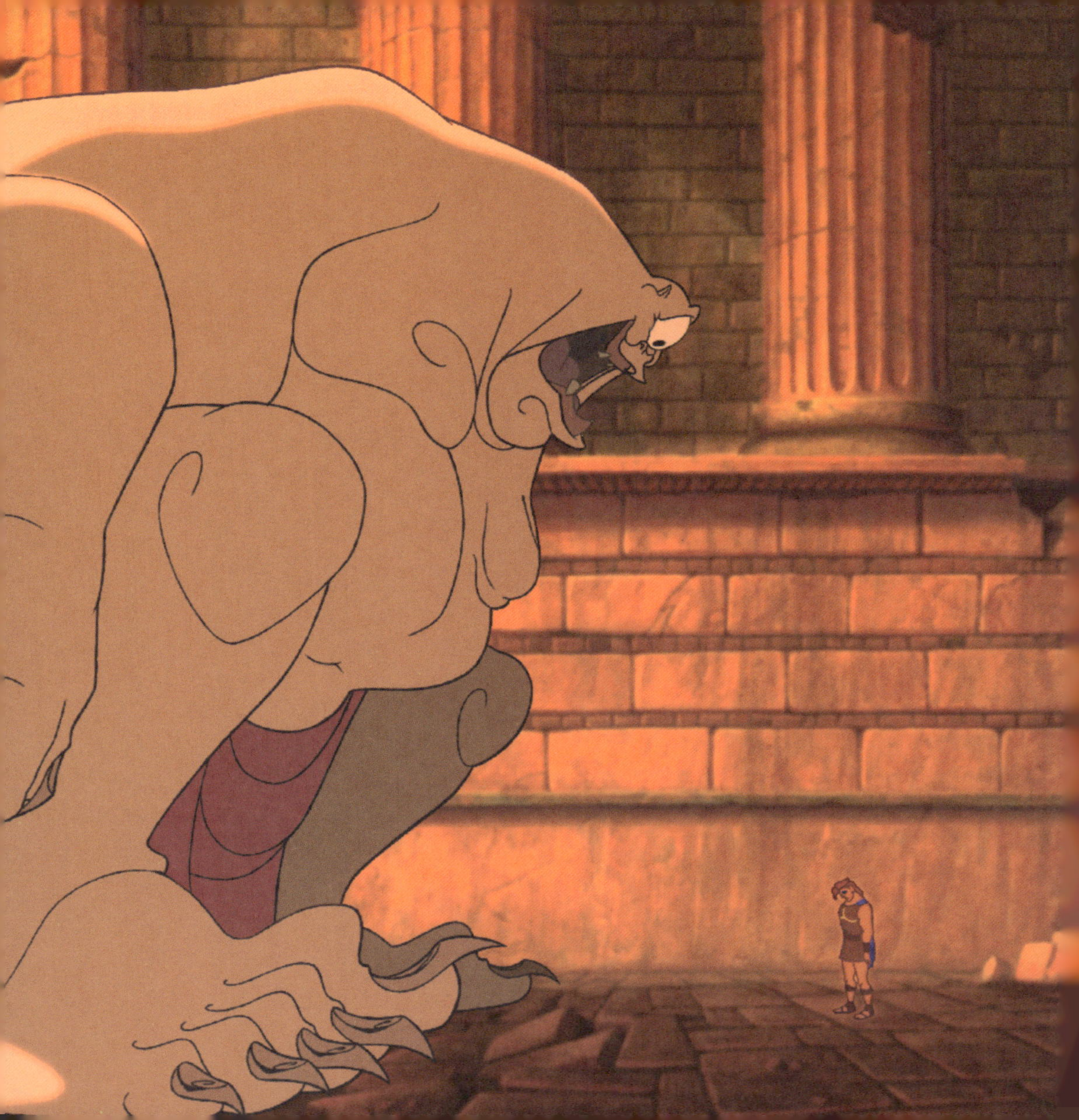

Cyclops knocked over a column and crushed Meg. Suddenly Hercules felt his strength return, and he was able to lift the column off Meg.

Then Hercules returned to Mount Olympus to kick Hades out. Battling with fire and ice, Hercules freed the gods and annihilated the evil Titans.

But Hades would not give up. Meg still belonged to him, and the time had come for the Fates to cut Meg's string of life. Hercules rushed to the underworld to save her, but it was too late. Hades had already thrown her into the Pit of Souls.

Hercules offered his life in exchange. Hades gladly agreed, knowing that no mortal could ever survive the Pit of Souls. So Hercules dove into the Pit. "You can't do this," raged Hades when Hercules climbed out with Meg. "You must be a god!"

It was true. Hercules had finally proved himself to be a true hero. The gods celebrated with great fanfare. But Hercules could not live without Meg. So, with blessings from the gods on Mount Olympus, Hercules returned to Earth with his true love and lived happily ever.

HERCULES

1. What do the three Fates share to see the past, present, and future?
2. What gift do Zeus and Hera give baby Hercules?
3. What does baby Hercules have around his neck when his adopted parents find him?
4. At the temple of Zeus, what does Hercules learn he must do to become a god again?
5. When do the Fates tell Hades to unleash the Titans?
6. What does the hydra do when Hercules chops off its head?
7. What kind of sandals does Pain wear?
8. Name the five Titans.
9. Which Titan does Hercules fight?
10. What does Hercules do to become a true hero and become a god again?

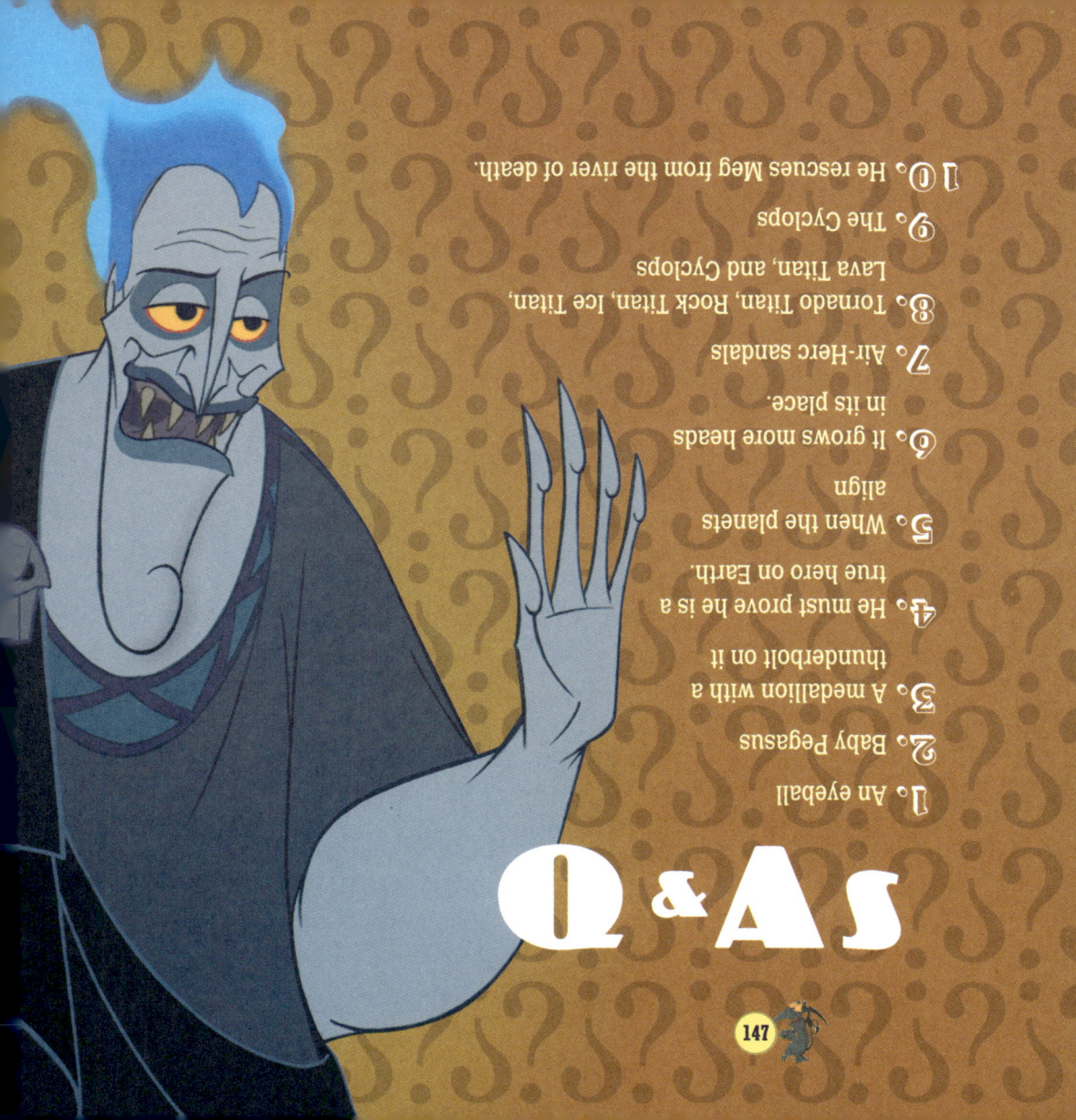

Q & As

1. An eyeball
2. Baby Pegasus
3. A medallion with a thunderbolt on it
4. He must prove he is a true hero on Earth.
5. When the planets align
6. It grows more heads in its place.
7. Air-Herc sandals
8. Tornado Titan, Rock Titan, Ice Titan, Lava Titan, and Cyclops
9. The Cyclops
10. He rescues Meg from the river of death.

Dress of the Gods

With a Herculean toga and head wreath, you can be a god or goddess (or just look like one). The next time Zeus and Hera throw a party on Mount Olympus, you'll be ready to walk among the immortals!

tape measure, old white sheet, scissors, double-stick tape, purple ribbon, purple sash, sandals, garden wire, pliers, green tape, bay leaves (real or cut out of construction paper)

TOGA

Measure body from shoulder to knee. Trim sheet to measure twice that length. Fold sheet in half lengthwise. Use double-stick tape to line the edges with purple ribbon. To wear, unfold the sheet to drape over the left shoulder. Open the sheet front and back to wrap around body and tie the sash around the middle. For small shoulders, gather the sheet at the shoulder and tie with ribbon. Wear the toga with sandals.

HEAD WREATH

Measure head circumference and cut a piece of garden wire the same length. Use pliers to bend the wire into a circle and twist the ends closed. Wrap the wire with green tape. Tape the leaf stems to the wire, fanning the leaves outward as you work your way around the wreath. Repeat with a second layer of leaves in the opposite direction. Place on your head and join the ranks of the gods and goddesses!

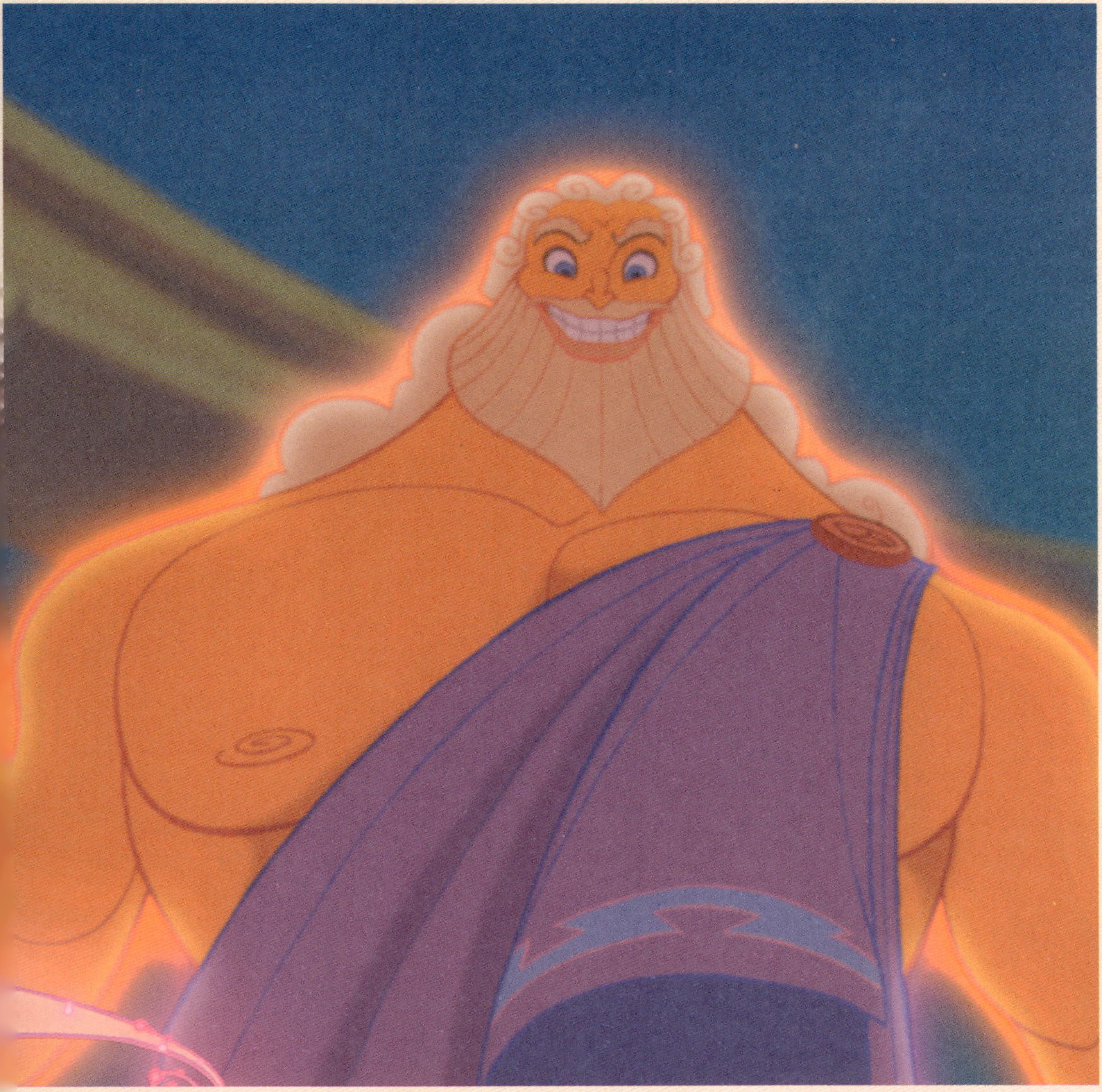

LINES FROM THE FILM

<Pain and Panic toss a Hercules vase in the air, and Hades flings a fireball at it.>

MEG: Nice shootin', Rex.

HADES: I can't believe this guy. I throw everything I've got at him, and it doesn't even—

<He looks at the new sandals on Pain's feet.>

HADES: What are those?

<The logo on the sandals reads "Air-Herc">

PAIN: Um...I don't know. I—I, I thought they looked kind of dashing.

HADES: I've got twenty-four hours to get rid of this bozo, or the entire scheme I've been setting up for eighteen years goes up in smoke...and you are wearing his MERCHANDISE?!

PANIC: <slurps a drink from a bottle with a Hercules logo on it> Thirsty?

<Flames shoot out of Hades.>

<Pain and Panic grunt and groan.>

Hercules' Strengthening
Sports Drink

A GOOD WAY to build up Herculean strength is to start the day with a bone-building breakfast. Try this delicious drink the next time you think you'll have a Titan-battling day.

½ cup orange juice
1 banana
1 apple, cored
½ cup yogurt
1 tablespoon wheat germ
3 to 6 ice cubes

1. Mix juice, fruit, yogurt, and wheat germ in blender.

2. Add ice cubes one at a time until desired level of frothiness is reached.

3. Pour into a tall glass and drink slowly with a straw.

Makes 1 serving.

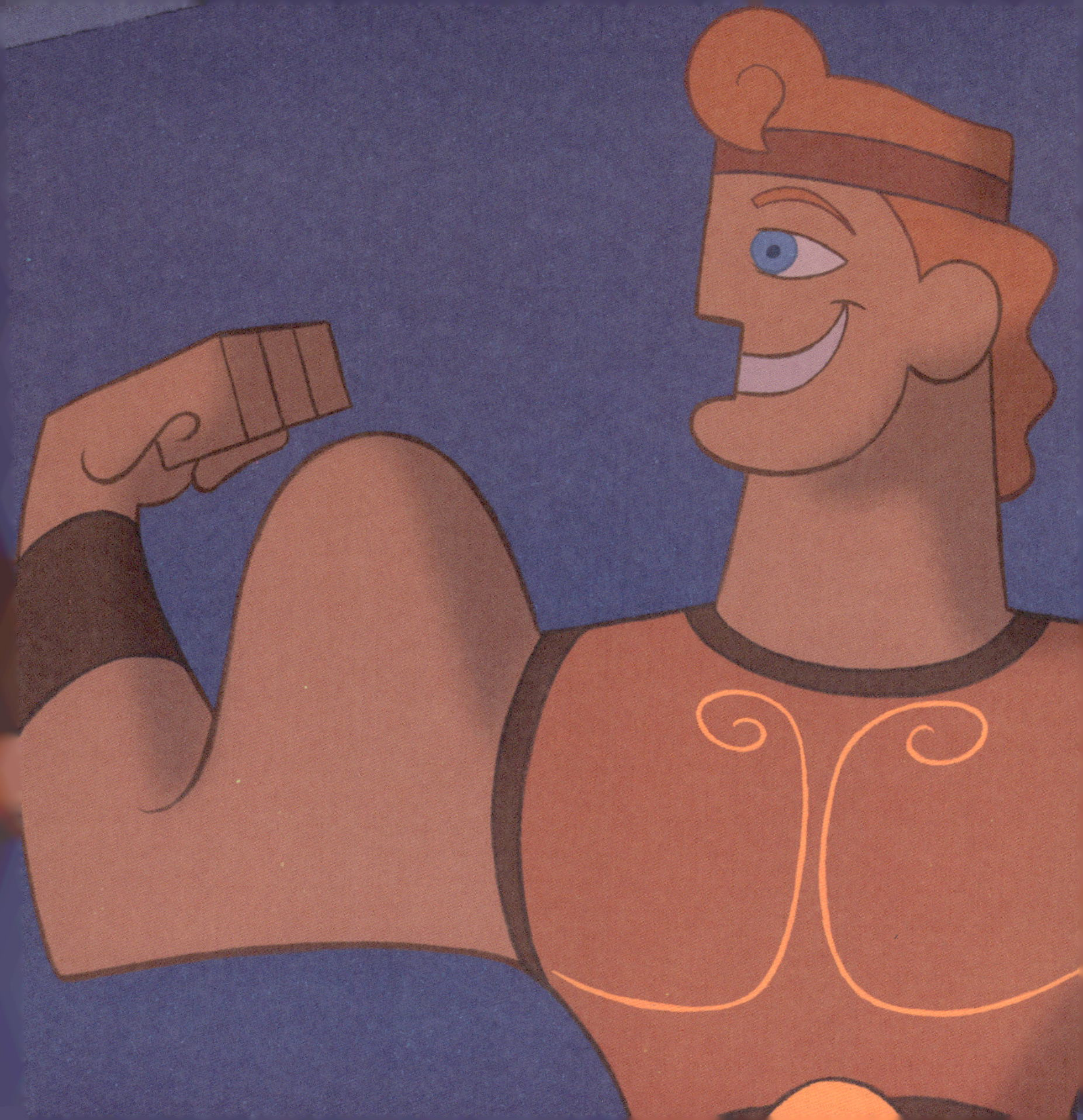

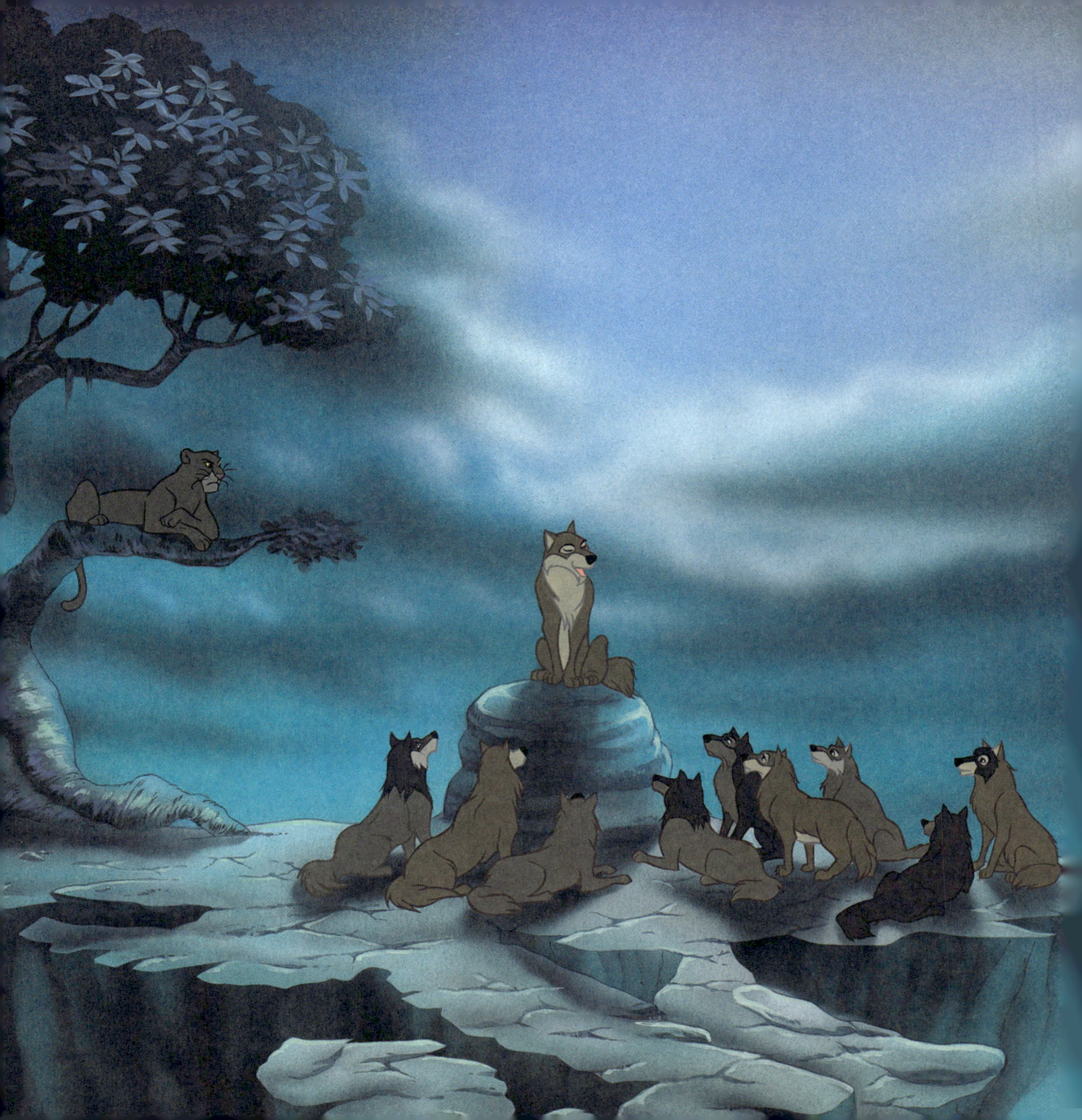

MANY STRANGE LEGENDS have been told about the jungle, but none so strange as the story of Mowgli. It began the day Bagheera the panther heard a strange sound from a basket on the riverbank.

The Jungle Book

"Why, it's a Man-cub!" he said.

Knowing the Man-cub would perish without a mother's care, Bagheera took the baby to a wolf family with a litter of cubs. The wolves adopted him and named him Mowgli. Over time, Mowgli grew with his wolf brothers and sisters. No Man-cub had ever been happier.

One night, the wolves held a meeting on Council Rock. The tiger Shere Khan had returned to their part of the jungle. He would surely kill the Man-cub. The strength of the wolf pack was no match for Shere Khan. Mowgli had to go.

Bagheera agreed to take Mowgli to a village, but Mowgli didn't want to go. "I can look after myself!" he said. Bagheera warned Mowgli of the dangers of being alone in the jungle, but even when Mowgli was nearly swallowed by Kaa, a python, and stamped on by an elephant, Mowgli did not want to go to the Man-village.

"Don't worry about me," he told the panther.

Bagheera gave up trying to help the Man-cub. "You're on your own," he said with a sigh.

Before long, Mowgli met a singing bear named Baloo. He quickly helped the Man-cub forget his troubles. Baloo taught Mowgli all about the good life: how to fight like a bear, dance like a bear, and eat like a bear.

Mowgli liked being a bear. But other animals in the jungle had their eyes on the Man-cub. A group of monkeys kidnapped Mowgli and brought him to their king.

"Word has it you want to stay in the jungle," said the orangutan king. "Old King Louie can fix that for you."

More than anything, King Louie wanted to understand humans. If Mowgli would show him the secret of man's fire, he would teach Mowgli how to live a monkey's life.

Bagheera and Baloo soon found Mowgli and rescued him from the monkeys. Mowgli was happy to see Baloo. But when Baloo told him they had to go to the village, Mowgli ran away.

    Bagheera and Baloo were on the lookout for Mowgli and asked the elephant brigade to help in the search. Nearby, Shere Khan lay low in the grass, watching and listening. A sinister smile spread across his face. He was soon on the hunt for the Man-cub, too.

    Meanwhile, Mowgli wandered into a desolate part of the jungle, where he was joined by a group of vultures. "Nobody wants me around," said Mowgli sadly.

    "We know how you feel," agreed the vultures. They offered to make Mowgli an honorary vulture and cheered him up with singing and dancing.

    Suddenly, all the vultures hid behind Mowgli. There, face to face with the Man-cub, stood Shere Khan. "Run!" shouted the vultures. But Mowgli stood firm.

    "You don't scare me," Mowgli told Shere Khan. "I don't run from anyone."

Shere Khan was not impressed with Mowgli's bravado. He closed his eyes and counted to ten to give the Man-cub a chance to run. The tiger opened his eyes to see Mowgli holding up a club, ready to attack.

Shere Khan pounced with a fearsome roar, but suddenly dropped to the ground. That moment, Baloo had grabbed the tiger by the tail, saving Mowgli from the swipes of the tiger's razor claws. The vultures quickly carted Mowgli to safety, while Shere Khan continued to run in circles with Baloo on his tail.

Suddenly a lightning bolt struck a nearby tree, setting it aflame. "Fire. That's the only thing Old Stripes is afraid of," said one of the vultures.

So Mowgli grabbed a burning branch and bravely tied it to the tiger's tail. Shere Khan roared with horror and ran off.

With Shere Khan gone, Mowgli would be able to stay in the jungle with Bagheera and Baloo. "Nothing's ever going to come between us again," Baloo told his friend.

Just then, Mowgli heard a strange song. He peeked through the trees and saw a village girl gathering water. Seeing the girl as she walked toward her village, Mowgli knew that he must follow.

Bagheera nodded wisely. Baloo and Bagheera smiled as they watched Mowgli go. Their Man-cub had finally found the place where he belonged.

1. Who raises Mowgli?
2. What secret does King Louie want Mowgli to tell him?
3. Where does Bagheera the panther agree to take Mowgli?
4. Why do the council of wolves decide Mowgli must leave the pack?
5. What does Kaa do to Mowgli and Bagheera?
6. How does Mowgli scare Shere Kahn out of the jungle?
7. Where does Bagheera find the infant Man-cub?
8. Who does Mowgli see that makes him want to leave the jungle?
9. Who does Bagheera call "Jungle Bum"?
10. What happens when Baloo and Mowgli float down the river together?

THE JUNGLE

Q & As

1. A pack of wolves
2. How to make fire
3. To the Man-village
4. Because Shere Khan the tiger has returned to the jungle and will kill Mowgli
5. He hypnotizes them.
6. He ties a burning branch to his tail.
7. In a basket inside a broken boat
8. A girl gathering water near the Man-village
9. Baloo, the bear
10. A monkey drops down from a tree and kidnaps Mowgli.

BOOK

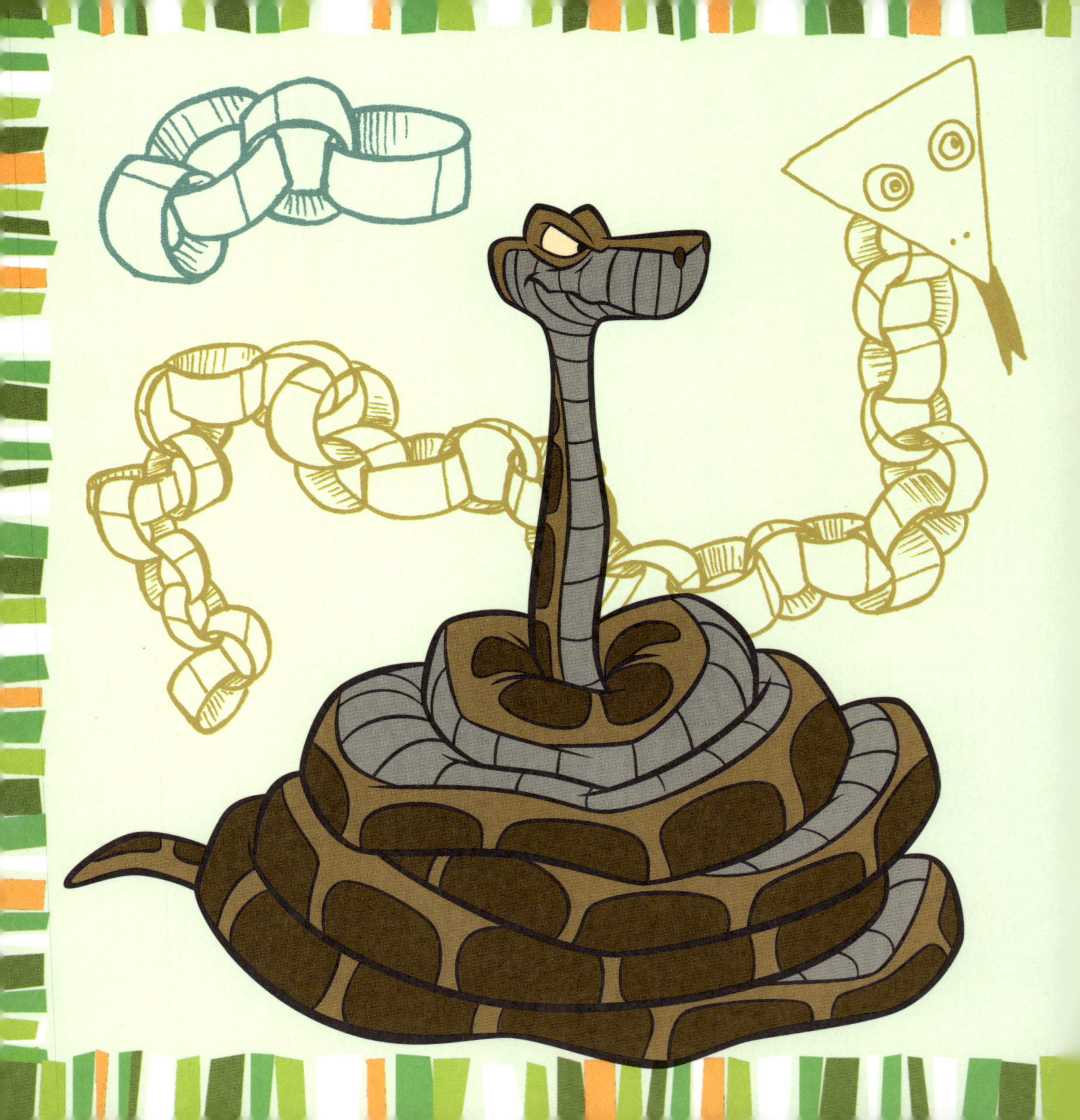

Slithering Kaa

Keep your eyes open for the hypnotic Kaa, the slyest python in the jungle. Before you know it, you might be wrapped up in his coils, ready to be a snake snack!

construction paper, scissors, glue, googly eyes

Cut strips of construction paper about 1 inch wide by 5 inches long. To make Kaa's body, glue one end of a strip onto the other end, forming a ring. Link the next strip through the ring and glue the ends together, starting a chain. Continue forming a chain until Kaa's body is as long as you like. To make Kaa's head, cut out a triangular snakehead shape about 3 inches wide by 4 inches long. To make Kaa's eyes, cut out 4 pairs of different colored circles, making each pair slightly smaller than the previous pair. Layer the circles on Kaa's head and glue them on. Glue googly eyes to the center of each eye. For Kaa's tongue, cut a strip about $1/2$ inch wide by 2 inches long. Fork the tongue by cutting out a triangle from one end of the strip. Glue the tongue onto the underside of Kaa's head. Then glue Kaa's head onto the first ring of Kaa's body. How many coils can Kaa wrap around you?

LINES FROM THE FILM

KAA: Sssay now, what have we here? It's a Man–cub. A delicious Man–cub.

MOWGLI: Oh, go away and leave me alone.

BAGHEERA: It's just what I should do, but I'm not. Go to sleep, Man–cub.

KAA: Yessss, Man–cub, please go to sleeep. Please go to sleeep.

<Mowgli is in a trance>

KAA: Sleep little Man–cub. Rest in peace. Sleep. Sleep.

<Kaa squeezes Mowgli>

MOWGLI: Ah…Bah…Bah… Bagheera!

BAGHEERA: Oh, no, no, look, there's no use arguing any more. No, no more talk till morning.

KAA: Ha, ha, he won't be here in the morning.

BAGHEERA: Ha…oh, yes he will. Ah…Kaa!

<Bagheera hits Kaa in head as he is about to eat Mowgli>

BAGHEERA: Hold it, Kaa.

KAA: Uhhh! Ohhh...Oh, my sinus. You have just made a serious mistake, my friend. A very... stupid...mistake.

BAGHEERA: Now, now, now, now, Kaa, I was...

KAA: Look me in the eye when I'm speaking to you.

BAGHEERA: Please, Kaa.

KAA: Both eyes, if you please. You have just sealed your doom.

<Kaa is suddenly yanked out of tree and falls onto ground below>

KAA: Ooooh!

MOWGLI: Look, Bagheera. Look.

<Bagheera is in a trance>

MOWGLI: Look. Bagheera. Wake up, Bagheera.

BAGHEERA: Ah, duh...ah...wha...

KAA: Just you wait till I get you in my coils!

MOWGLI: Bagheera, he's got a knot in his tail.

KAA: Ha, ha, he's got a knot in his tail. Oh. Oh. Ohhh, this is going to slow down my slithering.

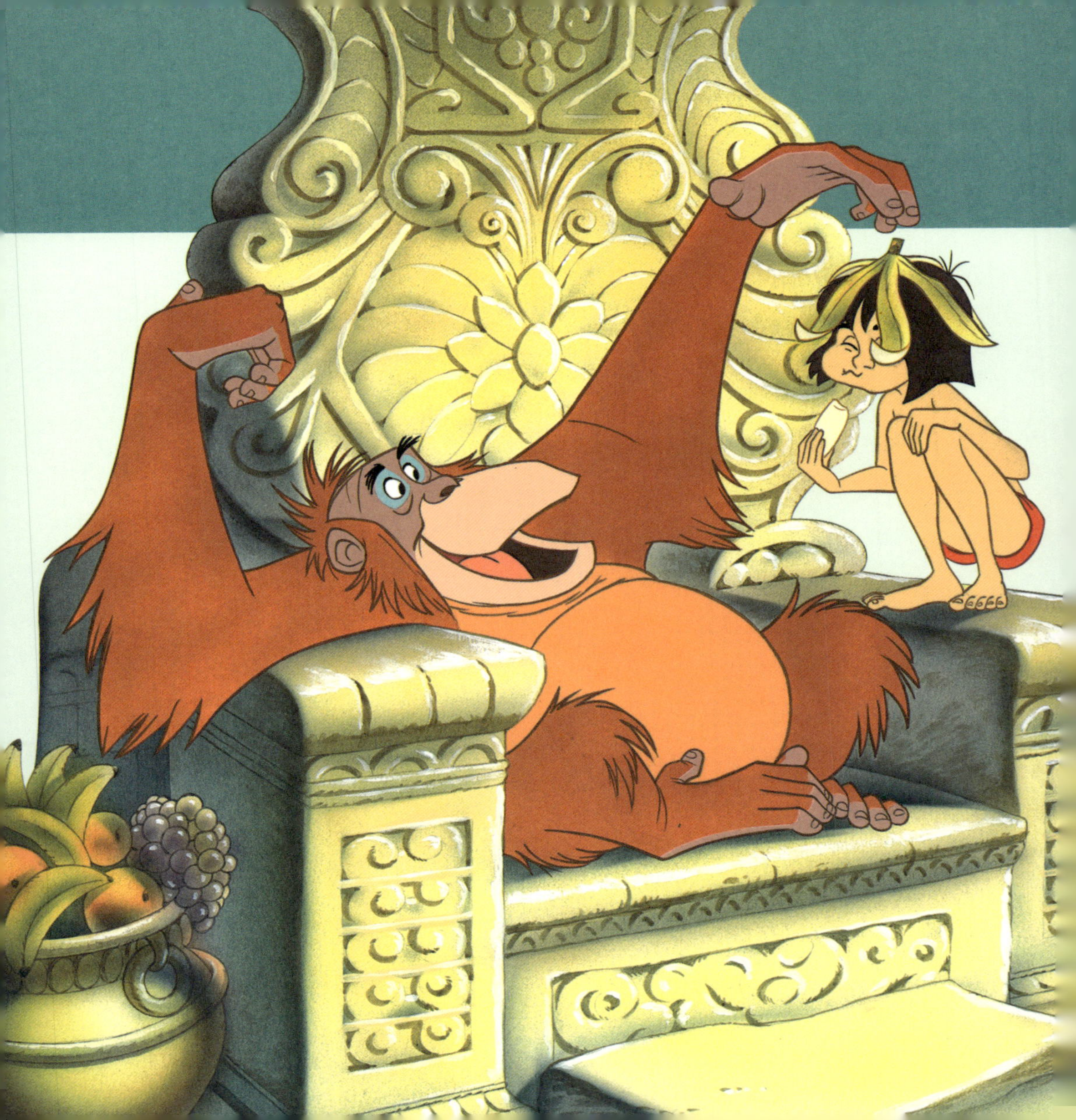

Bare Necessities
Banana Bread

MOWGLI KNOWS how to find Mother Nature's best ingredients in the jungle. Try this tasty treat, made with Mowgli's favorite jungle fruits.

1. Preheat oven to 350° F.
2. In a large bowl, cream butter and sugar until light and fluffy. Beat in eggs.
3. In a small bowl, mash bananas, milk, and vanilla together.
4. In another bowl, sift flour, salt, and baking soda together.
5. Alternate adding flour mixture and banana mixture into egg mixture. Stir in nuts.
7. Pour into greased 9 x 5 x 3" loaf pan and bake for 60 minutes or until top springs back when touched and test knife comes out clean.
8. To make glaze, combine confectioners' sugar, grated coconut, orange juice, and butter in saucepan. Cook over low heat until butter is melted.
9. Drizzle glaze over warm banana bread. Cool 10 minutes before serving.

Makes 12 servings.

BREAD:
- ½ cup butter
- 1 cup sugar
- 2 eggs
- 4 ripe bananas
- 1 tablespoon milk
- 1 teaspoon vanilla
- 2 cups flour
- ¼ teaspoon salt
- 1 teaspoon baking soda
- ½ cup chopped macadamia nuts

GLAZE:
- 1 cup confectioners' sugar
- 2 tablespoons grated coconut
- 2 tablespoons orange juice
- 2 tablespoons butter

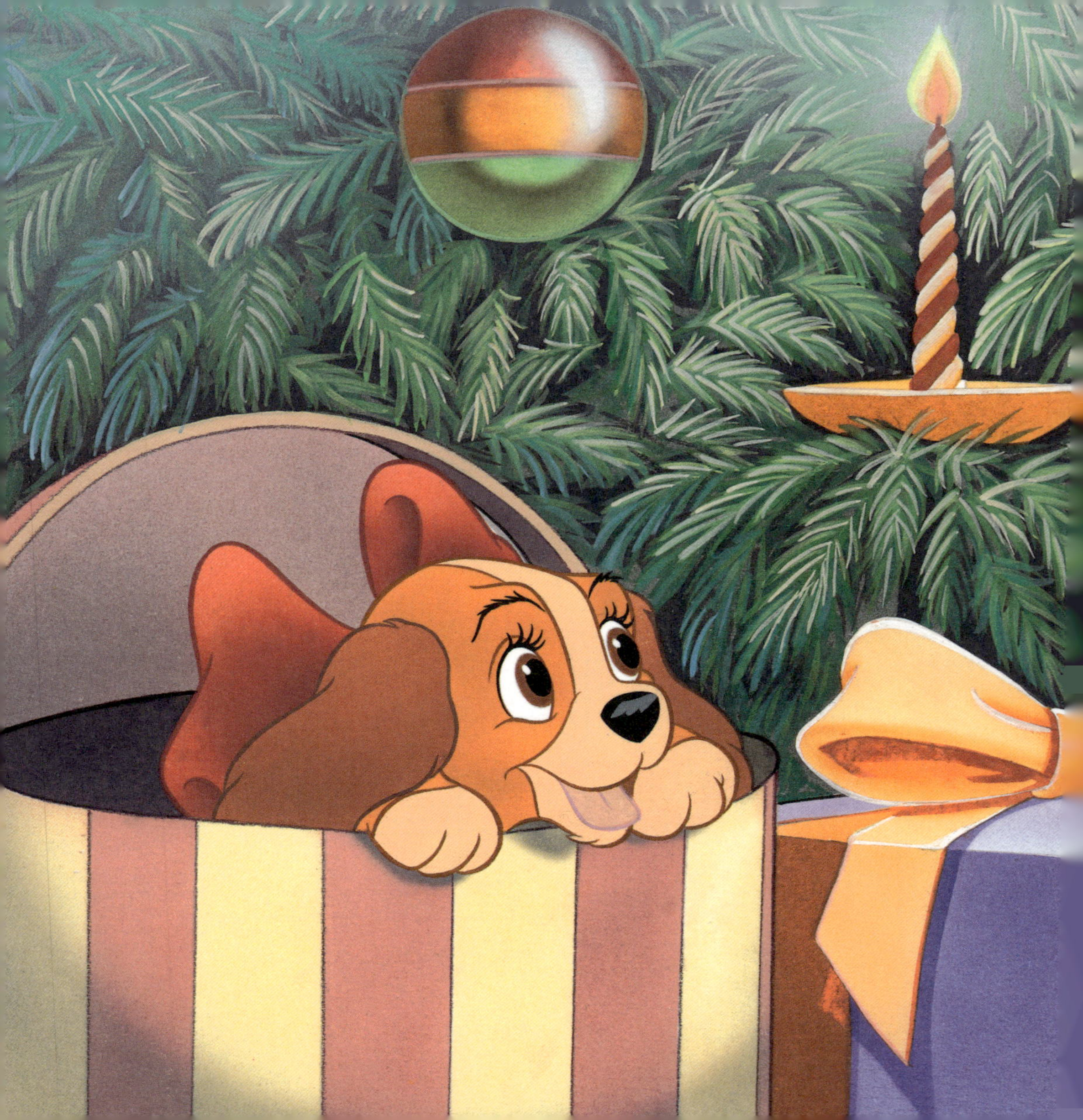

Lady and the Tramp

ONE CHRISTMAS MORNING, in a quaint little village, Jim Dear gave his wife, Darling, a very special gift. Darling opened her present to find the cutest cocker spaniel puppy she'd ever seen. "What a perfectly beautiful little Lady," said Darling.

Lady lived a very happy life with Jim Dear and Darling. She fetched newspapers, buried bones, and kept the garden free from rats. In the afternoons, she enjoyed long walks in the park. And every night, as Lady curled up by the fire with Jim Dear and Darling, she thought there could be no happier family than this.

One day, an old Southern bloodhound named Trusty and an elderly Scottie dog named Jock came by to visit Lady. "Jim Dear and Darling have been acting very strange lately," Lady told them. She went on to tell how Jim Dear pays her no attention when he comes home—he just fusses over Darling's condition. What's more, Darling is always too busy knitting booties to go for walks any more. They even called Lady 'that dog.'"

Jock and Trusty looked at each other knowingly. "It's nothing to worry your wee head about," said Jock.

"They're expecting a baby!" said Trusty.

A scruffy mongrel named Tramp came by and joined the conversation. He had no family and no home, and lived every day as he pleased. "Just you wait," he told Lady. "When a baby moves in, the dog moves out. You'll have nothing but trouble."

Soon Jim Dear and Darling were the proud new parents of a baby boy. At first, Lady was worried that Tramp's warnings might come true. But she soon discovered that the baby brought even more happiness to their home. Now she had one more person in the family to care for and love.

Sometime later, Jim Dear and Darling planned a trip. Aunt Sarah came to watch the baby while they were away and brought her Siamese cats with her. The mischievous cats climbed up the birdcage, clawed the curtains, broke a flower vase, and tossed the goldfish out of its bowl. When they heard the baby cry, they trotted upstairs, thinking of milk.

When Aunt Sarah saw the mess, the cats whimpered innocently. "You vicious dog," she accused Lady, "attacking my little angels!" Aunt Sarah immediately took Lady to the pet store and had her fitted with a muzzle.

Terrified, Lady broke away and ran out of the pet store, wearing the muzzle. She ran down a back alley, where suddenly she was surrounded by a pack of mean dogs. Just then, Tramp appeared and fought off the dogs, rescuing Lady.

"We've gotta get that thing off," he said, pointing at the muzzle. "I know just the place." Tramp took Lady to the zoo, where they met a beaver who chewed right through the strap and freed Lady.

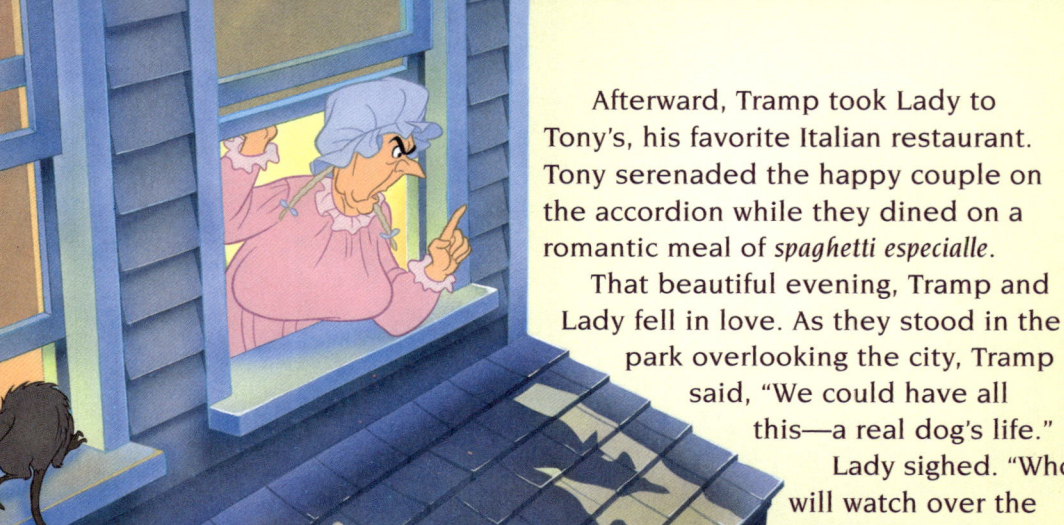

Afterward, Tramp took Lady to Tony's, his favorite Italian restaurant. Tony serenaded the happy couple on the accordion while they dined on a romantic meal of *spaghetti especialle*.

That beautiful evening, Tramp and Lady fell in love. As they stood in the park overlooking the city, Tramp said, "We could have all this—a real dog's life."

Lady sighed. "Who will watch over the baby?" she asked.

"You win," said Tramp. "I'll take you home."

When Lady got home, Aunt Sarah chained her in the backyard and locked her out of the house. Before long, Lady saw a rat scurry up the trellis into the baby's room. She barked and barked, but Aunt Sarah didn't understand. "Shush! You'll wake the baby," she scolded.

Tramp heard Lady's barks and came running. "There's a rat in the baby's room," she told him. Tramp ran upstairs. Lady broke away from her chains to help Tramp fight the rat.

When Aunt Sarah found them, she thought they were going to harm the baby. "You vicious brutes!" shouted Aunt

Sarah. "I'm calling the dogcatcher!" Soon Tramp was locked up in the dogcatcher's wagon on his way to the pound.

That night, Jim Dear and Darling came home from their trip. When Lady showed them the dead rat in the baby's room, they knew that she and Tramp had saved their baby. They were so thankful for what Tramp did that they drove right to the pound and adopted him.

Once again, Christmastime came to Jim Dear and Darling's house. Their baby had grown, and so had their family. Lady and Tramp were now the proud parents of four little puppies. Lady wagged her tail, for she knew there could be no family happier than this.

1. What does Jim Dear give Darling for Christmas?
2. How old is Lady when she gets her license?
3. What is wrong with Trusty?
4. What happens to any dogs without licenses?
5. What does Lady discover about Jim Dear and Darling?

LADY AND THE TRAMP

6. What does Tramp say happens to a dog when a baby moves in?
7. Who does Aunt Sarah bring when she comes to baby-sit?
8. Where does Tramp take Lady for a romantic dinner?
9. Who does Tramp get to help Lady take her muzzle off?
10. How many puppies do Lady and Tramp have?

Q & As

1. A cocker spaniel puppy named Lady
2. Six months
3. He's a bloodhound who's lost his sense of smell.
4. They will be impounded.
5. That they are expecting a baby
6. The dog moves out.
7. Her two Siamese cats
8. To the back of Tony's restaurant
9. A beaver at the zoo
10. Four

Clothespin Doggy

It may be a dog's life for Tramp living footloose and fancy free, but Lady knows that any dog without an owner could end up behind bars. Clip on this attachable clothespin dog and there will be no reason for the dogcatcher to make an appearance.

markers, construction paper, scissors, glue, felt, googly eyes, two wooden clothespins (with metal springs), ribbon

Draw and cut out a dog head about one inch in length and height out of construction paper. Be sure to include about a $1/4$-inch-wide neck. Then draw a dog trunk without legs or tail about 1 inch high and 2 inches wide. Cut out a tail and ears from felt. (For contrast, you can use different-colored felt.) Glue the tail and ears onto the body and head. Glue googly eyes to the dog head.

To assemble your dog, glue the head to the body. Then glue the front end of the body to the top of a flat side of a clothespin. The bottom of the clothespin should stick out from under the body, creating the front legs. Glue the second clothespin to the back end of the body, creating the back legs. Tie on a ribbon collar, then clamp your doggy onto your backpack or coat and take him for a walk!

LINES FROM THE FILM

LADY: It didn't hurt, really, but Darling has never struck me before.

JOCK: Ha! Ha! Now, Lassie, dinna take it too seriously. After all, at a time like this—

TRUSTY: Why, yes. You see, Miss Lady, there comes a time in the life of all humans when, uh, well, as they put it, uh, the birds and the bees? Or, well, er, the stork? You know, ah, no? Well, then, er, ah—

JOCK: What he's trying to say, Lassie, is…Darling is expecting a wee bairn.

LADY: Bairn?

TRUSTY: He means a baby, Miss Lady.

LADY: Oh. A—what's a baby?

JOCK: Well, they resemble humans.

TRUSTY: But ah'd say a mite smaller.

JOCK: Aye, and they walk on all fours.

TRUSTY: And if I remember correctly, they beller a lot.

JOCK: Aye, and they're very expensive. You'll not be permitted to play wi' it.

TRUSTY: But they're mighty sweet.

JOCK: And verra, verra soft.

Tony's
Spaghetti Especialle

FOR THE BEST ROMANTIC MEAL in town, it doesn't get better than a night at Tony's. This recipe is heavy on the meat'sa ball'a and best served with a kiss. Kids can help mix and shape the meatballs.

Sauce
2 tablespoons olive oil
1 small onion, minced
2 cloves garlic, minced
1 16-ounce can chopped tomatoes (with juices)
4 tablespoons fresh basil, chopped
2 teaspoons dried oregano, crumbled
salt and pepper, to taste

For Sauce:
1. Heat oil in heavy saucepan. Add onion and garlic; sauté about 5 minutes.
2. Add tomatoes, basil, and oregano and bring to a boil.
3. Reduce heat; simmer until sauce thickens, about 1 hour.
4. Season with salt and pepper.

FOR MEATBALLS:
1. Combine all ingredients except olive oil and mix thoroughly.
2. Shape into 1½-inch balls.
3. Heat oil in heavy saucepan. Add meatballs in batches and cook until brown on all sides, about 8 minutes. Drain off the fat. Combine meatballs with sauce and serve over spaghetti.

Makes 8 servings.

MEATBALLS

1 pound ground beef

¾ cup bread crumbs

1 large egg

1 clove garlic, minced

¼ cup finely chopped onion

2 tablespoons minced parsley

2 tablespoons fresh basil, chopped

½ teaspoon salt

¼ teaspoon ground black pepper

½ cup grated Parmesan cheese

2 tablespoons olive oil

1 pound spaghetti, freshly cooked

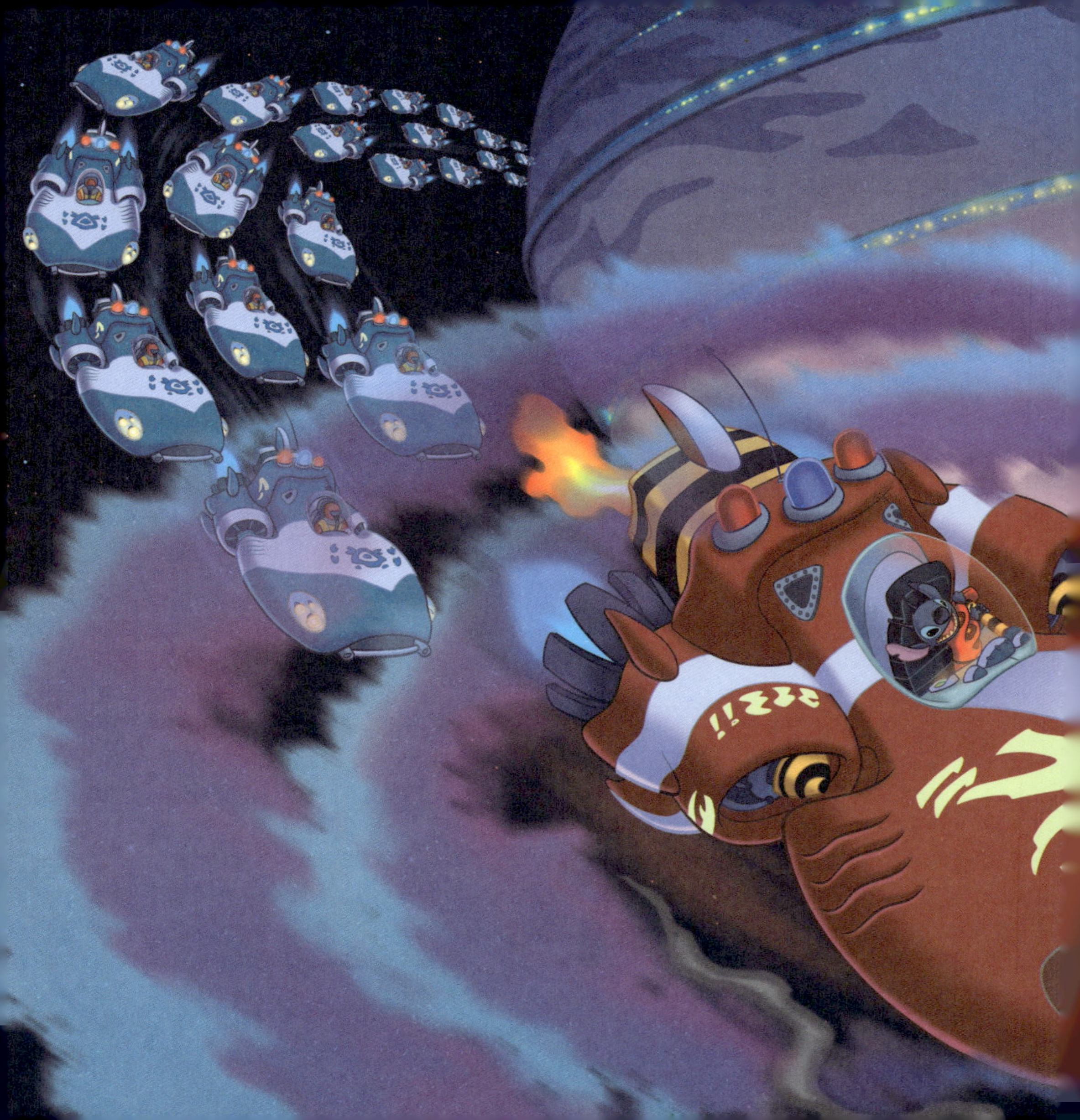

Lilo & Stitch

FAR AWAY, ON THE PLANET TURO, at the Galactic Federation Headquarters, Dr. Jumba Jukiba unveiled his new creation: Experiment 626. It was faster than a super computer, could move objects three thousand times its size, and was indestructible. Its only instinct was to destroy everything it touched.

Appalled at this unethical monstrosity, the Grand Councilwoman banished Experiment 626 to exile on a distant asteroid. But on the way there, Experiment 626 escaped Captain Gantu's ship and fled to Earth.

The Galactic Federation was enraged. "That monster must be destroyed!" said the Grand Councilwoman. So, Earth expert Agent Pleakley and Jumba set out to capture it.

Meanwhile, on the island of Kauai, Nani had left her little sister Lilo home alone again. Social worker Cobra Bubbles threatened to take Lilo away if circumstances didn't improve. "You have three days to change my mind," Cobra told Nani.

The next day, Nani tried to cheer Lilo by taking her to the pound to adopt a dog. Lilo picked out Experiment 626. "We thought he was dead when we found him this morning," said the rescue lady. Lilo thought he was a dog, and named him Stitch.

Lilo took Stitch through town, to the beach, and along the boardwalk. Everywhere they went, Stitch behaved like a monster.

At Nani's place of work, Lilo and Stitch watched their friend David perform his live fire dance. Nearby, Jumba and Pleakley disguised themselves as tourists and tried to capture Stitch. But Stitch fought back and tried to eat Pleakley. When the restaurant manager heard about the attack, he fired Nani.

"We have to return Stitch," Nani told Lilo that night.

"What about 'ohana?" Lilo asked. "'Ohana means 'family,' and that means nobody gets left behind."

Nani agreed. 'Ohana meant that Stitch could stay.

In the morning, Lilo and Stitch went with Nani to help her look for a new job. At the vegetable stand, Stitch danced the hula and knocked over the produce. At the hotel, Stitch played guitar and broke all the windows. And at the beach, as Nani asked about a lifeguard position, Stitch drew a huge crowd with his Elvis impersonations.

But when people started taking pictures of Stitch, he lost his temper and frightened everyone away. Nani had lost all her chances for finding a job. And tomorrow she would lose Lilo, too. They went home, and for the first time, Stitch saw Lilo's sadness and felt sad, too.

The next morning, Lilo awoke to find Stitch missing. "We don't need him," she told Nani sadly. Suddenly David arrived with urgent news about a job for Nani. "Lock the door and don't answer for anyone," Nani told Lilo as she and David hurried out.

Moments later, Jumba blasted his way through Lilo's house with laser guns. Pleakley tried to stop the destruction. Stitch had come home after running off in the night, only to come under attack by the aliens. Lilo and Stitch fought back, but in the explosive battle, Lilo's house burst into flames. Nani rushed home when she heard the fire trucks. When she arrived, Cobra was ready to drive away with Lilo. Nani pleaded with Cobra. When Lilo overheard, she slipped out of the car and escaped.

In the woods, Lilo ran into Stitch and Captain Gantu from the United Galactic Federation. Before they knew it, Lilo and Stitch had been captured by Gantu and were blasting off into space. With his super strength, Stitch was able to escape, but Lilo couldn't.

Meanwhile, Nani followed Lilo into the woods and met Jumba and Pleakley. She demanded to know where Lilo was, but the aliens refused to tell her. Suddenly Stitch appeared and convinced them to rescue Lilo. "'O*hana*," he said. "Nobody gets left behind."

After a hair-raising rescue, Lilo, Nani, and the aliens made it safely back to Earth. There, the Grand Councilwoman waited to take Experiment 626 away. "This is my family," Stitch told the Councilwoman. "It's little and broken, but still good. I found it all on my own."

"Then you may serve your sentence out on Earth," the Grand Councilwoman told Stitch. "And as caretaker of the alien life form, 'Stitch,' this family is now under the official protection of the United Galactic Federation."

Cobra, Pleakley, and Jumba happily worked together to build a new home. Lilo, Nani, and Stitch finally had their family and they filled their home with laughter, dancing, and a lot of love. From that day forward, no one would ever get left behind.

1. What miniature city does Stitch build in Lilo's room?
2. What is Stitch?
3. What does Bubbles have printed on his knuckles?
4. Where do Lilo and Nani find and adopt Stitch?
5. What does *'ohana* mean?

LILO & STITCH

6. What does Lilo hide under her pillow?
7. What is the one thing Stitch cannot do?
8. Who does Stitch impersonate on the beach?
9. What are Stitch's special powers?
10. How much did Lilo pay for Stitch?

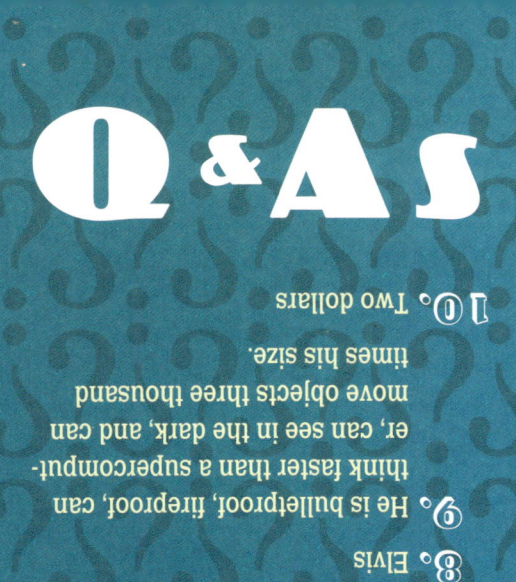

Q & As

1. San Francisco
2. He is Dr. Jukiba's genetic experiment number 626.
3. His first name, Cobra
4. At the dog kennel
5. Family
6. A photograph of her family
7. Swim
8. Elvis
9. He is bulletproof, fireproof, can think faster than a supercomputer, can see in the dark, and can move objects three thousand times his size.
10. Two dollars

Lilo's Hawaiian Hula Skirt

Join Lilo and Stitch for a fun day in the sun and sand. All you need is a long grass skirt and a little bit of Elvis, and you'll be ready to sing and dance—Hawaiian style.

brown wrapping paper, tape measure, scissors, stapler, glue, self-adhesive Velcro fastener

To make the skirt, measure and cut two sheets of wrapping paper about 6 inches longer than your waist size. Stack one sheet on top of the other and staple along the side that will wrap around the waist. To make a waistband, cut a 5-inch strip of paper the same length as the stapled side of the skirt. Fold the waistband in half lengthwise, place over the stapled edge of the skirt, and glue in place. Stick one half of a Velcro fastener on the outside of one end of the waistband, then stick the other half of the Velcro fastener on the inside of the other end of the waistband. Cut the skirt into 1-inch strips from the hemline to the waistline. Wrap the skirt around your waist and fasten in place. Then turn on the music and dance the hula!

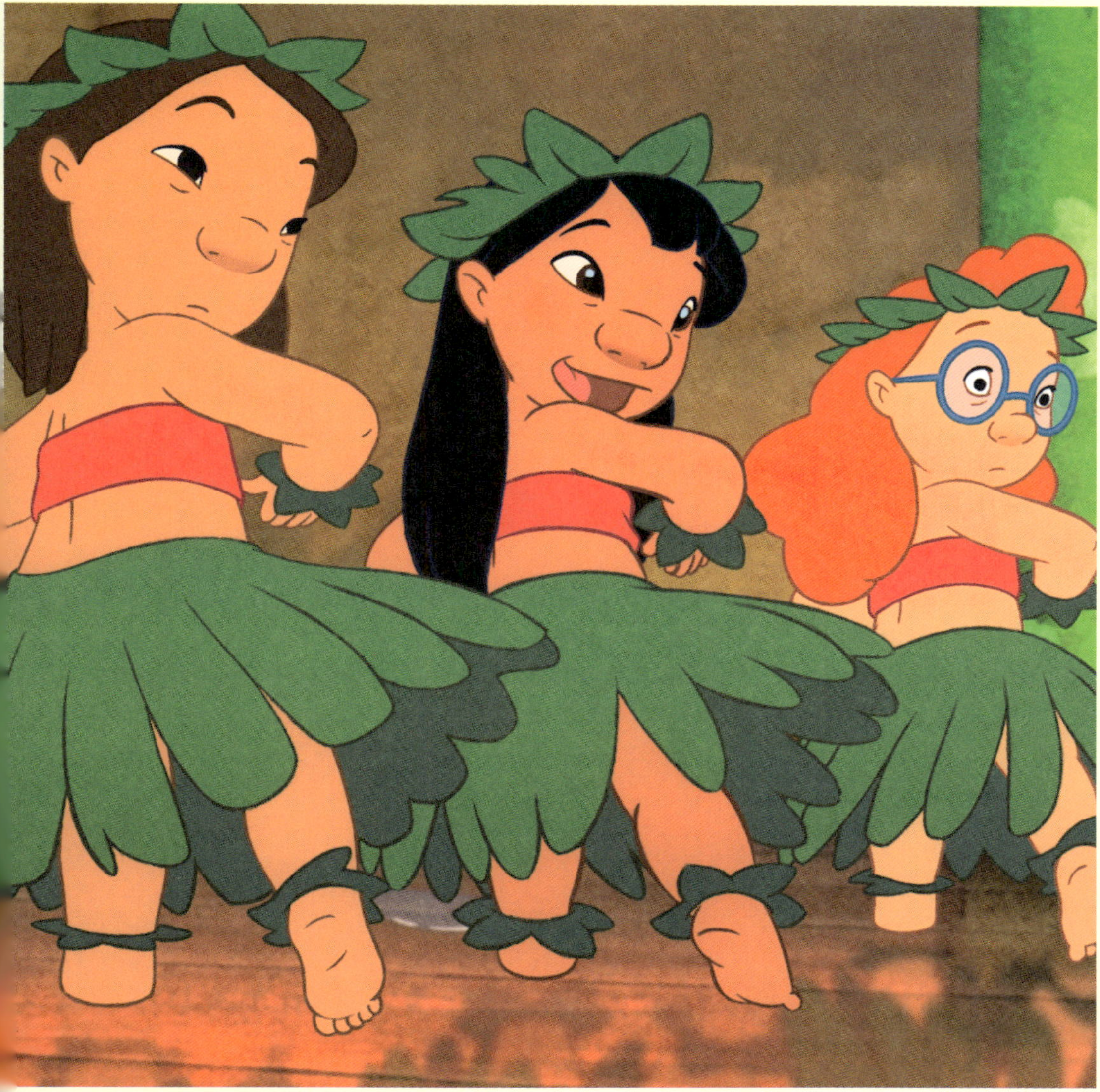

LINES FROM THE FILM

<Stitch kicks open Lilo's door.>

LILO: Look how curious the puppy is! This is my room!

<Lilo points to a cardboard box with a pillow and blanket.>

LILO: And this is your bed.

<Lilo pulls out a bottle and doll.>

LILO: This is your dolly and bottle. See? Doesn't spill. I filled it with coffee.

<Stitch gulps it down.>

LILO: Good puppy. Now get into bed.

<Stitch pushes Lilo down and climbs into her bed.>

LILO: Hey! That's mine! Down!

<Stitch throws a pillow at Lilo. He sees photo underneath and picks it up.>

LILO: Be careful of that!

<She yanks photo out of Stitch's hand.>

LILO: You don't touch this! Don't ever touch it!

STITCH: Raarwlfglligle! Bmaaarrrghh!

<Stitch tears at doll's head.>

LILO: Don't pull on her head, she's recovering from surgery!

<Stitch tears up Lilo's drawing.>

LILO: No! That's from my blue period!

<Lilo puts a lei on Stitch and calms him.>

LILO: There. You know, you wreck everything you touch. Why not try and make something for a change?

<Stitch thinks for a moment, then turns objects in Lilo's room into a detailed city.>

LILO: Wow. San Francisco.

<Stitch then acts like Godzilla and stomps through city, destroying it.>

LILO: No more caffeine for you.

Stitch's Hawaiian Fruit Smoothies

FOR THIS 'OHANA TREAT, it's a good idea to have mom or dad in the kitchen to help whip up the smoothies. Otherwise, if you make them the way Stitch does, things could get a little bit messy!

½ cup cubed mango
½ cup cubed papaya
½ cup cubed pineapple
2 scoops pineapple sorbet
⅓ cup milk or soy milk
¾ cup orange juice
1 cup crushed ice

1. Put all ingredients in blender and mix until smooth.
2. Pour in tall glasses and serve with straws.
3. Drink immediately.

Makes 4 servings.

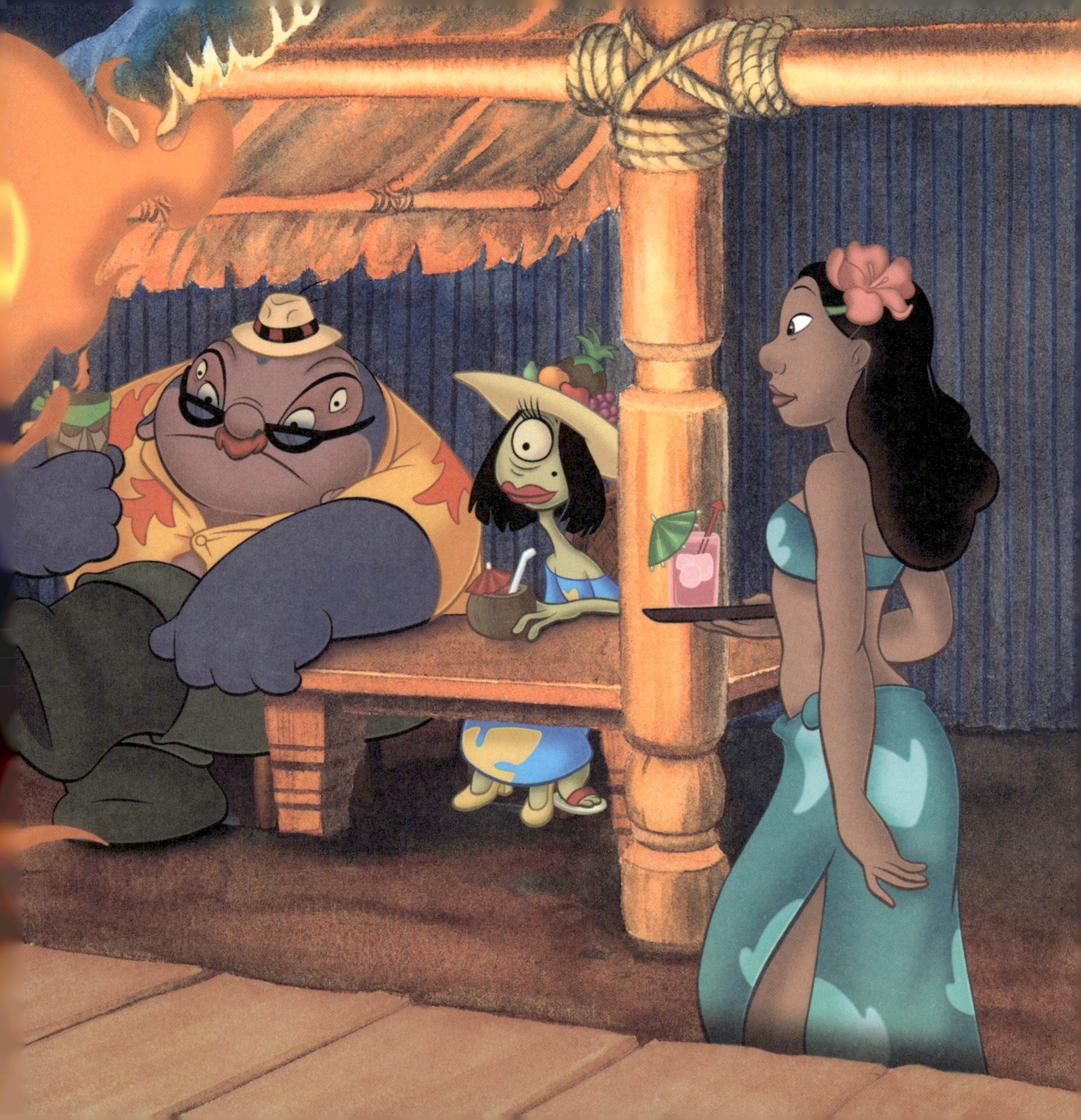

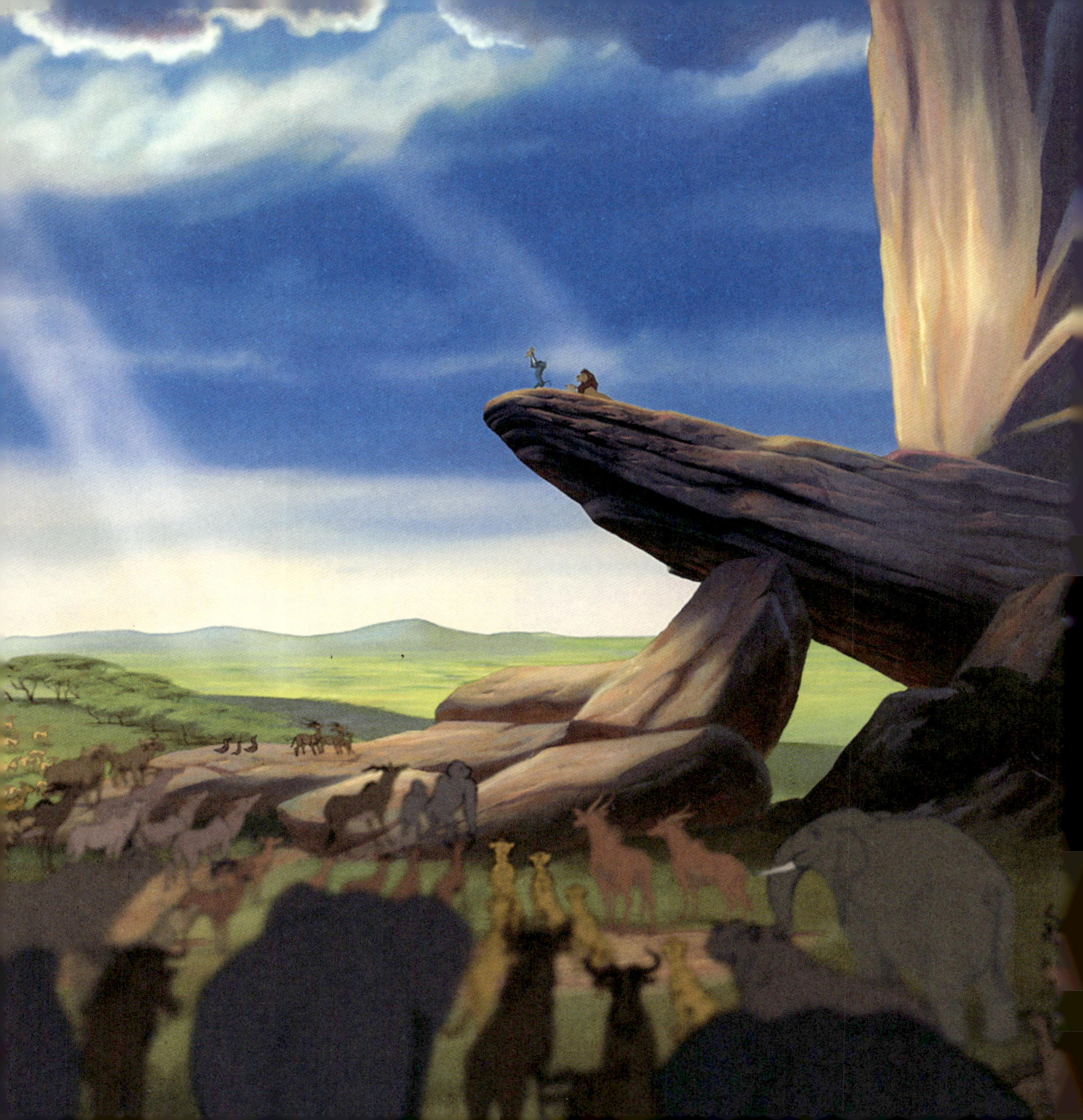

ONE MORNING, as the first rays of sun kissed the open African savanna, all the land's animals knew this day marked the dawning of a new era. Elephants, gazelles, hippos, giraffes, and all creatures great and small assembled at Pride Rock.

The Lion King

On this day, King Mufasa and Queen Sarabi honored their newborn lion cub, Simba. The animals bowed in awe as the wise baboon Rafiki held the young prince high above his head for all to see.

Only the king's brother, Scar, did not come. "I was first in line to be king," he muttered. "Until now."

The next day, the king took his prince to a special place at sunrise. "Everything the sun touches is our kingdom," Mufasa said. "One day, all this will be yours."

But Scar had ideas of his own. When he was alone with Simba, he told the prince slyly, "Never go to the Elephant Graveyard. Only the bravest lions go there."

Simba raced to tell his friend Nala this new secret place. The cubs' mothers agreed to let them go play only if Zazu the hornbill went along.

Before long, the cubs lost their guardian and found the graveyard. Simba strutted up to an elephant skull just as three nasty hyenas came out. The hyenas' mouths watered as they bared their ugly teeth and charged. Suddenly Mufasa filled the graveyard with a huge R-O-O-A-A-R-R-R!

Scar watched from a ledge as Mufasa led the cubs safely home.

Scar was angry his plan had failed. Then he told the hyenas his new, evil plan!

The next day, Scar took Simba for a walk in the gorge. "I have a special surprise for you and your daddy," he told the young prince. "Wait here." Soon, Simba felt a rumbling beneath his paws. A gigantic herd of wildebeest poured into the gorge in full stampede.

Simba clung to a tree branch with all his might. Just in time, Mufasa appeared in the gorge, picked up his son, and tossed him to safety. The king hung onto the tree branch for dear life and struggled to pull himself up out of the gorge, too. He called to Scar for help. Instead of helping his brother, though, Scar swiped Mufasa's paws off the gorge wall, and Mufasa fell under the trampling hoofs of the wildebeest. Simba, who saw his father's fall but not the cause of it, screamed.

The young cub wept at his lifeless father's side. Scar pretended to blame Simba for the king's death. "You must run away and never return," he told Simba.

A vicious smile came over Scar's face as he watched the crushed prince disappear into the desert. Then he returned to Pride Rock to assume the throne.

Sometime later, a warthog named Pumbaa and a meerkat named Timon found young Simba passed out in a dry lakebed. They took him to a lush jungle, where they taught him their motto, *hakuna matata*—"no worries."

Simba lived with his new friends for many years, growing up, eating grubs, and leaving his worries behind. One day, a lioness charged Pumbaa and Timon. Simba counterattacked, and soon found himself pinned to the ground by the lioness.

"Nala?" said Simba.

"You're alive!" Nala gasped. "And that means that you're king." Nala told Simba how Scar let the hyenas take over the Pride Lands. "There's no food or water," she explained.

"I can't go back," Simba told Nala. "I don't want to be king." And he wandered off to be alone in the jungle.

Rafiki soon found the disenchanted prince and led him to a vision of Mufasa. "You have forgotten me," the old king said. "And so you have forgotten who you are. Remember who you are. My son, the one true king."

Simba returned to the Pride Lands with his friends. He couldn't believe his eyes. Everything was gray and barren. Hyenas and dry bones littered the land.

Simba asked Scar to step down so that he could take his rightful place as king. Scar would not give up the throne without a fight. In the struggle, he divulged his secret to Simba: "I killed Mufasa." Lightning struck Pride Rock, and soon the Pride Lands were aflame. As the two lions roared in ferocious battle for the throne, Scar fell off a cliff into the hungry jaws of the hyenas.

Rain returned to the Pride Lands and the fires died down. Simba, the true king, stood proudly at the edge of Pride Rock with his queen, Nala. Next to them stood the wise Rafiki, holding up their new cub, the future king, for all to see. Once again grasses grew in the savanna, and all the animals returned to find their place in the Circle of Life.

1. Who introduces the new prince to the animals of the Pride Lands?
2. Why is Scar jealous of Simba?
3. Where do Simba and Nala go against Mufasa's wishes?
4. What does Mufasa call the delicate balance of all creatures from the ant to the antelope?
5. Why does Simba run away from the Pride Lands?
6. Who discovers Simba passed out in the desert?
7. What does *hakuna matata* mean?
8. What do Timon and Pumbaa love to eat?
9. How does Rafiki show Simba that Mufasa lives?
10. What happens when Scar becomes king?

THE LION KING

Q & As

1. Rafiki the baboon
2. Because Scar was first in line to the throne until Simba was born
3. The Elephant Graveyard
4. The Circle of Life
5. Scar convinces him that he is at fault for Mufasa's death.
6. Timon the meerkat and Pumbaa the warthog
7. No worries
8. Grubs
9. By showing Simba his reflection in a pool of water
10. The hyenas live among the lions in the Pride Lands and soon there is no food or water.

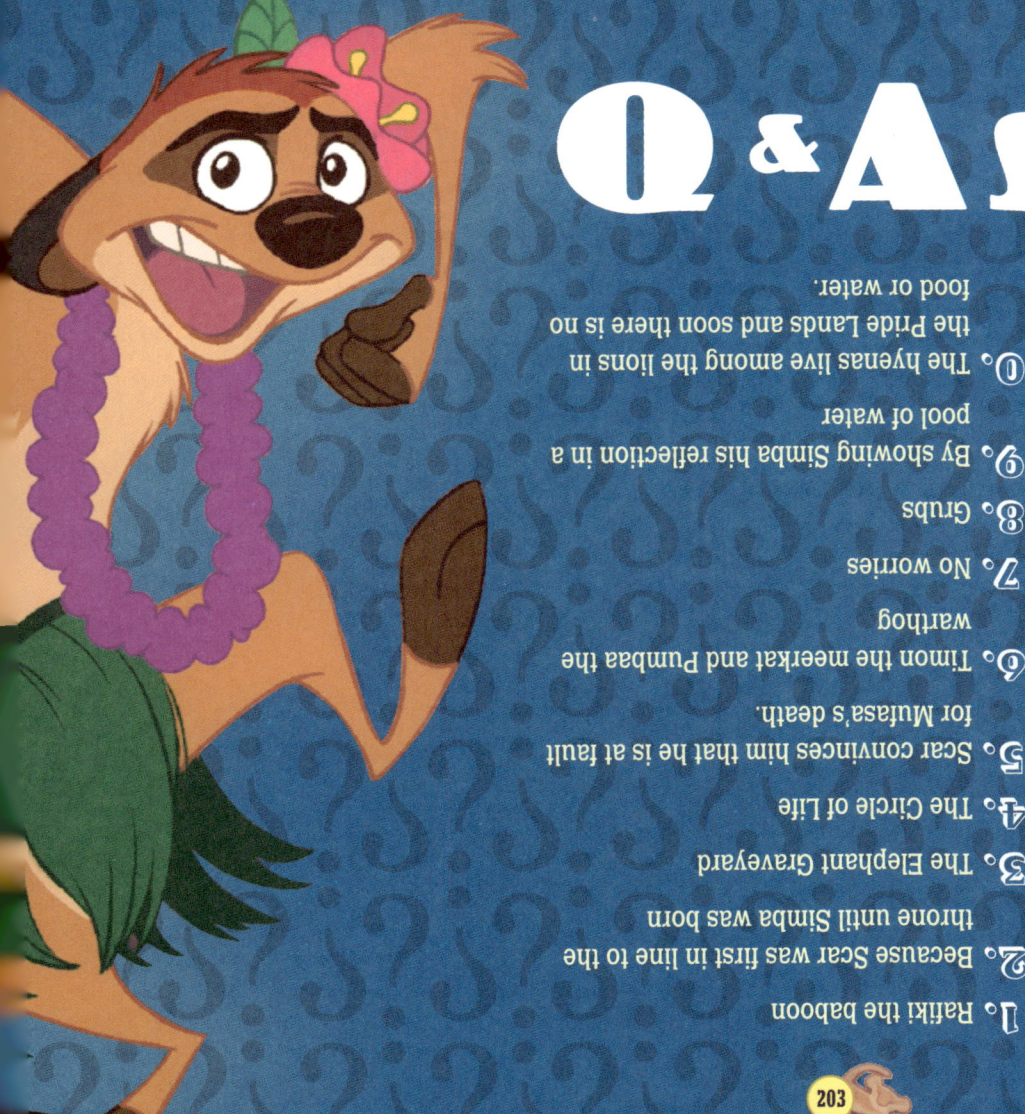

Savanna-drama

All the animals of the savanna gather at Pride Rock to welcome Simba, the new lion cub-prince who will one day be king. Create your own Pride Lands and show how the Circle of Life brings harmony to all the creatures from the smallest to the largest.

shoebox or other medium-sized box, tempera paint, paintbrushes, glue, cotton balls, scissors, construction paper, pebbles, modeling clay, toothpicks, seeds, rocks

Paint a background on the inside of your shoebox that depicts the sky and grassy plains of the African savanna. When the paint has dried, glue cotton ball clouds to the sky. To make grass, cut 2-inch-wide strips that are 3 to 6 inches long out of green construction paper. Fold in half lengthwise. Fringe half of the strip to the fold line by cutting slits about $1/8$ inch apart. Glue the unfringed half to the bottom of the box. To make trees, draw and cut out tree shapes from construction paper with additional two-inch flaps at the base. Fold the flaps under and glue to the bottom of the box. Glue small pebbles to the bottom of the box in between the grass and trees. Create animal bodies by rolling chunks of clay into little balls. Make smaller balls for heads. Use toothpicks to reinforce legs, giraffe necks, or elephant trunks. Add seeds for eyes. Add a nicely shaped rock for Pride Rock. Arrange the animals in your diorama and watch the Pride Lands come to life.

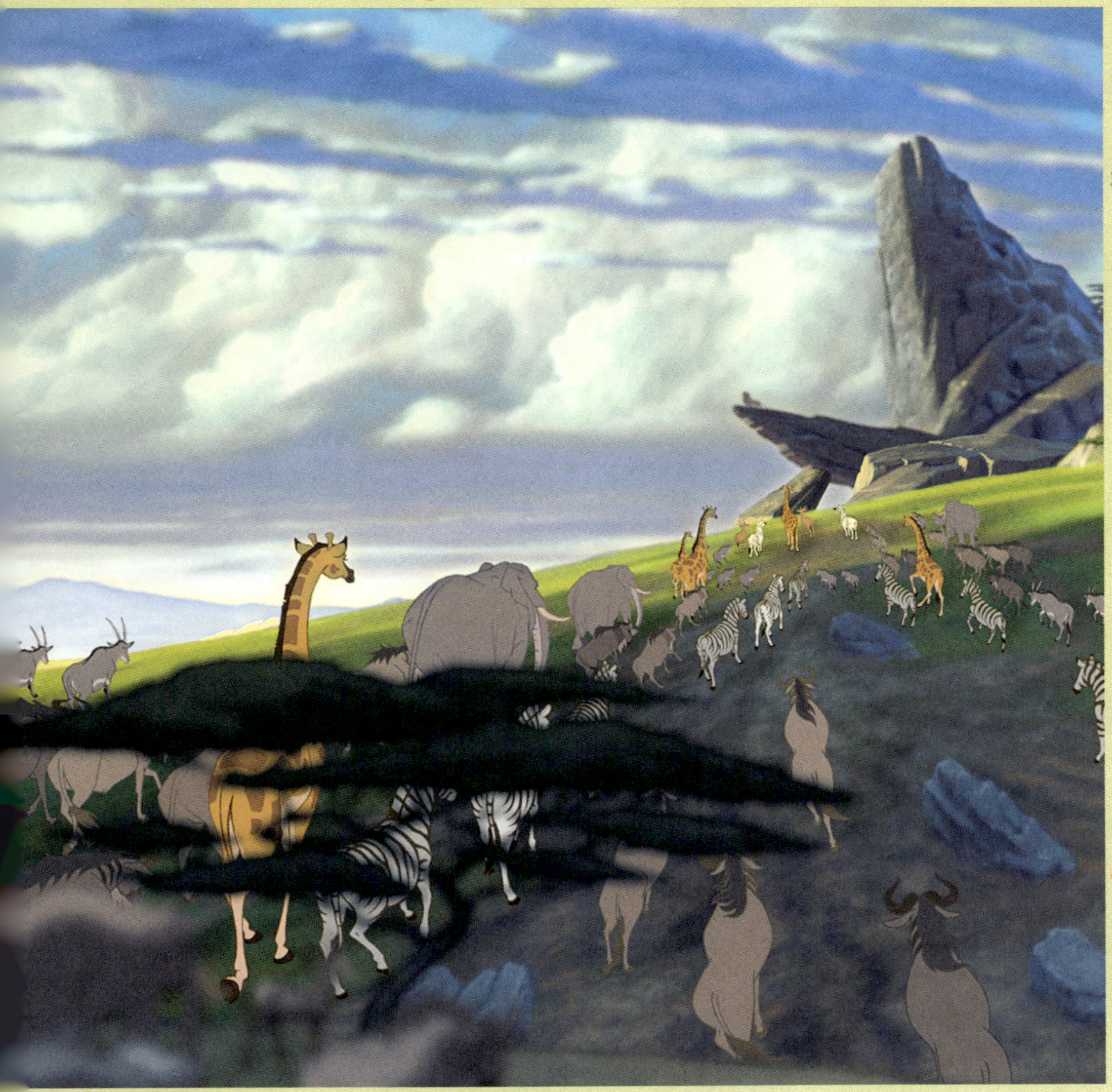

"Run away, Simba. Run. Run away."

"You know, kid, my buddy Timon here says: 'You got to put your behind in your past.'" —Pumbaa

"The question is, who are you?" —Rafiki

"...and **never** return." —Scar

"Home is where your rump rests." —Pumbaa

"Repeat after me. Hakuna matata." —Timon

"Remember who you are." —Mufasa

LINES FROM THE FILM

Timon & Pumbaa's
Hot & Gooey Grub Logs

AS ANY MEERKAT AND WARTHOG KNOW, some of the tastiest grubs are hidden away in rotting logs. Make your own "log" with bananas and have a grubby feast.

banana
chocolate chips
walnuts
marshmallows
gummy worms
granola
tin foil

1. Preheat oven to 350°F.

2. Leave the peel on the banana and cut a long slit along the inside curve.

3. Press chocolate chips, nuts, marshmallows, gummy worms, and granola into the banana halves with a spoon.

4. Wrap the banana in foil and bake in the oven for about 10 minutes, or until the chocolate and marshmallows are nice and gooey.

5. Grab a spoon and dig in!

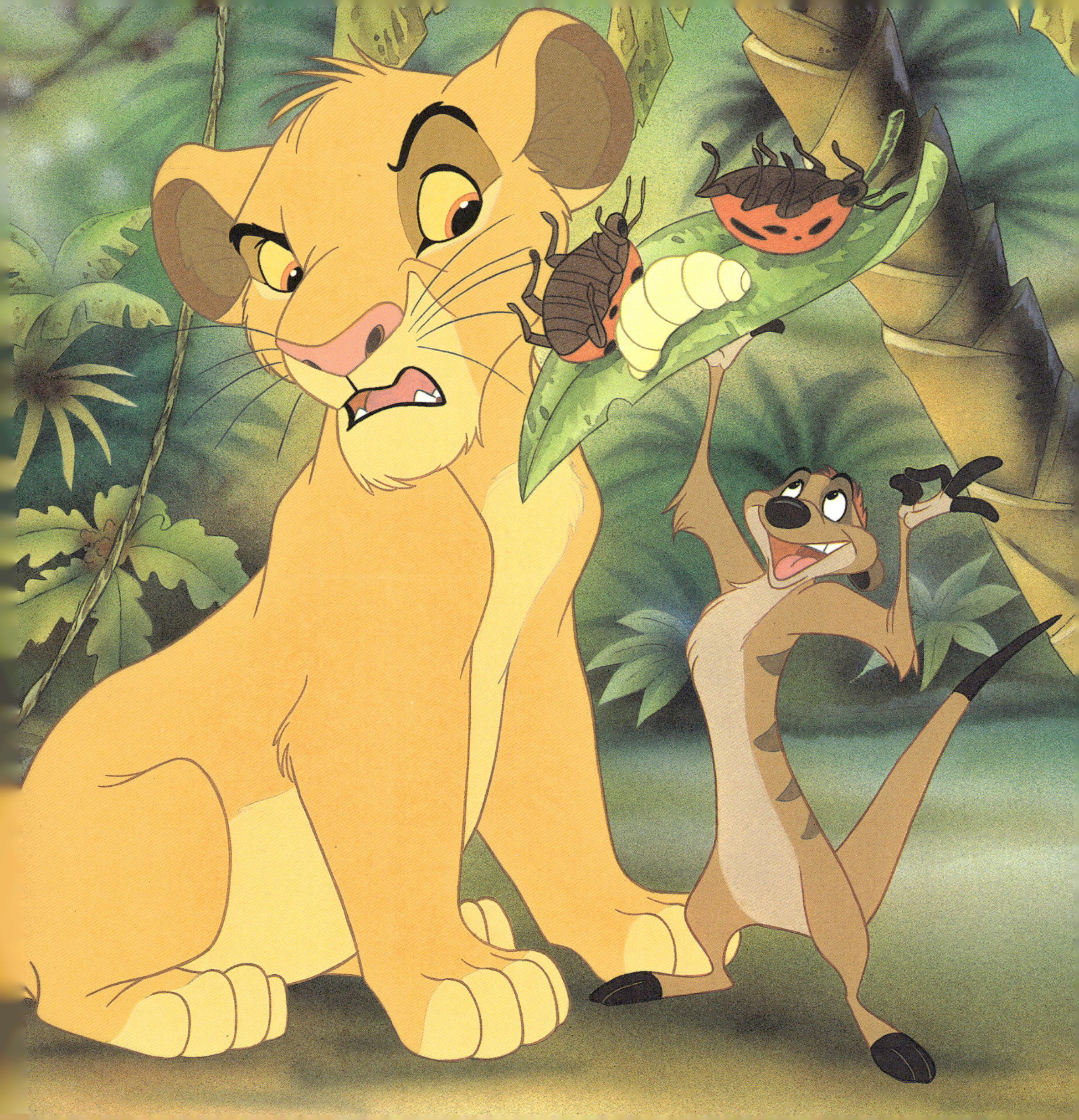

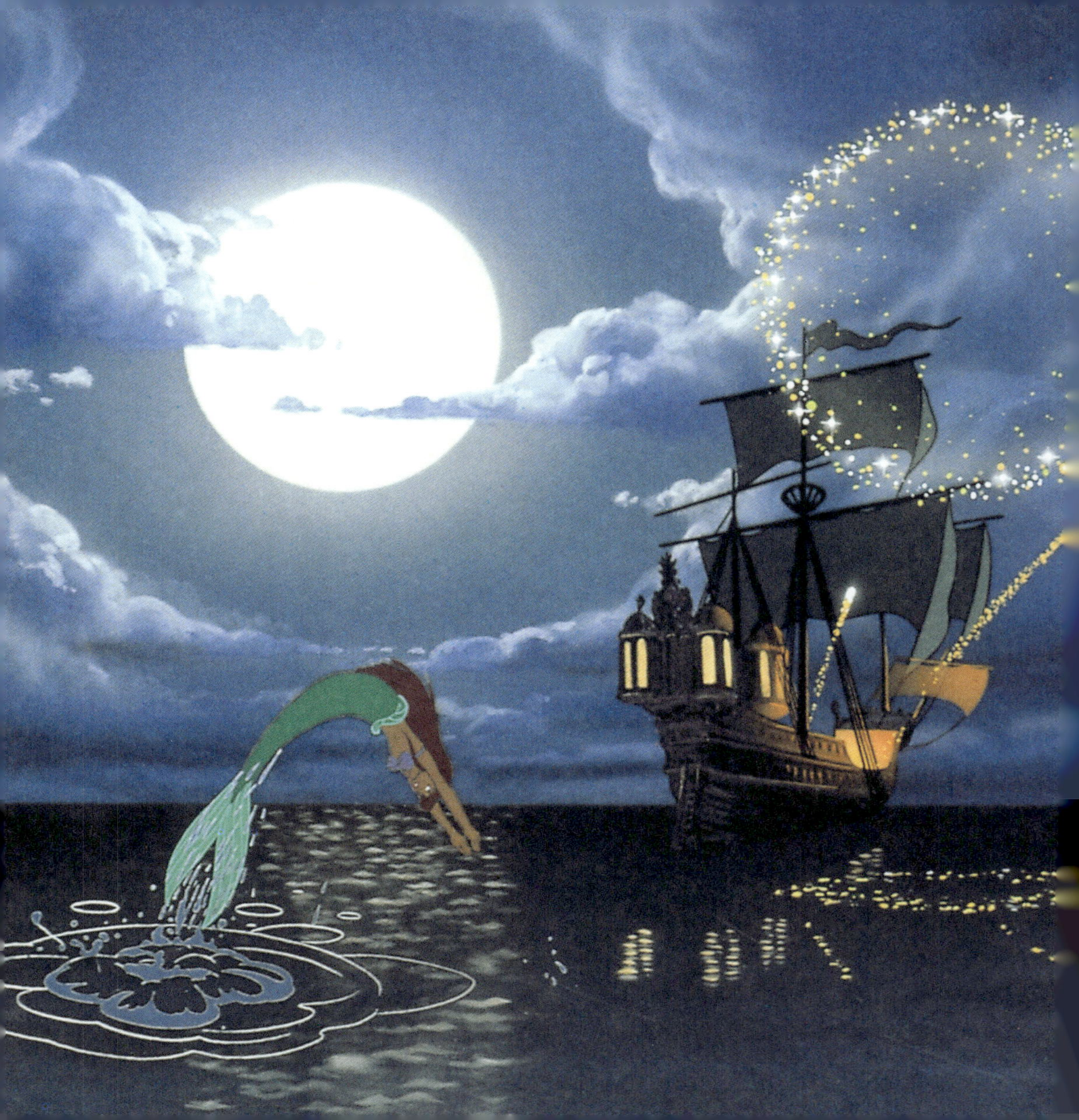

The Little Mermaid

IN AN ENCHANTED PLACE under the sea lived a world of merpeople governed by good King Triton.

The king's youngest daughter, Ariel, had always been curious about the world above the sea. On the day of the royal concert, Ariel and her fish friend Flounder explored a sunken ship. They swam to the surface and told Scuttle the seagull about their findings. When Ariel missed the concert and the king found out where she had been, he was very angry. He forbade Ariel from ever going to the surface again. He assigned the court composer, Sebastian the crab, to watch Ariel.

Ariel swam to her secret collection of human treasures. "I just want to be a part of the human world," she told Sebastian and Flounder. "My father will never understand." Before long, she was swimming to the surface again, and Sebastian could do nothing to stop her.

Ariel swam up to a passing ship and watched everyone on board with delighted interest—

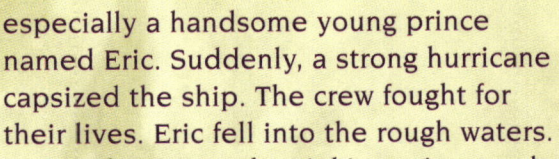

especially a handsome young prince named Eric. Suddenly, a strong hurricane capsized the ship. The crew fought for their lives. Eric fell into the rough waters.

Ariel swam to the sinking prince and dragged him to shore. She cradled him and sang to him until she saw that he was okay.

Meanwhile, lurking in darker waters, Ursula the sea witch and her evil eels Flotsam and Jetsam kept an eye on Ariel's every move. The sea witch wanted King Triton's crown.

King Triton began to notice a change in Ariel's behavior. "I suspect she's in love," the king told Sebastian, unaware of who had stolen Ariel's heart.

"I tried to tell her to stay away from humans," Sebastian stammered.

"Humans!" The king flew into an angry tirade. He found Ariel and destroyed her secret treasured collection.

Angry and determined, Ariel swam to the sea witch.

"Here's the deal," Ursula told Ariel. "I'll turn you into a human for three days. If the prince falls in love with you by the time the sun sets on the third day, you can stay human. If not, you turn back into a mermaid and you belong to me!"

Ariel looked at the trapped souls of all the merpeople who had been tricked by the witch's sinister ways. "As for payment," Ursula said with an evil smile, "it will cost you your voice." Ariel reluctantly agreed. She sang for the witch, who captured Ariel's voice in a shell and rendered her completely mute.

In moments, Ariel surfaced...with legs! Prince Eric found Ariel on the beach and thought she was the one with the beautiful voice who had saved his life. But when Ariel couldn't speak, he knew she couldn't be the one.

Nevertheless, Prince Eric took Ariel to the castle for dinner. The next day, he gave her a tour of his kingdom.

During a romantic boat ride on the water, Ariel could see that the prince was falling in love with her. They almost kissed, but Flotsam and Jetsam whipped the boat over, capsizing them.

The next morning, Ariel awoke to news that the prince had promised his heart to another. The jealous sea witch had transformed herself into a beautiful young lady named Vanessa. She wore the shell that held Ariel's trapped voice around her neck. When Eric heard the voice, he immediately wanted to marry this "Vanessa."

The wedding took place that afternoon on board the prince's ship. Scuttle and many of his seagull friends stormed the ship in a surprise attack. In the scuffle, Vanessa's necklace shattered, and Ariel's voice returned to her. Vanessa turned back into evil Ursula.

Eric ran to Ariel and kissed her, but it was too late— the sun had already set. Ursula grabbed Ariel, who had turned back into a mermaid, and dove into the sea. To save his daughter, King Triton offered his own life. Ursula greedily accepted. The evil Ursula finally ruled the waters! "You insignificant fools!" Ursula cried, stirring up the waters with her powerful new trident.

Yet, all was not lost. Brave Prince Eric pulled himself aboard a sunken ship that had resurfaced in the stormy waters. He aimed the bow at Ursula and plunged it through her middle, destroying her forever.

With the sea witch's spells broken, King Triton and all the trapped merpeople swam free. The king finally understood how much Ariel loved Eric, and granted her legs so that they could be together. For the first time in her life, Princess Ariel felt truly happy, for all her dreams had come true.

1. Ariel finds two human objects in a sunken ship and shows them to her friend Scuttle. What are they, and what does Scuttle tell her they are?
2. What is Sebastian the crab's full name?
3. What kind of creatures are Ursula the sea witch's spies and what are their names?
4. What was Prince Eric trying to do before Ariel saved him from drowning?

THE LITTLE MERMAID

5. What does King Triton do when he discovers that Ariel rescued a human?
6. What price does Ariel pay to Ursula to become human?
7. What happens to Sebastian at Prince Eric's castle?
8. What must happen for Ariel to remain human?
9. How does Ursula trick Eric into wanting to marry her?
10. What does Ursula want more than anything?

Q & As

1. Scuttle tells Ariel that a fork is a dinglehopper that humans use to comb their hair and that a pipe is a musical instrument called a snarlblatt.
2. Horatio Felonious Ignacious Crustaceous Sebastian
3. They are eels named Flotsam and Jetsam.
4. Rescue Max the dog from his sinking ship
5. He destroys her collection of human objects.
6. She gives up her voice.
7. Ariel rescues him from being served as "stuffed crabs" on Grimsby's plate.
8. Prince Eric must kiss her within three days.
9. She disguises herself as a young woman named Vanessa who sings with Ariel's voice.
10. King Triton's crown and trident, so that she can rule the ocean

Ariel's Wishing Stars

Ariel knows that dreams really do come true, when you wish on a star. If mermaids can become princesses, then whole new worlds can never be too far away. What do you dream about when you wish upon the stars at night?

posterboard paper, scissors, glow-in-the-dark pens (available at craft stores), glue, glitter, tape, ribbon

Cut large star shapes out of posterboard paper for each wish. Write your wish in glow-in-the-dark ink on one side of the star. Dribble glue around the edges of each star and sprinkle glitter over the glue. When the glue dries, shake the excess glitter off. Tape a long strand of ribbon to each star and hang from the ceiling or curtain rod. Make your wishes, and may they all come true!

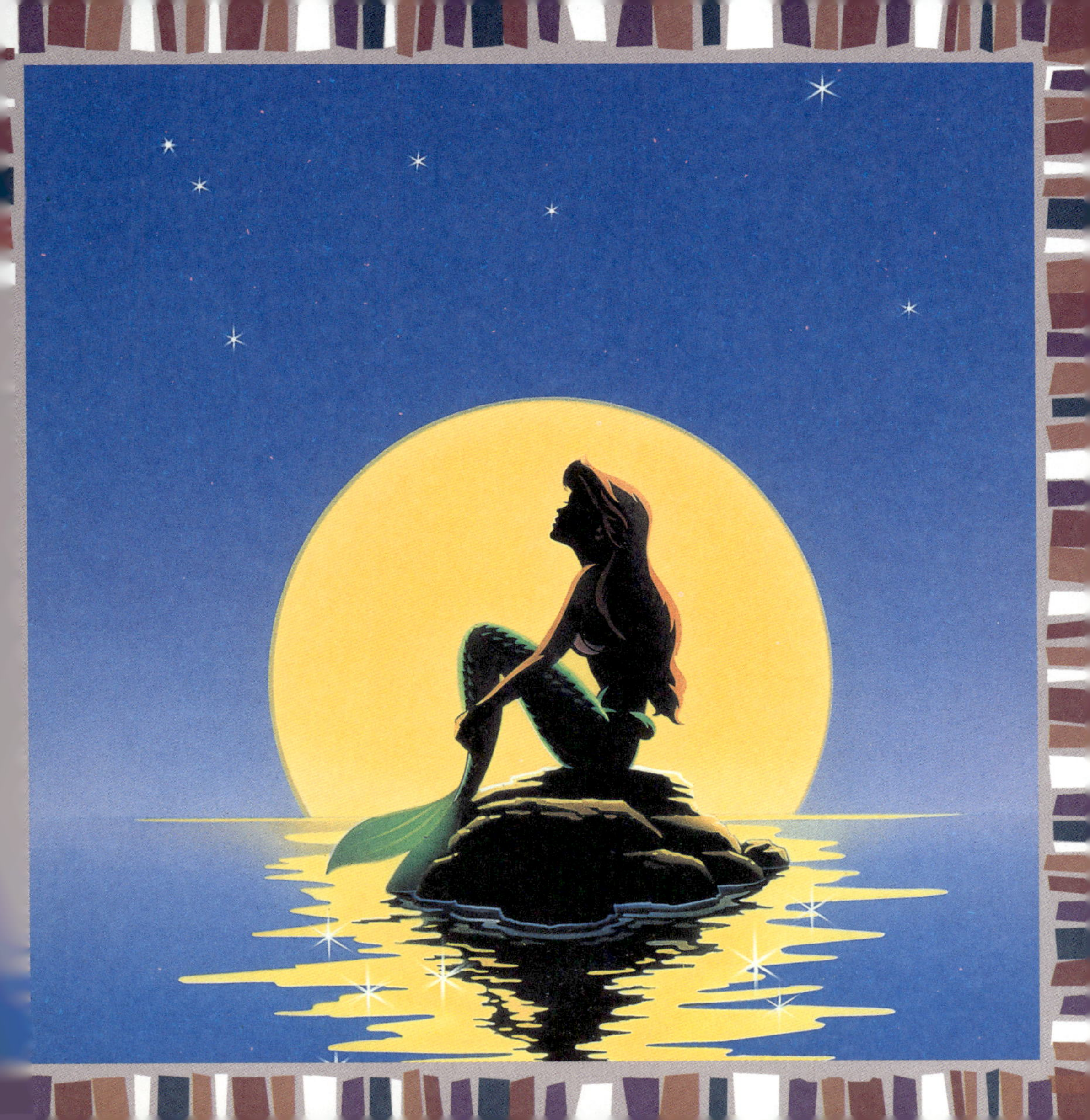

ARIEL: Look what we found.

FLOUNDER: We were on this really creepy sunken ship.

SCUTTLE: Human stuff. Let me see.

<Scuttle holds up fork.>

SCUTTLE: Look at this. Wow! This is special. Very unusual.

ARIEL: What is it?

SCUTTLE: It's a dinglehopper. Humans use these little babies to straighten their hair. Just a twirl here and a yank there, and viola! You got an aesthetically pleasing configuration of hair that humans go nuts over.

ARIEL: A dinglehopper!

LINES FROM THE FILM

FLOUNDER: What about that one?

<Scuttle holds up pipe.>

SCUTTLE: This I haven't seen in years. This is wonderful! A banded, bulbous snarfblatt. The snarfblatt dates back to prehysterical times when humans sat around and stared at each other all day. It got very boring. So they invented the snarfblatt to make fine music. Allow me.

<Scuttle blows on the pipe, causing seaweed and foaming water to erupt from its bowl.>

ARIEL: Music!

<Scuttle tries to play the pipe like a musical instrument.>

SCUTTLE: It's stuck.

ARIEL: The concert! My gosh! My father's gonna kill me!

FLOUNDER: The concert was today?

<Scuttle looks thoughtfully at the pipe.>

SCUTTLE: You could use it as a planter.

ARIEL: I'm sorry. I've got to go. Thank you, Scuttle.

SCUTTLE: Anytime, sweetie. Anytime.

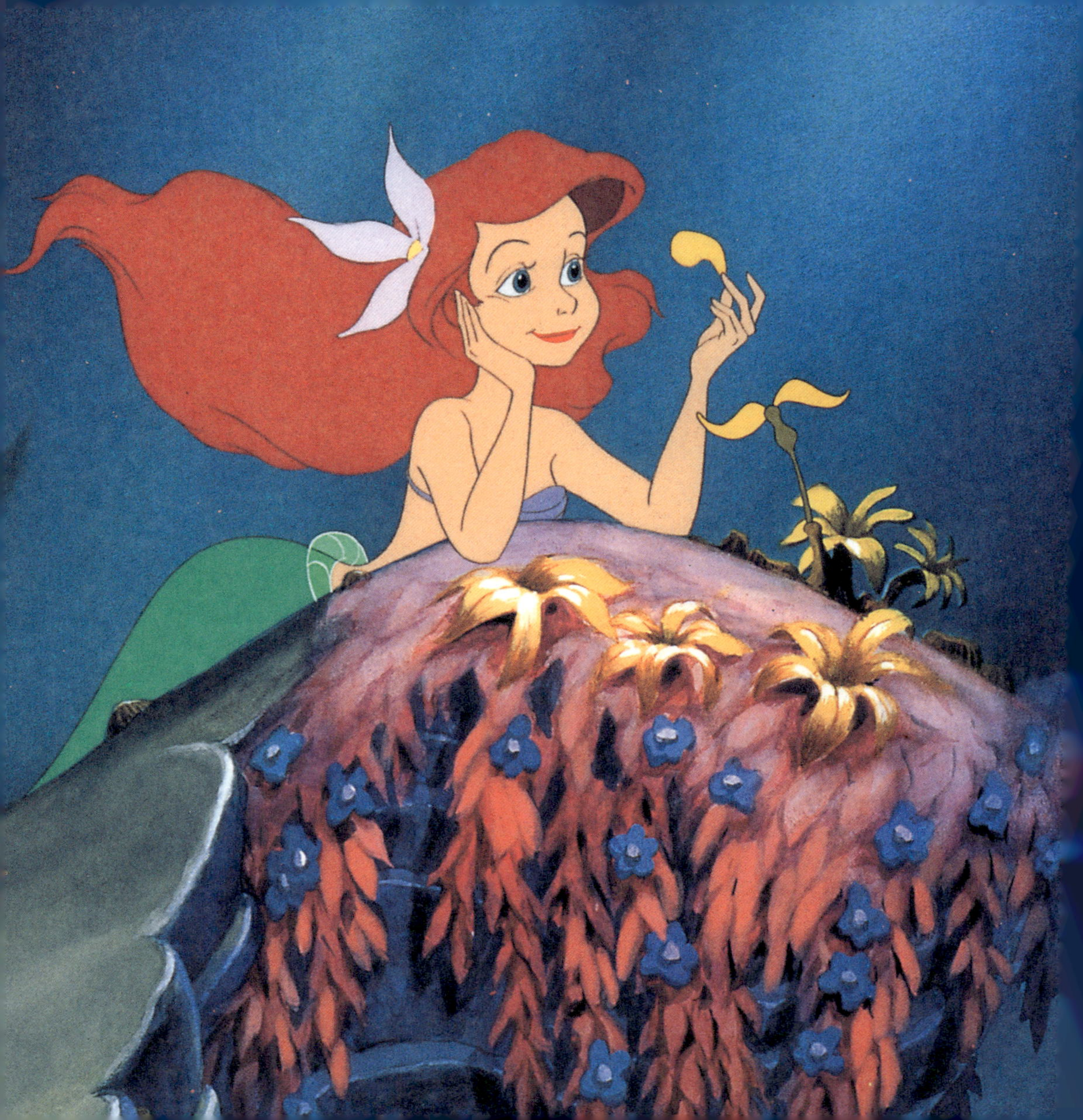

Ariel's
Bottom-of-the-Sea Soup

EVERY MERMAID KNOWS the tastiest and healthiest treats come from the sea. Ariel keeps her new legs strong with this yummy soup filled with "seaweed," seashells, and sea creatures.

6 cups chicken broth
8 ounces mini pasta shells
4 cups spinach, rinsed well and sliced into strips
2 cups goldfish-shaped crackers

1. In a large soup pot, bring chicken broth to a boil.

2. Add pasta shells and continue to simmer for the length of time indicated in pasta cooking instructions.

3. Add spinach strips to soup and stir slowly for 1 minute.

4. Pour soup into bowls and top with goldfish-shaped crackers. Serve immediately.

Makes 4 servings.

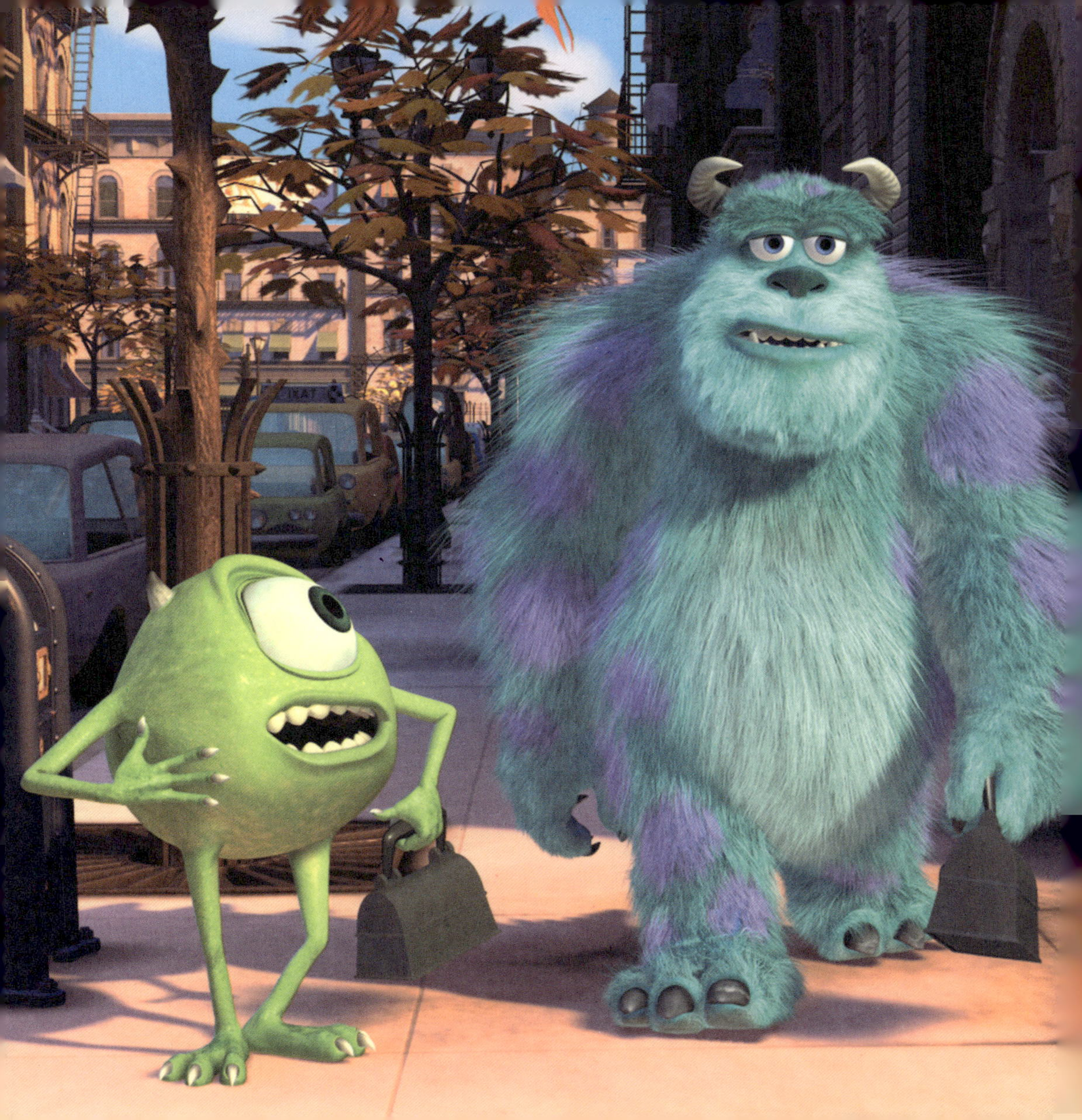

IN A DIMENSION BEYOND THE CLOSET doors of sleeping children around the world lies Monstropolis, the city of monsters. The scariest monster ever to walk through those doors, to the horror of screaming children, was an eight-foot-tall blue monster named James P. "Sulley" Sullivan.

Monsters, Inc.

Sulley collected screams for Monsters, Inc., a scream-processing factory that powered the entire city. It was a tough job, for everyone knew that children were toxic and direct contact with them could be deadly. To make matters worse, Monstropolis faced a huge energy shortage because children were getting harder and harder to scare. But Sulley was the top Scarer, thanks to the help of his hard-training roommate and scream assistant, a one-eyed green monster named Mike Wazowski. One night, while working late on the Scare Floor, Sulley discovered a closet door that hadn't been returned to the vault. "Hello? Anybody scaring in here?" he said, peeking inside.

"Boo!" said a voice behind him. It was a little girl grabbing his tail.

Sulley panicked. The girl squealed with delight. He tried to get rid of her by putting her back in her room, but she ran off in a game of hide-and-seek. Sulley finally caught her and put her in a bag.

When he returned to her door, he spied Randall Boggs, the snaky chameleon monster and number-one rival for the top scare record. Before Sulley could do anything, Randall sent the girl's door back to the vault, leaving Sulley stuck with a human child in Monstropolis!

Sulley ran to the restaurant where Mike was eating dinner. The girl climbed out of the bag before he could explain what had happened. "A kid!" someone screamed. Instant pandemonium broke out, and Mike and Sulley had to make a run for it with the girl.

"How could I do this?" Sulley said when they got home. "This could destroy the company!"

"The company!" Mike said, horrified. "What about us? That thing is a killing machine." The power surged every time she screamed—whether from laughter or tears.

But after a while, the girl seemed harmless—lovable even.

Before long, Mike had a plan to send her back. So they dressed her in a monster costume and snuck her into work.

Meanwhile, Randall had his own ideas for the missing kid. With his Scream Extractor, he planned to revolutionize the scaring industry. When he got wind that Mike and Sulley knew where the girl was, he offered to help them send her home. But instead of helping, he tricked them. Soon the little girl, who Sulley named Boo, was on her way to meet the Scream Extractor, and Mike and Sulley were on their way through a one-way door to the Himalayas.

Mike and Sulley landed in the middle of a raging blizzard inside the cave of the banished but friendly Abominable Snowman.

"Because of you, we are now stuck in this frozen wasteland!" Mike screamed at Sulley.

"You mean wonderland!" said the Abominable Snowman, and he told them about a cute village that lay at the bottom of a mountain.

"If you want to go out there and freeze to death, you be my guest," Mike said angrily. But Sulley couldn't stand the thought of Boo being in trouble, so he braved the blizzard alone. In the village, he found a door that led back to Monsters, Inc. just in the nick of time. Boo was strapped to a chair, with a vacuum contraption ready to suck the screams out of her mouth.

Sulley grabbed her and they ran into Mike, who had come back to help. He and Mike ran off to the door vault, where Randall chased them through millions of closet doors that traveled along overhead tracks. Finally, Sulley and Mike sent Randall through a closet door in a bayou swamp house, where the residents mistook him for a gator and beat him silly with a shovel.

It was time to send Boo home. "Nothing's coming out of the closet to scare you any more, right?" said Sulley, tucking her into bed. "Good-bye, Boo." He left sadly, and shut the closet door. Boo ran to the door and opened it to find her friend, but the portal to the monster world was gone.

"Cheer up," Mike told his sulking friend later. "We did it. We got Boo home! At least we had some laughs, right?"

That gave Sulley a revolutionary idea. Every time Boo had laughed, the power surged. In no time, Sulley proved that laughter produced ten times more energy than screams, and he turned Monsters, Inc. from a scream factory into a laugh factory. The city's energy shortage had finally come to an end.

1. What is Celia's hair made out of?
2. Which monster is Boo afraid of?
3. What happens to Mike and Sulley when they get banished?
4. What happens when Boo screams?
5. What does the Abominable Snowman offer Mike and Sulley?

MONSTERS, INC.

6. What eventually happens to Randall?
7. Why are monsters afraid of children?
8. What is Mike's favorite odorant?
9. Where and when does Boo get spotted in Monstropolis and cause a "Kid-tastrophe"?
10. What is Sulley's idea to change the way Monsters, Inc. supplies power to Monstropolis?

Q & As

1. Snakes
2. Randall
3. They end up in the Abominable Snowman's cave in the Himalayas during a blizzard.
4. The power surges
5. Lemon snowcones
6. He ends up in a house by a swamp where the owners think he's a gator.
7. Because they think children are toxic and deadly
8. Wet dog
9. At Harryhausen's sushi restaurant when Mike is taking Celia out for her birthday
10. To collect children's laughter instead of their screams

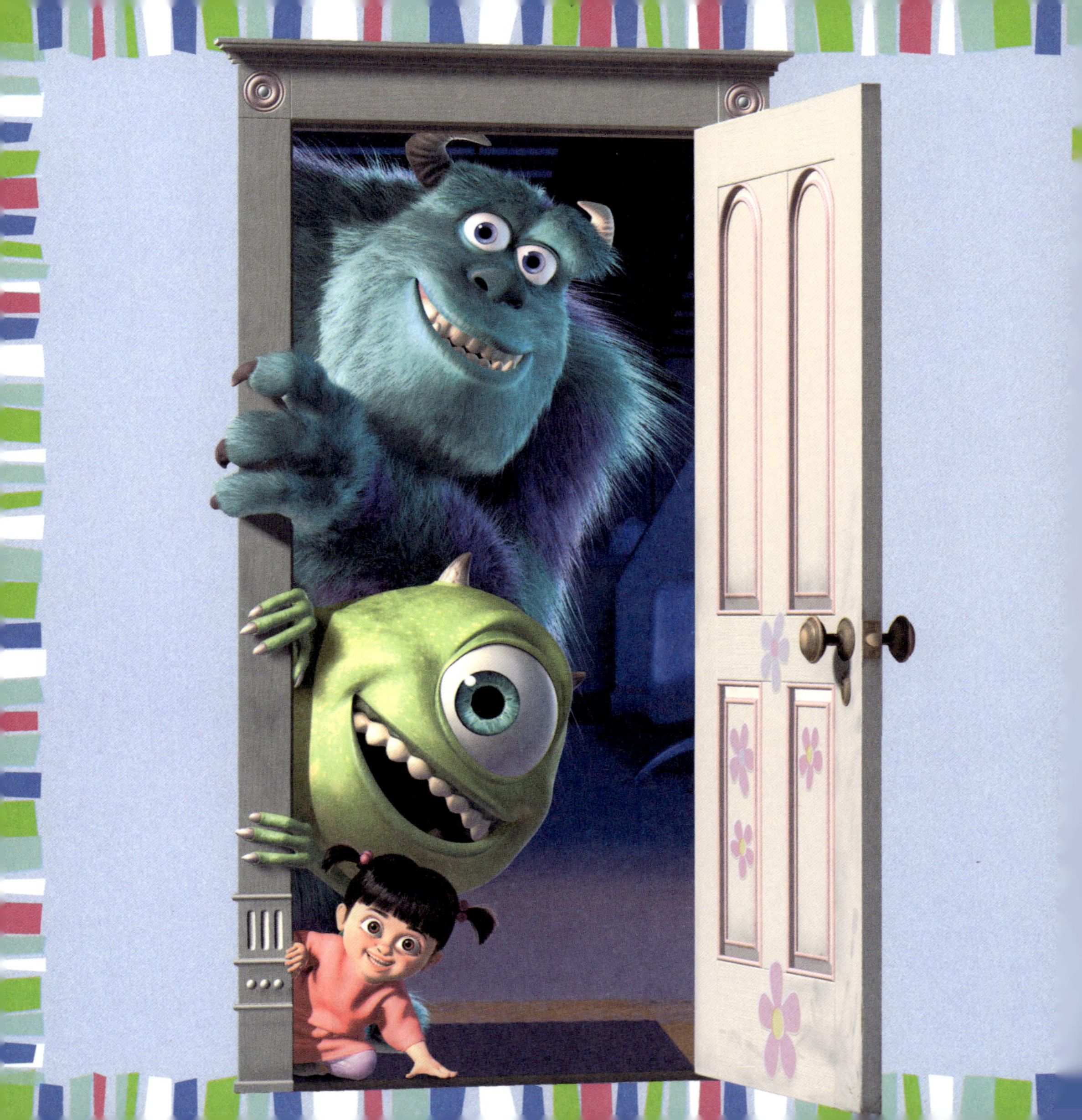

Boo's Closet Door

Do you ever wonder what's behind your closet door at night? Boo knows that her closet is the secret passageway to meet her favorite monsters. Here's how to make your own closet door portal that could lead the way to Monstropolis.

large shoebox with lid, masking tape, scissors, plastic soda bottle lid, poster paint, paintbrushes

Turn your shoebox into a closet and the lid into a closet door. Place the lid on the box and tape one long side of the lid to the outside of the box. Cut the top and bottom flaps off the lid so that the lid can open and close like a door. Cut a small X into the box where the doorknob should go. Place the soda bottle lid over the X and fold the triangular flaps into the underside of the lid. Tape the flaps to the inside of the lid to secure the doorknob. Paint the box with poster paint. Add flowers to make it look like Boo's or add your own decorations to attract your favorite monster. Set the closet on end and open the door. What will be inside?

"I bet it's just waiting for us to fall asleep and then, WHAM! We're easy prey, my friend, easy prey! We're sitting targets!" —Mike

"You know, I am so romantic, sometimes I think I should just marry myself." —Mike

"You know, there's more to life than scaring!" —Mike

"Kids these days. They just don't get

"Oh, actually, that's my cousin's...sister's...daughter, sir." —Sulley

"Hey Mike, this might sound crazy, but I don't think that kid's dangerous." —Sulley

"Nothing's coming out of the closet to scare you anymore. Right?" —Sulley

scared like they used to." —Waternoose

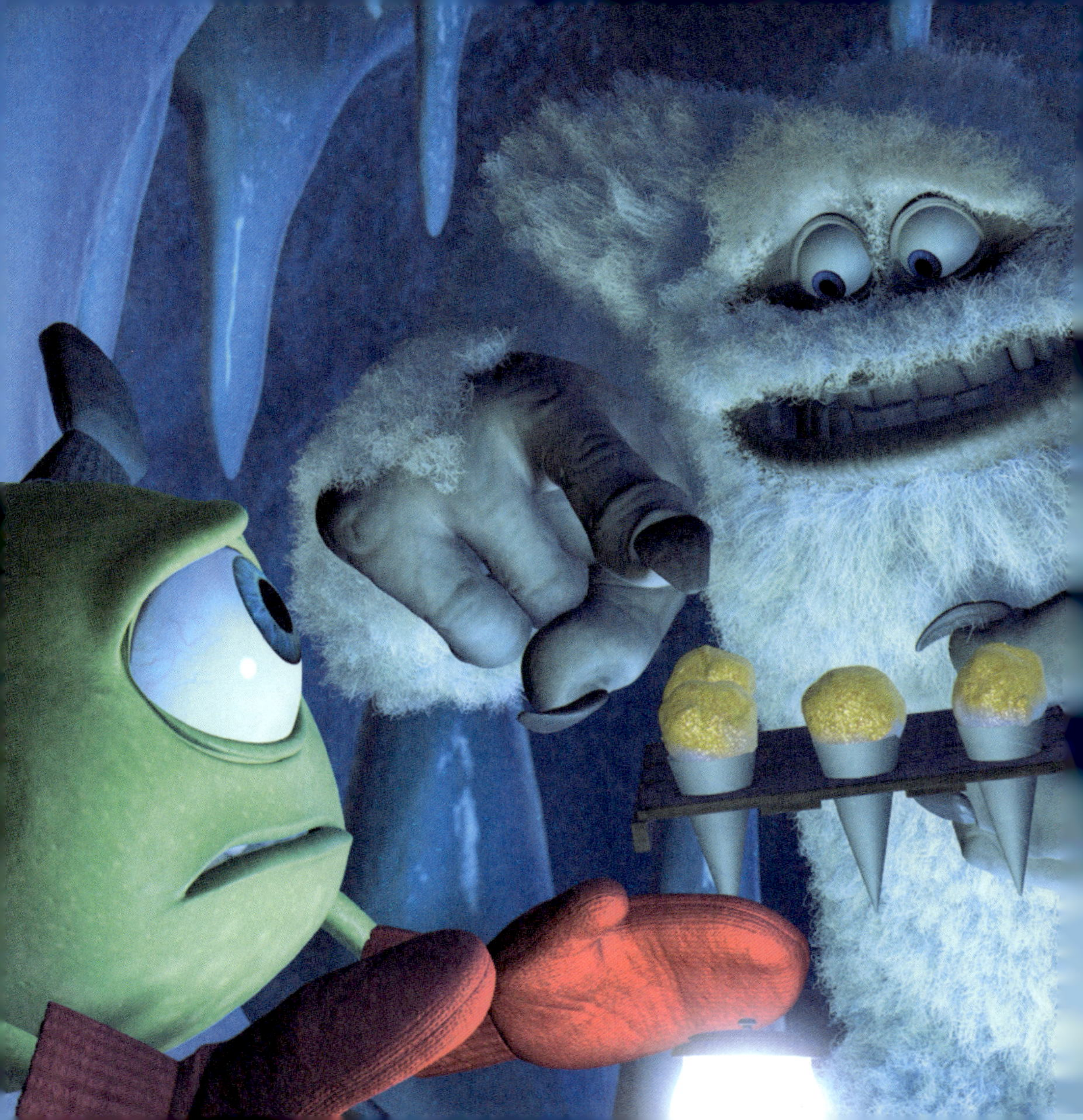

Abominable Snowman's
Lemon Snowcones

THE NEXT TIME you end up with a banished monster in the middle of a Himalayan blizzard, chill out with some of the Abominable Snowman's icy treats.

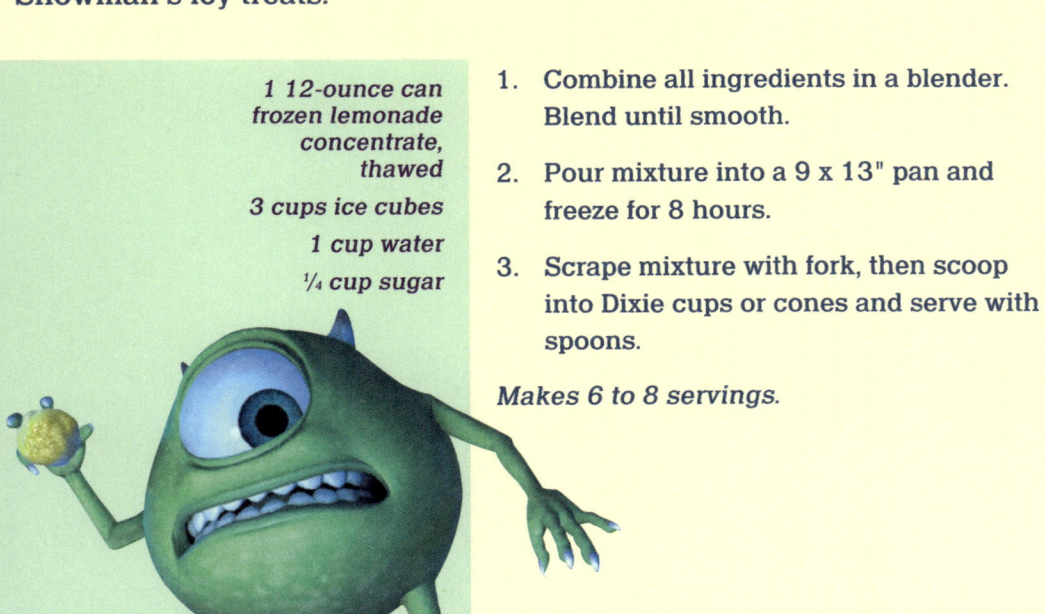

1 12-ounce can frozen lemonade concentrate, thawed

3 cups ice cubes

1 cup water

¼ cup sugar

1. Combine all ingredients in a blender. Blend until smooth.

2. Pour mixture into a 9 x 13" pan and freeze for 8 hours.

3. Scrape mixture with fork, then scoop into Dixie cups or cones and serve with spoons.

Makes 6 to 8 servings.

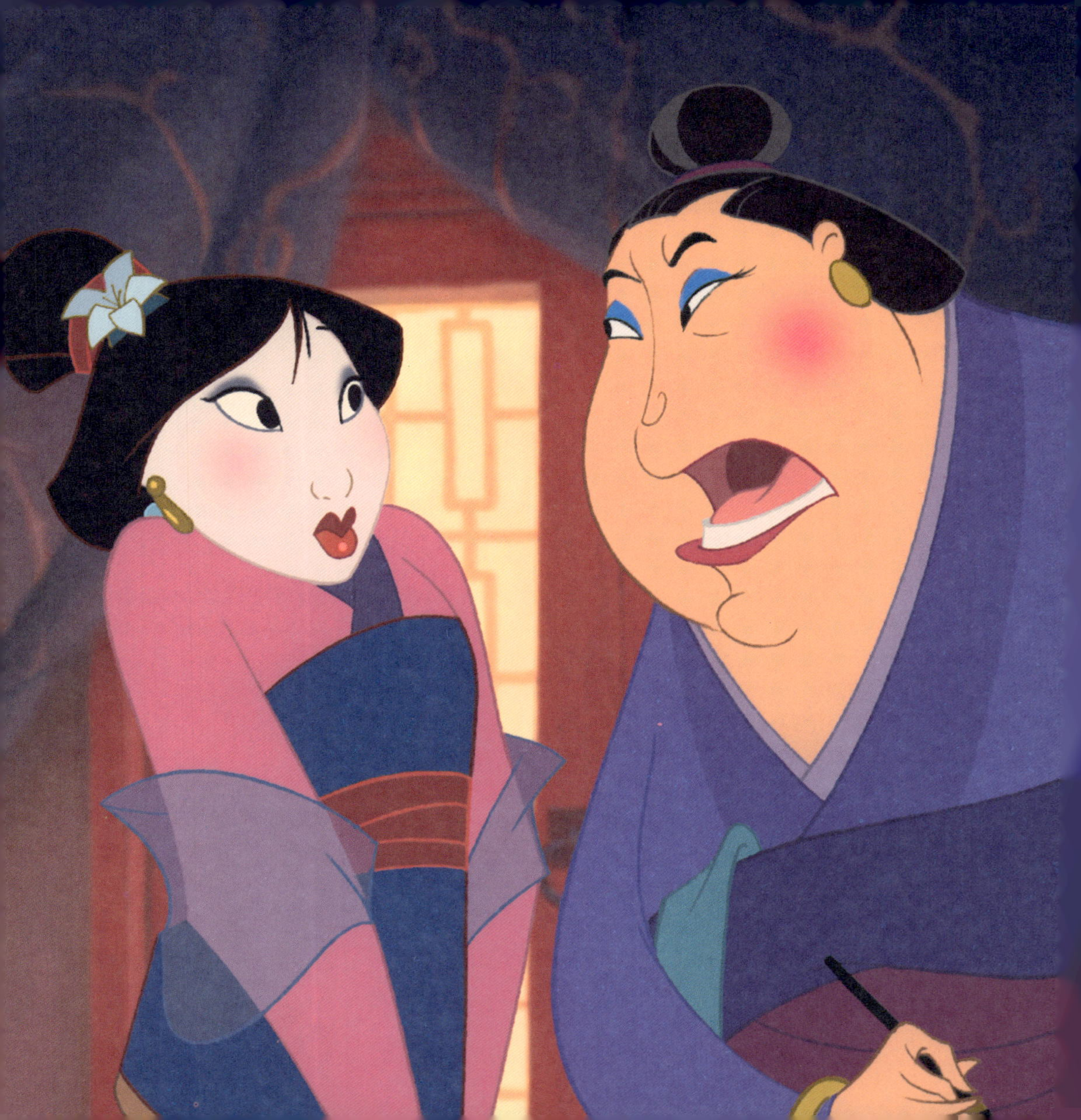

Mulan

ONE NIGHT, along the Great Wall of China, an Imperial Guardsman heard the cry of a strange bird. It was the falcon of Shan-Yu, the leader of the Huns. Suddenly, hundreds of invaders jumped the Wall. The Huns had invaded the northern border!

In a nearby village, Fa Mulan poured tea for the matchmaker. Unfortunately, her lucky cricket, Cri-Kee, caused the matchmaker to spill her tea and fall on a bed of hot coals. "You will never bring your family honor!" she told Mulan.

That afternoon, a proclamation arrived from the Imperial City. "One man from every family must fight the Huns." Fa Zhou threw down his walking stick and stepped forward.

"Father, no!" Mulan shouted.

"You dishonor me," he said, looking away from his daughter. That night Mulan prayed to her ancestors. She cut her hair, dressed in her father's armor, and took her father's sword. Disguised as a young man, she rode into the night to fight in place of her father, who had suffered a leg injury from a previous war.

Mulan's ancestors summoned the little dragon Mushu to awaken the Great Stone Dragon, to protect Mulan. But instead of awakening, the Great Stone Dragon crumbled to bits. So Mushu and Cri-Kee set off to protect Mulan themselves.

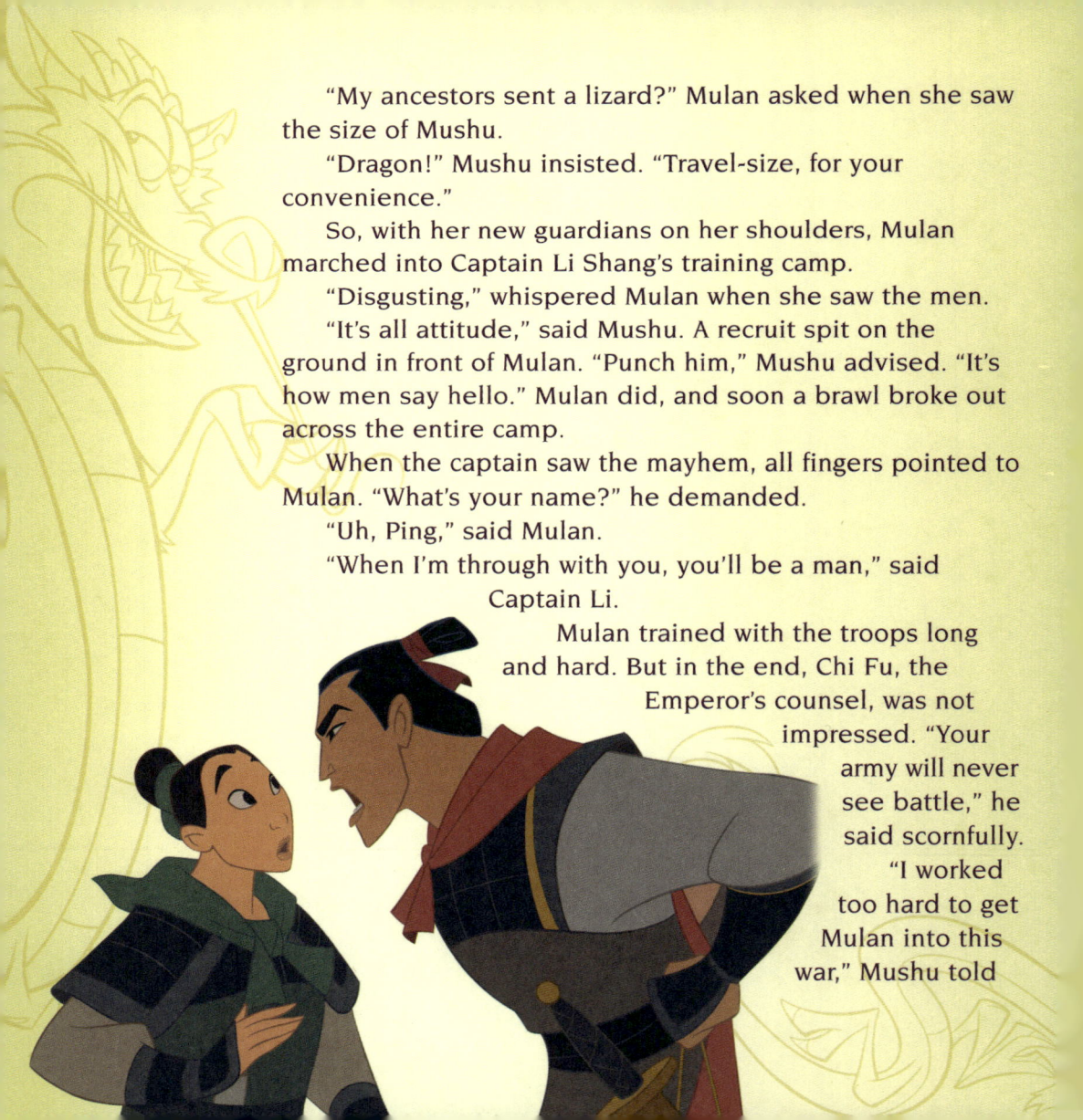

"My ancestors sent a lizard?" Mulan asked when she saw the size of Mushu.

"Dragon!" Mushu insisted. "Travel-size, for your convenience."

So, with her new guardians on her shoulders, Mulan marched into Captain Li Shang's training camp.

"Disgusting," whispered Mulan when she saw the men.

"It's all attitude," said Mushu. A recruit spit on the ground in front of Mulan. "Punch him," Mushu advised. "It's how men say hello." Mulan did, and soon a brawl broke out across the entire camp.

When the captain saw the mayhem, all fingers pointed to Mulan. "What's your name?" he demanded.

"Uh, Ping," said Mulan.

"When I'm through with you, you'll be a man," said Captain Li.

Mulan trained with the troops long and hard. But in the end, Chi Fu, the Emperor's counsel, was not impressed. "Your army will never see battle," he said scornfully.

"I worked too hard to get Mulan into this war," Mushu told

Cri-Kee. So they wrote a fake letter from the battlefront to Chi Fu: *Captain Li's troops are urgently needed*!

Soon, Mulan and the troops were marching to war. When they got to the Tung-Shao Pass, they found the village completely burned down. "We're the last hope for the Emperor now," said Captain Li somberly.

Suddenly the mountain echoed with the thunder of Shan-Yu's approaching troops across the divide. Captain Li's small army was no match for the enemy. "Prepare to fight. If we die, we die with honor," he said.

As Shan-Yu's army got closer, Mulan got an idea. She aimed her rocket at the highest mountain peak and fired. The blast set off a massive avalanche that buried Shan-Yu's entire army.

Captain Li nearly lost his life in the battle with Shan-Yu, and Mulan helped him to safety. "I owe you my life," he told Ping.

Mulan had been wounded too by Shan-Yu's sword, and needed help. In the medical tent, Mulan's identity became known. "A woman!" said Chi Fu. "Ultimate dishonor!"

"I did it to save my father," Mulan tried to explain, but it was no use. She had broken the law, and the punishment was death.

Captain Li drew his sword, then threw it in the snow. "A life for a life," he said. "My debt is repaid."

Ashamed, Mulan left for home. On the way, she spied the Huns emerging from the snow. "I have to do something!" she said to Mushu and Cri-Kee. Off they galloped to the Imperial City, before it was too late.

By the time she arrived, the Huns had invaded the Imperial Palace and captured the Emperor. Mulan bravely snuck into the palace with her fellow soldiers to fight Shan-Yu's men. They reached the Emperor just in time to rescue him from Shan-Yu's sword. But in the struggle, Mulan got trapped on the roof with Shan-Yu.

Mushu and Cri-Kee came to the rescue. They fired a rocket that blew the evil Hun into a stack of fireworks. China was saved from the Huns!

The Emperor thanked Mulan for her bravery with a gift of the Imperial Pendant and Shan Yu's sword. "Remember," said the Emperor, "a flower that blooms in adversity is the rarest flower of all." Mulan presented the gifts to her father upon returning home. She had finally brought honor to her family.

Captain Li Shang, too, realized that girls like Mulan don't come around every dynasty. To Mulan's surprise and joy, he honored the Fa household with a visit. She invited him to stay for dinner and Grandmother Fa invited him to stay forever.

MULAN

1. How does Grandma Fa know that Cri-Kee is one lucky bug?
2. Why does Mulan disguise herself as a man to fight for the Imperial Army?
3. What seemingly impossible task does Captain Li Shang ask his army recruits to do at the training camp?
4. What do the ancestors tell Mushu to do to help Mulan?
5. What happens to the matchmaker during her interview with Mulan?
6. What do Mushu and Cri-Kee do when Council Chi Fu tells Shang that his army is unfit for war?
7. What does Mulan tell Shang that her name is?
8. How does Mulan defeat the Huns at Tung Shao Pass?
9. What does the Emperor give Mulan as thanks?
10. What does Mushu do to scare Mulan's fellow soldiers out of the river when Mulan is bathing?

Q & As

1. She crosses the street blindfolded with him and doesn't get hurt.
2. To go in place of her father, who fought in a previous battle and must use a cane to walk
3. To retrieve an arrow from the top of a tall pole
4. Awaken the Great Stone Dragon to be her guardian
5. She gets an ink mustache, becomes soaked in hot tea, and sits on a pile of hot coals.
6. They dress up as a fake soldier to deliver a fake urgent document stating that Shang's troops are needed at the front.
7. Ping
8. She fires a rocket into the mountain peak, causing an avalanche to bury Shan Yu's troops.
9. The Imperial Pendant and Shan Yu's sword
10. Mushu bites Yao, who mistakes him for a poisonous snake.

The Indestructible Mushu

When the Great Stone Dragon crumbles, the little dragon Mushu comes to Mulan's aid. With a few chopsticks and construction paper, you can bring Mushu to life and make Mulan's ancestors proud.

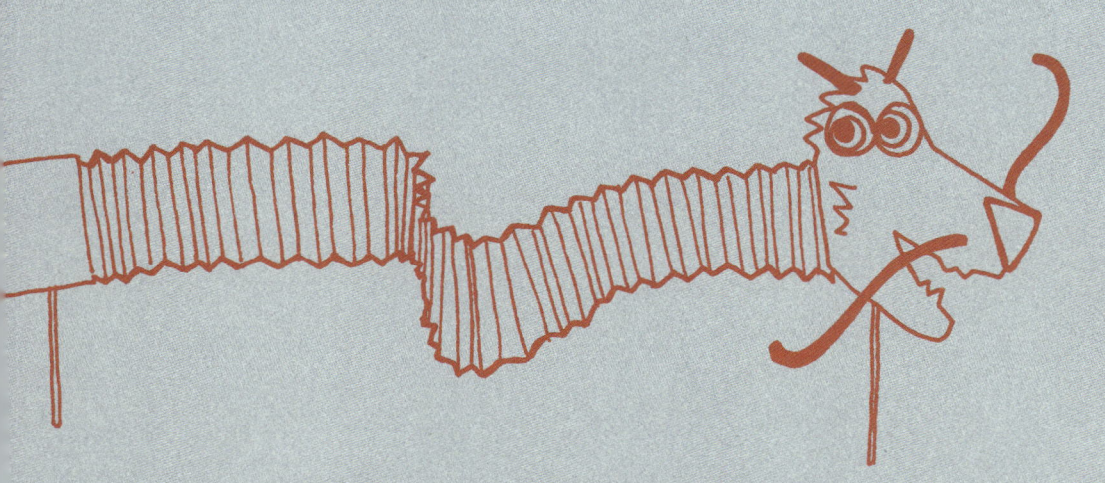

red construction paper, scissors, tape,
crayons, glue, googly eyes, 2 yellow and
2 blue 3 x12 pipe cleaners, wooden chopsticks

Cut two strips of construction paper about 3 inches by 12 inches. Fold each strip accordion style. Tape the two strips together to make Mushu's long body. Draw Mushu's head and tail on a piece of construction paper about the same width as Mushu's body and cut it out. Glue googly eyes and yellow pipe cleaners for whiskers and short blue pipe cleaners for horns on Mushu's head. Tape Mushu's head and tail onto the ends of the body. Tape the end of one chopstick onto the bottom of Mushu's head, then tape the other chopstick onto the bottom of Mushu's tail. Hold each chopstick to make Mushu move, then get ready to help Mulan kick some Hunny buns!

"I have a name. It's a boy's name, too." —Mulan

"Looking like a man doesn't mean I have to smell like one." —Mulan

"My little baby is all grown up and saving China." —Mushu

"You don't meet a girl like

hat **every dynasty."**

—Emperor

LINES FROM THE FILM

249

Mushu's Happy-to-See-You Porridge

FOR THOSE DAYS when you feel like you have to take on an entire army, it's best to start the day with a smile. And as Mulan knows, it's easy to smile when your breakfast is smiling back at you—even if your mouth is full.

1 cup milk
½ tablespoon butter
¼ cup brown sugar
⅛ teaspoon salt
¼ teaspoon cinnamon
½ cup rolled oats
¼ cup raisins
¼ cup chopped walnuts
4 small eggs, fried sunny side up
2 cooked strips bacon or turkey bacon

1. Combine all ingredients except eggs and bacon in a saucepan. Bring to a boil, then turn heat to low.
2. Simmer on low for about 10 minutes, stirring often.
3. When oatmeal has reached desired consistency, scoop into bowls.
4. Top oatmeal with eggs and bacon to look like a smiley face.
5. Eat while it's hot!

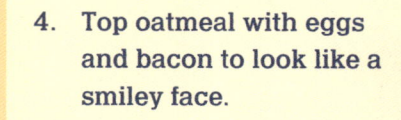

Makes 2 servings.

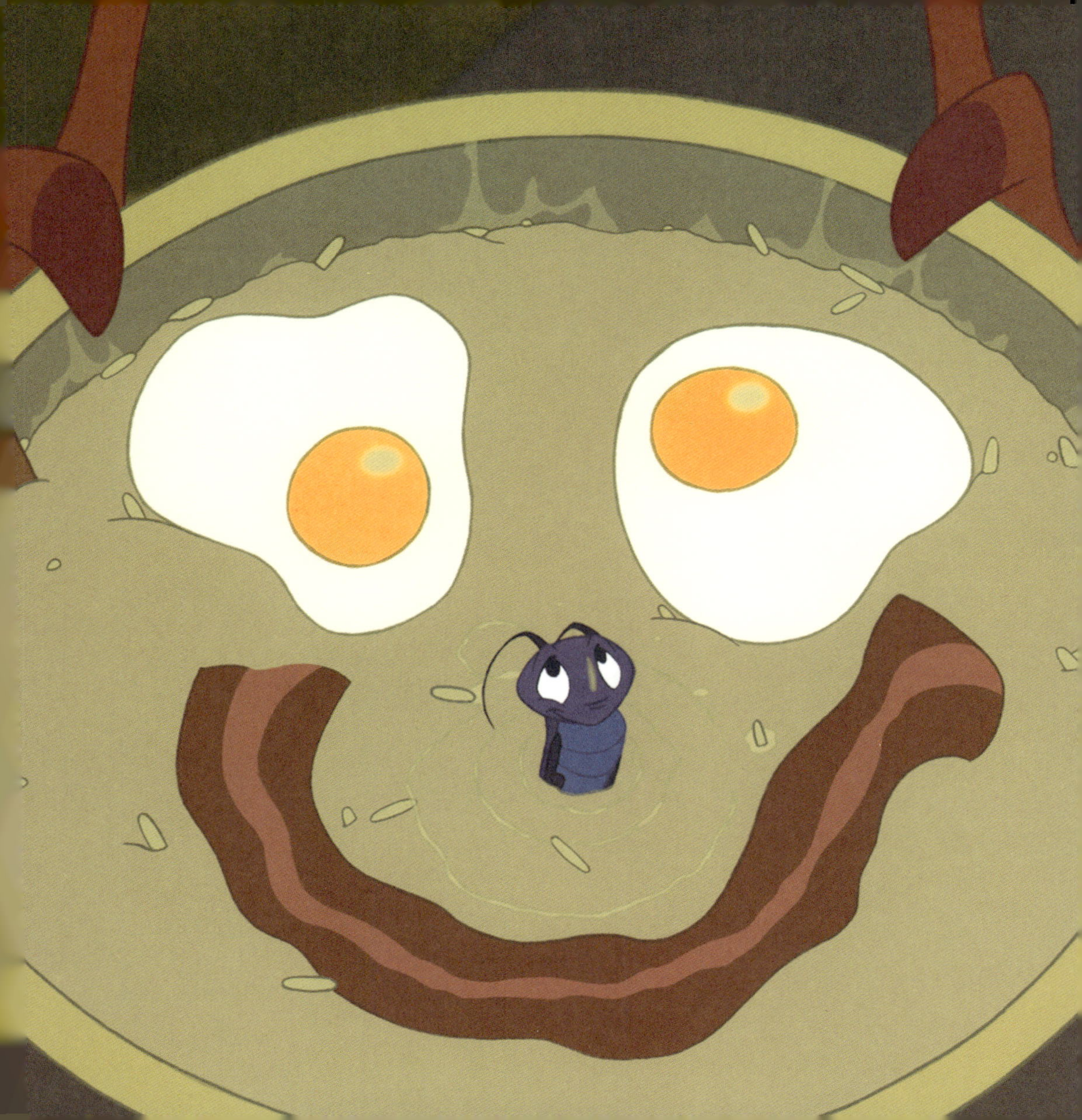

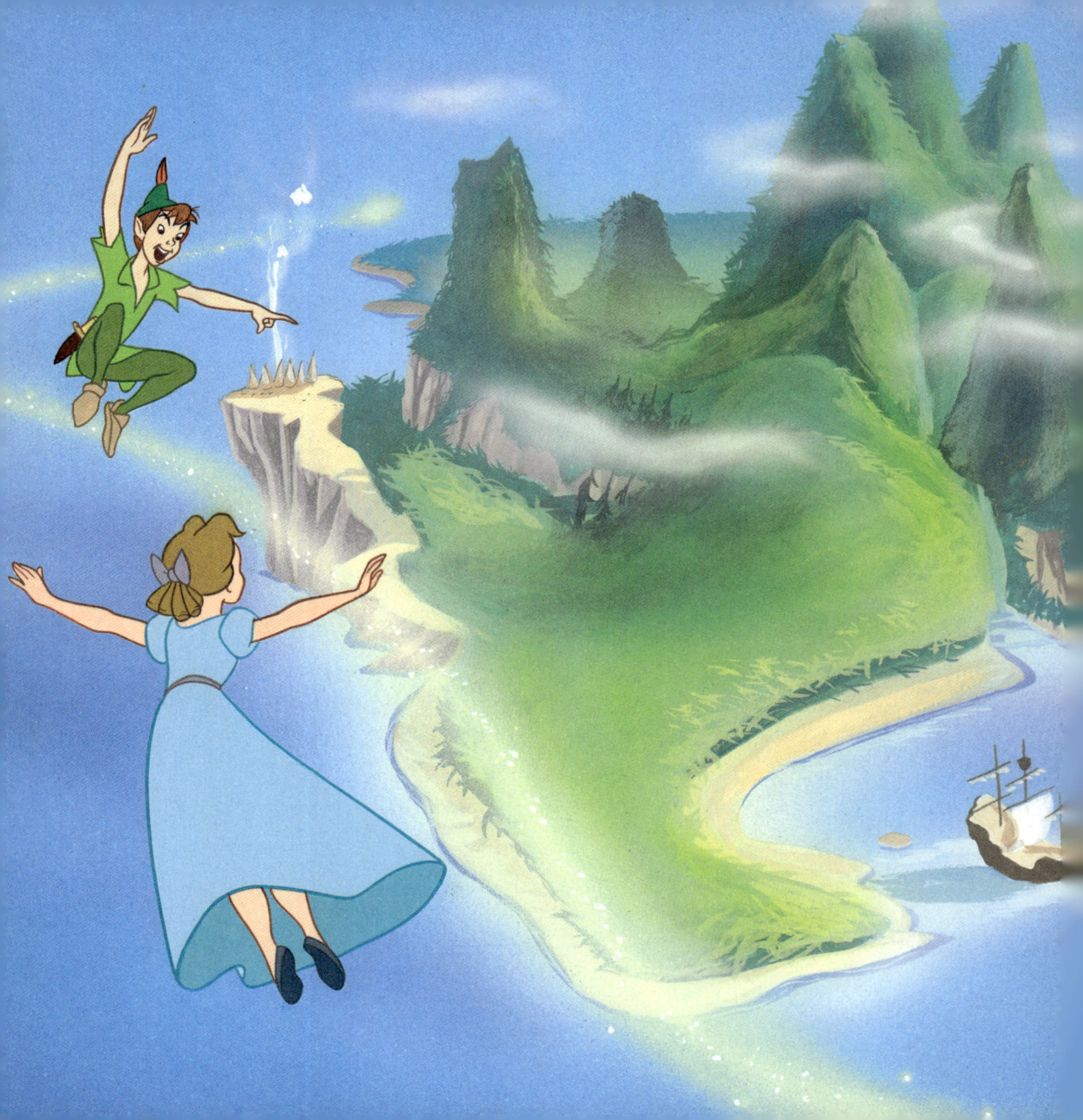

Peter Pan

ONCE UPON A TIME, nestled away on a quiet street in London, lived Mother and Father Darling and their children, Wendy, John, and Michael.

Every evening, Wendy told stories about Peter Pan and his adventures in Never Land. Michael and John loved acting out the swordfights between Pan and Captain Hook.

Father Darling did not approve of such play. "It's high time you had a room of your own," he told Wendy. "Tonight is your last night in the nursery."

Later that night, Peter Pan and Tinker Bell snuck into the nursery looking for Peter's lost shadow. "I might have never seen you after tonight," Wendy said. "For I must grow up tomorrow!"

"Come with me to Never Land!" Peter said. "You'll never grow up there."

The children were eager to go, but they needed to learn how to fly.

"Think of the most wonderful things," said Peter. Then, with a sprinkle of Tinker Bell's pixie dust, the children could fly. Soon they were soaring over London on their way to Never Land.

The children got their first glimpse of Peter's home from the top of a cloud. "It's just as I dreamed it would be!" Wendy said happily.

Meanwhile, in Pirate's Cove, Captain Hook had been looking for Peter's hideout. He was after Peter for cutting off his hand in a duel and tossing it to a hungry crocodile. Ever since, the croc followed Hook everywhere he went, licking his chops for more.

Peter took Wendy, Michael, and John to Hangman's Tree, where the Lost Boys lived. While Michael and John explored the island, Wendy and Peter visited Mermaid Lagoon.

There, Peter and Wendy spied Captain Hook and his first mate, Mr. Smee, in a rowboat headed for Skull Rock. "They've captured Princess Tiger Lily!" exclaimed Peter.

"Tell me the hiding place of Peter Pan, and I shall set you

free." Hook threatened the princess, but brave Tiger Lily refused to speak.

Peter Pan challenged Hook to a daring duel. They crossed swords at the edge of a cliff, where Hook slipped and fell. He dangled above the water, just out of reach of the crocodile's snapping jaws.

Peter scooped Tiger Lily up in his arms and returned her to the Indian camp. The chief was so happy that he christened Peter "Chief Flying Eagle."

Captain Hook fumed with anger and plotted to get rid of Peter Pan for good. He kidnapped Peter's pixie friend Tinker Bell and tricked her into revealing Peter's secret hideout before locking her up in a lantern.

At Hangman's Tree, Wendy told her brothers and the Lost Boys stories about Mother. Before long, everyone wanted to go home with the Darlings.

"Go on," Peter scowled. "Once you grow up, you can never come back!" He turned his back as the children left.

Outside the hideout, Hook and his crew lurked in the bushes. One by one, as the children came out, the pirates snatched them up and took them away.

Then Captain Hook delivered a specially wrapped package for Peter. Once Peter unwrapped it... KA-BOOM! It would explode.

Meanwhile, a terrible fate awaited Wendy and the boys on the pirate ship. "Sign up as a pirate," warned Hook, "or walk the plank!"

"Peter Pan will save us," Wendy said.

But Hook just cackled. "Pan will soon be blasted out of Never Land," he told her.

Hook pointed to the plank. "Ladies first," he sneered. As Wendy bravely walked the plank, Tinker Bell escaped from her lantern cage and sped off to warn Peter.

Thanks to Tinker Bell, Pan arrived at the pirate ship just in time. "This time you've gone too far!" he shouted, and chased Hook up the rigging in a fierce fight. In the most exciting duel ever, Peter agreed not to fly, and battled Hook—man to man.

Peter narrowly escaped, but in the end he knocked Hook's sword away and forced him to surrender. Hook swam away with the hungry crocodile close behind.

"Heave those halyards! Hoist the anchor!" shouted Peter as he took command of Hook's vessel. Tinker Bell sprinkled the ship with pixie dust, and soon they were soaring through the skies back to London.

"Michael, John," Wendy called. "We're going home!"

Back in London, Peter Pan bid the children farewell and sailed off into the moonlight. In the nursery, the Darlings waved good-bye, knowing that Peter Pan and all the excitement of Never Land would stay alive in their hearts forever.

1. Why does Peter Pan sneak into the children's nursery at night?
2. Where does Hook take Princess Tiger Lily?
3. What does Peter Pan tell Wendy, Michael, and John all it takes to fly?
4. Who is Captain Hook's first mate?
5. What happened to Captain Hook's hand?
6. What does Tinker Bell tell the Lost Boys to do when Wendy flies to Peter Pan's hideout?
7. What name does the Indian Chief give Peter Pan for rescuing Tiger Lily?

PETER PAN

8. What does Captain Hook tell Wendy, Michael, John, and the Lost Boys they must do when he kidnaps them?
9. What does Hook do to Tinker Bell after he tricks her into telling him where Peter Pan's hideout is?
10. How do you get to Never Land?

Q & As

1. To find his lost shadow
2. To Skull Rock
3. To think the happiest thoughts and a sprinkle of pixie dust
4. Mr. Smee
5. Peter Pan cut it off in a sword fight and threw it to a hungry crocodile.
6. To shoot down the terrible Wendy Bird from the sky
7. Little Flying Eagle
8. Join the crew or walk the plank
9. He locks her up in a lantern.
10. Fly past the second star to the right and straight on till morning.

Tick-Tock Croc

If a certain crocodile hadn't swallowed a clock, Captain Hook would never hear the tick-tock-tick-tock to know he was being followed. Here's how you can make your own tick-tock croc and chase Captain Hook all the way out of Never Land.

extra large Styrofoam cup, scissors, green, pink, and white construction paper, glue, yarn, stapler, newspaper

Cut the bottom of the cup off, then cut a large "V" slit into each side from the bottom to the top to make the croc's snout. Use construction paper and glue to add on scales, jagged teeth, and a tongue. Poke holes on both sides of the cup and add yarn to tie crocodile snouts over nose. For the tail, cut and glue several pieces of green construction paper to make two triangles about 2 ½ feet long by about 1 foot wide. Staple the sides together and stuff with shredded newspaper, then staple opening shut. Glue on green construction paper scales and other decorations. Poke holes in the base of the tail and loop enough yarn through to tie around the waist or belt loops. Now Tick-Tock Croc can snap his jaws, swish his tail, and lick his chops when he's swimming after Captain Hook.

"Ah! Hangman's Tree! So that's the entrance to his hiding place! Thank you, my dear. You've been most helpful." —Captain Hook

"Come down, boy, if you've a taste for cold steel!" —Captain Hook

"I'll fight you man-to-man with one hand behind my back!" —Peter Pan

"Nobody calls Pan a coward and lives!" —Peter Pan

LINES FROM THE FILM

"I'm a codfish!" —Captain Hook

Watermelon Pirate Ship

YOU DON'T HAVE TO WAIT for Tinker Bell to give you a sprinkle of pixie dust to get to Never Land. Here's how you can turn a watermelon into Captain Hook's pirate ship and sail all the way to Pirate's Cove.

1 oval-shaped watermelon
3 celery stalks
carrot sticks
grapes
cherries
olives
radishes
bell peppers
pineapple chunks
cheddar cheese
toothpicks
paper
marker
tape

1. To make a pirate ship, cut away the top third of the watermelon lengthwise. Trim the side edges of the boat with a notched pattern.

2. Hollow out the watermelon with a melon baller, but leave about 3 inches of watermelon on the bottom and about 1 inch all around. Set the melon balls aside.

3. Press celery stalks into the hull of your watermelon ship until the stalks stand up to make masts.

4. Cut a long, flat carrot stick to use as a plank. Cut a horizontal slit in the side of the ship to insert the end of the plank.

5. Create a pirate crew by using toothpicks to skewer fruits and vegetables together to make people. Heads can be made from melon balls, grapes, cherries, or olives. Bodies can be made from carrot sticks,

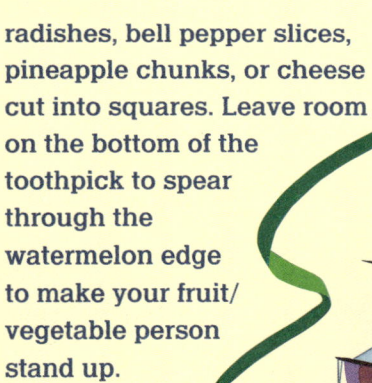

radishes, bell pepper slices, pineapple chunks, or cheese cut into squares. Leave room on the bottom of the toothpick to spear through the watermelon edge to make your fruit/vegetable person stand up.

6. Use a marker to decorate sails and a skull-and-crossbones flag on paper. Tape the sails and flag to the celery masts. Ahoy, mates, Never Land awaits!

Makes 8 to 12 servings.

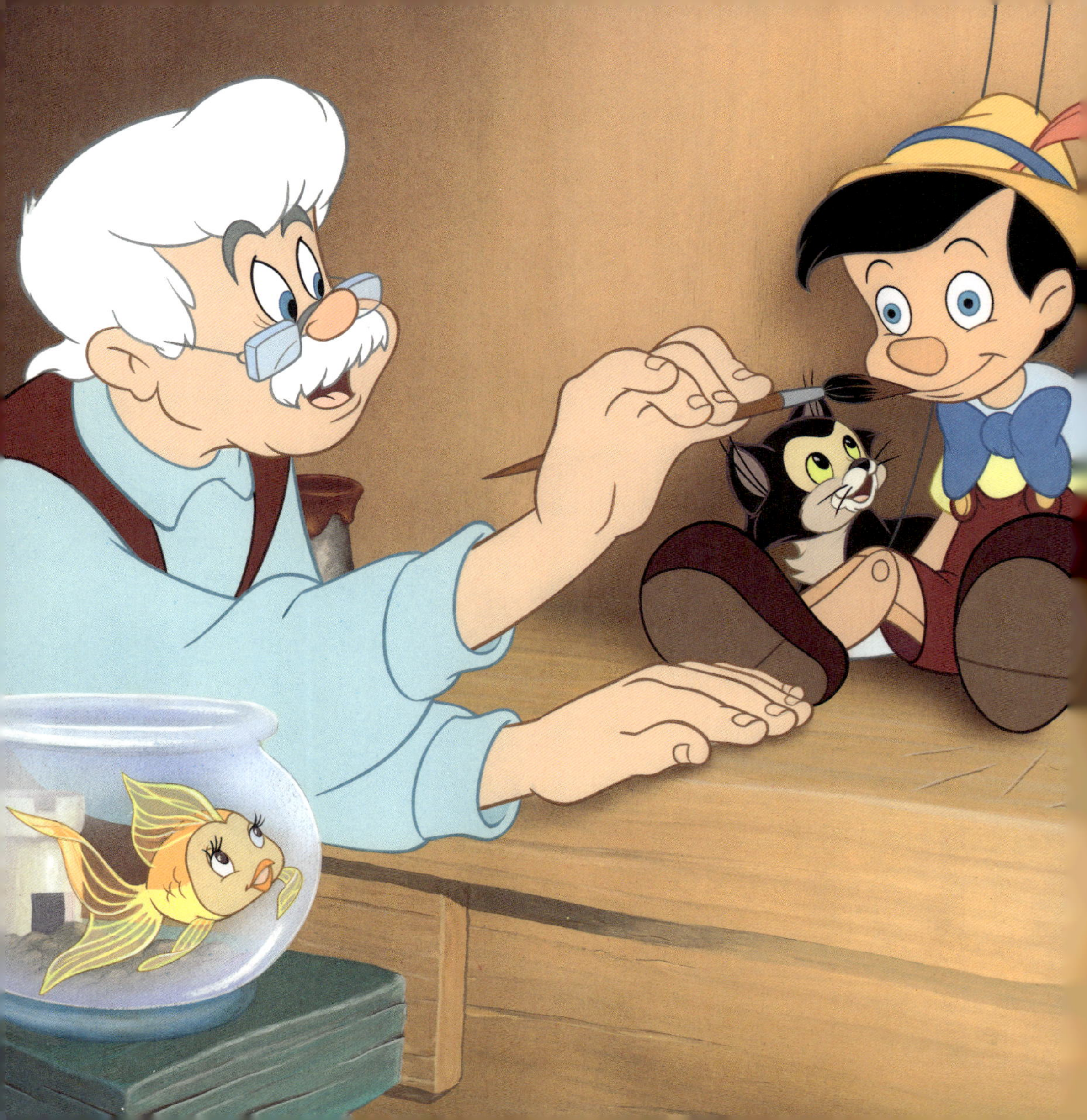

Pinocchio

ONCE UPON A TIME, in a quaint little village, there lived a kindly woodcarver named Gepetto. He lived with his sweet cat, Figaro, and a fish named Cleo. Gepetto's shop was filled with clocks, dolls, and toys. But his favorite creation was a wooden marionette named Pinocchio.

When Gepetto went to bed, he saw the wishing star outside his window. "I wish my Pinocchio would be a real boy," he said.

That night, a bright light filled the room. It was the Blue Fairy. "Good Gepetto, you have given so much happiness to others that you deserve to have your wish come true," she said. She woke Pinocchio with a touch of her wand.

"I can move!" said the wooden puppet.

"To make Gepetto's wish come true, you must prove to be brave, truthful, and unselfish," said the Blue Fairy to the boy. A poor cricket named Jiminy who had come in to escape the cold watched everything happen from the shadows. The Blue Fairy saw him, too, and said, "I dub you Pinocchio's conscience."

As the Blue Fairy waved good-bye, she reminded Pinocchio to be a good boy and to let his conscience be his guide.

When Gepetto discovered that Pinocchio could walk and laugh and talk, he danced with joy. "Now you can play with real boys and girls," he said.

On the way to his first day of school, Pinocchio met a scheming fox named Foulfellow and a cat named Gideon. They convinced the wooden boy that a life in the theater was the easy road to success. Jiminy Cricket tried to stop Pinocchio, but Pinocchio wouldn't listen.

Soon Pinocchio was working for an evil puppeteer named Stromboli, who made the wooden boy dance in a marionette show as a puppet without any strings. Stromboli made more money than ever. He locked Pinocchio in a cage to make sure he wouldn't run away.

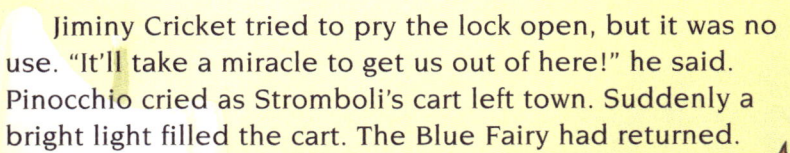

Jiminy Cricket tried to pry the lock open, but it was no use. "It'll take a miracle to get us out of here!" he said. Pinocchio cried as Stromboli's cart left town. Suddenly a bright light filled the cart. The Blue Fairy had returned.

"Why didn't you stay in school?" she asked.

Pinocchio started to tell her, but everything that came out of his mouth was a lie. Each time he lied, his nose grew longer, until it sprouted leaves and a bird's nest!

"I will forgive you," said the Blue Fairy, "but remember, a boy who won't be good might just as well be made of wood." She set him free, and Pinocchio and Jiminy ran home.

Before long, he met Foulfellow and Gideon again. They convinced him to vacation on Pleasure Island. Jiminy Cricket tried to stop him once again, but Pinocchio boarded the coach anyway. Soon he and Jiminy were on their way to Pleasure Island with a group of rowdy boys.

At Pleasure Island, the boys could eat all the candy they wanted, destroy things, and run wild. But the fun did not last long—soon all the boys started turning into donkeys. Even Pinocchio sprouted ears and a tail.

Fortunately, Jiminy Cricket found a way for them to escape, and they jumped in the water and swam away.

When Pinocchio finally got home, no one was there. He found a note saying that Gepetto had gone to look for his son and was swallowed by a whale named Monstro.

So Pinocchio and Jiminy went to the bottom of the sea to find Monstro.

Meanwhile, Gepetto, Figaro, and Cleo had been fishing inside the whale's belly for days with no luck. Just then, Monstro swallowed a huge school of fish—and Pinocchio, too!

Gepetto couldn't believe his luck. What a happy reunion for father and son!

Pinocchio made a big fire to make Monstro sneeze so they could escape on a raft. The plan worked, but Monstro was very angry and capsized them.

Gepetto was drowning. He told Pinocchio to swim for shore, but Pinocchio dragged his father to safety, saving him from Monstro's last attempt to swallow them alive.

When the waves died down, Gepetto found his wooden son lying facedown in the water. Gepetto sadly brought his lifeless little boy home.

That night, the Blue Fairy appeared again. "You have proven yourself to be brave, truthful, and unselfish," she told Pinocchio. "Today you will become a real boy." And with a touch of her wand, she brought Pinocchio to life.

Soon everyone was singing and dancing. Figaro kissed Cleo, and Jiminy even got a special "official conscience" award. Gepetto's wish for a son had finally come true!

PINOCCHIO

1. What does the Blue Fairy dub Jiminy Cricket?
2. What will it take for Pinocchio to become a real boy?
3. What does Gepetto give Pinocchio on his first day of school?
4. What happens when Pinocchio lies?
5. What does Pinocchio do instead of going to school?
6. What happens when Gepetto goes to sea with Figaro and Cleo?
7. What does Stromboli do to keep Pinocchio in his show?
8. Where does the Coachman want to take disobedient boys?
9. How does Pinocchio free Gepetto from Monstro?
10. What happens to Pinocchio on Pleasure Island?

Q & As

1. Pinocchio's conscience
2. To prove himself to be brave, truthful, and unselfish
3. A book and an apple
4. His nose grows into a tree branch with a bird's nest on it.
5. He joins Stromboli's marionette show.
6. He gets swallowed by Monstro the whale.
7. He locks him in a birdcage.
8. To Pleasure Island
9. He lights a fire to make the whale sneeze.
10. He sprouts donkey ears and a tail.

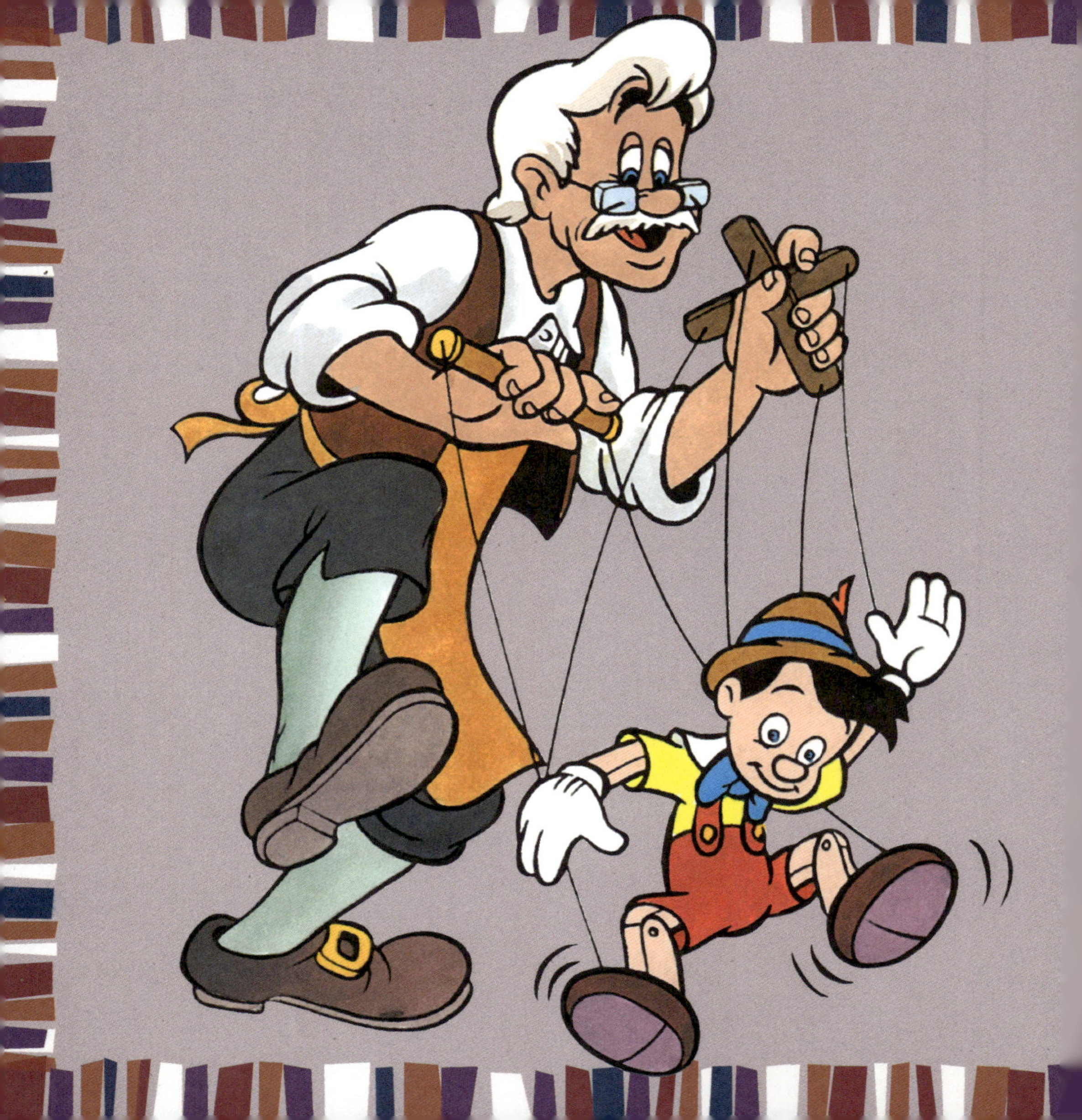

Marionette & Puppet Theater

When Pinocchio joins Stromboli's act, he becomes the star of the show. Here's how to make your own puppet theater and find out how well Pinocchio dances.

empty cereal box, scissors, poster paint, paintbrush, construction paper, glue, markers, brads, ice-pop sticks, string, tape

To make the puppet theater, cut the top off a cereal box, then cut a rectangular hole out of one side of the box. Paint the box with poster paint and allow to dry. Draw and cut out construction paper theater curtains and glue them to the sides of the rectangular hole.

To make the marionette, draw a head and body shape on construction paper and cut the shape out. Poke four holes in the body where the arms and legs will connect. Draw and cut out two arms. Draw and cut out two pieces for each leg, separating them at the knee. Poke holes in the tops of the arm pieces, the tops and bottoms of the thigh pieces, and the tops of the lower leg pieces. Attach the arms and upper legs to the body with brads. Attach the lower leg pieces at the knees. Draw a costume on the marionette with markers.

To make marionette controls, cross two ice-pop sticks into an X and glue them together. Cut four eight-inch strands of string. Tape one end of each string to one end of the ice-pop sticks. Tape the other end of each string to the hands and knees of the marionette. Dangle the marionette inside the theater and tilt the ice pop stick controls to make your puppet dance!

"I wished that my little Pinocchio might be a real boy! Wouldn't that be nice?" —Gepetto

"Prove yourself brave, truthful, and unselfish, and someday, you will be a real boy." —Blue Fairy

"Perhaps you haven't been telling the truth, Pinocchio." —Blue Fairy

"I'm a real boy!" —Pinocchio

"Oh, I think it's swell!" —Jiminy Cricket

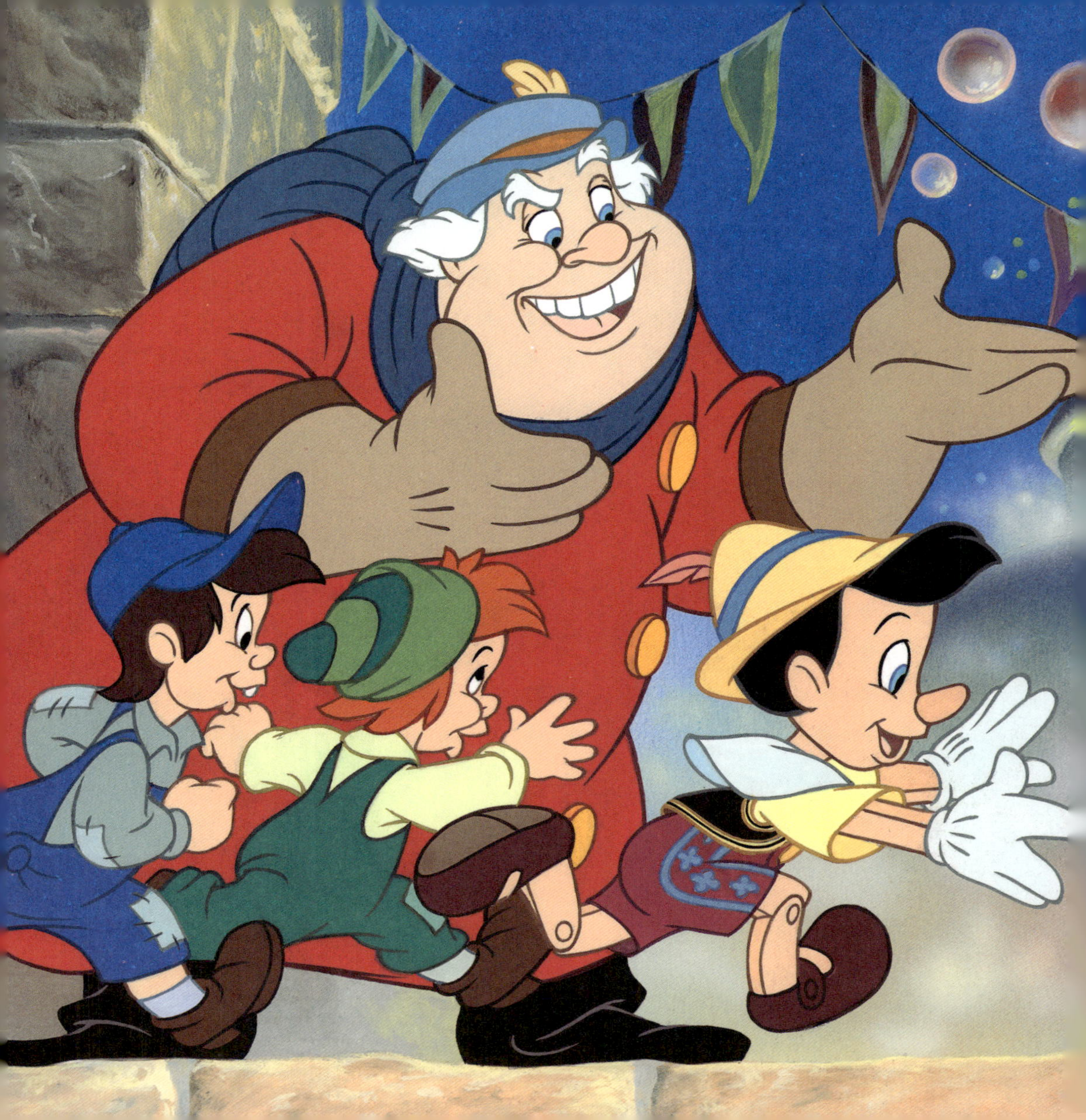

Pleasure Island
Root Beer Floats

EVERY DAY may be a holiday at Pleasure Island—but sometimes too much of a good thing can turn lazy children into donkeys, as Pinocchio knows. These root beer floats may not turn you into a donkey, but be warned: ice cream makes root beer extra foamy and your glass may overflow. That's part of the fun, so sip slowly and enjoy!

4 scoops vanilla ice cream
16 ounces chilled root beer

1. Pour 3 ounces of root beer into each of 4 tall glasses.
2. Carefully add a scoop of ice cream to each glass.
3. Top off each glass with the remaining root beer.
4. Serve with straws and ice-cream sundae spoons.

Makes 4 servings.

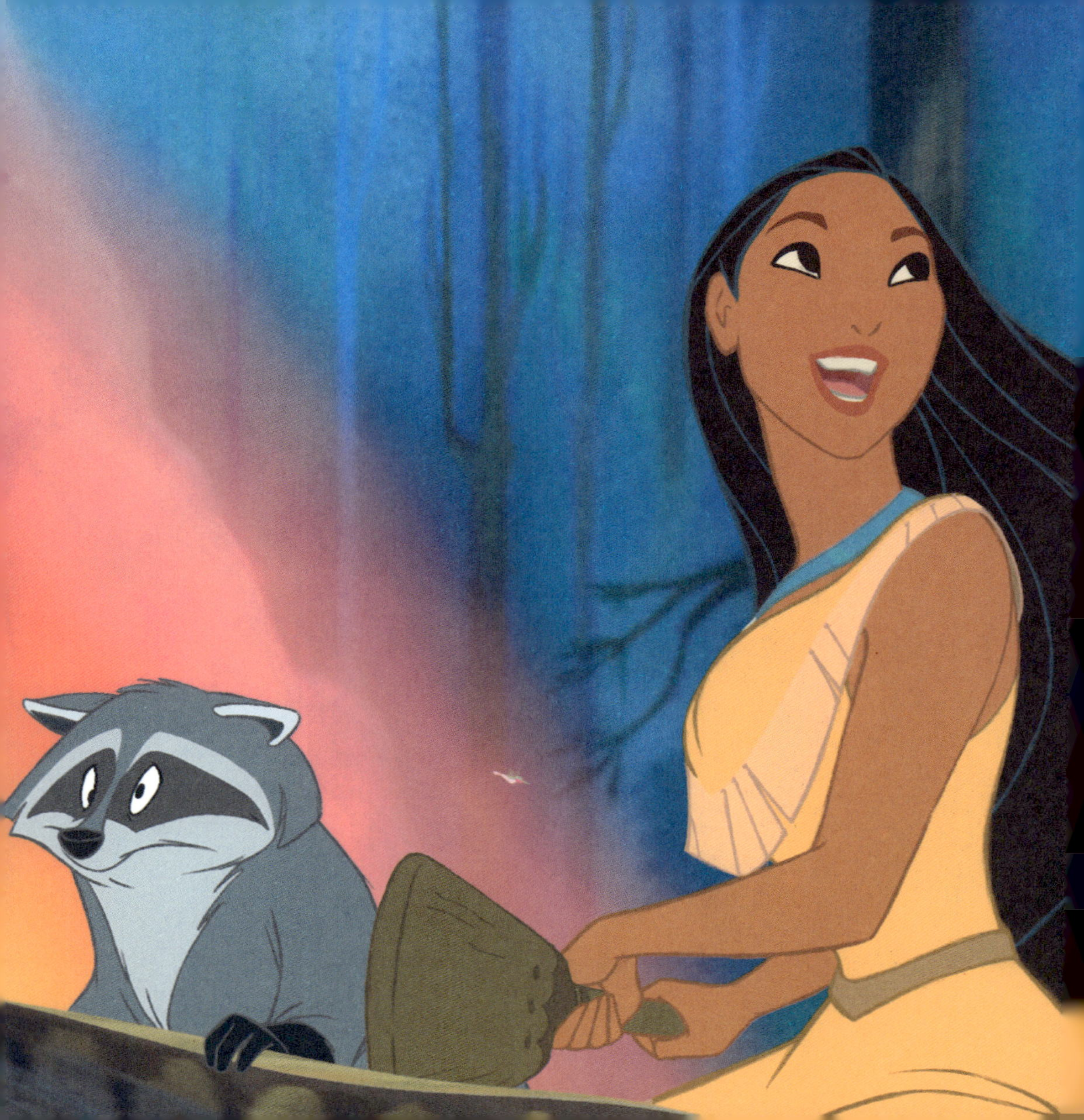

IN THE BEAUTIFUL and fertile land of the New World, a young woman named Pocahontas was paddling her canoe along a forest stream. She was troubled because her father, Chief Powhatan, had told her that the brave warrior Kocoum had asked for her hand in marriage.

Pocahontas thought Kocoum was too serious. She'd been dreaming about a spinning arrow that she thought foretold a different fate for her. Pocahontas asked the tree spirit, Grandmother Willow, for advice.

Pocahontas

"This spinning arrow is pointing you to the right path," said Grandmother Willow.

"What is my path?" asked Pocahontas. "How will I know?"

"The spirits are all around," answered Grandmother Willow. "Listen to your heart and they will guide you."

Pocahontas listened to the wind. "Something is coming," she said. She climbed a tree and saw strange clouds billowing in the bay.

The clouds were really the sails of a ship arriving from England. Governor Ratcliffe had come to the New World in search of gold. When they landed, he ordered Captain John Smith to scout the area.

Pocahontas spied on the pale-skinned man as he sipped from a stream. John turned to see the radiant figure watching him. Startled, Pocahontas fled, but John followed. "Don't run!" he shouted.

At first Pocahontas did not understand him, but then she remembered Grandmother Willow's words. She listened with her heart. "My name is Pocahontas," she told him. "My name is John Smith," he answered.

Meanwhile, Chief Powhatan had sent warriors to observe the newcomers. As the Indians spied on the white men,

Governor Ratcliffe's dog started barking. The air quickly filled with a spray of arrows and bullets.

In the woods, Pocahontas and John Smith were becoming friends. He told her about London, and the tall buildings in the city. "We're going to build those things here," he told Pocahontas.

But Pocahontas didn't think they needed a city in the middle of their village. She told John about her world, and how all the creatures are one with the sun, the moon, and the stars.

Pocahontas took John to see Grandmother Willow. He was amazed. "And to think we came all this way just to dig it up for gold," he said.

"Gold?" Pocahontas asked. John showed Pocahontas a coin. "There's nothing like that here," she said.

The sound of warrior drums interrupted them. "I must go," Pocahontas said.

At the village, Chief Powhatan called for more warriors to help them fight the invaders. They were preparing for war.

Pocahontas pleaded with her father. "If one of them wanted to talk, you would listen, wouldn't you?" she asked.

"Of course," said Powhatan. "But nothing is simple."

In the settlers' camp, John told Ratcliffe that there was no gold to be found. "We don't have to fight them," John said. "They can help."

"Lies!" Ratcliffe scowled. He thought the Indians must be hiding gold, and he planned to take it by force. "If you see any Indians, shoot them!" he told his men.

John snuck away to tell Pocahontas about the attack. "Come talk to my father," Pocahontas pleaded. John agreed, and they kissed.

Without warning, an Indian named Kocoum jumped out of the trees and attacked John. A young settler named Thomas had also been hiding in the trees, aiming his gun. He shot Kocoum, killing him.

The next moment, warriors captured John and carried him away to the village. "At sunrise, he will be the first to die," said Chief Powhatan.

Pocahontas went to Grandmother Willow. There she found John Smith's compass. "The spinning arrow from my dream!"

Grandmother Willow smiled. "Your dream was pointing you to John Smith," she said. "But you must hurry!"

Pocahontas ran like the wind to reach John. "If you kill him, you have to kill me, too," she said. "Is this where the path of hatred has brought us?"

Chief Powhatan saw that Pocahontas had wisdom beyond her years. He agreed to release John.

"Now's our chance," said Ratcliffe. "Fire!" But none of the settlers obeyed his order. "I'll settle this myself," he said and fired his own gun at the chief. At that moment John dove in front of Chief Powhatan and took the bullet.

Soon the ship was ready to set sail again. John needed to return to London for medical care. "Come with me," he asked Pocahontas.

"I am needed here," she told him. "But I'll always be with you forever."

Pocahontas had chosen her path. From high on a cliff, she waved good-bye to her friend. As the wind blew by, she knew they would always be in each other's hearts.

1. What does Pocahontas see in her dream?
2. What advice does Grandmother Willow give Pocahontas?
3. What are the strange clouds Pocahontas sees for the first time?
4. Why does Governor Ratcliffe come to the New World?
5. What is the name of Captain John Smith's ship?
6. What kind of gold does Pocahontas tell John Smith they have?
7. Who has asked Chief Powhatan for Pocahontas's hand in marriage?
8. What does John Smith do when Ratcliffe tries to shoot Chief Powhatan?
9. What is Grandmother Willow?
10. Who is the first one to greet John Smith in the New World?

POCAHONTAS

Q & As

1. A spinning arrow
2. To listen with her heart to the spirits in the earth, water, and sky
3. The sails of John Smith's ship
4. To search for gold
5. The Susan Constant
6. Corn
7. The brave warrior Kocoum
8. He jumps in the way of the bullet and saves the Chief's life.
9. A tree spirit
10. Pocahontas's raccoon friend, Meeko

"Colors of the Wind" Leaf Rubbings

Grandmother Willow teaches Pocahontas to listen with her heart to the spirits in the earth, water, and sky. Make a string of colored leaves that will blow in the wind, and find out if you can hear the spirits, too.

various-shaped leaves, tracing or parchment paper, crayons, scissors, tape, yarn

Collect a variety of nicely shaped leaves and place them on a flat surface. Cover each leaf with a piece of paper. Remove the paper wrapper from each of the crayons. Rub the long side of the crayon on the surface of the paper over the leaf. Repeat with different colored crayons until the image of the leaf comes through onto the paper. Cut out the leaf shapes and tape them to a long string of yarn. String the leaves in a window or along a wall. The next time the wind blows, what do the "colors of the wind" tell you?

LINES FROM THE FILM

GRANDMOTHER WILLOW: Is that my Pocahontas?

POCAHONTAS: Grandmother Willow, I must talk to you.

GRANDMOTHER WILLOW: Good morning, child. I was hoping you'd visit today. Why, your mother's necklace.

POCAHONTAS: That's what I want to talk about. My father wants me to marry Kocoum.

GRANDMOTHER WILLOW: Kocoum? But he's so serious.

POCAHONTAS: My father thinks it's the right path for me, but lately I've been having this dream—

GRANDMOTHER WILLOW: Oh, a dream! Let's hear all about it.

GRANDMOTHER WILLOW: <to the animals> Quiet! Quiet!

GRANDMOTHER WILLOW: <to Pocahontas> You were saying?

POCAHONTAS: Well, I'm running through the woods. Then, right in front of me is an arrow. As I look at it, it starts to spin.

GRANDMOTHER WILLOW: A spinning arrow. How unusual.

POCAHONTAS: Yes. It spins faster and faster and faster, then suddenly stops.

GRANDMOTHER WILLOW: Well, it seems to me this arrow is pointing you down your path.

POCAHONTAS: But what is my path? How am I ever going to find it?

GRANDMOTHER WILLOW: Your mother asked me the very same question.

POCAHONTAS: She did? What did you tell her?

GRANDMOTHER WILLOW: I told her to listen. All around you are spirits, child. They live in the earth, the water, the sky. If you listen, they will guide you.

Meeko's Cornmeal Crackers

WHETHER YOU'RE crossing the Atlantic or going for a walk in the woods, these crispy crackers will last long enough for the journey. If you're like Meeko, you'll enjoy eating these with berries on top.

2 cups shredded cheddar cheese

6 tablespoons butter

¾ cup flour

½ cup cornmeal

¼ teaspoon ground cumin

⅛ teaspoon cayenne pepper

¼ teaspoon salt

BERRY SPREAD

¼ cup cream cheese

¼ cup blueberries

1. Blend cheese and butter together in a food processor.
2. Add flour, cornmeal, and spices. Continue mixing until dough forms into a ball.
3. Divide the dough evenly and roll each half into cylinders about 1 ½ inches in diameter.
4. Wrap each cylinder in plastic and refrigerate for 8 hours.
5. Preheat oven to 350° F.
6. Cut the dough into slices about ⅛ inch thick and place on cookie sheets.
7. Bake for 10 minutes or until slightly brown around the edges.

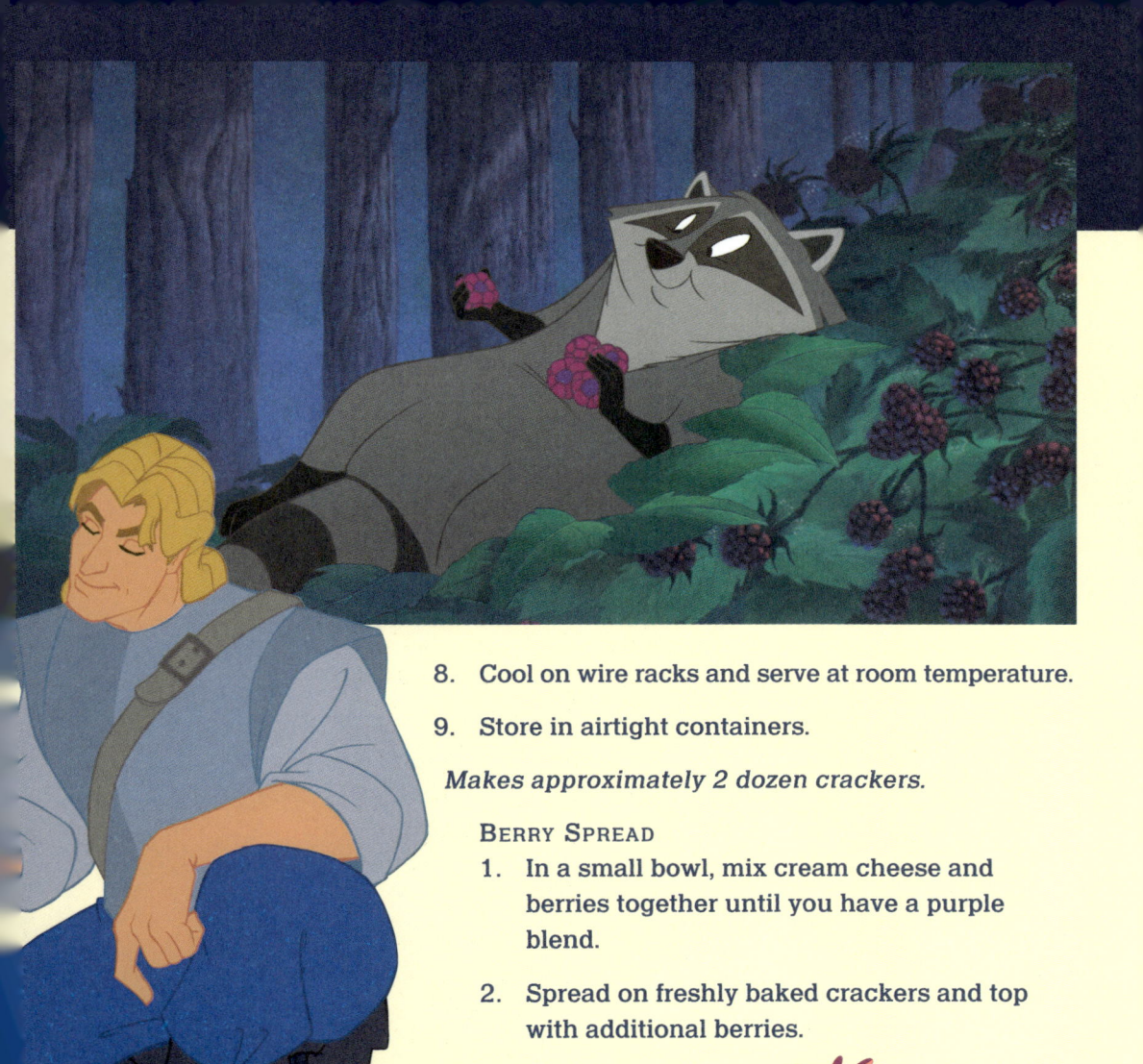

8. Cool on wire racks and serve at room temperature.
9. Store in airtight containers.

Makes approximately 2 dozen crackers.

BERRY SPREAD
1. In a small bowl, mix cream cheese and berries together until you have a purple blend.
2. Spread on freshly baked crackers and top with additional berries.

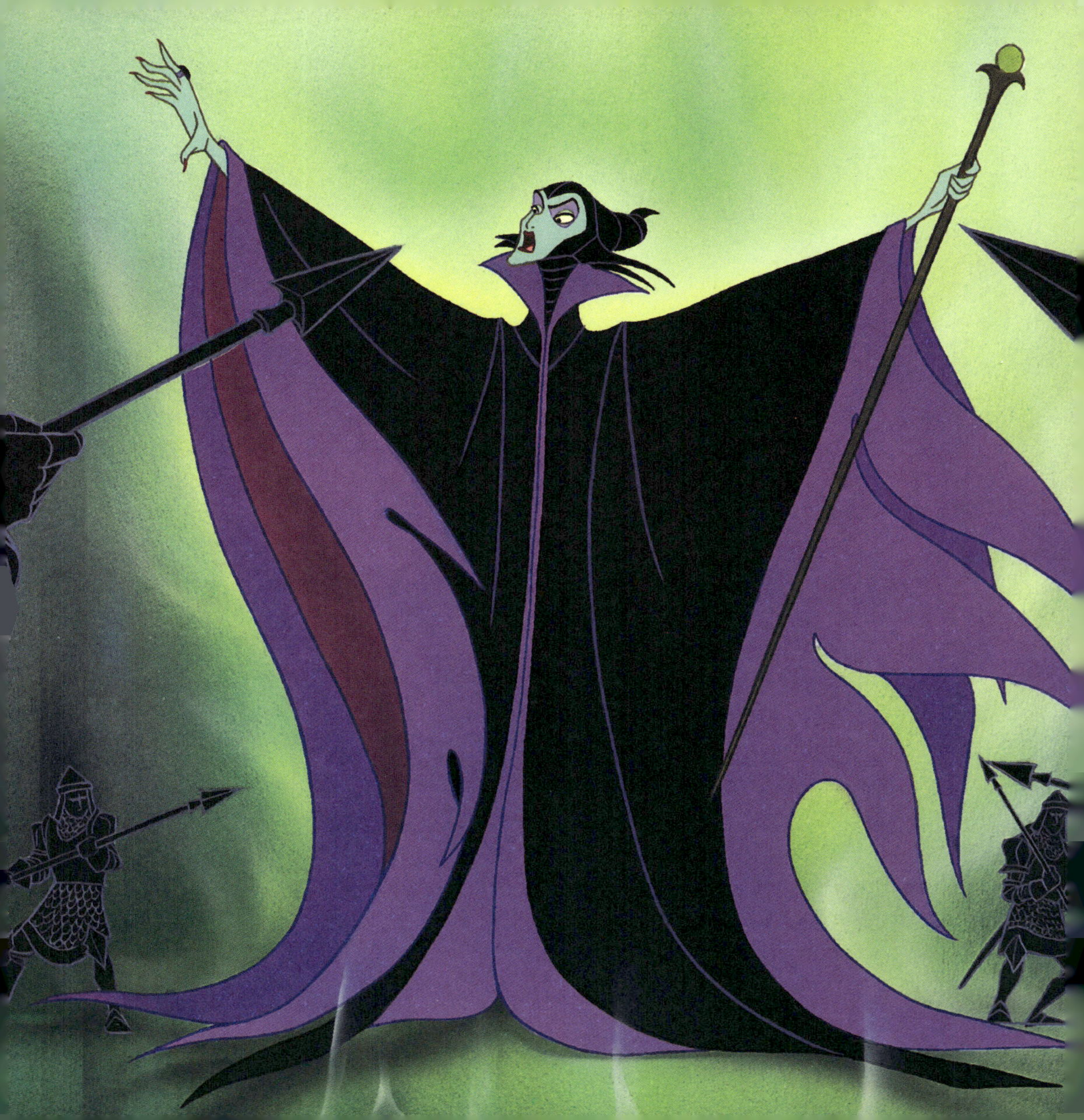

LONG AGO, IN A FARAWAY LAND, lived King Stefan and his fair queen. They waited many years for a child. One day a daughter was born. They named her Aurora, after the dawn, for the light she brought into their lives.

Sleeping Beauty

All came from far and wide to celebrate the child's christening. King Hubert and his young son, Prince Phillip, came from a neighboring kingdom. This was the day on which the prince and princess would be promised to each other in marriage.

The three good fairies Flora, Fauna, and Merryweather, bestowed very special gifts upon the young princess. The first one gave her beauty; the second one, the gift of song. As Merryweather raised her wand to grant the third gift, a horrible wind blew into the room. The evil fairy Maleficent appeared in a ball of fiery light, enraged that she hadn't been invited to the christening party.

"To show no ill will, I too shall bestow a gift," said the wicked fairy. "The princess will grow in grace and beauty. But before the sun sets on her sixteenth birthday, she will prick her finger on a spinning wheel and die." In a cloud of smoke, Maleficent disappeared.

All hope was not lost, for the third good fairy had not yet given her wish. "Not in death shall you fall, but in sleep—until True Love's Kiss breaks the spell," said Merryweather.

King Stefan ordered all the spinning wheels in the kingdom to be burned. Meanwhile, the good fairies, living as peasant women, raised the royal babe in the woods. They named her Briar Rose, and swore off magic so that Maleficent would never find them.

Briar Rose's sixteenth birthday finally arrived. The good fairies wanted to celebrate this special day with a surprise. So they sent her into the woods to pick berries.

The fairies spent all afternoon trying to sew a dress and make a cake. None of them knew how to do such things without magic. After a while, they gave up on the sagging dress and lopsided cake, and got out their wands.

Meanwhile, the princess sang joyfully with her animal friends as she filled up her basket with fruit. Prince Phillip rode through the woods and heard her sweet voice drifting through the trees. When he discovered Briar Rose dancing with the animals, he joined them. Soon the two were in each other's arms, falling in love.

When Briar Rose returned to the cottage, the fairies surprised her with the gown and cake. But she was more excited about the young man she'd met. "He's coming to the cottage tonight," she told the fairies.

"But you're betrothed to Prince Phillip!" they said. The princess did not know the young man she had met was actually the prince, and she wept.

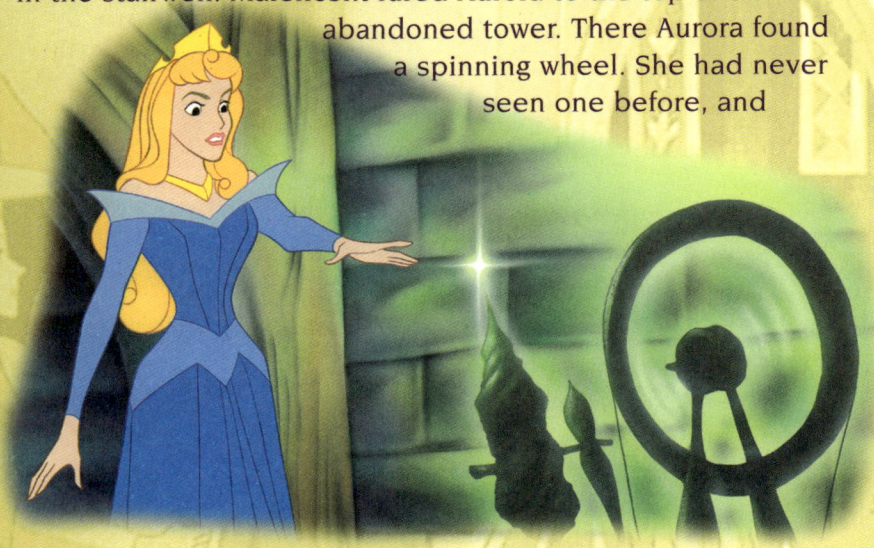

The princess returned to the castle that night. Evil lurked in the stairwell. Maleficent lured Aurora to the top of an abandoned tower. There Aurora found a spinning wheel. She had never seen one before, and pricked her finger on it. In an instant, Princess Aurora dropped to the floor and fell into a deep sleep.

When the good fairies found Aurora, they cast a sleeping spell over the whole castle so they could figure out what to do. The last words King Hubert muttered before he nodded off were, "My son wants to marry a peasant girl…." The fairies then knew who could awaken the princess.

That evening, Maleficent's goons captured Prince Phillip and chained him in the dungeon. The prince didn't have to stay a prisoner for long. The good fairies bravely found their way to him and burned his shackles with their wands. They armed the prince with an enchanted Shield of Virtue and a mighty Sword of Truth. "The road to true love may be barred by still many more dangers," Flora warned.

Prince Phillip galloped back to the castle on his horse, only to find that Maleficent had cast a spell covering the castle with a wall of thick, thorny branches. He battled his way through the thicket, where he met the fiercest creature of all. Maleficent turned herself into a huge fire-breathing dragon. The dragon hissed a spray of fire, but it was no match against Prince Phillip's shield and sword given to him by the good fairies. In a fierce battle, the prince plunged his Sword of Truth deep into the dragon's heart.

When the prince finally found Aurora, he kissed her tenderly. Her eyes gently opened, and the entire castle became awake.

The kingdom celebrated the couple's happiness with a grand ball. With each spin of the waltz, Flora and Merryweather changed Aurora's dress from blue to pink to blue to pink.

A dream come true, the Prince and Princess lived happily ever after.

1. What curse does Maleficent put on Princess Aurora?
2. What gifts do the three good fairies bestow upon Princess Aurora?
3. What does King Stefan do when Maleficent curses his daughter?
4. What plan do the good fairies come up with to protect Aurora?

SLEEPING BEAUTY

5. Why do the good fairies give up their magic?
6. What do the good fairies give Prince Phillip to fight Maleficent?
7. What does Maleficent turn herself into to fight Prince Phillip?
8. What name do the good fairies give to Aurora when they live in the woodcutter's cottage?
9. What does Maleficent do to Prince Phillip so that he can't break her spell?
10. What happens to Princess Aurora's dress when she dances with Prince Phillip at the castle?

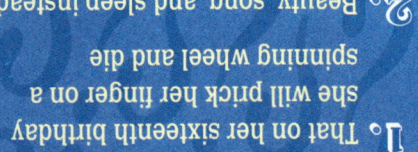

Q & As

1. That on her sixteenth birthday she will prick her finger on a spinning wheel and die
2. Beauty, song, and sleep instead of death that will last until True Love's Kiss breaks the spell
3. He orders every spinning wheel in the kingdom to be burned.
4. They become peasant women and raise her in the woods.
5. So that Maleficent can't find them
6. The Shield of Virtue and the Sword of Truth
7. A fire-breathing dragon
8. Briar Rose
9. She chains him in a dungeon at her castle on the Forbidden Mountain.
10. Flora and Merryweather keep changing the colors from pink to blue to pink to blue.

301

Prince Phillip's Shield of Virtue and Sword of Truth

Without the help of the Good Fairies Flora, Fauna, and Merryweather, Prince Phillip would have never been able to kiss his Sleeping Beauty and wake her from Maleficent's wicked spell. With the prince's mighty shield and sword, you, too, can fend off the evil fire-breathing dragon Maleficent and save the kingdom.

cardboard, scissors, poster paint, paintbrushes, duct tape, 2 empty paper towel rolls, tape, aluminum foil

To make the shield, cut a shield shape large enough to cover your chest out of cardboard. Decorate the shield with poster paint and allow to dry. Use two 24-inch strips of duct tape to make shield handles. Carefully fold each strip in half, sticking the tape to itself, to make two 12-inch strips without any sticky part exposed. Use more duct tape to attach the handles to one side of the shield. The ends of each strip should be about 6 inches apart to create a loop for the hand and arm. To make the sword, flatten the paper towel rolls. Tape the edges closed to hold flattened shape, then tape the ends of the two rolls together. Trim off two corners on one end to create a point on the sword. Tape the edges together. Wrap the sword with aluminum foil to make a steely blade. With your new shield and sword in hand, you'll have the magic tools to make all evil fairies vanish.

LINES FROM THE FILM

FAUNA: <Lights candles on Aurora's birthday cake> There! Oops! Well, what do you think of it?

FLORA: Why, it's, it's a very unusual cake, isn't it?

FAUNA: Yes, of course, it will be much stiffer after it's baked.

FLORA: Of course, dear. And, what do you think of the dress?

FAUNA: Well, it…it's…it…it's… it's not exactly the way it is in the book, is it?

FLORA: Oh, I improved it. But perhaps if I added a few more ruffles, what do you think?

FAUNA: Uh huh, I think so. Uh, what do you think, Merryweather?

MERRYWEATHER: I think we've had enough of this nonsense. I think we ought to think of Rose and what she'll think of this mess. I still think what I thunk before. I'm going to get those wands.

FAUNA: You know, I think she's right.

MERRYWEATHER: Here they are, good as new.

FLORA: Ca-ca-ca-careful Merryweather. Quick! Lock the doors. Fauna, you close the windows. Plug up every cranny. We can't take any chances.

<Flora points wand.>

FLORA: And now, you take care of the cake…

MERRYWEATHER: While I…

FLORA: Clean the room, dear, and I'll make the dress. Now hurry.

MERRYWEATHER: Oh! C'mon bucket, mop, broom. Flora says, clean up the room.

FLORA: And now to make a lovely dress, fit to grace a fair princess.

FAUNA: Eggs, flour, milk. Just do it like it says here in the book. I'll put on the candles.

MERRYWEATHER: <points wand at dress> Oh, no, not pink! Make it blue.

FLORA: Merryweather! Make it pink.

MERRYWEATHER: Make it blue.

FLORA: Pink!

MERRYWEATHER: Blue!

<Their magic turns the dress multi-colored.>

FLORA: Oh, now look what you've done.

Aurora's Sweet Sixteen
Birthday Cake

FAUNA THE GOOD FAIRY learned the hard way that it's a good idea to remove eggs from their shells before baking a cake. Let Mom or Dad be your magic wand, and watch this yummy angel cake come together in a snap.

For cake:
1 cup cake flour
1 ½ cups superfine sugar
10 large egg whites at room temperature
1 ¼ teaspoons cream of tartar
¼ teaspoon salt
1 teaspoon vanilla extract

1. Preheat oven to 350°F.
2. In a large bowl, sift flour with ½ cup of the sugar two times.
3. In a separate bowl, beat the egg whites, cream of tartar, and salt until the whites form soft peaks. Add ½ cup sugar and beat for 1 minute.
4. Continue to add 2 tablespoons of sugar at a time, beating after each addition. Stir in vanilla.

5. Fold the flour mixture into the egg whites ¼ cup at a time until just blended.

6. Pour the batter into an ungreased 10-inch tube pan and bake for 1 hour, or until cake is golden brown and springy to the touch. Let cake cool completely before removing from the pan.

7. For the sauce, puree the berries and lemon juice in the blender. Add sugar a tablespoon at a time until desired sweetness is reached.

8. Strain sauce through a fine mesh strainer. Pour over cake and serve.

Makes 14 servings.

FOR BERRY SAUCE:

2 cups mixed berries (such as blueberries, boysenberries, raspberries, blackberries, and strawberries)

2 tablespoons fresh lemon juice

4 to 6 tablespoons sugar

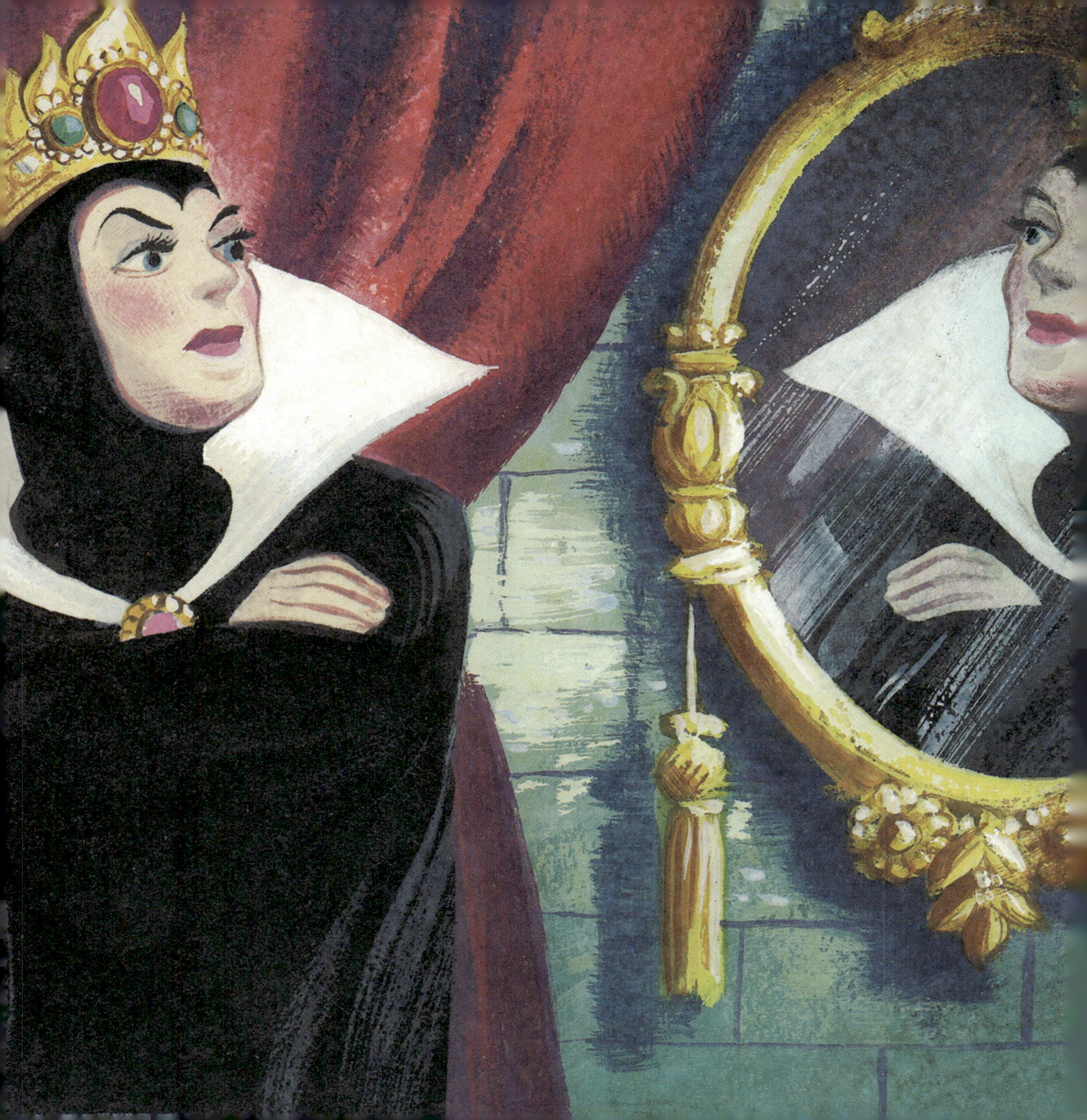

ONCE UPON A TIME there lived a beautiful princess with skin pure as snow, hair black as ebony, and lips red as a rose. Her name was Snow White. The Queen was also very beautiful, but she was a vain and jealous stepmother. Every day, the Queen looked in her Magic Mirror, and asked:

"Magic Mirror on the wall, who is the fairest one of all?"
And every day, the mirror answered:
"You, O Queen, are the fairest one of all."

Snow White
and the Seven Dwarfs

As long as the Queen heard this, Snow White remained safe from her stepmother's cruel jealousy. But to be sure that Snow White's beauty never surpassed her own, the Queen dressed the princess in rags and forced her to work as a scullery maid.

Rags could not hide Snow White's grace, and every day, she worked with joy and song. Her singing was so beautiful that a prince, passing by on horseback, fell in love the moment he heard her voice.

The Queen heard the princess's song, too, and in a rage, flew to her Magic Mirror.

"Magic Mirror, on the wall, who is the fairest one of all?"

"Lips as red as blood, hair as dark as night, skin as white as snow, her name...Snow White."

The Queen could not stand it. She ordered her huntsman to take the princess into the woods to pick wildflowers. "You shall not return until you bring me Snow White's heart in this box!"

The huntsman dared not disobey the Queen, but when the time came, he could not kill the girl. "You must hide and never come back!" he confessed.

Snow White ran and ran. Finally, the poor princess collapsed in the spooky forest and cried herself to sleep. When she awoke, friendly forest animals led her to a little cottage.

No one was home. Everything inside was very tiny and very messy. Snow White thought that seven children must live here without a mother to care for them. "Maybe if I tidy up, they'll let me stay," she thought. Snow White cleaned the entire cottage, and when she got upstairs, she found seven little beds with names carved in each one: Doc, Happy, Sneezy, Sleepy, Grumpy, Bashful, and Dopey. "What funny names for children," thought Snow White, just before she fell asleep.

The cottage was really home to the Seven Dwarfs, who worked in a nearby diamond mine. When they came home they saw a clean house! And some big creature asleep in their bed! "Maybe it's a monster," said one of the men. Bravely, they pulled back the covers and saw no monster, but a sleeping girl. Snow White awoke and told them her story about the wicked Queen. The Dwarfs invited her to stay and made her promise never to let any strangers in while they worked in the mines.

Back in the castle, the Queen's magic mirror said that Snow White was still alive. The huntsman had tricked her! The Queen was consumed with fury. She cast a spell to change herself into an old hag and make a poisoned apple to give to the princess. Now she was sure to be rid of Snow White forever!

That afternoon, Snow White was baking pies for the Dwarfs when an old peddler woman came by to sell apples. Snow White couldn't resist the biggest, shiniest apple. She bit into the fruit and instantly fell into the Sleeping Death!

The forest animals rushed to alert the Dwarfs. As fast as they could, the Dwarfs ran to the cottage and chased the Queen into the rocky cliffs. Suddenly, a thunderbolt struck the boulder below the hag's feet. With a horrible scream, the evil Queen tumbled into the darkness to her doom.

Even in death, Snow White was so beautiful that the Dwarfs could not find it in their hearts to bury her. So, they built a glass coffin and kept vigil by her side.

Prince Charming soon heard about the maiden who slept in the glass coffin. One day, after searching far and wide, he finally found the sleeping princess. With deepest sorrow, he gave her a good-bye kiss. Snow White's eyelids fluttered. True Love's first kiss saved her! The Dwarfs wished the happy couple farewell as the prince led Snow White to his castle where they lived happily ever after.

1. Who has lips red as a rose, hair black as ebony, skin white as snow?
2. Why is the Queen jealous of Snow White?
3. What does the Queen order her huntsman to do?
4. Who finds Snow White crying in the forest?
5. What are the names of the Seven Dwarfs?
6. Who has big bulging eyes, a wart, and one tooth?
7. What does the hag make for Snow White to give her the Sleeping Death?
8. What is the only thing that can cure the Sleeping Death?
9. What happens when the Dwarfs chase the Queen up the mountain?
10. Who comes into the forest to wake Snow White with Love's First Kiss?

SNOW WHITE

Q & As

1. Snow White
2. Because the Magic Mirror tells her Snow White is the fairest in the land
3. To take Snow White into the forest and kill her
4. The forest animals: rabbits, deer, raccoons, skunks, squirrels, birds, and a turtle
5. Doc, Dopey, Grumpy, Happy, Sleepy, Bashful, and Sneezy (Other names considered for the Dwarfs were Wheezy, Puffy, Stuffy, Biggo-Ego, Burpy, Deefy, Jumpy, Baldy, Nifty, Gabby, and Stubby! Can you think of other funny names?)
6. The Queen, who has turned herself into an evil hag
7. A poison apple
8. Love's First Kiss
9. The Queen falls off the cliff and dies
10. The Prince

SLEEPY

SNEEZY

DOC

BASHFUL

Dopey

Grumpy

Happy

Stick Dwarfs!

Trace each Dwarf onto paper and color. Cut out and glue tracings onto seven ice-pop sticks. Write names on the bottom of each stick. Try marching your sticks to a tune or act out the scene on pages 318–319.

DOC: Why, it's a girl.

SNEEZY: She's mighty purty.

BASHFUL: She's beautiful, just like an angel.

GRUMPY: Ah, angel! She's a female and female's is poison. They're full of wicked wiles!

BASHFUL: What are wiles?

GRUMPY: I don't know but I'm against them.

DOC: Shh! Not so loud, you'll wake her up!

GRUMPY: Oh let her wake up! She doesn't belong here anyhow.

SLEEPY: Shh!

BASHFUL: Look out!

LINES FROM THE SCRIPT

HAPPY: She's waking up!

SLEEPY: What will we do?

HAPPY: Hide!

SNOW WHITE: Oh dear! I wonder if the children are…Oh! Why you're little men!

SNOW WHITE: How do you do? I said, "How do you do?"

GRUMPY: How do you do what?

SNOW WHITE: You can talk! I'm so glad! Now don't tell me who you are! Let me guess…I know you're Doc!

DOC: Oh oh, why, yes, yes, that's true!

SNOW WHITE: And you're, you're…Bashful!

BASHFUL: Oh…oh gosh!

SNOW WHITE: And you…you're Sleepy!

SLEEPY: <Yawn> How'd you guess?

SNOW WHITE: And you…

SNEEZY: Ah, ah choo!

SNOW WHITE: You're Sneezy! Yes! And you must be…

HAPPY: Happy, ma'am! That's me! And this is Dopey. He don't talk none.

SNOW WHITE: You mean he can't talk?

HAPPY: He don't know. He never tried.

SNOW WHITE: That's too bad! Oh…you must be Grumpy!

DOC: Yeah, that's him.

GRUMPY: Heh! We know who we are! Ask her who she is and what she's doing here.

DOC: What are you and who are ah, ah, who are you, my dear?

SNOW WHITE: Oh! How silly of me! I'm Snow White!

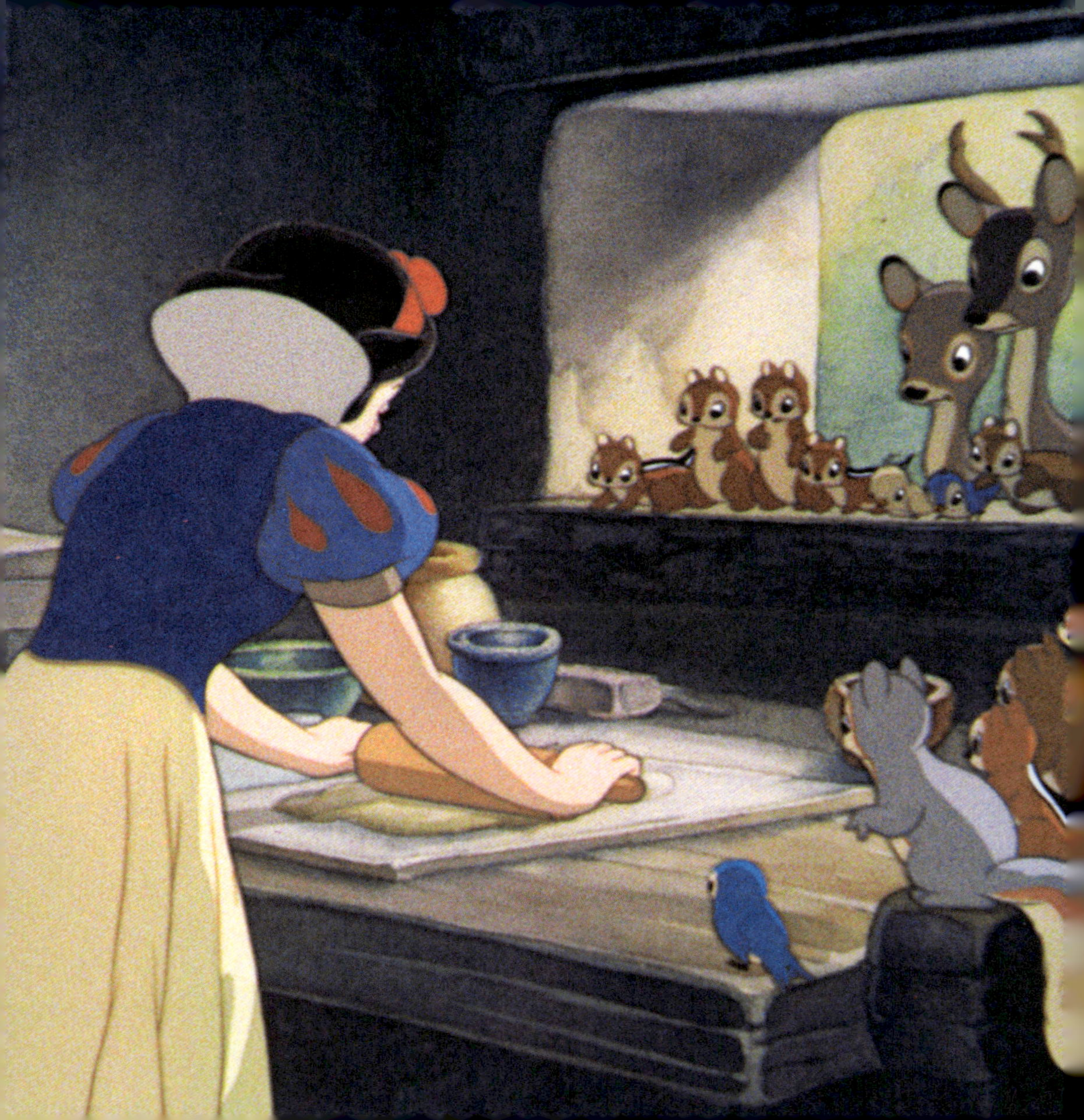

Snow White's
Gooseberry Pie

GOOSEBERRY PIE IS SO EASY TO MAKE, and the perfect treat if you feel like you've spent a day in the diamond mines. If you can't find gooseberries, blueberries will work just as well. And take a tip from Snow White—the secret to making a good pie is to bake it with love.

2 pre-made pie crusts

3 cups gooseberries (or blueberries) rinsed and stemmed

1 3/4 cups sugar

3 tablespoons quick-cooking tapioca

1/4 teaspoon salt

milk

sugar

1. Preheat oven to 425° F.

2. Line pie pan with pie crust.

3. In a saucepan, smash about 1/2 cup of berries and combine with sugar, tapioca, and salt. Cook and stir mixture until it boils. Stir for another 2 minutes, then remove from heat. Stir in remaining berries.

4. Pour filling into pie crust.

5. Put top pie crust over berries and pinch edges together decoratively.

6. Cut 3 or 4 decorative slits in top pie crust. Brush crust with milk and sugar.

7. Bake for 35 minutes.

8. Allow pie to cool for about 15 minutes, then serve while still warm.

Makes 8 servings.

The Adventures
Great Places for Children
SCOOTER RU
ANT AND BE GO ON A VACATION
Red's Dream
LASSETER
Toy
Smyrl
Twirl
L. MONEY
inkertoy®
nstruction System
Children can build lots of big creations,
The Big Builder
Set Contains
35 Pieces
14 Rods
PLAYSKO

Toy Story

EVERY DAY, six-year old Andy Davis played with his toys in a make-believe world. His favorite toy and the hero of all his adventures was a pull-string cowboy sheriff named Woody.

One day, Woody called a staff meeting among the other toys. "The Davises are moving to a new home in one week," he said. "I don't want any toys left behind." Hamm the piggy bank and Rex the dinosaur hadn't picked their moving buddies yet and started to fret when Woody passed along even more disturbing news: "Andy's birthday party has been moved to today."

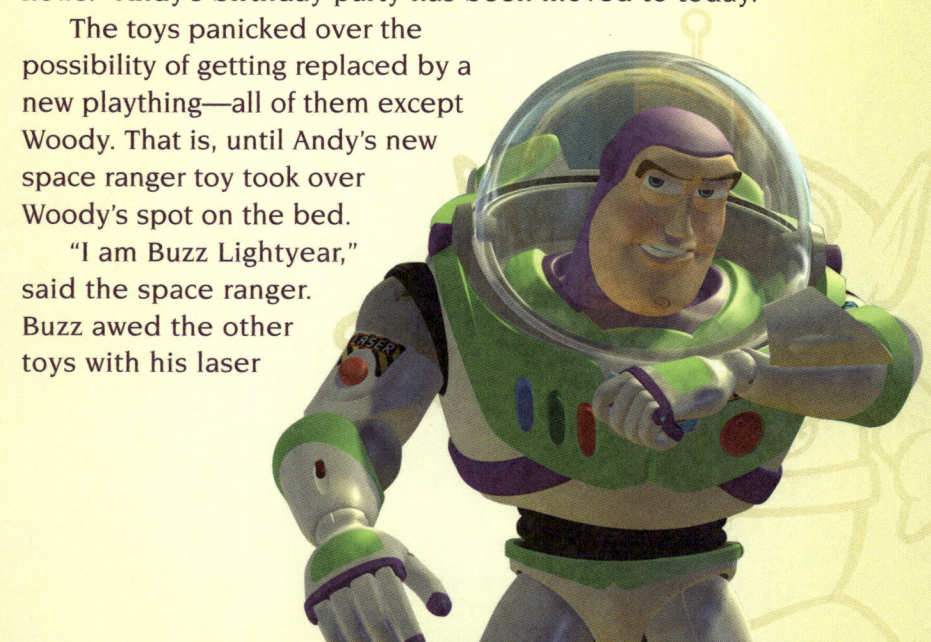

The toys panicked over the possibility of getting replaced by a new plaything—all of them except Woody. That is, until Andy's new space ranger toy took over Woody's spot on the bed.

"I am Buzz Lightyear," said the space ranger. Buzz awed the other toys with his laser and his retractable wingspan. Woody was not impressed. "He doesn't fight evil, or really shoot lasers, or fly!" he said.

"I can fly," said Buzz. He jumped off the bed, bounced off a ball, and catapulted off a racecar track back onto the bed.

"That wasn't flying! That was falling with style," said Woody angrily. After that, Woody's jealousy grew more and more each time Andy forgot about him in favor of Buzz.

A day before the move, Mrs. Davis announced dinner at Pizza Planet. "You can bring one toy," she told Andy. Woody overheard and suddenly got the devious idea to trick Buzz into helping a trapped toy behind the bed. Then he "accidentally" knocked Buzz out the window.

The toys worried that Buzz might have fallen into the backyard of Andy's evil neighbor, Sid. Everyone knew that Sid mutilated and destroyed every toy he touched.

"It was an accident, guys," said Woody to the angry mob of toys. "Come on, you have to believe me."

Just then, Andy came into the room looking for Buzz. When he couldn't find him, he grabbed Woody instead.

But instead of falling into Sid's backyard, Buzz had landed in a bush. He climbed out and leaped onto the rear bumper of the car, just as Mrs. Davis was pulling out with Andy, his sister, and Woody inside.

By the time they reached the gas station, Buzz had jumped through the window of the car and landed next to Woody. The two toys started fighting and tumbled out of the car. The next moment, Mrs. Davis drove away, stranding them at the gas station!

As luck would have it, a pizza delivery truck drove up. "It's a spaceship, Buzz," said Woody. They climbed aboard and soon were on their way to Pizza Planet.

"Good work, Woody," said Buzz as they entered the Pizza Planet arcade. Woody spotted Andy and was about to rejoin him when Buzz disappeared into a crane game filled with aliens. Knowing that he couldn't return to Andy without Buzz, Woody climbed in after him.

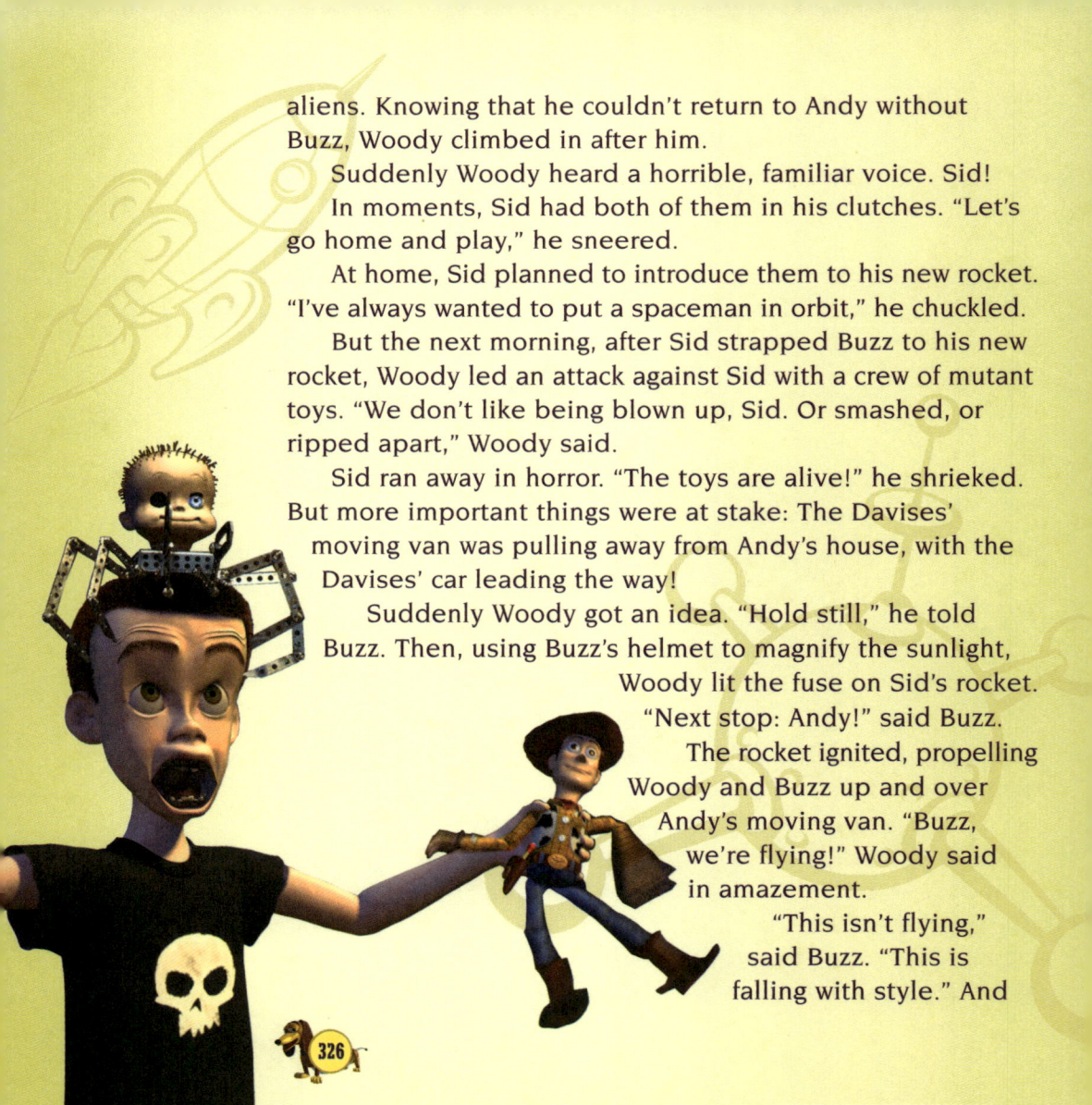

Suddenly Woody heard a horrible, familiar voice. Sid!

In moments, Sid had both of them in his clutches. "Let's go home and play," he sneered.

At home, Sid planned to introduce them to his new rocket. "I've always wanted to put a spaceman in orbit," he chuckled.

But the next morning, after Sid strapped Buzz to his new rocket, Woody led an attack against Sid with a crew of mutant toys. "We don't like being blown up, Sid. Or smashed, or ripped apart," Woody said.

Sid ran away in horror. "The toys are alive!" he shrieked. But more important things were at stake: The Davises' moving van was pulling away from Andy's house, with the Davises' car leading the way!

Suddenly Woody got an idea. "Hold still," he told Buzz. Then, using Buzz's helmet to magnify the sunlight, Woody lit the fuse on Sid's rocket.

"Next stop: Andy!" said Buzz.

The rocket ignited, propelling Woody and Buzz up and over Andy's moving van. "Buzz, we're flying!" Woody said in amazement.

"This isn't flying," said Buzz. "This is falling with style." And with style, Woody and Buzz landed next to Andy in the car on the way to their new home.

By Christmas, all had returned to normal in the play world of Andy and his toys. "You're not worried, are you?" Woody asked Buzz as Andy unwrapped his present. "What could Andy possibly get that is worse than you?" Suddenly Woody and Buzz's eyes grew wide. They saw the joy on Andy's face as he hugged his new puppy!

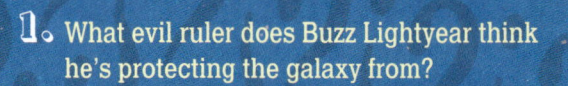

1. What evil ruler does Buzz Lightyear think he's protecting the galaxy from?
2. Where does Sid find Buzz and Woody?
3. What does Andy get for Christmas that could be a threat to Woody and Buzz?
4. How does Woody light the rocket strapped to Buzz's back?
5. What does Buzz learn when he sees the TV at Sid's house?
6. Who does Woody send to establish a recon post during Andy's birthday party?
7. Where do Woody and Buzz get stranded together?
8. How do Woody and the mutant toys save Buzz from Sid?
9. Why does Woody call a meeting with all of Andy's toys?
10. What does Hannah do to Buzz after he finds out he can't really fly?

TOY

Q & As

1. Emperor Zurg
2. In the Rocket Ship Crane Game filled with aliens at Pizza Planet
3. A puppy
4. He uses Buzz's helmet shield to magnify the sunlight and spark the fuse.
5. That he's actually a toy that can't fly, not a real space ranger.
6. Sergeant and his Bucket o' Soldiers
7. At a Dinoco gas station
8. They scare him by showing him they're alive and telling him to take good care of his toys.
9. To make sure everyone has a moving partner and to tell them about Andy's birthday party
10. She calls him Mrs. Nesbitt and dresses him in a frilly apron and hat for a tea party with her headless dolls.

Alien Squishies

In the galactic space station known as Pizza Planet, the Alien Crane Game Claw chooses who will go and who will stay. Here's how you can surround yourself with an entire population of aliens. (Little kids love squeezing these!)

construction paper, markers, scissors, tape, yarn or tissues

Draw an alien on construction paper and color it. Lay it on top of another piece of construction paper and cut it out. You should have the front and back of an alien. Tape the two pieces together around the edges, leaving a one-inch opening. Stuff pieces of yarn or tissues into the hole, then tape the hole closed. Now you can be the Claw and squeeze the alien squishies. Who will be the chosen one?

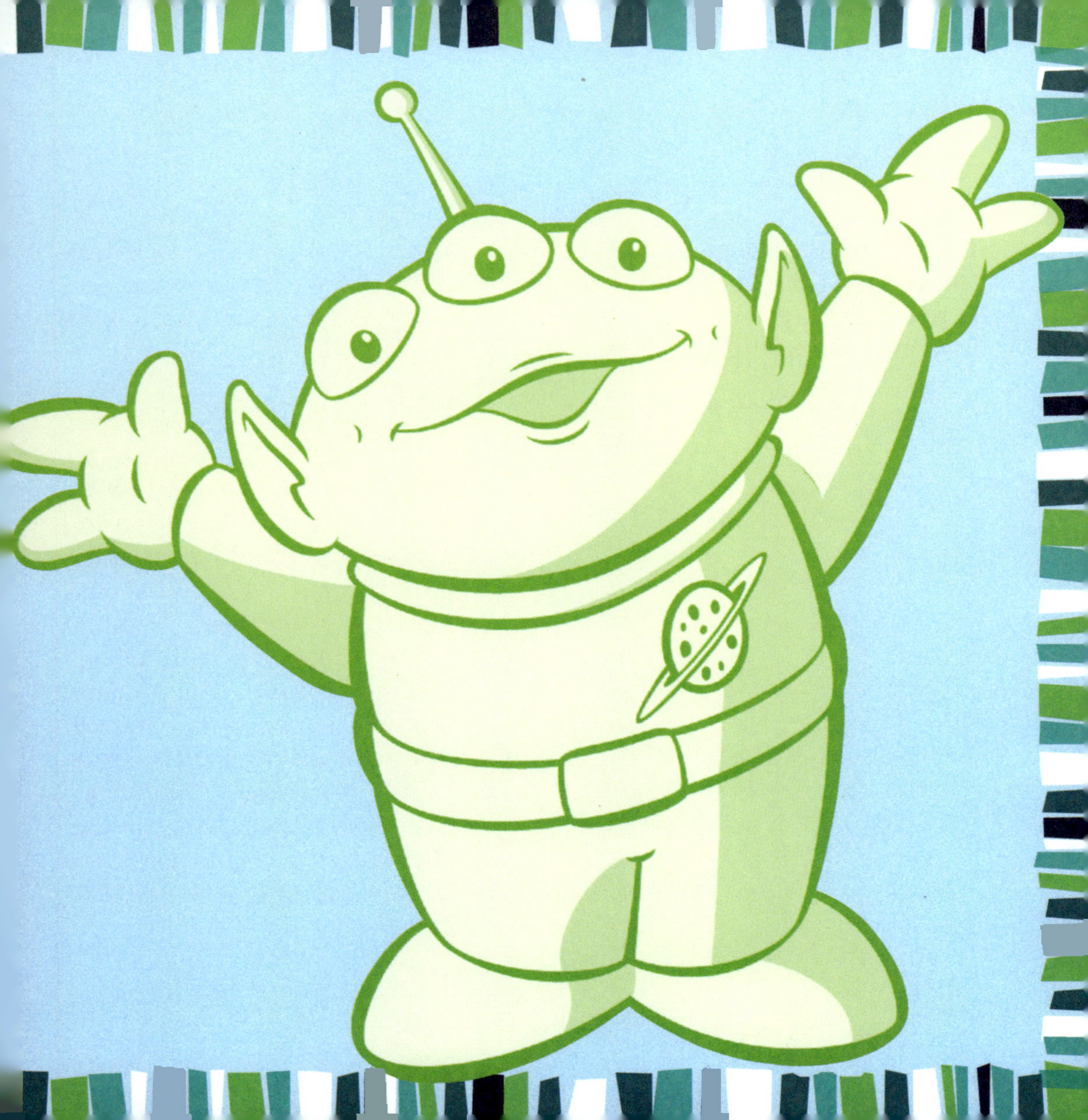

LINES FROM THE FILM

BUZZ: Greetings! I am Buzz Lightyear. I come in peace.

ALIENS: Ooooooooh.

BUZZ: This is an intergalactic emergency. I must commandeer your vessel to Sector 12. Who's in charge here?

ALIENS: The Claw. The Claw is our Master. It chooses who will go and who will stay.

WOODY: This is ludicrous.

SID: Hey Bozo…you got a brain in there? Take that! And that!

WOODY: Oh no, Sid! Get down!

BUZZ: What's wrong with you?

ALIEN: The Claw. It moves.

<Claw grabs alien>

ALIEN: I have been chosen! Farewell my friends. I go to a better place....

SID: Gotcha!

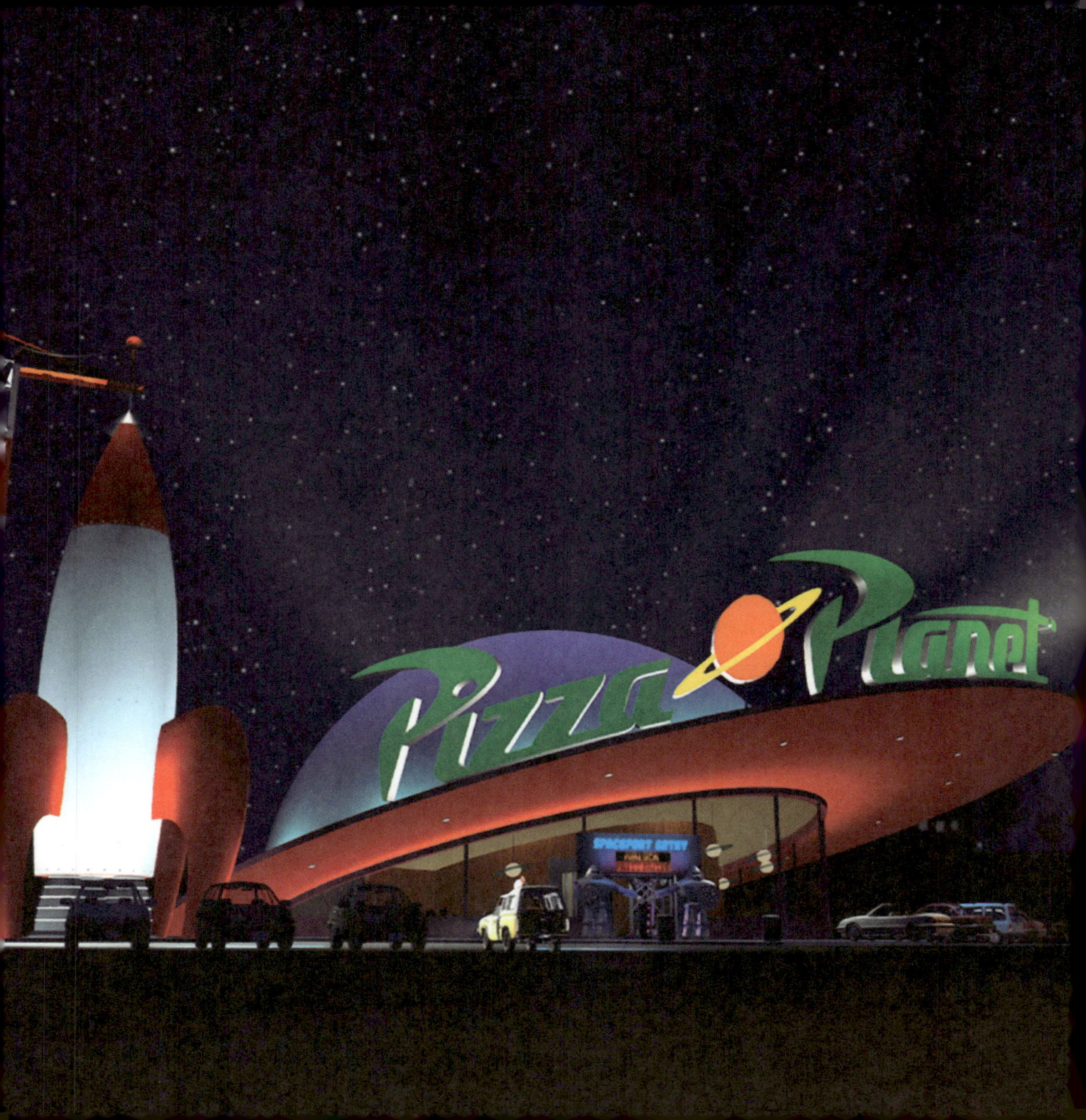
Pizza Planet

Pizza Planet
Mini Pizzas

THE NEXT TIME you're ready for an intergalactic refueling experience with Buzz and Woody, these quick and easy mini pizzas are hard to beat.

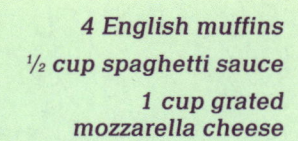

4 English muffins
½ cup spaghetti sauce
1 cup grated mozzarella cheese

OPTIONAL:
pepperoni slices
sliced olives
sliced mushrooms
green pepper slices
broccoli florets
Canadian bacon slices
pineapple slices

1. Preheat broiler.
2. Split muffins and arrange them on a baking sheet.
3. Spread about 1 tablespoon of sauce on each muffin half. Layer with 2 tablespoons of cheese.
4. Add optional ingredients on top, if desired.
5. Broil for 5 minutes, or until cheese is bubbling and golden.

Makes 4 servings.

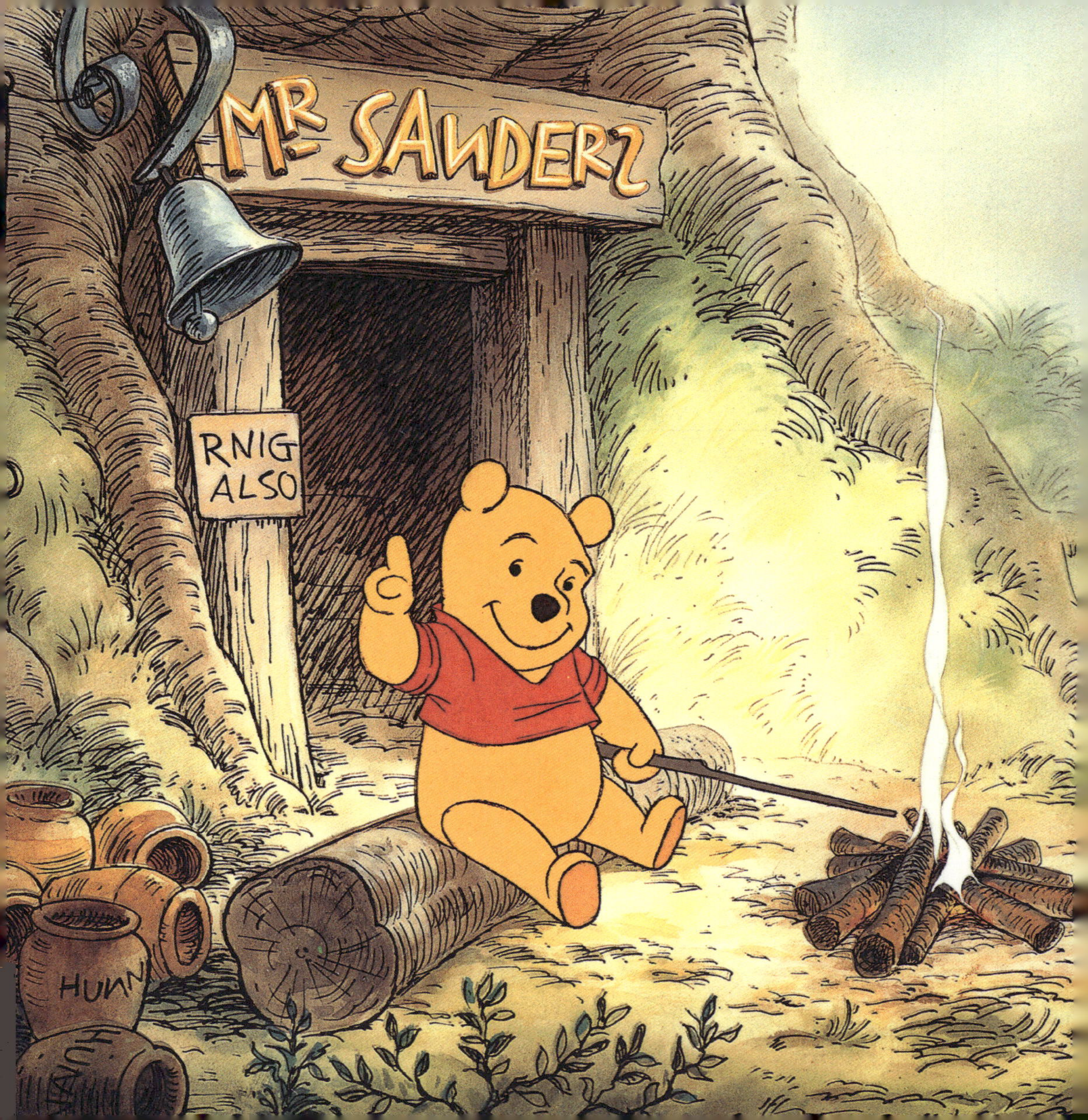
MR SANDERZ
RNIG ALSO
HUNN

WINNIE THE POOH LIVED in the Hundred-Acre Wood. Being a bear of very little brain, Pooh thought in the most thoughtful way he could think.

Winnie the Pooh

"Think, think, think," Pooh said. "Oh yes, time for my stoutness exercises." He stood in front of the mirror and touched his toes until he heard a rumbling in his tummy.

"Time for something sweet," said Pooh. So he went to the cupboard and stuck his nose in his last honey pot.

"Oh bother, empty again." said Pooh. Then a bee buzzed by. Pooh decided to follow it to its home in a tall oak tree. Up the tree he climbed and climbed and climbed until…SNAP! Pooh's branch broke and he fell right into a prickly bush.

Pooh brushed the prickles from his nose and began to think again. And the first person he thought of was his friend Christopher Robin.

Pooh asked his friend if he happened to have a balloon. "What do you want a balloon for?" asked Christopher Robin.

"Honey," said Pooh. "I shall fly like a bee up to the honey tree." So Christopher Robin gave Pooh a balloon. Then they went to a very muddy place and Pooh rolled around until he was black all over.

Now cleverly disguised as a little black rain cloud, Pooh floated up, up, up to the honey.

The bees buzzed angrily. "Christopher Robin, I think the bees S-U-S-P-E-C-T something," said Pooh.

"Perhaps they think you're after their honey," said Christopher Robin.

Suddenly they attacked. The air fizzed out of Pooh's balloon and he came tumbling down into Christopher Robin's arms. The swarming bees chased them all the way to the mud-pool, where Christopher Robin and Pooh hid happily under an umbrella.

At lunchtime, Pooh visited his friend Rabbit. At first Rabbit pretended not to be home, for he worried about sharing his lunch with a hungry bear. Then Rabbit decided to be polite, and invited Pooh in for some bread with honey. Pooh tried to be polite too, and asked for a small helping of both, but never mind the bread.

Pooh found his small helping of honey to be too small and asked Rabbit for a larger small helping. Rabbit gave Pooh the whole jar, and Pooh ate and ate and ate and ate and ate.

At last, Pooh said good-bye to Rabbit in a rather sticky voice. But when Pooh tried to leave, he couldn't fit through Rabbit's door. "Help and bother!" Pooh cried. "I'm stuck!"

Rabbit pushed and pushed and pushed, but could not squeeze Pooh out the door. "There's only one thing to do," Rabbit said. "I'll get Christopher Robin!"

In the meanwhile, Pooh's Hundred-Acre Wood friends came by to visit. "You are a bear wedged in great tightness," said Owl. Gopher suggested blasting Pooh out. Kanga and Roo brought honeysuckle for Pooh to smell, but Pooh tried to eat it. Christopher Robin and Eeyore tried to pull Pooh out, but there was no use.

"Pooh Bear, there's only one thing we can do," said Christopher Robin. "Wait for you to get thin again."

While Pooh's bottom was stuck on the inside of Rabbit's house and his top was stuck on the outside of Rabbit's house, both ends waited to get thin again—day after day and night after night.

Then one morning when Rabbit was beginning to think that he'd never be able to use his front door again, it happened! Pooh budged. "Today is the day!" Rabbit said, and ran to tell Christopher Robin.

So Christopher Robin and all their friends pulled Pooh with a heave…ho! Heave! Ho! H…E…A…V…V…V…E!

It worked! Pooh flew out of Rabbit's doorway and sailed up into the sky, straight into the top of a tall oak tree. But this time Pooh was in no hurry to be rescued. He landed smack-dab in the middle of a big, sticky store of honey!

Of all the happy endings to Pooh's adventures, this one was one of the happiest—and yummiest—endings of them all.

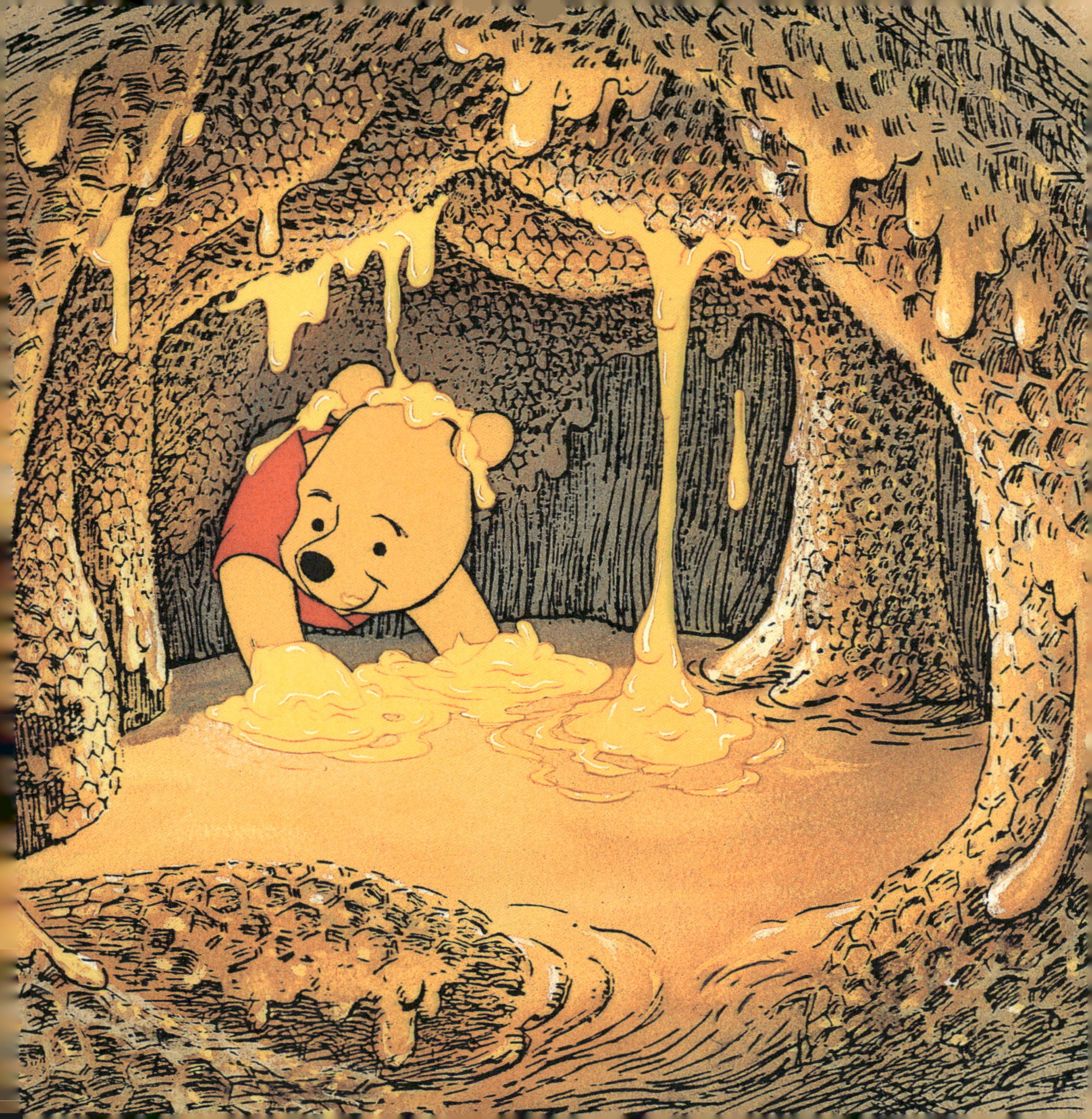

1. What is the name above Winnie the Pooh's door?
2. Why does Winnie the Pooh roll around in a mud puddle?
3. What kind of bush does Pooh land in when he falls out of the honey tree?
4. What happens when Pooh visits Rabbit for lunch?
5. What kind of flowers do Kanga and Roo bring for Pooh to smell?

WINNIE THE POOH

6. How does Rabbit decorate Pooh's back end?
7. Where does Pooh land when Christopher Robin and all his friends pull him out of Rabbit's door?
8. What does Gopher suggest they do to get Pooh out of the rabbit hole?
9. What is Christopher Robin doing when Pooh finds him?
10. How does Winnie the Pooh start his day?

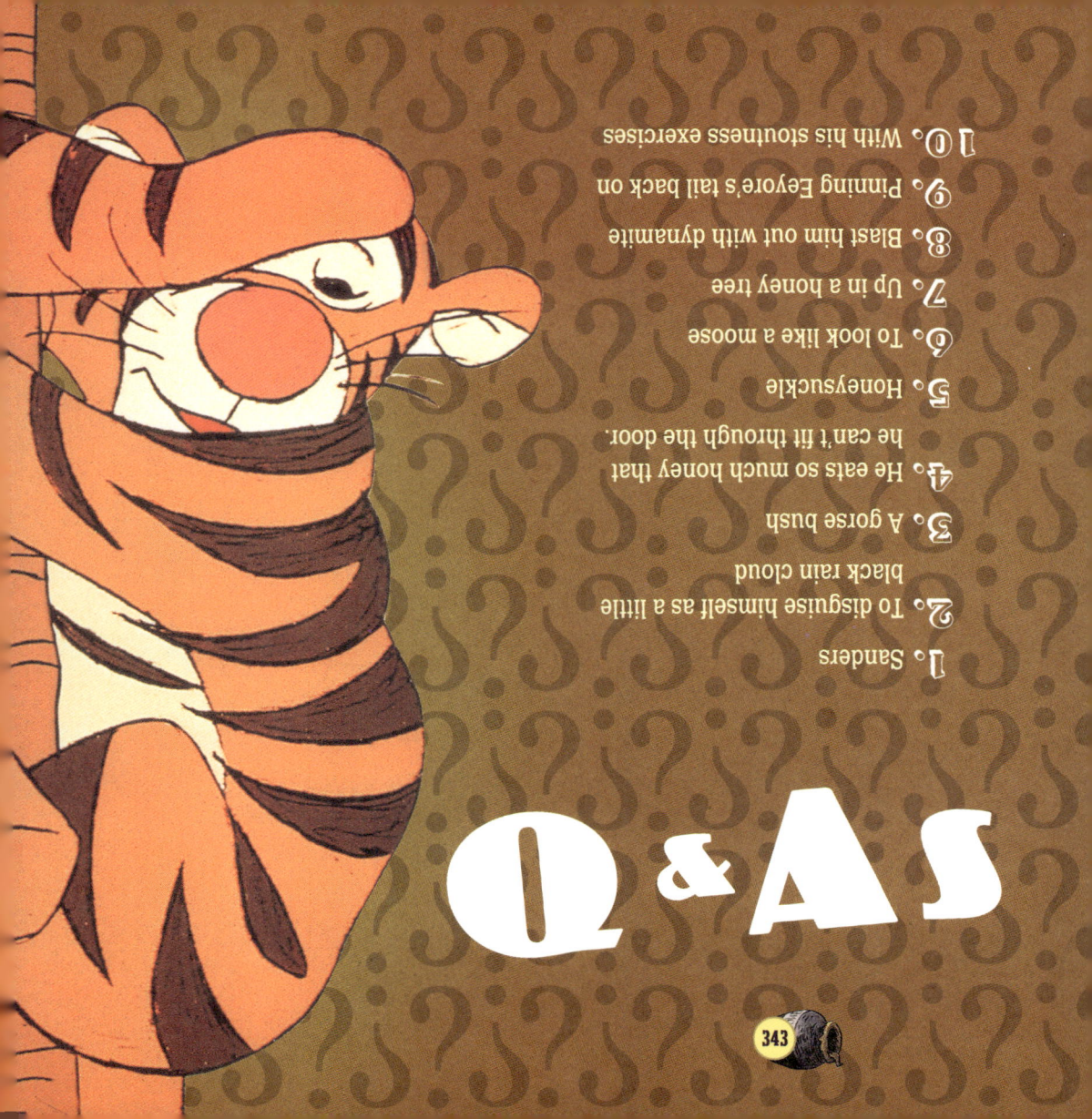

Q & As

1. Sanders
2. To disguise himself as a little black rain cloud
3. A gorse bush
4. He eats so much honey that he can't fit through the door.
5. Honeysuckle
6. To look like a moose
7. Up in a honey tree
8. Blast him out with dynamite
9. Pinning Eeyore's tail back on
10. With his stoutness exercises

343

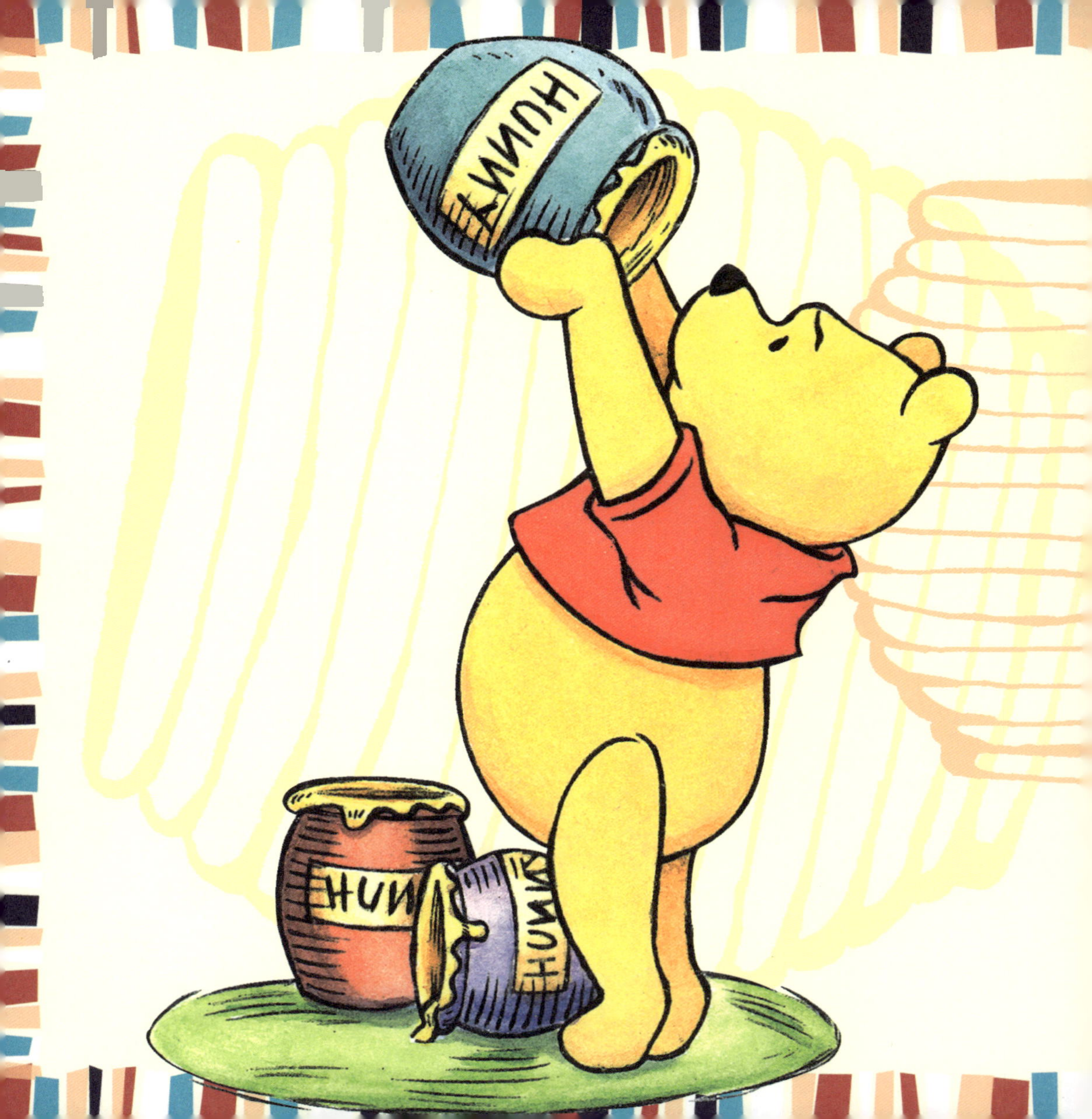
HUNNY
HUN
HUNN

Pooh's Honeypots

Winnie the Pooh can never have too many honeypots. Here's how to make your own honeypot, when you need to store a little smackerel of something.

FOR PLAY CLAY: *1 cup flour, ½ cup salt, 1 tablespoon oil, 1 teaspoon cream of tartar, ¾ cup water, 3 to 5 drops food coloring, paintbrush, food-safe varnish (available at craft and cooking-supply stores)*

In a large bowl, combine all the ingredients for play clay and mix thoroughly until you can form a large ball of clay. Press a piece of clay about the size of a Ping-Pong ball into a flat disk. Take another piece of clay about the same size and roll it into a long snake shape. Press the ends together to make a ring. Press the ring onto the disk to make the first layer of the honey pot. Continue rolling out long snakes of clay. Add about five to seven more snake rings on top of each layer until the honeypot is complete. Let the clay dry thoroughly, then paint the pot with a layer of varnish. Will your pot hold enough honey for a bear with a rumbly tummy?

I'm rumbly in my tumbly, time for something sweet.

Say, "Tut Tut, it looks like rain."

Now would you aim me at the bees...please?

I wasn't gonna eat it, I was just gonna taste it!

I haven't thought of anything,

Well, I did mean a little larger small helping.

Oh bother, empty again—only the sticky part's left.

346

That buzzing noise means something.

have you?

Oh, stuff and fluff!

LINES FROM THE FILM

Sticky Pooh Bear Buns

SOMETIMES THE BEST snack can be a glass of milk with a bit of bread and honey and the company of a good friend like Rabbit. Although Winnie the Pooh might prefer just the honey, these sticky buns are sure to satisfy any sweet tooth.

FOR BUNS:
1/4 cup warm water (100° to 115° F)
1/4-ounce package active dry yeast
1/4 cup honey
2 1/2 cups bread flour
1 teaspoon salt
2 large egg yolks
1/2 cup milk, room temperature
1/4 cup butter, melted

FOR GLAZE:
2 tablespoons honey
1/2 stick unsalted butter
2/3 cup confectioners' sugar

1. In a large bowl, sprinkle yeast over warm water and stir in 1/2 teaspoon honey. Let stand until foamy (about 5 minutes).

2. Add the remaining honey, flour, salt, egg yolks, and milk gradually to yeast mixture until blended. Add butter, and beat until smooth.

3. Scrape dough from side of the bowl and form into large ball. Cover. Let rise in warm, draft-free place until dough is doubled in size (about 1 hour).

4. Preheat oven to 350° F.

5. Prepare glaze by heating glaze ingredients in small saucepan until butter is melted. Remove from heat and cover. Keep warm.

6. Punch dough down. Roll onto floured surface into a 9 x 11" square and brush glaze on surface. Roll up dough, jellyroll style. Cut into 12 equal pieces and transfer to greased baking sheet. Brush more glaze on rolls. Cover and let rise in a warm place until doubled in size (about 45 minutes).

7. Heat remaining glaze and brush on rolls. Bake for 15 to 20 minutes, or until golden. Transfer to racks to cool.

Makes 12 buns.

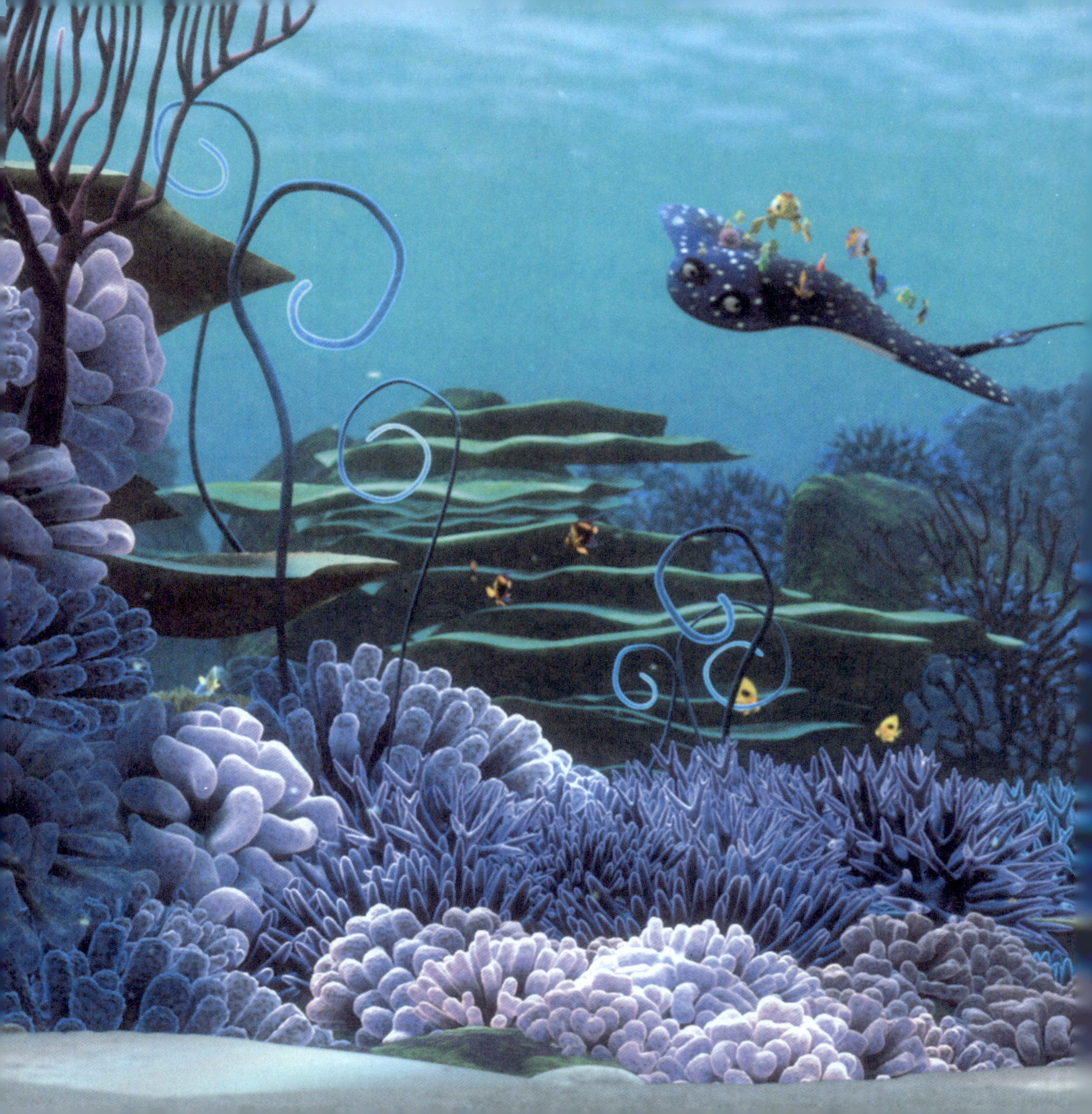

ACKNOWLEDGMENTS

This Little Big Book could not have been possible without the assistance and dedication of an entire team of crackerjack people. From Disney Publishing Worldwide, Hunter Heller for quick negotiations, Lisa Gerstel for her careful guidance, and Esther Kim for her patience and efficiency. Graham Barnard was indispensable in the approval process. Many thanks to him for responding to constant lengthy emails and telephone messages with prompt action. Thanks to Annie Auerbach, Nancy Parent, Vickie Saxon, and Deborah Boone for their good eye and attention to detail in editorial and design. Thanks to Tim Lewis for digital still selection, color correction, and fulfillment. Appreciation goes to Dave Smith at the Walt Disney Archives for his knowledge.